MAGPIE LEAVES THE NEST

JOHN GILLENDER & DENISE BEATON

Order this book online at www.trafford.com
or email orders@trafford.com

Most Trafford titles are also available at major online book retailers.

Printed in the United States of America.

ISBN: 978-1-4669-4481-7 (sc)
ISBN: 978-1-4669-4480-0 (e)

Trafford rev. 06/17/2013

www.trafford.com

North America & international
toll-free: 1 888 232 4444 (USA & Canada)
phone: 250 383 6864 • fax: 812 355 4082

To our individual families who kept the faith through all these twelve years.

ACKNOWLEDGEMENTS

WE WOULD LIKE TO thank Joy Gillender and Duncan Beaton our respective spouses who encouraged, cajoled and criticized us as the years passed but did not lose faith that we would complete this project. We want to thank our children Anne and Tracy Gillender (who were young adults when we began) and Janna, Erin and Leigh Beaton (who were in their teens) for their patience as we took over the computer one night a week for an entire evening to work on our manuscript.

We also want to thank Ed Griffin who provided honest feedback and wonderful suggestions on our first 50 pages. Shannon Beebe-Cembrowski who was studying Law in Chicago and who took time out of her busy schedule to edit the early parts of our book and who also provided valuable feedback on our content and sentence structure. The one person who has persevered from start to finish and has provided detailed editing for us from an American perspective is Andrea Gilbert from Birmingham, Alabama.

We do not want to forget our many friends both past and present who encouraged us to keep on going and to finish what we began.

Contents

CONTENTS

PREFACE

WE SAT IN BILLY MINER'S PUB located on the Fraser River in Maple Ridge British Columbia with our respective spouses. John entertained the rest of us with stories of his growing up years in England. The comment, "John, you should write a book" was made by me, Denise. John replied that many people had said this very thing and he would love to do so but did not have the knowledge of where to start or the expertise of writing or knowledge of the computer. Denise responded, "I've got the expertise of the computer and writing is my strong suit. After all, I've completed a degree and then some so you know I can write. I've always wanted to write a book but have not had the subject matter. If you talk, I'll type."

The partnership was formed that day. Many beers and hours later, the story was mapped out from start to finish. With the blessings of their respective spouses, the duo began their twelve year project. The result is this book. We hope the readers enjoy their experience as they see Canada through Gilley's eyes; Gilley whose personality parallels the Magpie.

We want to reassure our readers that we researched all the background and histories of our story to ensure our memories were accurate. Funnily enough, many of our memories needed to be tweaked by the search engines we used to verify our respective histories.

MAGPIE FOLKLORE

MAGPIE—A BIRD (GENUS PICA) having a very long, graduated tail. The European magpie (P. pica or caudata), the common magpie of folklore, has iridescent black plumage with white scapulars, belly, sides. It has often been tamed and taught to say a few words; it is famous for its love of small bright objects which it will steal and put to its own devices. The American magpie is closely related to the European.

In the British Isles a widespread (mainly found in England and Scotland and less common in Wales and Northern Ireland) traditional rhyme records the myth (it is not clear whether it has been seriously believed) that seeing magpies predicts the future, depending on how many are seen. There are many regional variations on the rhyme, which means that it is impossible to give a definitive version.

Magpie personality—A person, who talks a great deal and collects or hoards things indiscriminately, especially objects of that glitter. Also a Magpie is a person who loves to take risks for a livelier lifestyle. The Magpie has often been noted as being courageous, inquisitive and adventurous as well as one who noisily talks a great deal, sometimes to the point of being a pest.

CHAPTER 1

THE BORDER ENCOUNTER

GILLEY LOOKED AT HIS watch and thought, "Eight-thirty in the evening and no plane. Four hours late." The excitement of his first airplane flight had faded due to the long delay. Turning to his bride, Gilley expressed, "Is this normal?"

"Well, I don't know. I've never flown charter before. With a regular ticket they are generally on time. What do they mean by *technical problem*, Gilley?"

"Well, generally it's a saying that buys you time with the customer so you can solve the problem. At least that's what it meant in the manufacturing industry with my past companies." responded Gilley.

"Yeah, but what does that usually mean?"

"Well, it could mean there is an engine malfunction or it could mean instrumentation problems or the toilets won't flush. It could mean any number of things. I wouldn't worry about it. After all, the pilots aren't going to put their lives in jeopardy. This airline had been flying for many years. We'll get to Seattle when we get there and knowing your mom, she'll be calling the airlines all the time asking for updates."

Even as Gilley said these things to ease his new bride's worries, he thought, "Fine for her because she's going back home to the familiar.

But, I'm leaving home, going to the unknown. BUT *going to Canada*! I've dreamed of doing this most of my life but never thought I'd actually get there. Where the hell's that plane?"

No sooner had he thought this than the announcement came over the loudspeaker, "Flight 342 from Amsterdam has landed. All passengers please proceed to Gate 12. We will begin boarding immediately."

"Alright," declared Gilley, "Finally!" With that, Joy and Gilley cued up with the other passengers for what turned out to be a life altering adventure. They were finally in the air and had settled down for what was supposed to be a nine hour non-stop flight to Seattle, Washington.

Gilley sat gazing out of the window into the darkness, hoping he could see the outline of the British Isles as he left them behind for the first time. As he lit his cigarette, he thought back to the months leading up to this moment and still had difficulty believing he was married and only four months after that actually was on his way to the new life he had only dreamed about.

"I wonder what Bill, Ray and Dave are doing right now," asked Joy, breaking into Gilley's reverie.

"Let's see, it's about 10:00 PM. I imaging Bill and Dave are standing at the Waggon holding up the Copper Bar thinking about us and Ray and Margaret are sitting nearby devouring two of Muriel's best sandwiches"

"You remember all of the sandwiches we could get at a bargain? If Muriel didn't think they were perfect, she'd let us have them for half price. No way she'd *give* them to us. No, she'd charge us. Muriel wouldn't miss a way to make a penny. And those 'Chicken in a Basket', she would sell us the rejects and still charge us half price. We'd eat them anyway and gladly pay her because it didn't matter how they looked, they still tasted wonderful."

"Lots of times I thought she spoiled her creations just so she could let us have them for a deal. There was many a sandwich I couldn't tell was a reject. They tasted alright to me. Then there were the "lock-in nights". You remember those and how much fun we'd have? As you know the pubs had to close at 10:30 PM or else they could be fined heavily. We had ten minutes to finish our drinks and things had to be locked up by 10:40 PM. But, the management could also choose to have after hours' guests. If the police came, the cash register would have to be locked up and there could be no money exchanged for drinks. The people left in the pub were *special* friends (or family) of the establishment.

You remember the first time you and I were part of a lock-in at Stan and Wynn's place, The Bay Horse? We had to stay overnight because it was a long way home. That was a lot of fun. Then there was many a night at the Waggon when Muriel would get Fred to manipulate the Ouija Board, talking and scaring poor Bill something terrible," chuckled Gilley.

"I wish I'd been there when Fred was doing that but you know Muriel—only male guests were allowed to stay over at the Waggon. I remember Fred would sell me a six pack of beer when I had to leave. I wonder if Muriel ever knew about that," chuckled Joy. As the conversation died, Gilley began thinking about when he and Joy met.

It was August of 1969—unusually hot for the Northeast. Joy entered his life at the Waggon Inn which was near Ponteland. The Waggon Inn was the local pub where Gilley and his friends met regularly. He could remember that evening clearly. He saw her standing by the bar and the Beatles 1964 song, "*I Saw Her Standing There*" came to his mind. He immediately went to see Muriel in the kitchen. Muriel, the manager of the Inn along with her husband Fred, knew everyone and everything about the patrons in her establishment and was a bit of a gossip. He found her making her famous sandwiches for the clientele. "Muriel, who is that new girl standing at the bar with those older people," Gilley asked?

"Gilley, what are you talking about? I've seen lots of girls standing at the bar this evening," replied Muriel.

In walked an older, elegant lady with *the* said girl in tow. Muriel said, "Hi, Joyce, I haven't seen you for ages. What brings you here tonight?"

"Hello, Muriel," said Joyce. "John and I were thinking of where we could take our guest, Joy. She's visiting us from Canada. Her parents are friends of my sister Ann. You remember Ann? She immigrated to Canada many years ago. Joy here wants a truly English pub experience and we knew this was the place to bring her for that very thing especially since you make those exceptional sandwiches people come for miles around to enjoy."

"Hello Joy. Welcome to the Waggon Inn. I'm pleased you've met me before meeting my husband Fred," said Muriel wiping her hands on her apron and extending one in a handshake. "I'd like to introduce you to Gilley, here, who's one of our customers and one of my favourite boys. He's a regular here. If anyone can help you have a truly English experience, its Gilley. He's a good lad and he was born and raised just south of here. He knows the area like the back of his hand." With that, she wrapped her arm around Gilley's shoulders, gave them a squeeze, winking at them both. "I like them young and strong and he fits the bill. How long are you planning to stay in this area, dear?"

Joy, smiling, said, "I'm only here in the north for a week. Otherwise, I'm staying in London with my aunt Peggy. I'll be in England for a year on a working holiday with my friend Liz. She's arriving next week and we have to do a job quest in London as soon as possible. After all, we're here to work and immerse ourselves in the English way of life."

"Well, that sounds very interesting, Joy," said Muriel with a twinkle in her eye. "I wish you all the luck."

At this point, not able to stand it any longer, Gilley, extending his hand, said, "Joy, I'm pleased to meet you." Turning to Joyce he said, "And you also, Joyce. Would it be OK if I bought you, your husband John and Joy a drink to welcome you to the Waggon?"

"That's very nice of you to offer," said Joyce, "We will accept, right Joy? See you in the bar, Gilley. But before we leave, Muriel, I'd like three of your special sandwiches, please."

"No problem. I'll get Gilley to bring them out for you," smiled Muriel.

"That would be wonderful." With that the two left the kitchen.

Muriel, looking at Gilley said, "I saw that glint in your eye. She's a pretty one. This is your chance. Here, take the sandwiches out and when you talk to her, offer her the chance to see some Northumberland castles. Remember, you've only got a week. Now, Joyce and John Lions are very wealthy. He is the managing director of Shanks Toilet and Bathroom Fixtures. Careful how you walk, Gilley. They live in Fenham, in the rich section. There is talk they are building a house in the most exclusive area around here, Darras Hall Estates. That gives you an idea of just how wealthy they are." With that advice, Gilley, sandwiches in hand, turned to leave. "Oh" interjected Muriel, "Don't forget to get them to pay for those sandwiches. If you don't, they go onto your tab."

Gilley grimaced. This venture was already proving to be expensive. First a drink and now he has to make sure he gets these people to pay for their sandwiches or else he'd be in more debt. As they were finishing their conversation, Gilley heard Jake, Muriel's Mina bird squawk, "Where's Fred. Where's Fred."

"That's my cue, Gilley. I'd better find Fred before he drinks the bar dry. You go and sweet talk that young lady. But be on your best behaviour."

The pilot's voice brought Gilley out of his reverie. "Ladies and Gentlemen, in approximately thirty minutes we will be making an unexpected stop to re-fuel at Reykjavik, Iceland. Due to heavy headwinds out of England, we won't have enough fuel to make it nonstop to Seattle. Our stopover will take about two hours and then we'll be on our way to Seattle. I apologize for any inconvenience. We have radioed Seattle International Airport to notify them of the situation and they will do their best to insure those of you with connecting flights will be looked after."

Joy, sitting in the seat beside him, looked over at Gilley with an exasperated expression, "Can anything else go wrong," she groaned? "This flight has been a nightmare since we boarded at Stansted. First, arriving four hours late in Stansted started us off on the wrong foot. I still can't believe they didn't have anything open so we could eat or at least have a cup of coffee while we waited. This wouldn't happen in Canada. Second, those vending machines . . . everything that came out of them was garbage," she fumed. "How do the English put up with that? And now we have to stop in Iceland to fuel up. This should have been a direct flight. Hopefully, Mother will be checking with the airlines."

"Joy," Gilley interjected, trying to distract her by changing the topic, "I thought you liked this kind of thing. From the time we met, you've talked about becoming an airline stewardess."

"Well, it's different when you're busy taking care of passengers. Time passes more quickly. I hate sitting and waiting for things to happen," she pouted.

"I have to admit you have a point. I don't like sitting around either but I guess that's the way of airline travel. The airline people have treated us like royalty since we boarded. Free food, free booze—we've been waited on hand and foot since we left. You can't complain about that. I only hope I can save a few of these neat little mini bottles. I may even start a collection. I've never seen liquor bottles so small."

"You might want to do that for yourself, but don't forget Dad. We have to keep some for his bar too. He'll be disappointed if we don't. You'll love his bar. It's just like a small pub in England. That's how he designed it to be."

"I can't wait. Does he have beer on draft, "teased Gilley, pleased his distraction worked?

"No, Gilley. You'll be disappointed in the beer in Canada. The beer we drink at home comes in bottles and it's lighter, more like your Lager. You can only get draft beer in the beer parlors and it's not like your English beer. You won't like it."

"I don't mind Lager. You know the old saying, 'When in Rome, do as the Romans do.' Learning to drink it cold will be interesting, though."

At this point the pilot came on to announce their decent into Reykjavik, "Ladies and Gentlemen, please fasten your seat belts as we are descending into Reykjavik International Airport. I would ask you to extinguish all cigarettes and refrain from smoking until you reach the arranged rest area. Our stay will be approximately two hours. We have to ask you to leave the aircraft during this time in order to comply with safety regulations. There is a lounge for your convenience so you may stretch your legs and enjoy a cigarette. It is imperative you remain in this designated area due to VISA restrictions. The local time is now 4:00 AM."

"Iceland! Wow," said Gilley as they descended the stairway onto the tarmac. It was cold and everyone hurried to the terminal. "Wow! Even though it's 4:00 AM, there's still light on the horizon. I wonder what it would be like to live in the land of the midnight sun. I wouldn't know whether to go to bed or go for a beer."

Joy giggled, "I'm sure you'd figure out when to go for a beer in no time flat."

As they entered the door to the airport, both of them realized they were facing the same experience they'd had at Stansted. Everything was closed and only the vending machines glimmered a welcome. "Oh no," dismayed Joy, "it looks like we're about to repeat our experience of Stansted. Do you think the Icelandic people have better coffee in their vending machines than the English?"

"We'll never know, Joy, because we don't have the currency and the money exchange is closed. We can't even buy anything to prove we've actually been in Iceland."

"I don't care that we won't have anything to prove we've been here. We know we've been here. Besides, all I want to do is get home."

The newlyweds finally found the lounge and seats and settled down to wait. Neither one would admit it, but they dozed off while they waited for the refueling to take place. It was the announcement over the loudspeakers which woke them up as it did many other passengers. All of them herded back to the aircraft, boarded and settled into their original seats without much conversation as all of them were so tired by this time. Off they flew to America and what awaited them there.

Conversation was minimal over the next few hours. The cabin lights had been turned down to allow the passengers to get some sleep. Joy and Gilley took advantage of this. At approximately 8:00 AM, they came on again and an announcement of breakfast awoke the weary travelers. The warm smell of coffee wafting through the cabin helped everyone to wake up.

"I can hardly wait for them to serve coffee. I'm dying for a cup. I wonder if they'll put a shot of whiskey in it. That's what we need," declared Gilley.

"What do you mean 'A shot of whiskey?'" How can you drink that stuff so early in the morning," grimaced Joy?

"My dad always had a shot of whiskey with his morning tea especially if he'd had a rough go of it the night before."

"I can't imagine your father ever getting drunk," stated Joy.

"I haven't seen him drunk either, but if he felt under the weather, it was his tonic. And I know he wouldn't argue with what we've been through tonight. He would agree with me and I certainly think this past night qualifies. Besides, it's an English tradition. You should try it," teased Gilley.

Joy, not one to be thought weak, stated, "If you can pull it off with the stewardess, I'll take you up on your suggestion."

Just then the stewardess came with her wagon of beverages, "Good morning. What would you like—coffee or tea?" she asked, addressing Joy first then Gilley.

"Tea for my wife and coffee for me," replied Gilley. "Would it also be possible for you to get us two miniatures of whiskey we could add to our tea and coffee?"

"Of course, sir. I have the whiskey right here. You aren't the first to partake in that very English tradition," she said as she bent to retrieve four miniatures of Thornton's Whiskey.

"Humph," grumped Joy. "There you go getting what you wanted. I said I'd give it a try and I will. I'm sure I won't like it." Sure enough, Joy after taking a sip declared the drink un-drinkable.

"Joy, try again. Just drink it. It may not go down quite so smoothly the first time, but mark my words it'll do you a world of good and you'll feel better for having it. Once we've had breakfast, you'll feel like a new woman."

"I don't want to feel like a new woman. I just want to feel like myself again. Alright, but if I get a headache before we land I'll know whose fault it is."

At that point the captain announced, "Ladies and Gentlemen, I'm happy to announce we've entered American air space and we are anticipating landing in Seattle within the next six hours. When we land, it will be 11:00 AM and the weather forecast is expected to be sunny and warm. We in the flight cabin hope you were able to capture a few hours sleep as we flew over the North Pole. Enjoy your breakfast which is about to be served. Thank you."

With that announcement, the stewardess appeared with the serving cart. Breakfast consisted of scrambled eggs, sausages and hash browns with copious amounts of coffee. Orange and grapefruit juice were on the menu as well. Joy, not that hungry, asked if there was something lighter. "Yes, we have a nice fruit salad with a scone and jam if you would prefer that for breakfast," offered the stewardess.

Gilley, seeing an opportunity possibly missed interjected, "Would it be possible for my wife to have both breakfasts? Of course, rest assured nothing will be wasted."

The stewardess smiled and Joy jabbed Gilley in the ribs, "Gilley I don't want a heavy breakfast.

The Stewardess, knowing what he wanted, said, "I'm sure your husband could help you eat whatever you can't. Sir, it's very generous of you to offer to help your wife." With that she passed Gilley two trays containing the full breakfast and Joy received the fruit tray.

"Gilley, is this how it's going to be for the rest of our lives? You're going to ask for my portions so you can eat a double helping?"

"Joy, I'm bloody famished, you know. You yourself acknowledged there was nothing in those vending machines at Stansted and the ones in Iceland, we didn't have the currency to get even a packet of chips. I haven't eaten anything substantial since that meal we had before we landed in Iceland."

Rolling her eyes, Joy conceded, "I hope you enjoy this breakfast because I'm quite embarrassed."

After the breakfast was finished, the stewardess came collecting the trays. She leaned over Gilley and said, "I hope you enjoyed your breakfast, Sir. You certainly kept your promise that nothing would be wasted. By the way we have extras of the egg breakfast and I was wondering if you'd help us with that so we don't have to unload it from the plane when we land? You look to me like a big guy who can handle it."

Smiling, Gilley said, "Sure, I can help you out. It seems flying makes one more hungry than usual."

Joy hadn't been paying much attention to the conversation until the stewardess appeared with the promised tray, "What the hell is going on here, Gilley? Did you wangle another breakfast? I won't be able to fly with this airline again, you've embarrassed me so much."

"No," defended Gilley. "The stewardess offered me this tray. She said I was a big guy and I could handle it. Besides, she'd appreciate it if I helped them by eating an extra one as they would have to unload it off the plane."

"Sure," stated Joy, "you bloody well talked her into another breakfast. I can't believe your nerve." With that she crossed her arms and stared out the window. The stewardess came to collect the tray and said, "Sir, I do appreciate you're helping us out by eating another breakfast. Others also cooperated and now we've none left to unload."

Joy, not believing her ears, harrumphed and retrieved the book she'd been reading. Gilley just smiled to himself. They didn't talk again until the captain announced their arrival to Seattle airspace and their impending landing. Joy looked up from her book and said, "Don't forget what Dad told you about our ticket. We're flying in on the return half of a charter. Complications arise if you don't play your cards right. You've embarrassed me enough this flight. Don't do it again. It's illegal to land in Canada on this type of ticket."

Gilley had pushed this fact to the back of his mind as he didn't quite understand the complicated arrangement but he did remember what Jim had said. By 1970, charter flights had become the way to travel. A charter flight was much more affordable than a scheduled round trip flight. Often it was a much better bargain for people traveling one way to buy a Charter flight ticket rather than a one way ticket. They would then sell the return leg of the flight to regain a portion of their original investment thus gaining even greater savings. Many travel agents accommodated this arrangement by changing the names on the ticket to reflect the buyer and to conform to the regulations. Joy and Gilley had been given two such tickets as a wedding gift from her parents so they could come to Canada.

Now this was all well and good for the most part. However, there was a catch. Jim had emphasized that Canada had made it illegal to land in the country using this type of ticket. Charters in Canada were a round trip and only those flying out of the country were allowed to return on that type of ticket.

Jim had further explained coming in as a landed immigrant to Canada on this type of ticket was totally illegal. Now this confused Gilley and put him in a bit a predicament. He wanted to impress his new in-laws and he did not want to land in jail or worse, be deported back to England away from his new bride. And he didn't really understand why Jim would buy them tickets which might lead to such a result.

He didn't know what he was facing or how to handle the encounter with the border guards. If he was in England, he felt confident he would be able to finesse the situation as he understood the rules and the English people. Now he was a stranger in a strange land and not familiar with the customs and the people. This created a bit of anxiety for him and of course a challenge. How would he handle this without looking the fool? He decided to put off thinking about the situation for another few moments hoping something would come to mind.

As the plane touched down in the Tacoma Airport in Seattle, Gilley could no longer avoid the issue. He thought, "Customs ... Hmmm ... Never been through any customs before. What sort of questions are they going to ask? MMMM ... Perhaps 'Where have I come from, where am I going, what is my purpose here and what am I bringing with me?' Yea, that's what I would want to know if I was a customs officer. Ah ... no problem, I'm just going to tell him the truth, mostly" (look up how to put the dots).

Getting off the plane and walking through the airport was an experience in itself. It was so much bigger than Stansted and Reykjavik. Fortunately, Joy seemed to know her way around and Gilley just tagged along, taking it all in. Before he knew it, they were at the luggage pick up. After that they were going through American Customs. This was where Gilley became worried. The Americans had a bit of a hard reputation allowing anyone into the country. To Gilley's surprise, things went fairly smoothly. The customs officer had asked Joy first for her passport, where her final destination was and what she was bringing back into the country. Joy showed him her passport and said, "I'm going to New Westminster, BC, Canada and I have a few presents for my family." The officer checked her declaration form and verified she wasn't over the allowable limit for bringing purchases into the country.

With that the officer let her through the gate. He then turned to Gilley, "What about you, Sir?"

Gilley responded, "I'm with her and we are going to New Westminster. She has all of the presents." He handed the officer his passport. The officer leafed through the pages looking for the Visa stamp and looked at Gilley, "So are you on holiday, sir, as I see your passport is from the UK, not from Canada? And here's your Visa."

"Yes, Sir, I'm on holiday."

"Very good. Carry on, Sir. Welcome to the United States of America. Have a good time. Thank you." He stamped the Visa with the date of entry.

"Wow," thought Gilley, "That was easy. What was I worrying about?" He didn't realize he was not home free yet as there was another border to cross.

Joy, with Gilley following, made their way to the exit looking for Jim and Veron. With finding them, there were lots of hugs and excitement and of course, the introductions to Joy's younger sisters Sally and Anne. Gilley had heard lots about them and was looking forward to meeting them. Jim said, "Boy, you finally got here and made it through customs. Your flight was overdue by eight hours. How did it go? It actually worked better for us as we didn't have to pick you up in the middle of the night."

"It was real easy," replied Gilley. "The officer was very accommodating and didn't ask any hard questions, Thank God. But we are tired from the flight."

"Not as tired as I am," said Veron. "I was up all bloody night checking with the airlines for your arrival time."

With that, Veron led the group out of the terminal and into the parking lot. "I can't wait to get you both home," she stated. "There is so much for you to learn and see, Gilley."

Gilley's response, after lighting a cigarette, was, "All I want is a beer. I am so thirsty."

"I have lots in the fridge for you, "interjected Jim, "but not what you're used to. You have to get used to Canadian beer and the way we drink it here."

Jim ushered the newly arrived couple to a car Gilley had only seen in movies-a 1968 Cadillac Fleetwood four door sedan. It was a massive, bronzy coloured car with leather seats and air conditioning and all the bells and whistles available. As he opened the trunk (boot to Gilley) it was so big Gilley thought they could have put four times the cases in there. The seats were like sofas as they made their way into the massive interior. Gilley had never seen anything like it. "How do you like your ride home, Gilley?" crowed Jim.

"Is this your car, Jim" replied an awed Gilley.

"No I borrowed it from a friend just for the occasion. It's not every day I bring my son-law home."

"I wish I had friends like you, Jim. The fanciest car my friends have is a Mini. My brother was a Vauxhall Cresta, which was based on the American style, but is no where the size of this. This is out of my world, Jim"

Everyone settled in for a smooth ride north. Veron, in the front passenger's seat, was pointing out the sights as Gilley was playing with the mod cons in the back seat. Power windows, interior reading lights and the intriguing fender lights that indicated the way the car was going to turn. He had never dreamed of riding in such a vehicle.

Gilley took this opportunity to quietly observe his new in-laws as everyone chatted excitedly. Sally and Anne sat in between him and Joy in the back seat while Veron occupied the spacious front seat. The girls were mesmerized by the Beatle like appearance of Joy's new husband and fought over who was going to sit beside him. Sally was about sixteen years old with long blonde hair that softly curled about her shoulders. She appeared to be nervous about this new member of the family and had difficulty understanding his accent. She kept giggling at Gilley's responses and asked Joy to explain what Gilley had said.

Anne on the other hand had light brown hair cut in a page boy style. She was more outgoing and confident and seemed to take things more in her stride even though she was the younger by a few years. Both girls were very attractive. Gilley thought, "Wow, how can one family have so many attractive girls in one go? Too bad my mates aren't here to meet them."

Veron was also attractive with ginger brown hair permed in the latest curly style. She was obviously the one in control and the one who made the major decisions. Gilley, having met her in England, knew this about his new mother-in-law already, but it was interesting seeing her in the setting of her family.

Jim was in his early fifties with a crew cut, was distinguished looking and obviously a man who had succeeded in his goals. He presented himself well as a man of culture and business. He was also very easy to talk to and this helped Gilley relax and become part of the family.

Viewing his new bride in her family's context, Gilley could see Joy's resemblance to Veron—definitely her daughter. At that point Gilley had a glimpse into the future.

Joy had told her sisters all about Gilley and had sent many photographs, but to actually see this Englishman, dressed in a suit and tie with a Beatle hair cut and speaking with that trendy accent was more than they could bear. They said they could hardly wait to get home to tell their friends about Gilley. Until now, the friends hadn't believed them. Now they had living proof.

Before anyone knew it they had reached the Canadian Border. Jim had announced it as they were approaching the wonderfully famous Peace Arch at the Douglas Border Crossing. He said, "Gilley, you made it through the first customs, but you've another to face. This is the one where you have to be on your toes. You are now entering Canada."

Gilley was paying attention now. "Another customs," thought Gilley? "I thought we had passed all the obstacles. Oh, oh."

What Gilley saw was nothing he could have imagined as a boundary between two major countries. A long roadway, bordered by trees showing their fall leaves, led to an arch like structure behind which were several gates. Above these were slowly flashing amber lights indicating which gates were open for service to the motoring public. Jim pulled up to a lineup that led to one of these gates. On the green light, he pulled forward to a booth in which a customs officer sat. The officer leaned out of the little window and asked. "All Canadian citizens?"

"We all are," motioning to his passengers, "but my new son-in-law isn't", answered Jim as he spoke through his open car window.

This was Gilley's cue. "I'm from England, Sir."

"What is your purpose in Canada" responded the officer.

Jim answering for Gilley, "He's on holiday. He's my new son-in-law."

"How long are you planning to stay in Canada?" Now the questions were directed at Gilley.

"Well, Sir, I'm not sure. I don't have a specified time. It's September and my new wife and I are staying at least until Christmas."

At this point, the customs official realized there was more to things than he first thought. He directed the vehicle to the parking on the left and directed Gilley to go into the customs office. He was to report to the official behind the counter there.

As Gilley entered the office, he was feeling apprehensive and this increased as he saw a long line of people waiting at the wicket. He began to feel more edgy as he wasn't sure what he should do. On top of this, the long flight was beginning to take its toll. His hands began to sweat. Anxiety was mounting as the line slowly crawled forward. Gilley was aware of his new family waiting in the car and didn't want them to become impatient. Gilley's usually optimist outlook on life had been seriously challenged now. What if he had come all this way only to be sent back to England without his wife? How would he deal with that? All of a sudden his thoughts were interrupted as it was his turn. The officer waved him forward to the counter.

The officer was a pleasant type and cheerfully asked, "What brings you to Canada today, Sir?"

"What does bring me to Canada?" thought Gilley. Responding out loud to the question, Gilley replied, "I'm visiting my new wife's parents who live in New Westminster." He then produced his passport.

As the officer perused the passport, he asked Gilley, "Where did you come from?"

Now Gilley remembered what Jim had told him about the charter flights and how they weren't allowed in Canada. He blurted out, "London, England, Sir."

"How did you get to the United States?"

"I flew into Seattle."

"Do you have your flight ticket?"

By now Gilley was really sweating. The line-up behind him was growing and he was running out of ideas. He reached into his pocket and slowly pulled it out and gave it to the officer. "I'm done for now," he thought.

Just at that time, Jim came into the office, walked up to the wicket and stood beside Gilley. "What seems to be the problem, Gilley?"

The officer interjected and said to Jim, "And who are you?"

Jim said. "I'm his father-in-law and I was wondering if there were any problems."

The officer said suspiciously, "Should there be any problems, Sir?"

"None whatsoever," said Jim, taking a step back.

Then the officer said, "It's his problem, not yours." At this juncture, Jim left Gilley to fend for himself.

This interruption had given Gilley time to think about his situation. The officer turned to Gilley and said, "Before you were in London, where were you?"

"Seattle."

"Good response. How did you get to Seattle originally," came the next question?

"I took a ship from Liverpool to New York and traveled by train to Seattle," lied Gilley.

"When did you arrive in New York?" pressed the officer, now on the offensive.

"August"

"Your passport hasn't been stamped other than the time you just came through the Seattle immigration on your Visa." The officer let the question just hang there.

Gilley realized he had been caught out in the lie. Now what? He also remembered Jim had said he couldn't land in Canada on a one way charter flight. BUT he had landed in the U.S. He realized he was going to be OK. He had landed in the United States and he had his immigration papers which were issued to him in England from

Canada. If he showed his immigration papers, it just might work. He reached into his breast pocket and said, "Perhaps I should have given you these first." With that he handed the officer his landed immigration papers. Just then, Joy burst through the door looking very worried.

The officer looking up said, "Is this your new bride?"

Gilley responded, "Yes, Sir it's been a long journey from England and I forgot about these immigration papers. I hope these help. It's an honour to come to Canada."

The officer looked at the ticket and the papers and realized Gilley had come in on a return charter, "Why didn't you say you had these papers in the first place? It appears you are not coming here for a holiday, but to spend some time here and, my guess is to eventually live here with your new wife. We don't care how you entered the United States, just how you come into Canada. I think you've come to North America via a return charter ticket and you know it's illegal to land in Canada through this method, so you've been stringing me along. You're lucky today because you landed in the United States on this ticket and not in Canada. My advice to you is to keep these papers with your passport at all times." With that, he tore off the appropriate section, stapled a receipt into Gilley's passport and said heartily, "Welcome to Canada." He looked at Joy and said, "You can now have your husband back. I hope you live happily ever after."

Gilley and Joy left as fast as they could and got into the car. Veron said. "Why did things take so long?"

Gilley said, "Well, let's just say I convinced him I was a good candidate to become a Canadian citizen. I didn't attempt to get into Canada illegally on a return charter. I came into the States and I just found out that the Canadian customs don't care how I got into the USA, just how I arrive into Canada. He asked me who advised me to avoid telling the truth as he could have sent me back to England with what I told. I didn't tell him it was my father-in-law, Jim. I just said I had been told not to say I was coming into Canada on a return charter ticket. And that it is illegal to come into Canada that way. But since I landed in the United States and then came to Canada, it didn't matter. He told me the person advising me should have informed me of this. It could have saved us all a lot of time and trouble."

With that Jim smugly declared, "Oh, You didn't have any worries. They wouldn't pay to send you back anyhow knowing this cheap government."

"Well, the customs agent figured out what was going on and let me go even though he knew I was stretching things," sparred, Gilley. "You wouldn't have wanted your daughter's new husband spending time in the slammer as it would have cost you money to get me out as you know I'm broke."

Jim, knowing he was fighting a losing battle at this point, changed the subject, "By the way, Joy, I got you a job at the Bank of Montreal. You know the one on the corner of 8th Avenue and 12th Street. You start Monday." Then looking Gilley straight in the eye, "So far we don't know what we are going to get for Gilley to do for a living."

Veron, who had been unusually silent interjected, "Well, Monday morning Gilley and I are going to Canada Manpower and register him with Unemployment Insurance. That's the fastest way for him to find a job.' Then looking at Joy and Gilley, she stated, "You two have two days to get settled at home and then your Grandma is expecting you both Saturday morning in Victoria."

With that, everyone settled into the luxurious seats for the hour journey to New Westminster. Gilley watched as the scenery flew by. The countryside was so different from England. The most impressive thing was its vastness. One could see for miles to the distant mountains. These seemed to surround the land he viewed. There were some trees which Gilley recognized but were so much taller. What was astonishing was he couldn't see any major buildings other than farm buildings, until they reached what Jim told him was the municipality of Surrey.

And the buildings, they were like nothing like he had imagined. They all looked very new and were of a very different design than he had seen even in photos. What really impressed Gilley was the space and sometimes the huge tracts of land between the buildings. The houses had large yards and the trees were very tall. The entire valley was surrounded by what Jim told him were the Coastal Mountains, some covered in snow, hanging in the background like silent guardians.

The hour had passed before Gilley knew it and they were crossing the mighty Fraser River on the Pattullo Bridge. Jim pointed this out to Gilley and added, "You are now entering the Royal City of New Westminster, the oldest city in British Columbia and the original capital of the province. It was built by the Royal Marines in 1858 and incorporated in 1860." They then proceeded down Columbia Street and Gilley saw buildings resembling the cities of the Wild West such as the San Francisco he had seen in movies. On the river he saw tug boats pulling long trains of logs tied together and some of these were anchored on the banks.

"Jim, where are all those tugboats going?" Gilley asked.

"They are going to the saw mills."

"Are the saw mills those cone shaped buildings belching smoke?"

"Well, they are part of the saw mill as they burn the saw dust that's used to feed the boilers. The boilers create the steam that powers the turbine generators which in turn produce the electrical power to run the mills. The bunches of logs you see floating in the river are called booms. This is one of the most efficient ways of moving the logs from the many logging areas to the producers of lumber and other wood products."

"I've never seen anything like this let alone heard of it. This is totally new to me and I find it amazing. I'm so pleased to see so much industry here. It bodes well for me to find employment in my field. These saw mills have to have machinery and there must be local engineering machine shops which service these industries along with these tug boats. There must be a fabulous opportunity in the ship yards as I can see all these tug boats need deck equipment like towing winches and capstans. It would be great to get a job in a company manufacturing these items." Canada was looking better by every step he took.

The Columbia Street itself was busting with the activity of Thursday shoppers-cars, pedestrians, buses—just like England, but on the other side of the road. This was a bit disconcerting for Gilley as he kept thinking how hard it would be to adapt to driving in this new country on the wrong side of the street.

Leaving Columbia Street, they traveled up Stewartson Way and Joy pointed out the A & W on the right hand side. "This is what I told you about, Gilley. This is the A & W. You drive your car up to the stall and the waitress comes out and gets your order. You eat in the car and the A & W is famous for their root beer (which is non-alcoholic, by the way). I could sure use a Teen Burger right now. It's been so long since I've had one and I can hardly wait. The burgers in England just don't do the trick." Gilley, not knowing what a Teen Burger was, could see this was something else he would have to adapt to—hamburgers and drive-ins and eating in the car. As they proceeded, Gilley saw more and more industry on the banks of the Fraser River. Finding a job shouldn't be too difficult.

Turning onto to Twentieth Street, Gilley saw how big the houses were, that they were all different designs and painted very different colours. Not like in England where one was much like the other. On top of that, everything seemed to be built out of wood, not like the stone, bricks and mortar of the UK. Turning onto Eighth Avenue, there was much the same type of housing. They pulled up at 1806 Eighth Avenue. In comparison to the other houses Gilley had seen, this house seemed quite small from the street.

Everyone piled out of the car, thankful to stretch their legs. The men retrieved the cases from the trunk and carried them into the house. The door was unlocked. This surprised Gilley—perhaps they had forgotten to lock it in their excitement to pick up the newlyweds. "Just leave the cases here in the hall," instructed Jim, "I could use a beer. Come on Gilley. Let me show you the best place in the whole house." With that he proceeded down a flight of stairs with Gilley following hard on his heels, as beer sounded so good.

What unfolded in front of his eyes was a sight to behold—an English pub right there in a house. It had everything—a dart board, a snooker table and the fully stocked bar. Jim walked behind it and opened the fridge which was hidden to the side. He pulled out two bottles of Labatt's Blue and took down two glasses. Gilley was taking all of this in as Jim handed him his glass. "Welcome to Canada." Just then Joy and Veron appeared. Jim repeated the ritual and handed the ladies two glasses. They toasted the safe arrival of the couple and were almost ready for a second round when the two girls, Anne and Sally came downstairs.

"Could we have a Coca Cola, please Dad and can we play a game of pool with Gilley?" They giggled a bit as they looked at him. He was still quite the novelty. Gilley knew how to play billiards and snooker, but had not played the American game of pool.

"Well, girls, I would love to have a game with you, but you'll have to teach me how to play as I've never played Pool." Amazed at this, Sally, the oldest said, "You don't know how to play Pool? Why don't Anne and I play a game and you can watch how it's done? Then you can play the winner. We'll give you pointers as we go. We usually play High-Low ball. I can't believe you've never seen a Pool table before."

"Well," said Gilley, "I've never seen one this small before. I'm used to playing on the larger tables. We play Billiards and Snooker in England, not Pool."

Jim said, "We've got Snooker balls. Let's play Snooker. The girls haven't played it too much yet, but we can play partners. You take Anne and I'll take Sally." With that, he gave the girls their cokes and got the ball out of the rack which was hanging on the wall. They flipped a coin to decide who got first break and the game was on. The girls forgot their shyness for awhile as they concentrated on their shots. This was a longer, more serious game than they were used to, but, they were playing with a guy that looked like the Beatles. Cool!

After the game was over, Jim took charge even further. "Gilley, you've seen my bar. Now I'd like to show you the rest of the house. I've renovated it myself. You should have seen it when we first moved in 1958. Everything was old and worn out. I've put all brand new things in. You couldn't get it any nicer than this."

At that Veron loudly cleared her throat, "You did the renovations yourself? Who painted and cleaned up after you? Who helped knock down the old plaster and held the gyp rock while you nailed it up? Who then cleaned the mess you left when you did the plastering? Who ran for your tools when you forgot where you left them? How soon you forget, Jim!"

Jim, winking at Gilley, "You're right, Veron, WE were the best team and OUR house is the best on the block."

With that, Jim turned and marched upstairs with Gilley on his heels. As they got to the top of the landing, Jim quietly said to Gilley, "Remember, appeasement costs you nothing. If she only knew how much it really entailed." With that, Jim led the way through the main floor, first to the Master bedroom, then the guest bedroom and then the den which was where the TV was located. This had been converted from a bedroom. Jim then took Gilley into the large living room which could comfortably seat twelve people and following that, onto the dining room. There they had a table which sat eight and with extra leaves, could seat more.

The kitchen came next. This room was small compared to the other rooms, but had the most mod cons Gilley had ever seen. There was a large refrigerator, a stove, a big toaster oven and incredibly, a dishwasher. In the large double kitchen sink there was the latest fad—a garburator! This was Jim's pride and joy. He explained to Gilley, "If you ever use this to dispose of garage, you have to run lots of water down the drain. Watch it devour this carrot! Don't tell Veron I've just wasted a carrot." With that Jim turned on the garburator and the water and pushed the carrot into the middle of the hole. There was lots of noise as the blades chewed up the carrot and it disappeared down the drain.

Gilley was duly impressed. "Wow, you have to make sure you don't get your fingers in the way." They then moved out to the outside deck. This covered seventy five percent of the back of the house and overlooked the Fraser River. Off in the distance, Jim pointed out this large white cone.

"That's Mount Baker. You know it's a live volcano and it's only about a hundred miles from here. Sometimes you can see white smoke coming from the top and you know she's active. Interesting that it's almost two miles high. It doesn't look it from here."

"Is that in Canada, Jim?" asked Gilley.

"No, that's in the States, in the state of Washington. That's the state we came through bringing you and Joy from Seattle," replied Jim.

"Wow, it's so breathtaking. There's almost too much for me to take in. I can't believe how big this country is and I know I've only just seen a very small part of it." Gilley said.

"You haven't seen anything yet, Gilley. Wait until you go to Victoria. You will see some sights and some spectacular scenery. One day you might get to see the interior of BC. Now *that's* big country."

Looking to the left, Gilley saw a large grassed area surrounded by tall cedar trees that screened it from the back lane. To the right there was an asphalt parking area large enough for two cars to park side by side. "Whose street is that back there," asked Gilley pointing to the lane.

"Oh, that's our access lane which runs behind all of the houses that face onto Eighth Avenue and onto Seventh Avenue," Explained Jim.

From the deck, Jim took Gilley back into the house through the kitchen and living room and up yet another flight of stairs. This was where Anne and Sally had their own bedrooms. They shared a complete bathroom. This was so unheard of to Gilley. Anne's bedroom was neat and orderly and Sally's was a mess. Jim commented, "Thank God I don't have to come up here too often. Let's go back to the bar. It's time for another beer. I'll show you the basement and where you and Joy will be staying." With that he headed off with Gilley close behind, fearing he might get lost in this house of many rooms if he lost sight of Jim.

Arriving once more at the bar, Joy was behind the bar acting as the bartender. "What will you two gentlemen like to drink? I'm sure after your adventures you're very thirsty." She handed them each a fresh beer and took one for herself. "Gilley, Come with me. I have to show you our suite. Mom and dad put it together for us from the rest of the basement."

Leading the way, Joy opened a door that was off to the side behind the stairs. What Gilley saw really surprised him. To the left there was a stove, a sink and a fridge and then an outside door. To the front and a little to the right there was a small eating area complete with a little table and four chairs in front of a window. Further to the right, there was an area Joy said was the living room with a couch and chair. Behind this was the bedroom with a double bed and a built-in closet. "This suite used to be Grandma's before she moved back to Victoria. Mom and dad have fixed it up just for us to use temporarily until we can get our own place. Mind you, we have to pay them rent. They've given us the first month free. Of course we still have to buy our own food etc. Mom has also made it quite clear to me the furniture in this room is on loan and if we want it when we move, we have to buy it from them. Mom really emphasized the rules around the bar. She said, 'It's not a free bar'. Meaning what we drink we have to replace."

"I never expected anything like this," said Gilley awed at all he saw. "This is fantastic. We actually have our own place to live separate from the family and with the added benefit of being able to play darts and pool and enjoy the atmosphere of an English pub. My friends would be jealous. Maybe I should talk to Jim and make sure we have all the rules so we don't spoil a good thing. I'll talk to Jim when he shows me the rest of the house. He said there was much more to see. I can't believe it. I'm totally flabbergasted at this place. It's not what I'm used to in England. Everything here is so big." Turning to Joy, Gilley asked, "How could you want to give all of this up and return to England where everything is small and crowded?"

"It may be small and crowded to you, but material things aren't everything, you know. I enjoy the history of England and the traditions. I really like the English humor and the times we had in the pubs."

"Yeah, I really liked the times in the pubs too. I can see we're going to be spending our time in your dad's 'pub'. I can hardly wait. Let's go back."

Returning to the bar, Gilley thanked Jim and Veron for what they had done for them. "It's amazing, Jim. In England parents do their best to help out their children and the most the kids can expect is a room in the family home. But here, you've given us a whole suite and privacy to boot."

Jim said. "It doesn't come free, you know, Gilley. That's why I got Joy a job at the bank starting on Monday and before the week's out, I guarantee you will have a job too. Veron will make sure of that. She had plans to take you to Man Power on this coming Monday."

"Now, I want to make sure you know the rules of the house. You *never* take the last beer out of the fridge. As a matter of fact, if you take any beers out of the fridge, you replace them immediately. We expect you to furnish your own fridge with beers and whatever beverages you would like to drink. Now, your fridge is open to me if I need to supply my guests. You are welcome to use the darts and pool table anytime as long as you bring your own drinks and of course one for Veron and me. Now, Veron doesn't drink beer that much unless it's really hot. She prefers Scotch or Vodka. The mix we have."

At that stage, Gilley, feeling as if he needed to add some of his own rules, said, "That's fair enough, Jim. You have been more than generous with Joy and me. *Our* rules are never leave our fridge totally empty of beer. You have to leave at least three, two for me and one for Joy. That's all, Jim. All I ask is that I have a beer when I want one. And I think that's fair enough."

Jim was about to reply when Veron jumped in, "It's time for supper. Joy and I will go up stairs and warm up the Minestrone soup and buns. Jim, show Gilley the rest of the basement and come right up. It will only be a few minutes until supper is served."

Gilley turned to Joy, "Is that wonderful smell the soup we are having for supper? I've never heard of Minestrone. What the hell is Minestrone soup? Whatever it is, it smells wonderful."

Joy replied, "Minestrone is Italian and Mom makes the best around. I'm sure if she took it to Italy they wouldn't be able to tell the difference."

With that, the women went upstairs and Jim said, "Come on Lad, I'll show you the rest of the basement." With that, he ushered Gilley into the laundry area which had a washing machine, clothes dryer, an ironing board and lines upon which were hanging clothes drying 'by air' Jim said. Gilley had never seen what Jim referred to as a dryer.

"So, Jim, are you saying you put clothes into this machine and they come out dry? My mother used to put her clothes into a spin dryer which was nothing like the size of this. But all it would do was take out the excess water. She would still have to hang the clothes on the clothes line to dry."

"If you're awed by the laundry room, let me take you to my work shop. This is where I spend as much time as I'm allowed." With that, Jim escorted Gilley into his workshop. It was amazing and Gilley gaped at all the tools on display and at the bench space and at the hand tools.

Turning to Jim he said, "Man, this is just great. I've never seen this in a home before. Woodworking was my favorite subject in school. There I learned to use many of these tools. Let me know if you need any help. I would be more than happy to lend a hand. Since leaving school, I've not been able to get back to it as my career focused more on the metal industry. But I do know how to use all these.

I wish my father was here to see all of these fancy tools. He was amazing at working with wood. All he had as tools was a saw, a hammer, a screwdriver, pair of pliers and a chisel. With these tools he built sheds, fences and kennels for every type of animal as well as repairing everything that needed it. I really admire his skill and his ingenuity."

Jim replied, "Well, Gilley. I have a few projects lined up. I didn't realize you would be interested. I haven't had another man about the house to help me out. I'd like it if you could. Besides, we are close to the bar where we can get a beer break when we feel the need." With that, both men could hear they were being summoned. "Supper is ready." With that, Jim motioned with his eyebrows and they headed for the stairs.

Veron directed everyone where to sit at the huge dining room table. This was another new experience for Gilley. This table was big enough to seat eight and he counted only six for dinner. That left lots of room between the diners for the foursome and Anne and Sally. This was so different from what he was accustomed to in England where his mother's table had to be unfolded and at the most sat six in very tight quarters. It seemed like everything in Canada was bigger.

The first bowl of soup came with a large piece of heavy bread smothered in real butter. Gilley hadn't realized how hungry he was until the first spoonful hit his mouth. Before he knew it the bowl and the bread were gone. Up jumped Veron, "Have another bowl Gilley. It's good to see someone with a good appetite. More bread?" As Gilley nodded his agreement to both, Jim subtly pushed his bowl ahead as well, indicating he too wanted a refill.

After the third bowl, Gilley actually considered a fourth. Jim, reading his mind, stated, "Veron, I hope you have enough left over for our lunch tomorrow."

"Don't worry, Jim, I'll make sure you never go hungry. Gilley's enjoying this soup. I wouldn't want our new son-in-law to go hungry on his first night in Canada." At that everyone laughed. Hungry was the last thing Gilley would be after that dinner. Jim said, "Come on, Gilley. I think you've had enough. It's time to go down stairs while the girls clear up. I think a nice cold beer and a game of pool would finish off a perfect day." With that, he towed Gilley to the basement and the women dutifully cleared up the table.

The men had about half an hour to themselves, playing pool and shooting the breeze. The women came downstairs and joined them for a night cap. After all, the newlyweds had been traveling for over 24 hours. On top of that there had been a lot of driving, the uncertainty of the border and excitement in getting them home. Everyone was ready for bed. Jim said. "Chop, chop! Time for bed! Joy, I'm sure you can find everything you need for the night." With that, Veron and Jim climbed the stairs and Gilley and Joy entered their suite.

It didn't take long for the new couple to find themselves in bed. Gilley, lying in bed, thought about his family back in England. He thought about the last few days, saying farewell to his family and the stay in London. "Here we are, 6000 miles from home and a new life to start. There are so many mod-cons, the place is so vast and the houses are so big! How can I remember all of this and adapt to this new way of life?" His last thought as he drifted to sleep was of his brother, Neil, standing at Newcastle train station saying, "Don't forget your heritage, Gilley. Come back home sometime soon. Don't be like your magpie, Pete who left never to return."

The following morning was quiet. Gilley awoke before Joy, cleaned up, dressed and quietly left their suite, finding his way to the kitchen. Veron was sitting at the kitchen table having a cup of tea. Gilley was surprised she was all made up and ready for the day. What time was it anyway? At that point Veron asked him what he'd like for breakfast. "A cup of tea and some toast would be fine, Veron. I'm still full of Minestrone soup. That was a great dinner."

Cup of tea in hand, Gilley made his way out to the deck. He had noticed it was after nine in the morning. Wow, he hadn't slept that late for a long time. He stood on the deck sipping his tea and enjoying his first cigarette of the day. The view was spectacular. The Fraser River wound before him and off in the distance was this large, snow covered mountain. There houses on the hillside of the river and traffic on the roads. People going places. Gilley wondered where they were going. Not too far in the distance, he heard a haunting sound. Just then, Veron appeared with the toast and more tea. Gilley said, "What's the name of that huge mountain in the distance again? Jim told me but I can't remember."

"That's called Mount Baker. It's over one hundred miles away in the United States and is over two miles high. If you watch it over time, you can see a steam plume coming from it at times as it's a live volcano."

"A live volcano right on your door step? I remember Jim telling me that. That's amazing. Has it ever erupted?"

"Not since I've been here, thank God. Actually, I think the last eruption was in late 1800's. As far as I know it was a small event and didn't threaten anyone living in the vicinity."

"Wow! One hears about such things, but to be living in the shadow of a volcano is truly unique. Another question, what is that haunting sound in the distance? I've been hearing it all night long."

"Veron says, "It's the bloody trains. They're noisy, things. They keep me awake all night. You'd think by now they would have figured out a way to silence them and keep them from making that noise, especially at night. It's a good job we don't live right on the track."

"They don't sound like that in England", replied Gilley. "It sounds quite romantic to me."

"Romantic?!?! Wait until you've been here a few years and they've kept you awake for nights on end. You'll change your mind about them."

This made Gilley giggle a bit, "Vernon, I'd like another cup of tea, if you don't mind. Oh, here comes Joy."

Joy was not in the greatest of moods. "I see married life hasn't changed your morning moods, Luv," Veron commented. "Come and have a cup of tea."

"You know I don't do mornings—not like the two of you. I could hear you two giggling and chatting all morning, especially you, Gilley with that penetrating voice of yours. It carries for miles." groused Joy. "I suppose Dad's gone to work?"

"That's right, Luv. It's Friday morning. He left the house at 7:45 as usual. He'll be back for lunch. That reminds me. I have to go to the bakery to get more of that bread. Gilley, you ate us out of it last night. I'm glad you liked it. I always thought that particular bread went the best with my Minestrone soup. I see you agree with me."

Gilley just smiled as Veron left to get more tea. Then he pulled Joy to one side. "Would it be possible to have a shower now?"

Veron saw them huddled together. "What are you two doing?"

Joy explained, "Gilley was just asking if he could try the shower downstairs."

"Sure he can. He can go right now. Jim has a shower most mornings and a bath at night. I think Gilley should get used to it."

Joy retorted, "He can have a shower in the morning but not a bath at night. That's my time whenever we have a bath tub. I can see I'll have to use your tub and make sure it's before nine o'clock so I don't' interfere with dad's bath schedule." Having gotten the go ahead, Gilley excused himself and headed downstairs.

He knew where the shower stall was. However, he had only ever had a shower at a facility after playing sports, never at home. Gilley found himself facing another new experience. It didn't take long to figure out how to turn the water on and to find the shampoo and soap that stood in the rack hanging from the overhead nozzle.

The water temperature was more of a challenge though. It was either freezing or too hot. Gilley bounced in and out a few times, laughing. There was more to this than he had thought. Eventually, he found that by adjusting the hot and cold taps correctly, he could get just the right temperature of water. Oh, that felt so good. The pressure of the water beating on his skin felt so wonderful. There was nothing like this in England that he knew of. Lost in revere, he suddenly heard Joy banging on the door and shouting, "How long are you going to be in there? It's been over fifteen minutes already." Gilley shouted back, "Joy, This is just magical. Two more minutes."

With that Joy returned upstairs. "He's gone daft in the head." She announced to Veron. "Now he thinks the shower is magic. I tell you it doesn't take much to make him happy."

Veron replied, "Well, that's good. He's in for a lot of new experiences. If he likes the shower so much, just think, Joy, he'll want to get up early in the morning to have a shower so he can go to work."

Joy hearing this, thought. "With all these new things and modern conveniences, will he every want to go back to England?"

Anne and Sally appeared at this time. They had overheard how Gilley was enjoying his shower. They then asked, "What was it like, living in England, Joy?"

"It's a lot different than here. They don't have the luxuries there like we do here. The shower is a good example. People there bathe once a week, whether they need it or not. Showers are almost unheard of, especially in the homes. Everything there is much smaller than here because the houses are so old and the modern appliances we have would hardly fit in even if they have the money to buy them. For example Gilley's parents didn't have a fridge or telephone at home. They have a spin washer but no dryer and Nelly has to hang their clothes on a clothes line to dry."

Anne and Sally found this hard to believe. "Well, why would you want to live there, then? Its sounds so old fashioned."

Joy said, "The people are so much fun. They don't' think twice about inviting you into their homes or out for a beer at the pub. The pubs are a lot of fun. Not like the ones we have here. People go there to meet their friends and they play darts, dominoes, cards and they had great sing-a-longs. All you needed was someone to play the piano. It was very different than here. Everyone knew everyone else and just had fun. Even if you were a stranger, it didn't' take long to be included in the fun."

"You play the piano, Joy. Did you ever do that," queried the girls?

"Nope. I didn't know the songs. Besides, I was having too much fun to bother playing the piano."

Veron chimed in, "Remember, you were just on holiday there, even though it was a working holiday, I'm sure you just wanted to listen to what others had to play."

At this point Gilley returned to the kitchen all fresh and clean. "WOW that shower is magical. I have never felt so good. Just think I can have one of these every day. I imagine I can have several if I really want to. Canada is so wonderful. What will come next?"

Joy eyed Gilley, "I told you he's gone totally daft over a stupid shower. What will happen when he comes across something really big?"

Anne and Sally looked at Gilley, who then looked back at them, "Aren't you supposed to be in school today?"

Together they responded, "No. Mom said we could have the day off to get to know you better. We've been doing pretty well in school. Besides, we have extra homework to do to make up for it."

Joy joined in, "These girls are so curious about you and your life in England. Why don't you start with the story of the Magpie? I'd like to hear it again. I know Mom would be interested."

"Oh, do you mean Pete? He was a character," said Gilley, settling in with his third cup of tea for the morning. "He came to us when I was about ten year old. My brother Neil had found him one day when he was walking through the woods close to his home in Lamesley. Now Neil and his wife lived with her mother in the Station Cottages. This was about twelve miles from our house which is in Throckley.

The bird had obviously been pushed out of his nest. Neil tried to put him back in but the nest was just too high and he was attacked by the parents for his efforts as well. He decided to bring him home and raise him as a pet. My father was known in the county for his ability with birds and animals. Many people brought sick ones to him and he just seemed to know what to do to make them better. Neil knew that the little bird stood the best chance with Dad looking after him so he brought Pete, well that wasn't his name at the time, over on a Sunday afternoon. It was common for Joan and Neil to come for Sunday tea and to have a bath."

At this point, Sally jumped in, "Why did he wait until Sunday, Gilley? Pete could have died."

"Sally, you have to understand that in England in 1955, most people took public transport. It would have taken Neil an hour and a half to get to our place from where he lived. He knew enough about birds to keep him alive till my father could take over. You see, Neil had wanted to be a Veterinarian as he enjoyed all types of animals. He had had everything from ferrets, rabbits, dogs, cats, pigeons and even the odd time a hedgehog he had found in the woods."

"This particular Sunday, Pete, as he was eventually called, came along with them in a shoe box. Neil explained how he had found him and what he hoped Dad could do. He also stated he thought this would make a good pet for me to distract me from my asthma (that's another story). Well, I was thrilled. It was the first time I had seen a magpie so close and the first bird I had ever had as a pet. Neil handed the bird over to my father and he made all the regular checks. He knew what he was doing as he had raised racing pigeons. Well, everything was well with our magpie. No broken wings or claws. His eyes were bright so we knew he didn't have internal damage. He was stressed though, due to his bus trip. Dad declared the best thing for him was to be able to fly around. The shed was idea. He said he could make a nice box with a nest inside for his comfort. The magpie could fly around inside the shed and stretch his wings. He would get over the stress of being separated from his family and would develop in a normal way.

Right away we all made a trip to the shed which was at the back of our yard. There dad quickly constructed the box, settled Pete inside and set about solving the next problem-food. "What have you been feeding him, Neil" Dad asked?

"I've given him bread soaked in milk. He seems to have taken to that."

Dad was glad to hear that. "What we have to do is slowly wean him off the bread and milk and introduce a more natural diet. We have to look for some worms after tea. I can mash them up and begin to mix it into the bread and milk. It won't be long before he'll start looking for his own food."

Anne squealed, "OOOH, you fed him worms and you mashed them up??? YUK! How gross is that!??!!?"

"Why did you call him Pete, Gilley?" Veron asked.

"Well, it had to do with the noise he made. Don't forget, I was only ten and he was a very young bird. He peeped instead of making adult birds sounds and the peeping sound he made sounded like PETE, PETE. I thought, 'What a smart bird, he knows his own name.'

Anyway, he seemed to like it as he responded to it right away. And everyone said it suited him."

"That's typical of a young boy," said Veron.

"As time passed, he grew and started to fly around the shed more often. He had taken on all of the characteristics of a magpie raised in the wild, so my father decided it was time to let him out of the shed to see what would happen. My father had forewarned me that Pete may just fly away and never be seen again when the time came. That would be the best thing for him.

The day eventually came for Pete's release. He was tentative in coming out of the shed. At first he sat on top of the door and looked around. Then he flew for a bit and came back to the door. Then he leapt to the roof and then went back inside where he knew it was safe. This went on a few times. Then I guess he decided the world was OK after all because he hopped onto the door one more time and then flew away. I stood there looking after him for a time and then I went to my room, sure that he was gone to find his rightful place in nature. The following day, when I woke up, I heard a pecking on my window. I opened the curtain and there was Pete. He pecked on the sill again as if to say, "Let me in." I opened the window and he jumped on my shoulder as he had often done before and nibbled at my ear.

With that we walked down stairs to my mother's astonishment. 'Well, he came back, eh? He must be hungry.' She made him a breakfast of bread and milk which he ate greedily while I had my porridge. He wanted to try that too. It was as if he was glad to be back and part of our family. After we had eaten, mother sent us outside. He immediately flew to the shed and to his perch. This was a spot he had adopted since outgrowing the nest dad had made for him when he was small. I felt he needed some time by himself, so I closed the door and went off to school.

The next morning was Saturday. Father went out to open the shed door for Pete before he went off to work. Many Saturdays I went to work with my father and helped to stoke up the boilers. Usually Pete flew out of the shed and would perch on top of the kitchen door as we finished our breakfast. This day was different. As he sat there a large gust of wind slammed the door shut trapping Pete's left claw. What a squalling he made. Father quickly opened the door, but the damage had been done. The claw hung there mangled. Father immediately took

Pete and calmed him down. Then he rapped the claw in bandages. He said that was the only way to save the claw if possible. If the claw could not be saved, then Pete would not survive.

Pete seemed to know he was being cared for. He accepted the bandage and didn't try to remove it. He just made the best of it by hopping around quietly in the shed. This recovery took several days. Father would patiently change the bandage daily. Pete would sit quietly while this took place. Eventually Father declared it was healed as best as it could be. Pete knew this too. Even though it looked crooked and out of place with his other claw, he managed to adapt quite well. He could land and perch as well as ever. This feature became his distinguishing trademark around village."

"With this injury, a new development had occurred though. He had become very attached to my father. He would follow him to the bus stop when he left for work and be waiting there when he arrived home again. Eventually, he became more adventurous. He would actually take the bus with him. It became quite the talk of the neighborhood as Pete would jump on the back of the bus and perch on the landing deck. These buses were double decker buses like the ones in London, but yellow.

Now, these buses had two employees, one the driver and the other the conductor. The conductor collected the fare from the travelers and he was also responsible for the welfare of the passengers. When Pete began riding the buses, these conductors were concerned he would somehow distract the driver or the passengers and cause an accident. Also, if he was so bold as to ride on the back deck, what would stop him from coming right into the bus and flying around? To solve the problem, they began to shoo him away, often as the bus came to a stop to let passengers on or off. Well, Pete being quite quick, came to expect this. Soon, he would fly off himself, sit on top of the bus roof and wait until the bus started again. Then he would fly down and perch on the platform again. Eventually the conductors realized he would do no harm and they began to joke with my father that he should be paying double the fare. My father would joke back, "And how much does it say in your manual what a bird's fare is for standing room only?"

Gilley continued, "One thing you may not know about magpies is that they like shiny objects. They are attracted to bits of silver paper, metal, glass etc, anything that sparkles. Well, we really knew about Pete's attraction as he would often return home with a bit of paper or glass and deposit it in the shed around his perch. Sometimes he would come to my school and become quite the nuisance, sitting on the window squawking and making quite the racket. I would often have to spend my recess time taking him home instead of playing with my friends in the school yard.

He began to be quite inquisitive and as a result of this, began to adventure through strange, open windows and into our neighbours' homes. Many of them began telling us he had flown into their homes, only to be shooed out again. Then one day a man appeared at our door. My mother thought he was a new insurance man as it was very common in those days for insurance men to come around and collect the insurance money on a weekly basis. It turned out that was an insurance man alright, but he was on a different mission. He was an investigator. He immediately asked my mother if we had a magpie as a pet. Of course she said "Yes". Then she asked why he was asking.

"Well, he said, "we have had many small claims reported to us of stolen jewelry. These reports state that the thief was a magpie who flew into their open windows and took these items. We have been told that you have such a bird and that your son has trained him to do become a thief."

My mother said, "I can tell you the bird is very inquisitive. And we have been told he has flown into peoples' houses. But how do you know he was the so believed thief? If you would like to know more, you should talk to my son. He should be home from school at any time." Just at that time, I came up the footpath with Pete flying around me. I was anxious to tell my mother of Pete's gift to me. When I saw my mother talking to a man, I hesitated. And a good thing that was too. As the man turned around to face me, Mother put her fingers to her lips indicating I should be silent. Then she said, "Let's all go into the house for a cup of tea and talk this over." With that, we went into the kitchen and Pete flew off.

After Mother had completed the ritual of pouring the tea, she said, "Gilley, this gentleman is here from the insurance company. He's an investigator. Apparently many people have reported they have been robbed of their jewelry by a magpie. This man is wondering if that magpie is our Pete. Would you mind answering his questions?"

With that, the man began his interrogation. "How long have you had your bird?"

"About seven months." I replied.

"Does he come to you when you call him?"

"Sometimes."

"Does he collect shiny objects?"

"I know he gets intrigued by silver paper and pieces of glass and what looks like pieces of pottery."

"What does he do with them?"

"He pecks at them, picks them up and drops them. Looks at them and picks them up again. Sometimes he flies off with them."

"Where does he fly off to?"

"He flies off in the direction of the dean. We often see him when we're playing over there, flying about the hedgerows."

"Have you ever followed him, when he carried something off?"

"No, he goes too fast. And when he goes, he comes back whenever he wants to."

"Do any of your friends see where he goes to?"

"None of my friends have said anything and no one has told me they have found anything like a hoarding place. You know they are renowned to have several of them as I've been told by my father."

"He does stay here sometimes, doesn't he? Can I see where that is?"

"Sure, he has his perch out in the garden shed." With that, we got up from the table and I led him to the shed. Pete was there, sitting on his perch. However, he would not let him into the shed. This man was a stranger. He squawked at him and flew to the door and back to his perch, clearly indicating his disapproval of this presence.

The man then said, "Well, obviously he doesn't want me to be here. What is he hiding?"

I replied, "If you leave and go back to the house, I will get him out of here. Then you can look around all you want to." He agreed. With that, I closed the door, settled Pete down and took a bit of extra time to collect the shiny bits that had accumulated on the floor. After all, I didn't want any evidence lying around that may provide the man with an excuse to take Pete away. When ready, I opened the door and Pete as normal, flew away. The man came and took his look around. He spent a while in the shed looking into every nook and cranny. I was hoping that Pete hadn't hidden anything I couldn't see. Eventually, he was satisfied and said so. He took his leave of us, but it was not to be a quiet one. Pete returned and let the man know he was not pleased with his intrusion.

Mother and I returned to the kitchen to have supper. I knew I should let her know about the gift Pete had given me that afternoon. I just wasn't sure quite how to approach the subject. I decided that the best way was the direct approach. "Mom, I have to show you the diamond Pete gave me today." With that I dug into my pocket and removed all the silver paper and the glass I'd collected from the shed floor. In amongst it all was the diamond that had weighed so heavily during the man's visit.

My mother said, "Where did you get all that paper from?"

"From the shed floor. I didn't want the man to take Pete away."

She saw the diamond. "We should wait until your father comes home and tell him the full story. Now enjoy your dinner."

Father arrived home at his normal time, 9:30 PM. It was past my bedtime, but I could not go to bed until I had this matter resolved. Upon hearing the door open, I jumped up ready for whatever came next. Mother took charge of the situation and handed Father his usual cup of tea and told him of the day's ordeal. Father said, "Let me have a look at that so called diamond."

I carefully handed it over, feeling confident that he would know what to do. He took the diamond, and said, "Hmmmm, looks like it's about half a carat. It also looks like it's fallen out of someone's ring. Now the way to test if it's a real diamond is to place it against the glass window and see if it scratches." Sure enough, it cut the glass.

"Now," Father said, "It appears that we have a diamond. There are two things we could do to find the owner. Firstly, when people lose anything they value, they often put an ad in the local stores. I'm sure you've seen those small papers in the windows of the various stores. Over the next few days, when you get time, go and check them out. The second thing we could do is hand it over to the local police in case somebody has notified them they've lost a diamond. You never know, Gilley, there could be a reward in it for you."

"Father, if we go to the police, would they take Pete away?" This was my biggest concern.

"No, they wouldn't take Pete away. It's typical of that breed of bird to pick up shiny objects. But you could always say you found it on the ground. And I wonder if that insurance man has had a claim for such a diamond. It would be interesting if he did. And after all, maybe Pete did steal it out of a bedroom. Now, Son, I'll leave the decision up to you. I'd like you to go to bed and go to sleep. While you're sleeping the solution will come to you." Father then took the diamond and put it into a little glass dish and placed this onto the sideboard. "It'll be safe there. Everyone can see it. We just have to wait. Time for bed."

With that we all retired to our respective beds. As I settled into mine, I realized it was up to me to solve the mystery of the diamond. I decided that first thing after school, I would check the local stores for adverts indicating lost diamonds. If I didn't find any of those, I would then check the local newspapers. Having decided on a plan, I fell asleep."

At this point, a noise at the front door brought them all back to reality. "Oh," said Veron, "That's Jim home already for lunch. I can't believe it's already twelve o'clock. I'd better get his lunch ready." With that, Gilley got up from the table to make way for Jim.

All of the women clamored at once, "You can't stop the story now without telling us what happened to the diamond."

Standing in the door frame, Gilley turned and said, "Well, I checked the ads like my father told me to and no one had reported a missing diamond. I even checked the local papers in the lost and found sections. Then one day, before I had had the chance to go to the police, I checked the glass dish again. Much to my shock and dismay, the diamond was gone! I asked my mother and father and they had removed it. Who could have taken it? Could it have been Pete? It was common for him to be in the house especially when the windows were open. When we have more time, I'll tell you the rest of the story." With that Gilley turned on his heel and headed down to their suite to get beers for lunch. After all, they were still on holiday.

Chapter 2

Victoria and Life in Canada

SATURDAY WAS A HARD start as Joy and Gilley had to be up early and on the road to Victoria so Gilley could meet Grandma and Aunt Rosa. The night before had seen an impromptu party of friends and neighbours who eventually went home after 2:00 AM. Much to Gilley's relief, Joy was doing the driving. She knew about driving on the correct side of the road for Canada and of course knew the way to the ferry terminal. Besides visiting Grandma and Aunt Rosa and seeing the capital city of BC, Gilley was to see where Joy was born and spent the first part of her life. Gilley was looking forward to learning more about Joy. After all, she had spent a great deal of time with his parents and exploring his history.

The couple was allowed to take Veron's white Datsun 510 to Vancouver Island instead of having to take the bus. This was on the condition they returned the car with a full tank of gas. Of course when they got into it, Joy realized their first stop before the ferry would have to be the gas station as there was only a quarter of a tank to begin with. "Typical of Mother," she grumbled after she started the car. "Not only will we have to fill the tank so we don't run out before we get back, but we'll have to return it to Mother with a full tank as well. There's always a price to pay with Mother. You'll learn that soon enough."

"Well, it's nice of her to lend us her car, Joy. We'd be paying more if we had to rent one for our trip. It's also more convenient than taking the bus. This way, we have more freedom to see where you grew up and as well as other sites."

"Putting it that way, I can see your point of view. It would be nice if she'd give us a break, though."

They drove through New Westminster, over the Queensborough Bridge (another bridge crossing the Fraser) and stopped at a small gas station. All of a sudden a young man ran out of the building and up to the driver's window. "How may I help you, Ma'am?"

"Please put five dollars of regular gas in, thank you," replied Joy. Turning to Gilley, she said, "That should about fill it up. We can stop here on our way back and top it up."

"Wow, man!!! This is impressive. Is this normal? You have attendants fill your petrol tank here in BC? That's unheard of in England. We have to do it ourselves. And the price of gasoline! You're asking for about two pound of petrol. That would only give me four gallons and that wouldn't take me very far. And," said Gilley, calculating quickly in his head, "That's nearly 16 gallons of petrol if it's only 32 cents a gallon."

"Just let's see what the gauge says after he puts five dollars in," said Joy. Sure enough, there were 16.3 gallons registered on the pump.

"Wow, how can they do that," asked Gilley, astounded? "That would get us 4 gallons in England. If I was to get 16 gallons in England that would cost me $20.00 Canadian dollars. That's incredible. Petrol or gas as you call it here is four times cheaper. At that price I could afford a big car like your dad picked us up at the airport with. Now I know why you don't see those in England."

At this point Joy was puzzled, "I don't know what you mean by that Gilley. The price has just gone up from 30 cents to 32 cents a gallon. When I started driving, I was paying only 27 cents a gallon. That's a huge increase just for gas."

Leaving the gas station, they carried on towards the ferry. The road wound along the Fraser River and through picturesque farmlands. Joy pointed out the various crops the farmers in the area grew. Gilley was fascinated by the roadside stands advertising fresh fruit and vegetables, especially corn on the cob. "Corn on the cob! Is that what you served us in England that night you tried cooking a typical British Columbian supper," asked Gilley?

"That's right! Now you'll get to taste the real thing," replied Joy. "Not like what I was able to get in England that night. Your mother said it was for pigeons and cows only. Having tried to eat English corn I understand what she was talking about. This is real corn. You'll love it when you get the chance to try it here. Mother is planning on serving it when we get home."

They eventually came to the Deas Island Tunnel. This, Joy explained had been a controversial and innovative accomplishment. Normally, the government built bridges *over* the numerous waterways the Lower Mainland was built around. However, this tunnel was an engineering feat. "But don't ask me anything about it. Talk to my dad. He'll be able to explain how they accomplished such a feat." Gilley did think it was odd seeing a small ship sitting on top of what normally would be a bridge while their little white car passed underneath it. It gave him a queer feeling and he was glad Joy was driving.

Eventually, after about forty five minutes, they reached the Tsawwassen Ferry Terminal. This again was new for Gilley. The Terminal was built on a long jetty that stretched out into the Juan de Fuca Strait. He could see cars lined up along the road as they approached the ticket booth. Joy said, "It's a good thing we got here when we did. It looks like there may be a line up in a few minutes. Then we would have to sit here for two hours and wait for the next ferry. That's how long it takes for a ferry to make a one way trip and unload the cars. Grandma wouldn't like it too much if we didn't arrive at the time we said we'd be there."

Sitting and waiting for the ferry, Gilley had a chance to take a look around. The water stretched out on either side of the road way. To Gilley's right, approximately a mile away he saw another long causeway stretching out into the water. To his left there was just water, but it was dotted by hundreds of boats of all kinds. "Joy, what is that land mass to our right? It looks like there's a train lined up all the way to almost the end. Obviously something is being unloaded onto the ships. It looks like coal to me."

"Oh, that's Robert's Bank. It is a coal terminal. The trains come from all over BC, Alberta and Saskatchewan. They carry coal from the mines in those areas and it gets loaded onto the ships that take it to

Japan. That's all I know. If you have more questions, ask Dad. He'll be able to tell you a lot more. Anytime I've seen these trains it's been when I've had to wait for them to pass at a crossing. It seems they are miles long and go on forever."

"Wow, I didn't realize BC had a coal industry. There's something in common with Newcastle. You've heard of the saying, 'Don't take coal to Newcastle.' Well, that's because coal was the main industry for the Newcastle area. I remember when I was younger and they were filling in the clay quarry in Throckley, I used to pick the coal that came with the fill from the mines. Usually we had to work hard to get enough coal to fill a wheel barrow, but sometimes the companies would send a lorry with a good percentage of coal for the people to pick. Those were the times when there was so much, I used to fill a wheel barrel up and then heap bags on top. We'd all use the coal in our fireplaces. It saved us a lot of money me doing that."

"Hold that story. Grandma will be able to relate to that," said Joy.

"What's that to our left," asked Gilley?

"Well, that's the waters off Tsawwassen. Tsawwassen is where a lot of rich people live. The homes there almost all have an ocean view. That's really sought after here. An ocean view property is wonderful to have and expensive too. Of course everyone here has a boat of some sort. Either a sail boat or motor boat for water skiing. One day we'll have to drive through there so you can see what I'm talking about."

Soon the call to board the ferry came over the loud speaker. The line where they were waiting moved forward. Again, Gilley was glad Joy was driving. Pulling onto the ferry over the ramp which stretched over the water was no small feat. Joy did it like an expert. She parked the car where the attendant directed, they got out of their vehicle dodging others trying to park and found the staircase leading to the Galley. Joy was emphatic that they have the clam chowder for lunch. BC Ferries were famous for this dish. They stood in line with their trays, got their food and were lucky enough to secure a seat by the window. Joy was right. The clam chowder was excellent. It came with homemade rolls and creamy butter to boot!

By this time the ferry had gotten underway and had traveled half way through the Juan de Fuca Straits. Gilley had a hard time focusing on his lunch though. "Joy, this is incredible. Right now we can't see any land. Where are we?"

"Don't worry, Gilley. This only lasts for a few minutes. We're in the middle of the Juan de Fuca Strait. It's the largest body of water between the mainland and Vancouver Island. Pretty soon we'll start seeing land again and it'll be Galliano Island."

"Juan de Fuca? Wasn't he Spanish? I thought Captain Vancouver discovered this part of the world."

"No, the Spanish were actually here before you Brits even though it's called British Columbia. The Spanish had circumnavigated the straits before Captain Vancouver. They were pretty close together though, so people get confused."

With that, Gilley took another spoonful of chowder. The scenery was breathtaking. The water was a brilliant shade of blue and sure enough, Gilley could see land up ahead already. As soon as they finished their lunch, Joy led them out onto the outside deck. They found a sheltered spot and gazed out over the blue waters. While they had their cigarette, Joy pointed out the small islands that had begun to appear around the ferry. "There's Galliano and Salt Spring Island. Over there is Pender Island and Mayne."

Then they entered a narrow channel where Gilley felt he could reach out and touch the islands on either side of the ferry. "We're now in Active Pass," said Joy. "This is the most dangerous part of the journey as there are many under water hazards and often the ferries encounter one another and have to pass each other. It's half way between the mainland and the Island." Just then Gilley jumped out of his skin. The ferry they were on blasted its horn. Sure enough another ferry was coming into view ready to pass them by. Both ferries came very close to the land and Gilley could see people sitting on their sundecks watching the spectacle in their small cottages. Joy explained, "These are summer cottages. Wouldn't it be great to have one here some day."

Gilley said, "Yeah, but how the hell do you get there?"

"Oh, there are ferries called Island Hoppers. These are smaller ferries and they travel between these small islands."

The trip took about an hour and three quarters and the entire way Gilley was mesmerized by the beautiful green of the trees, the blue of the sky and water and the gulls as they swooped through the sky. He even thought he saw a bald eagle. Not being sure, he decided to watch for it on the way back and ask Joy about it if he saw it again. After all, they were more American than Canadian, he thought.

They arrived at Swartz Bay on time. Disembarking was an adventure as well. As soon as the announcement came over the speakers for those traveling by bus, Joy said, "That's our cue. Let's get ahead of the crowd." Sure enough, everyone else got up at once as soon as the announcement came for their departure and headed for the descending staircases. The passages to the car parks were tight and everyone seemed impatient to get on their way. Gilley wondered what the hurry was because there was a ten minute wait in the cars while the ferry docked.

Once in their car, Gilley asked, "Is it always like this here? What was our hurry? We could have stayed on deck and enjoyed the scenery coming into Swartz Bay?"

"Oh, Gilley, we'll see it on the way out. It's not like in England where everyone accepts queuing for everything and no one dare jump their turn." Once everyone was off the ferry and on land again, the challenge came to get into the right lane in order to take the appropriate exit which led to the right highway taking them to their destination.

The drive to Victoria was another experience of the BC country side which was very similar to the rolling hills and farm land of England with one difference. Here, running on both sides of the road were large billboards advertising hotels, tourist attractions and tours along with restaurants.

The outskirts of Victoria didn't look any different to Gilley than the other Canadian cities he'd seen already. However, once they got to the downtown core, he was amazed at how much the architecture and gardening resembled the British style. Joy pointed out the Empress Hotel and told him they held High Tea there every day at 4:00 PM. "And they do it just like they do in England. They pride themselves on retaining the British way of life and attitude."

Gilley looked over to another set of buildings, "What are those? They look very much like an English castle."

"Oh, those are our parliament buildings. The legislature sits there. We're just about at Grandma's. She'll be anxiously waiting for us and you can bet she has our arrival time down to the minute. You can ask her all kinds of questions. She likes that and will take us on a walking tour of the city. She has all kinds of information stored in her mind.

Pulling up at Grandma's house on Menzies Street (right behind the parliament buildings) they saw Grandma already heading down her front stairs. She was at the car before the couple could get out. She just had to greet her favourite granddaughter and the new husband right away. Grandma, in her early 70's was full of energy. With her strong Birmingham accent, she welcomed them into her home. "There are a couple of beers in the fridge for you both, Luvs. After that, you have to go to the liquor store and get your own."

"We brought lots with us, Grandma," Joy said.

"I'm pleased that you've come prepared. While you finish your beers, I'll finish my cup of tea. Then we've got to go and see Rosa. She's anxiously waiting to meet Gilley."

The beers and tea went down quickly and the three of them set out for Rosa's. Now Rosa lived in Toronto Street, just a few blocks away. Oddly enough to Gilley, Grandma didn't lock her doors. As they walked along he wondered about this. However, he didn't get a chance to ask as Grandma dominated the conversation asking questions about the wedding and the trip over from England.

Rosa, who had obviously been waiting as anxiously as Grandma, greeted them with open arms. "Joy, it's good to see you and here, this must be Gilley. I've heard so much about you, Gilley. Let's take a look at you and see if they were telling the truth." Turning back to Joy, she said, "It looks like you've done alright, Joy. He's a big strong man."

Impatiently, Grandma cut in. "Where's your manners, Girl? Offer these two a beer before you expect any answers and get me a brandy."

"It's a little early for a brandy, don't you think?"

"It might be for you but not for me. A wee nip never hurt anybody at any time of the day."

With that, Rosa went to the fridge and returned with three bottles of beer and a glass of brandy. She handed the bottles out, keeping one for herself. Gilley politely took his and wondered what to do, as Rosa had made herself comfortable on her favourite chair, bottle in hand. She raised it to her company and said. "Cheers."

Grandma said, "What, no glasses?"

Rose responded, "Gilley's going to have to get used to the Canadian way of life sooner or later. You're not teaching this guy the right thing. Cheers."

Joy comes back, "A glass is nice and the way they do it in England is so civilized."

Rosa quipped back, "He'd better get used to it, because I'm not going to wash any bloody glasses. Now tell me about yourself, Gilley. What do you do for a living?"

Joy interrupted, "Where's the kids? What's Doug doing these days?"

"He works at the local sawmill during the day and delivers prescriptions for the local pharmacy on the evenings and on weekends—mainly to the elderly. I never see him. He's got his own apartment now in James Bay. I'll phone him and see if he's got time to come over for a visit. I know you two used play together when you were kids.

Janice is at her friends place for the weekend and David, who knows where he is. He's got a local paper delivery and hangs out with all his school buddies on the weekends. We may see him when he gets hungry. By the way, Mum, what are we doing for supper tonight?"

"What do you mean 'we'? I've got a chicken in the oven for these two. I'm not feeding you as well. But you're more than welcome to come over for a drink later on. I may have enough wine, but I may be short of brandy. So you can bring the brandy. Then we can have our special drink, brandy and wine."

"Well, I suppose I should make something for David and leave it in the fridge just in case he comes home for dinner. I'll leave him a note and I don't mind joining you for supper, Mom."

Grandma retorted, "It's not a very big chicken. You'd better bring something to add to the dinner if you expect me to feed you also."

"I'm sure you've made enough, knowing you, Mother. I'll see what I have on hand." Looking at Joy, she said, "I just have to tell you, you have a keeper there. If I was a bit younger, I would fancy him for myself. As a matter of fact, I do fancy him. Take care or you may find you have competition." With that, she candidly winked at Gilley, who looked down at his beer, not knowing what to do about that.

Grandma, looking at Gilley said, "Don't worry, son. She's all talk." Looking at Rosa, said, "Besides, you're far too old for him. If anyone's going to take him away from Joy, it'll be me."

"Now who's calling the kettle black?"

Joy interrupted, "OK you two. Gilley has been asking me all kinds of questions about Victoria and I told him you were the expert. He'd really like you to show him the parliament buildings and tell him about some of the history."

"Yes" declared Grandma. "Hurry up and finish your drinks. Let's get going as there's a lot to see and I want to be home in time to cook supper. Rosa, I'll see you in a few hours. Don't forget to bring the brandy and something edible for dinner."

She led them down Government Street passed the parliament buildings to the Empress Hotel. Grandma walked them through and spouted off the history of the hotel like a regular tour guide. She told them about High Tea, led them to the Bengal Lounge explaining how it was modeled after the East Indian Trading Company and through the lobby to the conservatory. "They grow lots of unusual plants here and look, there are lounges where guests can sit and relax." Their next stop was Madam Tussaud's Wax Museum. As time was getting short and Grandma didn't want her chicken to be overdone, she led them past the museum explaining how the figures inside were very life-like and to the parliament buildings. "You can come back and see the museum tomorrow. The parliament buildings are my favourite. Hurry up so we can look through the public part before closing time. They're not open on Sundays."

Gilley mentioned, "It's so much like England here, especially when you see those red double-decker buses."

Grandma explained, "Watch out for those. They may look like they're English, but they charge you a fortune to go for a ride. One day, the guy asked me if I wanted to have a ride on one. I said, "Is it free?"

"No bloody way is it free," said the driver.

"Then I'm not interested. It doesn't cost me to walk so why should I pay to ride your bus? I've ridden enough of those buses in England. I know what they're like to ride on. As a matter of fact, my husband used to be a bus driver in Birmingham."

Grandma led the couple on a quick trip through the Parliament Buildings. She talked about the Premier of British Columbia, WAC Bennett whom she called Wacky Bennett. She said it wasn't unusual for her to walk through the parliament buildings and run into him. He always remembered who she was and what she did. Often he would say, "Hello Luv, what's new today? Have you acquired any new antiques?"

"I would say, 'Hey Luv, you can't get any new antiques, antiques are old.' He'd get a chuckle out of that." Then he would say, "I should get you a job in the government, you can talk circles around people."

"Then I'd say, 'What with all you bloody antiques? I have enough antiques in my store to look after." He'd get a chuckle out of that too and wish me well as he went about his business. Well, enough of that; my chicken is almost done so let's get back to the house."

Rosa came over with a nice apple pie for dessert. "Apple pie, Rosa. Did you make it or did you pinch it?"

"As a matter of fact I went to the Empress Bakery and bought it just for this special occasion. It's nice to have a new man in the family." With that she also produced a half bottle of brandy. After supper the two of them got into their favourite drink, brandy and wine. Grandma, Joy whispered to Gilley, rolled her own cigarettes when she got to drinking. These home-made cigarettes were continually going out. Grandma declared, "I don't know why I bother with these things. They're always going out. But they're cheaper than those tailor-mades you three smoke."

Gilley spoke up, "And yet I don't think we spend as much on our cigarettes as you do on matches."

"Cheeky bugger, you've got there Joy. We'll have to put him in his place," she said as they all laughed. Around about 9:00 PM, Grandma announced, "That's it. You two take Rosa home while I get ready for bed. I'll leave the door unlocked but make sure you lock it when you come in."

"That's odd, Grandma. Why don't you lock it during the daytime when you go out?" Gilley inquired.

"Well," Grandma replied, "Victoria is safer than where you come from. You can trust your neighbours to watch out for you during the day, but at night everyone's asleep. Remember where your room is and try not to make too much noise during the night. I know what young couples get up to," she said with a knowing wink.

The following morning, breakfast was served at 8:00 AM. It was poached eggs on toast whether you liked it or not. That was Grandma's favourite. She took the couple on a walk around Beacon Hill Park and along Dallas Road. This brought lots of memories back for Joy and she recounted them to Gilley on the way. There was a late lunch at Rosa's that David and Janice attended, but alas, no Doug. Rosa couldn't get in touch with him to let him know about the lunch invitation. "He will be upset to have missed you two."

After lunch, with bags packed, Gilley and Joy bid farewell to the Victoria group and made their way back to Schwartz Bay for the 3:00 PM sailing. Joy had to get home in time to get ready for her new job at the Bank of Montreal that started the next day. Gilley wondered what was in store for him. He knew Veron had plans and would not stand still until he was fully employed.

The following day Joy left for her new work and Gilley had his magical shower. He was dressed and standing there wondering what to do next when there was a knock at the door of the suite. Opening it, he found Veron, all dressed and looking purposeful. "Come on Gilley, no time to waste. We're going down to Manpower and see what jobs they can give you."

"Alright! I'll just lock this door. Do you have the key for it? I think Joy took the other one."

"Oh, don't bother with that. We never lock our doors here. Who would break in anyhow?'"

"Well, in England, we always lock up. We would never make it easy for a thief."

"Well, you're in Canada now. Things are different here and you're going to have to adjust to our ways."

With that, the pair set off walking to downtown New Westminster and the Manpower office. It was a beautiful day and quite hot for September. Gilley enjoyed seeing, on foot, the different architecture of the buildings and the novel way the city was laid out. It was in a grid fashion, quite different from Newcastle.

"Veron, this is a wonderful experience for me. I really appreciate seeing New Westminster on foot. It's helping me get my bearings. I'm getting a better idea of how the city is laid out and how to get around here. How much further is the Manpower office?"

"Well, that's one of the reasons I thought we'd walk. After all, you and Joy don't have a car yet and walking never hurt anyone. You need to learn how to get around. I won't be there to hold your hand forever you know. Its about a half hour from our place to Manpower but longer coming back as its all uphill. It'll help you work off all the food you've been eating since you arrived here. I don't want you getting fat after all," retorted Veron. She led the way into the Manpower building and headed straight for the receptionist, presenting herself as the spokesperson. "My Dear, who do we see about getting my son-in-law here a job?"

"The receptionist looked up from her typewriter and said, "Do you have an appointment?"

"No. How do we get an appointment?"

"Well," the receptionist replied, "generally we set up an interview for the candidate where we find out his or her skills. Once we know what type of work the person is qualified for, we then set up an appointment with an employment officer."

"Oh! We don't have time for an interview. I have to get this young man a job. He just married my daughter and I don't want to support them much longer than I have to?"

"I'm sorry, Ma'am but I have to follow the rules. You do need an interview but today you're in luck. If your son-in-law fills out this form, an interviewer can see him at 10:30. Then you can come back at 12:30 for an appointment with an employment officer. That's the best I can do for you today."

Veron, not to be put off, said, "I don't have time for that today. I can see lots of people in here not doing any interviewing. I'd like my son-in-law to see an employment officer right away. He can tell him what his qualifications are at that time without having to go through all that rigmarole."

"Ma'am, please have a seat. I'll talk with my supervisor. I can't make that decision." With that the receptionist stood up and left her position. Veron smiled slightly to herself and then turned to Gilley, "You have to be in charge here in Canada. You can't let anyone tell you what to do. If you push hard enough you can get what you want."

"I see," said Gilley understanding more than what Veron had intended.

The receptionist returned in a few moments, "Ma'am, my supervisor has authorized the next available employment officer to see your son-in-law without the necessary paperwork and pre-interview. He will see Mr. Summerville at 10:00 AM. Could you please fill out this information form for the employment officer? It will speed things up for you." With that, she handed them the form and answered the phone, which had been ringing intermittently since Veron and Gilley had arrived. Veron steered Gilley to the waiting area and smiled at him again. This time she didn't have to say anything. Gilley filled in the required form with Veron's assistance and returned it to the receptionist.

Promptly at 10:00 AM a balding, sharply dressed man came over to the pair, "Mr. Gillender come with me. I understand you are looking for a job."

Gilley stood up and extended his hand, "Mr. Summerville, please call me Gilley. That's what I'm most comfortable with. And, yes, I am really looking forward to working in Canada. I've heard so much about your country and its endless possibilities."

Veron couldn't understand why she wasn't allowed to accompany Gilley into the interview. Mr. Summerville, seeing the situation, was most insistent he see Gilley alone. "After all, Ma'am, it's Gilley who is looking for the job and he looks quite capable of doing an interview on his own."

Sitting down across from his desk, Mr. Summerville explained to Gilley that the best way to get employed would be to have a resume, "Do you have one?"

"What is a résumé? We don't have that in England."

"A résumé is a brief outline explaining your qualifications, your work history and your personal information along with any hobbies or other interests you have, "Mr. Summerville explained, "Is there someone you know who can help you create one? Here's a format for you to follow. It would be best if someone could type it out rather than having it handwritten. It looks more professional. Something on paper allows us to circulate the information to more employers, that way getting the word out about you. If they have questions, they can call us and we will get in touch with you to ask if you are interested. Try and get one back to me in a few days and I will post it on our board as well as begin to circulate it to possible employers. Before you leave, let's talk about your qualifications and what you want to do with them. After all, I don't want your Mother-in-law to be disappointed in our office."

"Thank you, Mr. Summerville. I'll do my best to get a resume done and return it to you within the time you want it. As for what I'd like to do, well, just having come from England, I don't know what fields you have here in Canada. With my training and my work experience I'm looking for a position as a mechanical design draughtsman. That's what I was doing when I left England. What do you have available here in British Columbia?

"That depends on your experience. When did you start working," asked Mr. Summerville?

"I started working at a proper job when I was fifteen, sir."

"What do you mean by a proper job?"

"Well, I started delivering papers when I was thirteen and did many other things like potato picking, coal picking and whatever I could make a penny at. At age fifteen, I was old enough for a regular forty hour a week paying job. That's when I started as a probationary apprentice Engineer's Fitter and Turner. Sixteen was the legal age to sign apprenticeship indentures which allowed me to become a journeyman fitter and turner by the age of twenty-one. After I did this, I was given the opportunity to spend another four years in the drawing office as a junior draughtsman, learning how to design and produce blueprints of the products to be manufactured by the personnel on the shop floor. I became a draughtsman last year at the age of twenty-five. This gave me the freedom to go anywhere in the world with two tickets—Fitter and Turner and Mechanical Draughtsman."

"Well now, that gives you about ten years experience and you're only twenty-five. You've covered a wide variety of the engineering fields we have here in Canada. I'd love to see your resume but do explain what a Fitter and Turner is. That's not a position we have here and I can see its value. I don't see you having any problem getting employment here."

"In England, an Engineer's Fitter and Turner is a machinist who can machine a part from a blueprint, take that part and assemble it into a machine so that the machine will successfully work."

"That's very interesting, Gilley. Please do your best to get me that resume. Just hand it into the receptionist to my attention. Here's my business card. I'll then call you with positions I think will match your qualifications and experience."

With that, Gilley thanked Mr. Summerville and left the office, returning to the reception area. Veron was sitting there waiting with her arms crossed.

"Well, do you have a job or not."

"No, I've got to do a resume first and get it back here in two days," declared Gilley.

Veron replied, "Jim's very good at writing resumes. He does it for everyone who asks. We have an hour before we need to leave for home, so I want to go to Eaton's to pick up a few items."

Turning to Gilley she said, "Come on Gilley, I'll show you downtown New Westminster. I've got some shopping to do." With that, she shoved the outside door open and set off at a brisk pace.

Gilley, not used to her mannerisms yet, took some time to catch up. He thought, "Wow, she's in good shape. It's a good job I'm a lot younger and used to walking."

A few blocks down the hill, Veron pointed out the Eaton's store and said they would try there first for what she wanted. Gilley not used to the traffic being on the other side and not knowing the rules of the road yet, darted across Columbia Street in the direction she pointed. After all, that's what everyone did in England. Turning around to see where Veron was, he felt a big hand on his shoulder. Looking up, he saw a tall police man frowning down on him.

"Just where do you think you're going, young man?" His grip tightened on Gilley's shoulder.

"I was going shopping with my mother-in-law, Sir," stuttered Gilley, unsure of what he had done wrong. Just then Veron came up beside the pair.

"Officer, I saw what happened with my son-in-law. He's just come from England and doesn't know our rules about jay-walking and how we have to wait for green lights. But I will make sure he's trained before the day is out."

With that, the officer released Gilley's shoulder. "Alright, young man, I'll let you go this time. Don't do it again. Jay-walking is an offence as it's very dangerous. You could get hit by a car. You need to listen to your mother-in-law because she knows the rules."

"Thank you, Officer," said Gilley. "I will listen to my mother-in-law."

Scowling at Gilley, Veron took his arm and said, "If you don't know what to do, ask before you do it. That way it saves us both a lot of trouble. Just wait until Joy finds out what you've done. Come on let's go into Eaton's and see if we can find what I'm looking for." With that, she steered him into Eaton's and made a bee-line for the men's department. To this point, Gilley wasn't sure just what Veron was looking for. However, when she looked at him and sized up his attire which consisted of a shirt and tie along with a sports jacket and pressed trousers, he understood the mission. "Your dress is very English and you need to be Canadianized. Let's start with your wardrobe." With that, she began handing Gilley casual shirts such as golf shirts, T-shirts and the like. "Here on the West Coast, we are more casual. If you want to fit in, you have to wear shirts like these. Ties are only for business and special occasions. If you want to mingle with the crowds, you have to be more relaxed."

Trying to regain some control, Gilley responded. "I can't afford to pay for this, Veron, till I get a job."

"Oh, I'll set you up with an account. You need to start getting your credit rating and now's the time to start."

With that she marched Gilley to the customer service desk to where she planned to supervise the filling out of the application. Gilley had other plans though. "Veron," he said firmly, "I don't believe in credit. If I can't afford to pay cash I don't want it. I would rather wait. Besides, I haven't had time to settle down to see what type of clothes I like. I think Joy should be here anyhow."

"Well, who do you think trained Joy?"

"I appreciate your concern, Veron. Don't forget I have clothes coming from England including ones that are more casual. Remember, North Americans are copying the British trend. I think I have to concentrate on getting a job first. How long is it going to take for us to get home in time for lunch with Jim?"

Looking at her watch, Veron said, "You're right. We have to get going now. Jim will be expecting his lunch so he can get back to work. This time follow me across the road. We don't want anymore police attention. The next time, they will fine you $10.00 on the spot"

"Oh, that's about 4 pound in England. Well, I won't be doing that again."

Relieved that he didn't have to try on the clothes, Gilley carefully put down the pile of shirts he'd been holding and followed Veron out of the store. At the pace she walked it only took them half an hour to get back home. They arrived just as Jim pulled up in his car. Gilley marveled at Veron's timing.

"Boy, Veron, you are in very good shape," puffed Gilley, "its taken me all my effort to keep up with you."

"That's because I got to the health spa and swim 30-50 laps a time and do this 4 times a week, along with all of the walking I do around here. Besides, you've got to stop smoking all those cigarettes."

As they entered the house, Jim said, "How did it go at Manpower today?"

Veron jumped in immediately, "He has to do a bloody resume. I thought you could help him out, Jim."

"Well if he comes back to the office with me, I can help him out and we can get the school secretary, Eileen, to type it up for you."

Lunch passed with Veron telling Jim all about their experience at Manpower and she especially embellished his jay-walking incident. This was a good source of amusement for everyone.

Jim said, "Gilley, you've had quite the morning today. Come on, let's get going back to the office. Eileen will know how you should do your resume. Everyone she's helped has gotten a job, she's that good.

On the way back to the school board office, Jim explained the layout of how a resume and the reason why it was used. "After all, Gilley, employers need to know what you can do and this is the method we use here to tell them that. I know it's different in England and you're not sure what I'm talking about but you'll see. Eileen will explain it all to you. I have a meeting to attend but will be back in an hour. By then you should have it done. She's really good and knows how to make things look professional. I've trained her well." With that, they entered through the back door of the school board offices and Jim walked straight toward an attractive woman sitting at a desk located at the back of the reception area beside a tall window. She smiled at the pair as they came toward her.

"Jim, this must be the son-in-law you've been telling us all about. My name is Eileen," she said in her soft English accent. Gilley wondered if half the Canadian population was made up of English immigrants. If so, this would be great. Already, he was feeling more at home than he expected to be.

"Eileen, you're right as usual. This is Gilley. Could you help him develop a resume? He's already been down to the Manpower office and they want him to come back with one in two days. I'm counting on you to help him out."

"I'd be happy to, Jim. Gilley, nice to meet you. What part of England are you from? I'm from Guildford, Surrey, myself."

"I'm from Newcastle and I have relatives living in Leatherhead which is not too far from Guildford."

"Wow, it's a small world we live in. Here, pull up a chair and sit beside me. I'm guessing you've never done a resume before and I can help you with that."

Gilley followed her instructions and she put a fresh paper in her typewriter getting ready to start. However, once Jim had left, all the staff kept interrupting Gilley wanting to chat with Jim's new son-in-law from England. They seemed so interested in getting to know him. When he chatted back in his English accent, used his native colloquialisms, it brought gales of laughter that Gilley only partly understood. He knew he had to get this resume finished or he would be in trouble with Jim. It seemed the harder he tried to focus on his assignment and ignore the staff, the more interested in him they became.

Eventually, Jim returned and saw what the situation was. "Gilley," he roared, "are you done with that resume yet? We have to get this completed before we go home or you'll have Veron to answer to, you know that don't you?"

"Yes, Jim," grinned Gilley. "It's finished as far as I'm concerned. Eileen and I have been working really hard on it and she's just about to type the final draft. Thanks, Eileen." Eileen, with lightening speed finished up the final copy and handed it to Jim.

Jim looked at it and said, "This is good, Eileen. You've done a good job putting this into a format Canadians can understand."

"Jim, do you think I could have a look at it before we go? I'd like to see what I look like to a Canadian employer as I've never ever done this before."

Gilley looked quickly through the finished product and was duly impressed, "Jim, I would hire this guy on the spot."

Jim took it back from Gilley and turned to Eileen, "Eileen, let's try out that new state of the art Xerox Photocopier. Can you run four copies please as I'm sure he'll be going to apply to more places than Manpower, if I know Veron, that is?"

"Now Gilley let's drop a copy of this off at Manpower. I have two more schools to see and we can go for a beer before we head home. I think Veron will be pleased with what we've achieved here today." With that they proceeded to Manpower dropping off the required resume to the attention of Mr. Summerville and then to the two schools in question. Getting business done as fast as possible they found themselves pulling into the parking lot of the King Edward Hotel by 3:30 in the afternoon.

This was Gilley's first experience at a Canadian beer parlor. It took his eyes a few moments to adjust to the darkness of the large room. He immediately noted little round tables dotting the floor and covered with yellow terry towel cloth. As they seated themselves at one, a waiter who obviously knew Jim, dropped four beers on the table.

"How's your day going, Sir?" he queried as Jim gave him a one dollar bill.

Jim replied, "Thanks for the beers, Jack. The day's done." With that, he took the change of 40 cents and dropped it on the table. Turning to Gilley he explained, "The reason why I brought you in here Gilley, is it's a lot different here than in England. When you go to a pub in England, you go to the bar straight away and get your own order then you find yourself a table. At times you return to the bar for refills and generally, they refill the original glass. Now, here its different. You have to find your table first as you can't go to the bar on your own. You must wait for the waiter to come and take your order, go to the bar for you and deliver it back as well. In this case the waiter has a full tray which he carries around with him as he walks around.

When he sees new customers enter, he'll come over and, if he doesn't know you, will ask if you'd like a beer. In this case, Jack and I go way back and he knows when I come here with someone, to leave two beers each right away. Now this is where the important part comes in. There's a way to communicate with the waiters without embarrassing anyone. You tip him ten cents and put the remaining change on the table. The immediate tip tells him you appreciate the service and the change says you want more when you're close to finishing. Now at the same time, if two of your friends came in and sat at another table, and waved at you, you cannot get up with your beer and go to sit with them. It's illegal for you to carry your own beer in a beer parlor. If you want to join your friends, you have to ask YOUR waiter to take your beer to the other table. If that table happens to belong to another waiter, you must give the original waiter a nice tip. Then the second waiter becomes yours and you start over with him. If you follow my advice, the waiters will get to know you and will really take care of you and your guests. That makes you look good and makes them look good and everyone is happy."

"Oh, I see. So you have to wait for service and pay them for it. It seems to me the better the service the more you pay so that service will continue. Is that right?"

"Yes, you catch on quickly, my boy. It's like that in most business transactions too. We call it 'you scratch my back and I'll scratch yours'.

"Strange little glasses, these are Jim. Can I get a pint instead? One of these barely gets a start on my thirst. Then Jack wouldn't have to come back as often.

Laughing, Jim said, "No, no pints here, Gilley. That's why I order two to start. That's equal to a pint. Another interesting point is the way the bartender makes his money. If he pours the beers just right, leaving a quarter of an inch of foam he attains the legal amount. If he leaves more than that, you can send your beer back. That's why you need a good waiter. The waiter makes sure you get your money's worth and the bartender gets his due as well. That man really earns the tip you give him. It does not pay to be stingy in these places."

"Now if you get a good barman and he can pour within a 16th of the quarter inch of the brim, with the foam sitting on top of the glass, not too much foam, he gets a bonus for the amount of additional beer he can sell per keg. Lots of places, the barman buys the kegs directly from the brewery. So if he can sell say five hundred and fifty glasses from a keg said to dispense five hundred glasses, he's making an additional ten percent for himself"

"Wow, there are a lot of rules and regulations about drinking beer here, Jim. On another note, Jim, why are only men in here. Where are all the ladies?"

"Ladies cannot come in here by themselves. They must be escorted by a man and then they can only sit over there in the Ladies and Escort section."

"Pouf, you'd never get away with that in England. How backward that is. Is this only in British Columbia?"

"No, I don't know for sure, Gilley, but I think other provinces can be worse. I've heard from friends that we are quite progressive here in BC. Every province has its own liquor board and its own rules."

Just at that time, Gilley noticed a man drinking what looked like red beer. It looked like tomato juice, but at the same time, looked too thin. What was that? Never one to be shy of course, He asked, "What is that man drinking over there?"

"That's red-eye," answered Jim, "its tomato juice and beer."

"Arrgh that sounds awful" groaned Gilley.

"I've tried it once and it's not too bad. Another round?" As he said that, Jack dropped two more beers onto the table. "Keep the change, Jack. This will be the last. I have to get home."

Leaving the beer parlor and driving home, they passed the bank where Joy had started her first day. "Ah, we can't pick her up just yet. Banks don't close to the public until 3:30 PM and then they have to balance their cash. If they're lucky they will get out before 5:00 PM. Let's go home. She'll enjoy the walk."

Arriving back home, Veron was waiting for them. "You two have been drinking, haven't you? Where's the resume?"

"We got the resume done at the office, took a copy to Manpower and then I finished my day. I took the boy to a Canadian beer parlor to show him how we do it here. Let's go downstairs and have a beer while we wait for Joy."

"I'll have my Scotch and ginger if you don't mind." With that they went to the bar and entertained themselves until Joy arrived home. Gilley, however, had a hard time concentrating. He was quite excited and pleased with himself at what he had accomplished today and he could hardly contain himself. He really wanted to begin to celebrate only when Joy arrived, which she eventually did. But she was not alone. She was accompanied by a stranger. They came down the stairs laughing and chatting. As they entered the room, Jim boomed, "Bryan, where did you come from?"

"I heard Joy was back home with her new husband and I thought I'd take this opportunity to say congratulations and introduce myself." With that he turned to the only stranger in the room, "You must be Gilley. I'm Bryan. Pleased to meet the man who captured this lovely lady's heart."

With that, Jim handed him a beer. "Glad to see you, Bryan. You must be back home from logging for awhile, eh?"

"Yeah, tomorrow I have to drive up to Whistler to return my brother's truck and pick my car up."

Joy said, "Gilley this is the guy I was telling you about. I used to play hooky with Liz, you met her in England and Lorraine who is now Bryan's wife. The three of us would forge each other's notes of explanation and plan afternoons at the Lamont's house. We'd listen to the latest hits from Bob Dylan, the Beatles and the Stones. We'd smoke and plan our futures. Next thing Liz and I knew, Lorraine asked if she could bring her friend, Bryan. Well, we knew what that meant. She was in love. Once we met Bryan, we all thought he was really neat and he immediately became one of the pack. It helped that he had all the latest records. After all, he was working."

"Yes, I knew all about these girls' truancy. They forgot I used to get the attendance records on a daily basis and I'd see Joy was absent. I knew where to look. Even though you three thought you were clever and would duck down, remember how I would pretend to come and check out the house, go back to the car and drive away. Then I'd drive slowly back and catch the three of you peaking out the window. I'd order you back to school."

"That's right, Dad. I hated that. You could only tell me to go back to school because you were my dad. The others could stay and have fun. It was so embarrassing."

"I had to make sure you kept your marks up and graduated. After all, you were a grade A student with University potential. I had to do my best. And that wasn't enough."

Bryan jumped in, "Um, things are getting a little too hot for me so I'm going to get going. Besides, Lorraine has dinner waiting. Gilley, how would you like to come with me to Whistler? I bet you have never seen a Canadian logging camp. You might even get to see a real Indian."

"What time do you want to leave?" replied Gilley, not wanting Bryan to think less of him.

"6:00 AM. I'll come by the front door, but I won't honk. Don't want to wake the neighbours you know." With that they lifted their glasses in a toast. This was the beginning of what came to be known as Gilley's first Encounter with Canadian Aboriginals.

CHAPTER 3

THE ABORIGINAL ENCOUNTER

FIVE-THIRTY CAME VERY QUICKLY for Gilley that morning. (He had to set the alarm that early so he could be ready for Bryan.) Thank goodness for that magical shower. No sooner had he gotten out of the shower, than a knock came to the outside door to the suite. Gilley knew it was Bryan. "Come on in", he whispered, not wanting to wake Joy up.

Bryan boisterous as usual, boomed in, "Gilley, you still naked? Has that Joy not got our coffee ready? Come on, time's passing."

A small groan came from the bedroom. "Shhh, you'll wake her up. You really don't want to do that," said Gilley. "If you really knew Joy you would know she's not a coffee person or a morning person."

Bryan giggled, "I know that. I just have to give her a hard time. We'll stop at the 7/11 for coffee and something to eat. Get dressed. Let's go." Turning toward the bedroom, he shouted, "Have a nice day, Joy. I'll return him in one piece, I promise."

The first stop before leaving New Westminster was the promised 7/11. Gilley really didn't know what that was until they stopped. It turned out to be a gas station with a grocery store attached. They did serve coffee and donuts and muffins. Wow, that was something. Gilley had heard of donuts but had never had one before. Another 'first' on a day of what would turn out to be a long list of 'firsts'.

Leaving New Westminster, they drove the most direct route to Whistler. Normally road trips were not Gilley's favourite if he wasn't in the driver's seat. However, this was a brand new country and the scenery he was seeing took his breath away. He was glad this time he wasn't driving as he could focus his entire attention on taking in the new countryside. Bryan proved to be not only an apt driver, but also an apt tour guide. He narrated almost every mile of their drive, telling Gilley what he was seeing and some of the history behind it.

While Gilley appreciated the information he was being told, he also decided to take a good look at his driving host. "Hmm, Bryan is a lumber jack. He certainly isn't as tall as I'd imagined lumber jacks to be. He's probably five foot eight inches, but his appearance certainly fits the bill. He's an outdoorsman for sure with his bushy beard, long, mousy brown hair and stocky build. He definitely fits. I can see him wielding an axe against a tree until it crashes to the ground. I wonder what the others look like." Gilley decided to ask Bryan, "Are you a lumber jack, Bryan? Like chopping trees and the like?"

"No, not really, Gilley," answered Bryan. "I've cut down lots of trees, but my main job is to clear the way for the roads and build them for the logging trucks and heavy equipment to get in and out and to take the trees out to the saw mills."

"Oh, thanks for telling me that, Bryan. I don't know anything about the logging industry. The only thing I know is in the north of England, my brother-in-law was involved in trucking loads of dirt into the Kielder Forest. This is the largest man made forest in the world. Or it was then."

"Interesting," said Bryan. "I thought the only forest in England was Sherwood Forest, where Robin Hood and his Merry Men harassed the corrupt Sherriff of Nottingham."

"I'm surprised you know that, Bryan. Robin Hood is a bit of a myth. One day I'll tell you the real story of Robin Hood who was most likely Hereward the Wake."

"Oh, that would be great. I love reading and have read lots of books. At night in the camps, there is no TV reception, you know and the only entertainment is a good book." Having said that, Bryan said,

"Look over there Gilley. Those are the North Shore Mountains. This bridge we're coming to is called the Second Narrows Bridge."

Travelling over the Second Narrows Bridge, Gilley could see Vancouver City and the harbor to his left. Boats of all kinds and sizes dotted the blue water. Gilley saw tug boats pulling barges, huge freighters waiting their turn to be berthed, and private sail boats skipping along on their way to the ocean.

Bryan pointed out landmarks and important locations. "To the right here, Gilley, you can see where the rich people live. It's called the British Properties. It was given to the Guinness family by the Crown for their service. At first it was only accessible by boat but in order to promote this fabulous location to residents and entice them to buy into the selective property on this side of the bay, the family built the first bridge to cross the Burrard Inlet. It was called the Lions Gate Bridge, named after the mountains behind it, known as the Lions and it was a toll bridge initially"

"Where are these mountains that you speak of? They must be impressive to be given such a name," asked Gilley?

"The Lions are that pair of pointed peaks you see over there," said Bryan, pointing to their location. "On a clear day in the winter they are covered in snow and resemble the face of a Lion. They are approximately 5400 feet high and can be seen from all over the Lower Mainland. The other name for the bridge is the First Narrows Bridge. The only people who could afford to buy over here were the rich who were mostly British. Hence it got to be known as the British Properties."

"To your left you can see the ocean and on the horizon, you can see Vancouver Island. I understand you've already seen the fine city of Victoria. What did you think? It's quite British, isn't it or so I'm told?"

"Yeah, it looks quite a bit like Britain, but you couldn't get a good pint of beer even there. This beer here is more like what we call a lager and isn't too bad, but it's nothing like we serve in England," replied Gilley.

"You guys drink your beer warm don't you? How can that be refreshing?"

"Actually, our beer is kept in the cellar, so it's not really warm—like room temperature, if you know what I mean. It's cooler. However, the flavour is more pronounced when it's served that way." With that, they came into Horseshoe Bay. "What's this place called? This is quite beautiful."

"This is called Horseshoe Bay. Yeah, there are some pretty nice houses here too. The BC Ferries dock here and you can get one to Nanaimo or to Sechelt from here. You took the ferry from Tsawwassen to Schwartz Bay in order to get to Victoria. That's in the opposite direction from here."

"Oh," was all Gilley could say as he was so taken by the scenery and the magnificent boats that were anchored there at the Marina.

As they left the Horseshoe Bay area, heading north again, Bryan asked Gilley, "Could you reach behind the seat there, Gilley? There's some beer back there and I'm getting thirsty."

"Oh," said Gilley again and he reached behind him and pulled forward a case of beer from which he took two as instructed.

"There's a bottle opener in the glove compartment. Thanks. Crack one each and put the case back. We don't want the RCMP to catch us drinking." Gilley did as he was told and sat back to enjoy this forbidden luxury so early in the morning. He looked at his watch and saw it was only just passed eight thirty. This was another first. "I don't think I've ever had a beer this early in the morning, Bryan. That is if you don't count drinking until the early hours of the morning. I've never heard of drinking beer in the car until I met Joy. When I left the pubs in England, she always asked if we could get beer to go. It was totally untraditional for us to drink beer while we were driving home but now I can see this is a Canadian thing."

They were heading north, when Bryan whispered, "Quick, hide your beer. RCMP to the right! We don't want to draw attention to ourselves as there's no one on the road but us right now." Gilley quickly put his beer onto the truck floor and buried it between his feet. Then he dropped his coat over his lap, just to make sure. Also, quick thinking on his part, he thought, "I'll light up two cigarettes to cover any smell.'

He did this, handing one to Bryan. "Tell me when it's OK again. I never thought I'd see the Royal Canadian Mounted Police way up here. He's in a car and not on a horse. I guess they're progressing too. Shame, though, isn't it. They are such a symbol when you see them on their horses. I remember when my brother gave me a knife with a Mountie on it. It was one of my proudest days. He picked it up when he was in the Merchant Navy and they stopped at Montreal. The blade said, 'Made in Sheffield' and the handle was made in Canada. The saying on the other side was 'They always get their man'"

"Well, today they didn't get their man. We passed them without any trouble. Thanks for the smoke. The most they would do to us anyway would be to make us pour our beer out. Not only what we're drinking, but the two cases I have in the back of the truck. That's punishment enough, don't you think? We're passed them now, Gilley. Finish up your beer and let's have another one to celebrate." With that, they fell silent and Gilley took in as much of the grandeur as he could while supplying Bryan and himself with beers and smokes.

"That's the Britannia Mines over there to your right, Gilley," said Bryan breaking the silence. "It's one of the oldest copper mines in BC. It's still operating. One day, when you have time, you should come up and really take a look around. There's quite the history to it. This doctor found copper in the late 1800's and it was a quite a large find too. Because they couldn't get electricity here for awhile, they sent the copper to Vancouver Island to smelt it. See that stream there and the colours along the sides of the rocks? That's from the copper. We're going to stop at Squamish to fill up the gas tank and get more smokes. I'm running low." Gilley just nodded, making a mental note to tell Joy about the Britannia Mines and that he wanted to come and see them in earnest. After all, he was an engineer and these things excited him, especially mining and gold mining in particular.

Soon they arrived at Squamish and Bryan drove into the gas station and told the attendant to "Fill it up with Regular, please. Come on Gilley, let's get some smokes and pay for the gas. Besides I don't know about you but I have to use the washroom. That's what happens when you drink beer on the road."

"I have to tell you Bryan, I can get used to having someone fill your car for you. You have to put your own petrol into your car back home. And I could never afford to fill it up. That would cost a fortune. Why, let's see, given that there's Three Canadian dollars to the Pound, I figure at home we pay about $1.25 Canadian for one gallon of gas. Here I see it's only 33 cents. Wow, what a difference."

They were standing at the counter by this time. Bryan said, "Give me two Export A's please and I want to pay for that gas too. What does that come to? The person behind the counter handed over the packages of cigarettes. "That will be 7.00 dollars for your gas and 66 cents for your cigarettes for a total of $7.66."

Gilley was astounded. He couldn't believe his ears. "Tell you what, Bryan, let me pay for the gas. You've bought the beer and you're driving"

"No, Gilley, keep your money. I was coming up here anyway. I'll get you back some other time. If we're lucky, we'll get lunch when we get to camp. Come on, let's go. It's another hour away from here."

"You're on. Um, could I have another pack of Export A too, while you're at it, please?"

Shortly after leaving Squamish, they turned onto a dirt road, leaving the breathless scenery behind. Trees! Trees everywhere. There was nothing but trees on either side of the road. Gilley's mind now turned to industry. "Bryan, no wonder you have so many bloody sawmills around here. You have so many trees. You people will never run out. I've seen piles of sawdust beside those mills. What do they do with it all?"

"You've also noticed those odd shaped burners, I'm sure. Those are called beehive burners and are used to burn the waste from the milling of the wood. Some of the mills have converted and use the heat generated to run their mills by utilizing the steam to generate electricity."

"Also, Gilley, some homes used to use the sawdust for heating until oil and Natural Gas took over. Right now, industry still uses most of what is produced. However, they've come up with a new idea called Presto Logs. The sawdust is mixed with wax and other ingredients and pressed into a log shape and sold in boxes to people with fireplaces who don't want to go chop their own wood."

"That sounds very modern. We burn coal at home because that's what we have lots of. But just lately, we've all been converting to North Sea Gas. My brother is one of the senior project engineers ensuring the gas delivery system. I worked a while with a company that built the substations for local delivery," replied Gilley.

"Oh yeah, cool. We're almost there. I'm getting hungry. It must be going on 11:00 AM by now. I hope the kitchen's open. It may not be too late for breakfast. Pass me another beer, Gilley, just in case," asked Bryan.

After another half hour of winding logging roads and more trees, sometimes so dense that Bryan had to turn on his headlights, the pair came to a large clearing that was definitely their destination. There were temporary buildings and machinery everywhere and looked like organized chaos to Gilley.

"Here we are, Gilley" boomed Bryan as he finished his beer. "Let's see who's left in camp besides my brother, Grant. Can you get the other two cases of beer? The boys will be looking forward to them." As he said this he produced a brown paper bag from under the seat. "And they'll really enjoy this—Canadian Rye Whiskey. Have you ever had this before?"

"No, Bryan. I can't say as I have. I've had some Scotch Whiskey a few times. Bloody expensive it was. Lead the way," said Gilley. As he followed Bryan, he wondered if Canadian loggers would be the size of Paul Bunyan with his scraggly beard, red and black plaid flannel shirt and baggy pants held up by suspenders and not forgetting his huge axe slung over his shoulder.

The noise of the truck pulling up had attracted attention of the inhabitants and before they reached the porch area, men were spilling out of the door, shouting greetings.

"It's about time you showed up, Bryan. Did you bring something for us? Who's the stranger with you today? Why is he dressed in city clothes all the way out here?" They all shouted together and it was hard for Gilley to make out what they were saying.

"Hey, Guys. Let me introduce Gilley. He's fresh off the boat from England and he's married Joy Wilson. You know that cute brunette—Lorraine's friend. She bagged herself a Beatle type if you can believe it. He hasn't had time to get Canadianized yet. Just wait till you hear him talk. You'll know what I mean as soon as he opens his mouth. I brought him with me to show him some real forests and what a Canadian logging camp looks like."

Gilley was so busy trying to take in the scenery as well as the camp that he hardly heard what was going on around him. Were these men the loggers or were they just the helpers? They looked quite ordinary. True they had the beard and plaid shirts, but did not have the size he expected. He followed Bryan into the bunk house with a case of beer in each hand. The men filed in behind them. Gilley took in the room. It was very basic. There were bunk beds against one wall and a table with four chairs in the center of the room. Everybody made themselves at home on the beds and available chairs making sure Gilley, as the guest, had one of the chairs. Grant cracked open the first case of beer and became the spokesman, "Welcome to our logging camp, Gilley. How did you like the trip up here? How long have you been in Canada?"

"Thank you, Grant," said Gilley taking the beer. "I've been in Canada just over a week and what a busy time it's been."

"Really, what have you been doing?"

"Besides looking for work at what you call Manpower, we've been over to Victoria and now I'm visiting my first logging camp. I can't believe how big your country is. The scenery is beautiful. Never seen anything like it. I've never seen as many trees in my life as I saw today."

"Don't you have forests in England?"

"Sure they do," interrupted Bryan. "They have Sherwood Forest, right Gilley? And they have the largest man-made forest in the world called Kielder Forest."

"How did you come to meet Joy," shouted Grant over the hubbub?

"She walked into my favourite pub one night and the rest, as they say, is history."

Just at that time, Bryan interrupted, "We're starving. Have you guys got anything to eat around here?"

"Nope, the cooks took off to town to get some supplies for next week. Most of the crew have left for the weekend and the kitchen is shut down until the cooks get back. Hopefully, that should be sometime later today or we'll be leaving camp too." Just then in came a small, dark man. He was very thin and had dark shoulder length hair. His distinguishing feature was his glasses. They were too large for his face and were held together with black tape over the large nose. Bryan immediately jumped to his feet to introduce the newcomer.

"Gilley, this is Willy. He's our local Indian handyman. If you want anything around here, you just have to ask Willy. How about some food, Willy? I'm starving," said Bryan.

"The cooks are in town and the kitchen is closed but I'll go and fix something for you," said Willy. With that, he went off to the kitchen.

"Was that a Native Indian, Bryan?" gasped Gilley. Everyone started to laugh.

"Yeah, Gilley. What were you expecting?" replied Bryan.

"Well, I always imagined they would be bigger and bronzed and more muscular as they're portrayed in the movies."

Laughing, Bryan said, "Well, Gilley. That's Hollywood for you. Here in Canada the Indians are just normal people, especially on the West Coast here."

Just then, Willy returned with a plateful of food. He had obviously raided the leftovers from the fridge. There were a variety of meats and a few slices of bread on the plate. "Here you go, guys. This is all I could find. We had a great breakfast of bacon and eggs and ham with toast and hash browns. Pancakes too. Whatever you wanted. But that's all gone. This is all I could find." Pointing to several pieces of breaded meat he said, "This is from last night's dinner. These are pork culets. We had them along with roast beef."

With that, Bryan made himself a roast beef sandwich with the bread that was on the plate and the beef. "Oh, Gilley. Did you want some of this beef? No? Ok, I'll eat it. Help yourself to the cutlets. Tom is a great cook."

Gilley looked at the cutlets left sitting on the plate. They looked as if they had seen better days. However, his stomach was calling to him and he ventured to take one of the offerings. It didn't taste too bad. Hmmm. The second one went down a bit slower, but seemed to do the trick in quieting Gilley's stomach. He was a bit embarrassed at the noises it was making.

After eating the second cutlet, he looked up and realized Willy was staring at him. It seemed Willy was as fascinated with him as he was with Willy. "You're English, eh. My Grandfather was Scottish and he married my mother who was a Native Indian. Pleased to meet you. You've come a long way and we need to welcome you properly." With that, he grabbed the unopened bottle of Rye, cracked it open and offered the whole thing to Gilley. "Here, have a drink. Welcome to Whistler."

Gilley, not wanting to offend anyone, but being a bit tense, took the bottle and had a healthy swig. Trying hard not to cough the entire drink up, he passed it back to Willy. With that, Willy took a swig too and passed it onto the next person. The bottle was passed around several times and Gilley had his opportunity to taste straight Rye again and again. Since he was the guest, it seemed that the bottle came his way more than anyone else's. Just when he thought that was the end of it, another one appeared from somewhere and everyone said, "Bryan, the magician, is at it again." And so did Willy with more pork cutlets, just for him. Of course, Gilley could not refuse anything that was offered him. That would be rude. He found that washing the cutlets down with a beer made them more palatable. It became a matter of Rye, cutlets then beer, round and round. Oh well, Gilley thought at one point, "I'm sure glad Bryan knows the way home."

Then the logging stories started with their encounters with bears—grizzly bears, black bears, and brown bears. Then they expanded to include cougars with huge fangs and then all manner of other wild animals that inhabited these forests. Next came the moose and deer hunting stories. "Whoa, man what a climax this is going to be!" Every story was about near misses and barely survived encounters. Each story was met with respect and knowing nods. It was as if everyone knew this was the absolute truth and survival was the only goal.

Gilley was spell bound. He took in every detail. The alcohol enhanced his perception. "This was the real Wild West. Bryan was right. Hollywood was wrong. How could anyone miss the drama of real life on the West Coast," he thought and as he looked around, the trailer took on the likes of a saloon filled with cigarette smoke and the smell of booze. The only things missing were the old piano plunking away in the corner and the girls in their saloon outfits.

Willy was fascinated by Gilley and sat beside him to make sure he was comfortable and had all that the camp could offer. Bryan saw this and said, "Willy, you're that close you may as well sit on his knee." And Willy did just that, much to Gilley's shock. Everyone laughed at Gilley's embarrassment. Willy didn't seem to notice. He just pushed more whiskey down Gilley's throat. It was as if he had made it his personal mission to give Gilley whatever he desired or whatever Willy thought he desired. Gilley began to wonder when this would end.

Eventually Bryan announced they had to get going because they had to have the car off the logging road before dark. "It's too difficult to get the car through these rough roads in the dark."

"Well, shit, Bryan, it was dark coming in. Can it be any darker going out?" slurred Gilley. Knowing laughter followed.

"You haven't seen dark until you've seen a forest in the dark, Gilley. Trust us. You want to be on the main roads by the time the sun sets. You need the light in order to see the animals on the road. They travel to the watering holes at dusk and sometimes stop to eat by the roadside on the way back." Gilley realized it was 4:00 PM in the afternoon already. Time to go and he was relieved to get out because another bottle of Rye had appeared from nowhere.

Leaving was not as easy as it sounded. Willy didn't want to let Gilley out of his sight. He proposed all manner of ideas in order for him to stay by his new found friend asking Bryan if he could come to New Westminster with them. Bryan cut Willy short, "We're not going to New Westminster, Willy. You have to stay here anyhow and help the cooks when they get back. They're counting on you to be here to help." With that Bryan and Gilley got into the car, waved good bye to everyone and took off into the forest.

On the way out, Gilley wasn't feeling any pain. Actually he was fairly looped. Well, what with the bumping of the road and the swaying of the car and his new taste experience of rye, they began having to stop the car every so often to let him get rid of those pork cutlets (or whatever they were). Bryan was laughing his head off. "Now you see why no one else ate them. I don't need to tell you it's not easy getting rid of things that way." After the first few times, Gilley began to sober up and the stories of the black bears and the brown bears and the grizzly bears and the cougars and whatever else they had in these bloody woods, began to flood his mind. And fear of being attacked while in a very vulnerable position began to make him reluctant to get out of the car to do anything.

However, much to Gilley's annoyance, Bryan stopped the car on his own. "Now it's my turn to get out, Gilley. Nature's calling." With that, he got out and headed to the side of the road.

"Nature??? Ahhh! That's a good idea!" With that Gilley got out too. However, the darkness and the stories took over. "I'm supposed to relieve myself with all the wild animals about?? Maybe I can hold it," thought Gilley. Suddenly the horn blasted so loudly that Gilley fell over in surprise. "Bloody hell," he yelled. "What was that?!?"

"Bryan, laughing so hard he could hardly speak, said, "Sorry about that. All I was trying to do was to protect you, you know. Scaring the wild ones away."

Gilley picked himself up, dusted himself off and jumped back into the car quickly, "What did you see, Bryan? I thought for sure I'd been attacked by one of Canada's most dangerous animals."

"Did you not see that black bear I chased away," said Bryan laughing?

"We don't have anything like this in England. I think the most dangerous things in England are some of the girls that come out of the pubs at closing time."

"Yeah, I know what you mean" laughed Bryan. With that he started the car and off they went. "That's your first experience at a logging camp. What do you think?"

"Well, Bryan, it was nothing like I'd imagined. That Native Indian was nothing like I'd thought. He was small and kind of scrawny. I thought Indians were tall, bronzed and muscular—kind of like Adonis. Another thing, I thought all loggers were the size of Paul Bunyan and looked like him too. At first I thought the men who greeted us were their helpers."

"No, Gilley, Paul Bunyan is like your Robin Hood. He's a myth and most loggers are like the guys you met today, just average men."

"Also," carried on Gilley, "I didn't realize how dark forests were, even in the daytime, let alone the night like now. We don't have anything like this at home and I've been out to our most remote places. You can always see the sky and then you can navigate your way home. That is unless it's covered in cloud and raining. But here, why I wouldn't know the first thing to do if I got lost."

"Don't worry yourself, Gilley. You won't get lost if you stay by the car. As for the Indians, you've been watching too much TV. Real Native Indians, especially here on the coast are often quite small. They've intermarried with Whites for generations. However, they all seem to have a problem with alcohol. They call it Whiteman's Poison. It seems they go crazy after they've had a few drinks. Not like us. It's different. They really go nuts. Even their Elders encourage them to stay away from it. Take Willy for example. I don't know if you noticed, but the boys and I made sure he didn't get as much of the Rye as the rest of us did. We'd grab the bottle when he was in your lap and you had him distracted. And I didn't want to bring him with us into town. If I had done so, he would have been on a bender for days and ended up in jail or even worse. No, we make sure he stays in camp as much as possible. He's a nice guy and we don't want to see anything happen to him."

Bryan, looking at him, offering him a cigarette and said, "You're looking a bit off color, do you want me to stop the car again?"

Gilley replied emphatically, "Not bloody likely."

Suddenly Bryan whispered, "Look Gilley, a deer up front there. You see lots of those out here." Slowing down, the headlights caught the deer as it was crossing the road. It stopped and stood stalk still. "This is why many of them get hit by cars and trucks. They freeze when they see lights. I guess it's a natural reaction, but Man, can they do damage to your vehicle." They watched as the deer stood there and then suddenly leaped away into the darkness.

"Wow," breathed Gilley. "That was great. Look, there's one looking at us now." With that they turned and sure enough a big buck was standing not two feet away from the car in the semi-darkness. It too, stood there watching. "What a beautiful animal!" As suddenly as it appeared it vanished into the darkness of the woods. With that, they carried on down the road.

In what seemed like no time at all, they reached the main road to Squamish. Gilley said, "It's still light out. What time is it? I thought it was very late at night. Oh, it's only 5:30."

"Yeah, being in the forest can be deceiving unless you know what to expect. Speaking of darkness, it looks like we're in for one of the famous West Coast storms. See those clouds ahead? Well, they're packing a good deal of rain. I'm sure, being from England, you've seen it pour. Well, I'd be interested in your opinion after we've gone through this one." In a few moments they were engulfed in a thundering downpour. It drummed on the roof of the car and bounced off the surface of the road. On top of that it was pitch black again. One could not see the road ahead. Good thing Bryan was driving as he knew what to expect. He did slow down a bit and Gilley saw that a few motorists had actually pulled over to wait out the storm. "Squamish is just around the corner. We'll stop for gas and see if there's any place open to eat. I'm famished."

With that, they turned the corner and there was Squamish. They took the turn off and headed for the gas station they had visited earlier in the day. Suddenly the rain stopped as fast as it had begun. It lightened up a bit and as they reached the gas station, it was beginning to return to normal daylight. "Please fill 'er up," Brain said to the attendant. "Gilley, I need to go to the washroom."

"Brain, I hope the attendant was correct. He said we only owed $4.50. You asked him to fill the tank and I got us two packs of smokes and it was under $5.00. I can't believe that. In England it would have cost me about $14.00 Canadian just for the gas."

"That's about right, Gilley. $14.00?!? That's Highway Robbery. You've come to the right country, Gilley. From what you've been telling me today, England is really expensive. I can't see how you can get ahead there.

Let's see if there's any beer left in here. I'm thirsty and it's a long way back to home. Everything's closed here so we'll have to go to my favourite place in North Vancouver. They serve the best hamburgers I've ever had." With that he opened the trunk of the car they were now driving and pulled out a half case of beer. "This will tide us over until we get there. My brother Grant would never let me down."

Getting back into the car and onto the highway, Gilley said, "Now I see why they call you the magician." He wasn't really sure if he wanted more alcohol to drink. After all, that was a large part of the problem he'd been having since they left the camp. "Oh well, it may help my stomach. It's acting a bit weird again. You never know," he reasoned to himself. With that he cracked open the bottle and took a long drink. It felt good and he began to feel better. Suddenly, he thought of the Mounties. Quickly he hid the bottle between his legs. "Bryan, are there a lot of police about this time of night. I suppose we should be careful again or is it OK?"

"We always have to be careful, Gilley. I'm glad to hear you thought about that after all you've learned today. But, I think most of them would be having supper about now. It's a good idea to keep it low just in case. By the way, just a tip from me to you-always keep a fresh supply of beer handy for company. You never know when it'll be needed."

Eventually, they arrived in North Vancouver and Bryan, as promised stopped at the 'Best Hamburger Place in Town'. Well Gilley had never had a real hamburger before, so how would he know this was the best one? But he'd heard about this Canadian dish from Joy and she had attempted to educate him while they were in England. This experience had been fine, but she said hers were nothing like the real thing because she couldn't get all the real ingredients.

Sitting down in a booth, Bryan ordered for both of them, "We'll have the House Special with Fries and two Labatt's Blue, please." Turning to Gilley, Bryan apologized, "I hope you don't mind that I ordered for you. I just thought you may not have the experience of ordering burgers yet and could use some advice from a pro. You'll like these, I know. Like I said, they're the best I've ever had. I don't know what they do to them. I've tried to make them myself but can't quite get it right."

The beers came first and then the burgers and fries on what Gilley knew as a meat platter. The size of this burger-Gilley couldn't get over it. And the mountain of French Fries, he could not believe his eyes. Turning to Bryan, Gilley said, "Bryan, there's enough here to feed both of us."

"I told you this was the best place for a burger. They look after the hungry man and after our trip today, we need all the replenishment we can get."

Learning to eat a Canadian hamburger was a whole new skill for Gilley. At first he watched what Bryan did as he didn't want to appear ignorant. First, Bryan ate the large, flat, soggy, green thing lying on top of the burger. "What the hell is this, Bryan?"

"It's a slice of dill pickle. Don't they have those in England?"

"Oh no! All I know is pickled eggs and onions. Joy eats something like this all the time. I don't want to even try them."

"Don't worry." With that, Bryan whipped it off the burger and popped it into his mouth. "Not only do they have the best burgers in town, but the best pickles too."

Next, Bryan picked the whole burger up with his hands and began to devour it, bite by bite. Copying Bryan, Gilley was not too far behind. As he bit into this delight he noted it had bacon, mushrooms, lettuce, tomatoes, onions, ketchup and other sauces. It sure tasted good (much better than those pork cutlets) and he began to feel better. Bryan knew what he was talking about. In no time flat, Bryan's burger AND fries were gone. Gilley couldn't believe his eyes. He'd just gotten half way through his burger. Bryan then ordered two more beer. "Do you want another burger? I'm thinking of having another. No fries, just a burger."

"No thank you. I'm having a tough time getting through this one. These are great! Joy made us hamburgers when we lived in England, but they didn't taste anything like these. She couldn't get all the right ingredients, but they were a hit anyhow. These are much better. Don't tell her I said so or I'll be in trouble."

Bryan's second burger came right away. This one took him a bit more time to eat and allowed Gilley to catch up. This guy, he never missed a beat; he never changed. Drinking all day, with little to eat and not showing it. "Boy, these Canadians can sure drink and eat, too" thought Gilley.

As if Bryan had read his mind, he said, "Gilley, you know you have to make the best of it when you get the chance to eat. In my business, you eat when you can as you may not get the chance to eat when you want to."

Eventually, they arrived back in New Westminster. It was about 9:00 PM in the evening, and surprisingly, looking no worse for wear as far as Gilley was concerned. He'd had his experience with the pork cutlets, beer and Rye and the helpful burgers and fries and as far as he could tell, he looked the same as he did when he left. It had been an incredible day with this new found friend and his day's adventures. Joy, however, was not impressed with the two of them. She knew something had been up. But Jim, being the host, invited Bryan in for a drink, "Come on down to the bar. I'm sure you two are thirsty after such a long day driving."

"Thanks, Jim," laughed Bryan, "We'd like that. Gilley had quite the adventure today, going to a logging camp for the first time and meeting his first Native Indian, Willy. Willy is now Gilley's best friend."

Around the bar, today's story was told. This rounded off another wonderful experience for this newly landed immigrant. Joy, however, was thinking to herself, "Canada really isn't the place for him especially the way he's dressed. Look how he went out to the logging camp dressed as though he was going to the office and Bryan in his flannel logger's shirt and jeans. They must have had a good laugh at his appearance."

Turning to Bryan, Joy said, "Thanks Bryan. I really appreciate you taking Gilley with you today. I wanted him to experience some Canadian culture."

"No problem, Joy. He had a bit of that today, you could say. We went to the logging camp at Whistler, he met Willy, had a sample of Canadian cooking and Canadian drink. But, we returned home safe and sound with lots of stories to tell. We had a good laugh at Gilley's reactions to the stories of bears, cougars and the like, if you really want to know. I'm sure he'll tell you all about it in due time." After finishing his beer, Bryan said he had to leave and go home. "Gilley, thanks for coming with me today. I hope you had a good time because I did and I'm sure I'll have more opportunities to introduce you to the Canadian lifestyle." With that, he turned to Joy and said, "You've got a good one here," and left for home.

Chapter 4

The Job Hunt

THE NEXT DAY GILLEY was sitting peacefully in their suite. Joy had already left for work. Drinking a second cup of tea, he thought, "What an experience I had yesterday! There are so many opportunities here in Canada for me to make my way. I wonder where I should start. I wonder if I could get on as a lumber jack?" Suddenly, a knock came on the door. "Who can that be," he thought? "Everyone should be at work by now." He muttered. He opened the door to find Jim standing there dressed as normal for work in a suit and tie. "Hi, Jim. What are you doing home this time of the morning?"

"Well, Veron has been after me to help you find a job. I have some free time today and I've taken the liberty of making a couple of appointments with people I know. I thought it best they could meet you as well as going through your resume. The first appointment is with Allen Pinky. He's the Chief Draughtsman at A & I Engineering on Annacis Island. No promises. The second interview we have is with Mickey Drake who has an engineering consulting company in Vancouver. No promises there either, but you never know who they know and it gives you a starting place. In my opinion, this will be better than going through Manpower."

"Why, thank you Jim. You've put some planning into this morning, I can tell. I'm ready to see whomever you think can help me. Just give me a moment to finish dressing and gather those resumes we copied at the school board."

Driving over Queensborough Bridge, Jim pointed out a little golf course. "You see that, Gilley? That's a nice little course to start you playing golf in Canada. We can slip away in the evening without too much hassle. By the way, our golf balls are bigger here. You have to get used to that."

"Everything is bigger in Canada, it seems, Jim. I'd love to play golf with you but I don't have clubs here."

"Don't worry about that, we'll come up with something for you," said Jim. Then he pointed out the industrial estate of Annacis Island and explained how it was created by a British group who specialized in designing such estates. "They chose to make this one with a combination of the American grid system and the British habit of using names for streets instead of numbers. You must have noticed in New Westminster we have both numbers and names as well as streets and avenues—kind of a combination of both countries. Generally speaking, streets in America are East to West and the avenues run North to South. Here on Annacis Island, the grid system makes it easier to find one's way around and yet the names of the streets don't help in that matter, but add some colour. You'll notice as you come into Annacis Island there's a big round-a-bout which, as you know, is very British. The Canadians had a bit of a time getting used to how it worked," explained Jim.

Gilley said, "This is similar to the Team Valley Trading Estate where I worked for Bren Manufacturing. They too had a large round-a-bout right in the middle of the Estate on the main thorough fare called Kingsway."

Shortly afterwards they arrived at their destination. It was quite a modern building and Jim led the way to the reception area. There he asked for Allen Pinky. They didn't have to wait long before a short, thin, energetic looking man rounded the corner, smiling at them. "Jim, good to see you. Right on time, as usual. I gather this is the son-in-law you've been bragging about. Here, grab a coffee over there. There's sugar and milk and come on into my office. It's just here on the first floor."

Jim smiled back, "We'll take you up on that, Allen. Yes, this is Gilley, fresh off the boat, so to speak, from England." With that they followed Allen to the huge metal urn which was set up to the left of the reception desk. It was on a stand by itself and had a black spigot at the base. Beside the urn was a stack of Styrofoam cups and on the other side were sugar and a can of something quite familiar to Gilley, Carnation Canned Milk. Finally something Gilley could refer to. Gilley, as was his new custom, stood back to watch how things were done here. Jim took one of the cups, twisted the spigot and held the cup under it as the strong black liquid poured into it. He then shifted to the other side and added ample sugar and canned milk. "Get used to this, Gilley. Everywhere you go, people offer you a coffee. Not like England. You'd be lucky if they offered you a cup of tea anywhere."

Gilley followed Jim's lead. The smell of the coffee was quite distinct and very different to what he was used to in England. He copied Jim and added the cream and sugar. "HMMM. That canned milk makes it taste pretty good. Quite different from what I'm used to, but I like it."

Sitting down in Allen's office, polite conversation followed. Then Allen asked Gilley, "Now Gilley, to the reason you're here. Jim told me you were a draughtsman but he wasn't sure what type of draughtsman you are and what experience you've had."

"My training in England encompasses many disciplines and I don't become a fully fledged draughtsman until I'm thirty. Now that I'm twenty-five, I'm no longer a junior draughtsman, I'm just called a draughtsman. I can't be classified as a design draughtsman until I'm thirty. Most of my work has been in the designing of parts that need to be machined in order to build the printing machinery manufactured at Bren, the company I worked for the majority of the time. I suppose my classification is a mechanical draughtsman. My resume explains my educational background."

"Let me see that resume then. I know you Brits go through a far more intensive program than we do here."

Gilley pulled out his resume. "Here it is, Allen."

Allen took his time and read it thoroughly, sipping on his coffee. "Well, Gilley, with this resume, I also see that you're a machinist and fitter by trade."

"Allen, the procedure in the north of England is to be on the tools before you can become a draughtsman. The belief is you have to have an understanding of what equipment is required to manufacture the parts you design."

"I think your qualifications are beyond what we need here in this company. You'd be better off working for a company that designed machinery or equipment rather than trying to adapt to structural drafting as it is a totally new discipline. Not that you couldn't in time do it, Gilley, but to start off, I think you'd become rather bored and frustrated. I don't think structural design will provide the stimulation you are used to. Leave this resume with me and I'll make some phone calls to see if anyone I know is looking for someone of your qualifications. Two places you could try in New Westminster are Durante Machinery and Brunette Machine."

"Thanks for your help, Allen," said Jim. "That gives me an idea of where to look. It's hard for me to understand Gilley's background because it's totally different to mine. I've always been involved in architecture and building maintenance with school boards. Gilley, Allen and I first met while upgrading the Vincent Massey/Lester Pearson School complex. That's a long time ago. Now it's known as New Westminster Secondary School which is the largest high school in British Columbia. There is an interesting history behind both schools, including ghosts haunting the corridors of them both. I'll tell you about it sometime, Gilley. Very interesting."

"I've heard some talk about that, Jim. I'd like to be there when you tell Gilley the whole story," said Allen.

Gilley looked from one man to the other, not sure how to respond, "Yes, thanks Allen. I appreciate your time and your advice. I will let you know how I make out and I'll remind Jim you'd like to be there for the full telling of the school's history. I have to confess, I didn't think haunting would be a part of such a new country." With that, they left and headed towards Vancouver and their next appointment.

Going back over the Queensborough Bridge and on to Vancouver, Gilley said "I really do appreciate all the help you're giving me today, Jim. I've never seen so many log booms in one place before. Is this the Fraser River?"

"Yes it is but there's a North and a South arm to the river. Right now, we're going over the North arm which has the majority of saw mills and of course log booms. There are over 30 sawmills on both sides of the river here and they produce BC's largest economy, lumber. These log booms are an efficient, cost effective way to transport logs from the forest to the saw mills."

Jim took Marine Drive to Vancouver. "I thought we'd go this way to our next appointment. It will give you a chance to see some of the industry along the Fraser River." After a time, they turned north onto Oak Street. "We're in the Shaughnessy area now Gilley. Look at those homes. They are owned by old, wealthy families who made their money from the good old days where furs, lumber and mining were pioneered as well as the companies which serviced them."

Heading north on Oak Street they crested a hill and the mountains came into view. "You see those two peaks in front of us? They are called The Lions. In the winter time you can see why. The snow really defines them."

"Bryan pointed those out to me yesterday. I didn't think they could be seen from so far away. What a country!"

Driving over the Cambie Street Bridge, they headed into downtown Vancouver. As they crossed this bridge, Gilley observed, on the right, how many industries were collected together along the banks of the water. "Jim, there's so much industry here. There's got to be a job for me somewhere. By the way, is this the Fraser River again?"

"No," said Jim. "This is False Creek and I'll tell you why later. I don't like driving in Vancouver, it's so busy. I always get lost, so I need to concentrate on where I'm going." With that Jim turned onto Nelson Street and found a parking spot. "Here's a good one. They are hard to come by at this time of day. We may have to walk for a bit but that'll give you a chance to see Vancouver on foot. Good parking spot, this—no meters and a two hour time limit. That will give us enough time to see Mickey, have lunch and get back before we get towed. That would be an embarrassment." With that they walked up Nelson, past Granville, and to Howe and found the building. Gilley saw that this area was full of industrial shops, office blocks and some old houses in the mix. The air smelled of freshly cut wood from the saw mills down by False Creek. Again, he had to wonder about life in BC.

Mickey met them at the door as he was expecting them and they were right on time. "Punctual as usual, Jim. Let's go for lunch. There's a small pub just down the street called the Nelson Arms. Best place in the area for food and drink. I've reserved us a table because it gets very busy this time of day."

"Thanks, Mickey. This is my son-in-law, Gilley," said Jim as they entered the pub door. Sitting down, Mickey ordered a round of beer and the lunch menus.

"I hope you brought his resume, Jim. I'll read through it while we're waiting for lunch. So Gilley, what do you think of Canada so far?"

Before he could answer, the waiter brought the round of glasses filled to the line with foamy beer. "Well, I like it quite a bit. It would be better though if they served beer in pint glasses. That way you wouldn't have to order so often." With that, he turned to the waiter and ordered three more. "It's been a whirl wind of experience since I arrived here. I've been to Victoria and the parliament buildings, I've seen the beautiful Gulf Islands as the ferry passed by and I've been to Whistler and seen my first logging camp and Native Indian. I don't think my family will believe I've done all of that in my first seven days. Why in England, it's an adventure just to go to the next village."

"Wow, you have been busy. Let's take a look at this resume. HMMMM, I see you served your apprenticeship as a machinist and you've also served five years as draughtsman. Most people coming from Europe are very well trained in their specific trades and it looks like you are no exception. It's going to be difficult for you to find a job tailored to your training. Remember Canada isn't like Europe and our industries are structured differently along with the fact that we don't have the traditional background Europe has."

Mickey finished reading Gilley's resume and paused, it seemed for a long time. Gilley waited. "Gilley, I don't really understand your qualifications. Most of what I get involved with is engineering facilities such as Jim's school. We work on the structural side of engineering with the Architects and we also focus on the functional side of things such as the heating and ventilating systems, lighting, draining and sanitary systems which cover a wide range of rules and regulations which require a great deal of expertise. In reading this resume, it looks like you've had more experience with designing machinery and with the knowledge you've gained as a machinist you are able to design the parts that will be machined to the specifications required to make a the machinery functional.

"I agree with you, Mickey. I'm having difficulty really grasping what Gilley's training will get him over here. Sometimes it's like comparing apples and oranges. However, I'm sure we'll find something for him. After all, he's very well trained and qualified."

"Jim, it's like I need to build a bridge and I need a special crane to do so. Gilley has the education to build that particular crane for my purpose. This is a specialized field. You may be able to pick up a job with the engineering consultants in town that look after pulp and paper, mining and saw mills. They do more of this kind of work—designing machines to do a specific job. It would be nice if we could equate your qualifications to a Canadian standard so you'd have a better idea of where to look and who to approach. I'll circulate your resume among some of my engineering friends and see what they come up with. I feel you should look more to people who build machines and equipment."

Lunch came at that point. Jim had ordered the daily special, fish and chips for himself and Gilley while Mickey had the beef dip. This dish fascinated Gilley. "Now there's something I've never seen before. Is that all beef between that bun? And what's that liquid you're dipping it all into? It looks so black."

"This is beef drippings flavored with a little onion and beef broth. And yes, this is all beef. I would think this is an English dish. I gather it isn't as you've never seen it before."

"No, we don't have beef in England like I've seen so far over here. In England, I wouldn't be allowed that much beef for my main Sunday dinner. My mother has beef roast every Sunday and it's about the size of what's in that bun Believe it or not, she feeds three of us all with that amount. I like Canada. Everything's so much larger here."

After lunch the three of them returned to Mickey's office as Jim had some papers to sign for the School Board. This didn't take long and they returned to the car. Jim looked at his watch, "Right on time. No one will tow us now. Gilley, it looks like it's going to be harder than I thought, to find you a suitable job."

"Jim, I could go back to the shop floor. I really don't want to, but I'll do what I have to get a job," replied Gilley, getting into the car.

"It's early days yet, Gilley. Something will come along. We're still waiting for the rest of your belongings to arrive from England including the instruments of your trade. You can't do too much without your tools." Jim steered the car into traffic and they were on their way home. "I'm going to take you home a different route, Gilley. We're going to go along Broadway. That will give you a different view again of the area." With that, Jim turned onto the Cambie Street viaduct and onto Broadway.

"Wasn't that False Creek, Jim? Tell me about it. How did it come to that name?"

"It's not that hard when you know the terrain. Quite a few mariners took that waterway thinking it was the Burrard Inlet as they look similar from the sea. It's quite shallow and many a ship got stranded as the tide changed. It got a bit of a bad reputation."

It wasn't long before they were back a Jim's office. Gilley did appreciate Jim thinking of him and giving him a different look at the land. He still wasn't sure where he was and how he got there, but figured he'd learn it all in good time.

Walking into Jim's office, his secretary informed Jim that Veron had called and to call him back as soon as he could. "I'd better take that call. She doesn't call that often."

Shortly Jim returned, "Canada Manpower called and you have an appointment this afternoon at 4:00 PM. It's a good thing we got back at this time. It's 3:30 PM now. We're going to have to leave right away so you can get there on time." Away they went again. Gilley couldn't remember when he had been in a car so much and traveled so far in so short a time period. Was this the way it would always be? "By the way, Gilley. I'll have to drop you off at Manpower and return to my office as I have a meeting at 4:30 PM that I can't miss."

"That's no problem, Jim. I can find my way back home. Veron and I walked home the last time I was there," said Gilley. "Besides, after sitting all day in the car, it'll do me good to have a nice walk." Thinking to himself, "That will give me some time alone to clear my mind. Things have been happening so fast, I can't keep up."

At Manpower, Mr. Summerville explained he had two opportunities for Gilley. One was in Trail at the smelter and one was for BC Hydro. "They are looking for a draughtsman with your qualifications. The person in charge there is English and understands your training. He would be glad to interview you and he indicated the job would be yours anyhow as he's been looking for someone like you for some time."

"That sounds promising. Where's Trail?"

"Well, it's about 700 miles due east of Vancouver in the Kootenay District. It's a small town primarily servicing the mining community. They smelter all kinds of ore including Nickel, Zinc, Gold and Copper. There are about seven thousand residents living there. Manpower would pay your bus fare both ways, an overnight stay at a motel and your food expenses if you were serious about taking the job."

"What do they pay?" asked Gilley.

"Depending on what your responsibilities would be, the range is between $400.00 and $800.00 dollars a month."

"Oh, 700 miles away from Vancouver. Um, tell me about the Hydro one," replied Gilley.

"The BC Hydro one is more complicated. You have to go for an interview and if that one is successful, you have to go to their main office in Vancouver. There they will ask you to do an IQ and aptitude test. If you pass that you get to start at the bottom as a meter reader. That entails going from house to house in a certain assigned area and reading the gas and electricity consumption for that month. The starting wage is $350.00 a month. But with your qualifications it wouldn't take you long to get into the engineering department and they start around $500.00 a month. I can get you your first interview next week if you want."

"They both sound promising. I was told that if I started at a job that paid between $350.00 and $500.00 a month, I would be alright. Let's start with the BC Hydro interview first. I'll have to talk to my wife about Trail before I go further on that one. We've just arrive here from England and she already has a job at the Bank of Montreal. I don't know if her parents would like it if she moved away again so soon."

"Good, then," said Mr. Summerville. "I'll give you a call tomorrow morning and let you know when and where the interview with BC Hydro is going to take place."

That night at supper, Gilley related his day. Of course, Veron was most interested in the Manpower interviews. However, she was not impressed with either prospect. "Trail!!! You can't go there! It's a smelly old place and too far away. I don't know how you could even consider it. And BC Hydro will take forever by the time you get through their bureaucracy."

And Joy—well she was even more appalled than Veron, if that was possible. "There is no way we are going to Trail. You have no idea how far away that is. And I will not have my husband reading meters for BC Hydro. I don't care if it's just a starting place. That's what kids from high school do. You're far from that. The weekend is almost here. Let's wait until Monday. Something better is bound to come along." With that, Gilley knew the topic was closed, at least for now. Joy continued, "Mom and dad are having a party for us on Saturday night with all of our friends to celebrate our wedding and our home coming. Even Grandma and Aunt Rosa are coming from Victoria. It's going to be a great time. I can hardly wait to introduce you to all my friends."

Friday was a quiet day for Gilley. It was sunny and everyone had gone to work and Veron to the spa. Gilley decided to take advantage of the September sun and this opportunity to lay out on the lounge chair sunbathing. He lay there thinking about his short time in Canada and how much had happened. He was in a whirlwind especially now that he had heard from Mr. Summerville. He had just found out before he lay down he had an interview the following Tuesday with BC Hydro. He also knew he should write a letter to his parents. "That's all fine and dandy but where would I start? Oh well, best to wait until after the party on Saturday night." He dozed a bit, feeling the heat of the sun and then a sound caught his attention. He opened his eyes to see a silhouette sitting on the railing. He thought it was a magpie at first "Pete, is that you?" But as his eyes adjusted to the light, he realized it was just a crow. However, was it just a crow? It cocked his head at Gilley and hopped along the railing, favoring his left claw, just like Pete would have done. "Is this Pete reincarnated," he thought? Gilley stood up and moved towards the crow. Just then a noise behind him scared him and the crow, which flew away.

It was Veron back from the spa. "Well, Gilley, taking to the sun, are you? It must be nice having a day off."

"Well you don't know what just happened to me. I thought my magpie had arrived back from the grave."

"What do you mean, 'back from the grave? Have you had too much sun? I don't have time for this. I have to get lunch ready. Jim will be here soon, expecting his meal."

Just then Joy and Jim arrived too. "I had to go to the bank and I invited Joy to come home for lunch too. Having a sun bath are we, Gilley," said Jim?

"That makes four for lunch. No problem. Joy, come and give us a hand setting things out. Can you imagine that Gilley thought his magpie had come back from the dead to visit him? That's a long way for anyone to come let alone a bird," laughed Veron.

"What's this about a magpie Gilley? A story I haven't heard yet no doubt," asked Jim?

Gilley briefly explained what had happened in England when he was a boy. "Pete is dead, no doubt. But for a brief moment I thought reincarnation was real."

Laughing, Jim replied sarcastically, "They say Newcastle United supporters have black and white eyes as you even call your team the Magpies, if I remember correctly."

Joy called, "Lunch is ready."

As soon as they all sat down for the mid day meal, the topic of the Saturday night reception came up. Of course, Veron led the discussion with a list of things that needed doing in order to ready the house and yard for the expected guests. "Gilley, I think you would be best used cutting the lawn. Then you can do a general clean up of the yard. You know, pulling any weeds from the gardens, picking up any trash etc. Jim, you're going to pick Grandma and Rosa up from the bus terminal about 4:00 PM, right after work. Joy, I know you have to go back to work, but when you get home, I'd like you to clean up the bar downstairs. It's always late on Fridays, isn't it? Rosa and Grandma may be here by the time you get home, so you could always do that in the morning,"

"No, I can't," retorted Joy, "I always sleep in on Saturdays and then get my hair done. This Saturday it's even more important that I look my best."

"Alright, just make sure the bar is dusted and tidy. I'm going to be busy getting the food for tomorrow night and starting the preparation. All of us women can help with getting the food ready." By the time Veron had finished giving her instructions, lunch was finished. She shooed them all out of the kitchen so they could go about their assigned tasks. "Gilley, I'll be watching you to make sure that magpie doesn't distract you again."

Gilley was going over the large lawn which Jim and Veron had around their house. He'd cut grass before at home, but never an area so large. He imagined himself pushing the manual mower over it. "It'll take me all afternoon and then some," he thought. "Well, Jim, before you leave, can you show me where you keep your lawn mower?"

"Right. That would be a good idea. Come on Gilley, there's a storage area under the deck where I keep my gardening equipment."

"Alright, Jim, I'll go and get it. I'm sure I can find a lawn mower."

Chuckling, Jim said, "On second thought I think I should come with you. I'm not sure you'd recognize a Canadian mower."

Sure enough, the machine Jim pulled from under the deck did not resemble anything Gilley would have associated with a lawn mower. "This is a gas mower, Gilley. It's a little bit sensitive to get it started and you have to have it adjusted just right. Also, you have to have this bag on the side. All the grass clippings get blown into the bag. Saves raking and your back. When it's full, empty it onto the compost pile at the back of the yard."

Awed, but trying not to show it, Gilley asked, "Thanks, Jim. Now that I know this contraption is a lawn mower, can you show me how to get it started?"

"That's easy. You pull this lever back and pull the cord here. Once it starts you throttle it down, right? No need to run it at full speed as then it uses too much gas and is very noisy. Don't worry, you'll be fine." With that he left for work.

"Right then," thought Gilley, "I'll start with the grass. I'm sure I can do this. If it works half as well as Jim says, it won't take much time at all." With that, he turned the lever, pulled the cord and the mower roared to life. Throttling back slowly, he got it to a nice speed. He completed the grass with no hiccups. "This is more like it. If I'd had this machine back home, I'd have made a bundle cutting other people's lawns." After that, he addressed the rest of his tasks. By the time Jim arrived with Grandma and Rosa, Gilley had put on a good sweat. "Is it that time already? I'd best go and have a magical shower and get cleaned up. That'll be two today," he smiled.

Dinner that night was a quick affair with homemade minestrone soup and bread. There would be lots of food at the party later on. There was still a lot to do to get ready. Jim offered, "Gilley and I will go down and clean the bar, Joy. You don't have to worry about it."

"Thanks, Dad. I'll come and make sure you two do a proper job," replied Joy. With that, the three of them went down to the bar. Arriving there, Jim offered beers all around and the work began. It didn't take long with three of them pitching in, so a game of pool was in short order. Anne and Sally surfaced from their rooms. They knew what their mother would ask them to do if they were visible and they also knew how to avoid the work. They arrived in the basement just in time to for a game of pool.

About 8:30, Rosa and Veron appeared (and Anne and Sally disappeared). "Well," Veron said, as if she hadn't seen them, "we've done all we're about to do tonight. Grandma's gone to bed. Jim, pour us the usual." After her first sip, she continued, "Gilley glad to see you did the yard work. But you're not done yet. Tomorrow I'd like all the windows washed and both of you men need to go to the liquor store to get supplies for the party."

"I thought Gilley and I could go out for a game of golf tomorrow morning. We could get going about 7:00 AM. It's just over the bridge. We'd be back by 10:00 AM."

"I don't care what you do, Jim. As long as this place is ready for tomorrow night. I want everything to be right for Joy's reception."

"Wouldn't that be mine too," quipped Gilley?

"Cheeky bugger! I'm going to keep my eyes on you." Looking at Jim as he giggled, she declared, "Don't think you're going to get away with anything now that you have a male supporter."

Aunt Rosa, on her second drink already joined in, "You tell them, Honey. Can't let the men get away with anything. Now you remember that, Joy. Keep your man in hand."

The following morning, after the game of golf, Jim and Gilley worked in harmony, cleaning the windows and getting the other chores done. Soon it was time to go to the liquor store, Gilley's favourite place. Jim allowed Gilley to drive and directed him to the King Ed Hotel on Columbia Street. "We must start the evening off right, Gilley. We've been working hard all day and it's time for a few beers out of those "silly little glasses" according to you. Then we'll get on with the next set of instructions."

Two beers each, the liquor store and the drive home later, the men were unloading the car into the bar. Beer and mix into the fridge, ice into the freezer and the hard liquor onto the shelves beside the glasses. "Boy, Jim, you sure have some booze, man. I've never seen so much alcohol in one's home before."

"I like to keep a well stocked bar, Gilley. That's part of being a good host in Canada. It's important to have something for everyone. What hard liquor do you prefer, Gilley? I like Rye and Seven, myself, answered Jim."

"I had Rye with Bryan and his lumberjack friends and I don't think I'll ever have Rye again. I'd best stick to beer I think. I don't think I'm cut out for hard liquor" replied Gilley.

"Just let me know when you change your mind, Gilley. You will, you know."

Just then, Veron entered. "Took you a long time at the liquor store. What were you up to?"

Gilley, quick on the draw, "It was very busy, isn't that right Jim? And Jim, here was showing me all the different types of beers they carry. I've never seen so many varieties. I had a hard time choosing." Just then, Joy appeared from the hairdressers, every hair in place. She was wearing an outfit Gilley had not seen before too. "I see its time for a beer."

"Anytime's good for a beer," replied Gilley.

"Be sharp about it. We still have lots to do before everyone arrives at 7:00 PM," ordered Veron.

By the appointed time, everyone including Grandma and Aunt Rosa, were sitting at the bar waiting for the guests to arrive. Joy's two sisters, Anne and Sally were not quite at drinking age but were both teasing Gilley to play pool with them and were trying to con him into slipping them a beer. The doorbell rang. Joy immediately ran up the stairs to greet the first guests. Harry and Gwen Marsh were standing there. An old friend of the family's, Harry soon proved to be quite the character.

Howie and Linda Gail came in next. Linda was Joy's best friend and Howie, her husband, was a commercial painter working for the school board. Bob and Jean Spencer were next. Bob was a building contractor who did a lot of work for the school board. Then there was Bill and Joan Hoskins. Bill was an agent for school grounds products. Uncle Paul, Veron's youngest brother, arrived with his wife Grace. Uncle Paul was Joy's special uncle and Gilley was very anxious to meet this man who took up so much of his wife's conversation. Paul was an electrician and Grace was an operating room nurse.

Next to arrive was Mickey and Elaine MacRorie. Mickey worked at the school board for Jim and was in charge of Grounds. Elaine worked for the local newspaper, The Columbian. Gilley soon found out that Mickey was also the bootlegger for beer and other things, as everyone thought the liquor laws in BC were antiquated. It was nice to know a man of this position. He was to come in handy at various times in the future. Following on their heels were Marva and Brian Turner, the local corner grocery store owners. Brian also worked for Seagram's Distillery. Next were Bill and Marg Donaldson, the local pharmacy (chemist's) owners. He was a handy man to know if you got sick. Terry and Marilyn Parsons came next. Terry was a dentist and Marilyn was his assistant. Terry was an eccentric guy. He was building his own airplane and he drove a Rolls Royce, which he repaired and tuned himself. They also had an indoor swimming pool. Interesting people, the Parsons were.

Anne and Eric Godden arrived next. Eric was a land appraiser and flew with Jim in the Second World War. Anne was responsible for Gilley and his wife getting together, as Joy had stayed with Anne's sister in Newcastle. People kept pouring in and Gilley lost track of who was who.

As each couple arrived, the party got livelier. Each one had brought a wedding gift, which Joy opened and displayed immediately on a table that was in the corner by the fireplace for all to see. Gilley couldn't believe his eyes at some of the presents. There was an electric frying pan, a mix master, many casserole dishes with lids, and an electric iron, an electric kettle, a coffee percolator and many other novel gifts. Each one was much more expensive than what would be given in England. Gilley was amazed at the variety of electric gadgets. In England, his family only had an electric iron and a washing machine with a spin dryer. "What would Mother have thought had she been here to see all these mod cons," Gilley thought. "Life is so different here, I wonder why Joy would want to stay in England where a housewife's life does not have these time saving appliances."

Each and every guest had to go to the bar, get Jim's attention and order the type of drink they wanted. After a little while, Jim pressed Gilley into serving behind the bar. Gilley felt right at home here, but Veron was watching every move and every drink he poured. When it came to her drink, she whispered, "Don't be stingy with the Scotch in mine, you bugger. You're not in England now."

Once everyone had two or three rounds Jim announced, "Dinner is ready. But before dinner, let's have a toast to the newlyweds. Here's to Joy and Gilley." With that everyone raised their glasses to the bride and groom. "Ok, Folks, now you can go and serve yourself upstairs in the dining room and sit wherever you feel comfortable. I will be behind the bar when you need another drink."

Gilley decided he would take advantage of this break as people were getting their food. He could not believe his eyes. The spread was unbelievable. There was a huge salmon, a large hock of ham, cold cuts, salads of every type, buns and breads and various cheeses. There was a very large chocolate cake waiting to be cut for dessert. After enjoying this wonderful spread, people began returning to the basement and the bar was busy again. Between the décor of the bar and the many English accents, Gilley could have sworn he was back home in England.

Helping Jim out behind the bar gave him an additional advantage. He was able to meet almost everyone who came and as he served them their drinks, he got to know how they were connected to the family. By 11:00 PM the party was in full swing and the conversation lively. Some were trying to dance to the music, while others were attempting to make good shots at pool.

Jim challenged, "Who would like to play darts with Eric and me?" Gilley and Harry took them on. It was Gilley's turn to throw. Just then, Veron descended the stairs carrying a tray of food. Gilley threw his dart. It hit the wire on the dartboard and ricocheted into her path lodging in the wall beside her. "Gilley, I hope that wasn't on purpose, you bugger. Are you trying to kill me already? Jim, did you see what he did?"

"Oh, oh! I'm in trouble now. I'm sorry, Veron" he smiled.

"This isn't over yet Gilley," growled Veron, "You watch yourself from now on." Unfortunately for Veron, there had been one of those lulls in the room's din and her voice carried. Everyone knew Gilley was in trouble. Gilley took the opportunity the silence provided and thanked everyone for coming and helping them celebrate the special occasion of their wedding. He thanked them for the wonderful gifts that would help them get their new life started. He also thanked Jim and Veron for their hospitality and for providing the suite. All of these gifts would help them establish their lives in Canada more easily. Everyone applauded and after the applause died down, Veron, glaring at Gilley, said, "Let's have fun tonight."

Jim, not wanting to be left out said, "Let this be the first of many parties to come."

The party continued until the wee hours of the morning. Jim and Gilley were the last ones in the bar. Jim went to turn off the lights, "Well, that was a night and a half. The beer is all gone. We're going to have to go and visit the bootlegger tomorrow because your mother-in-law and wife will want a touch of the hair of the dog, if I'm not mistaken."

"I know that saying. I have a few in the fridge in the suite. Let's have one more before bed," offered Gilley. "Then we can offer them a token to hold them over until we get to the bootlegger."

"That's a good idea," said Jim. "A beer and a smoke. Tomorrow's going to be a long day." It was close to 4 AM when they finally turned off the lights.

The following day was Sunday and Gilley woke with a fuzzy head. His muscles and bones were numb from drinking, laughing, dancing, coughing and smoking—all the good things that come with a great party. As he scrambled from bed, Joy asked, "What time is it?"

"It's 8:00 AM."

"What are you doing?"

"I'm going to have that magical shower then make some breakfast."

Joy responded, "Make it for yourself. You're going to make points with mom getting up at this stupid time on a Sunday." With that she turned over and went back to sleep.

Gilley's shower was fantastic and did what he wanted—it washed away the cobwebs and left him refreshed and ready to start the clean-up Veron had demanded the night before. He made a cup of tea and some toast in one of the Canadian pop up versions of a toaster. He really got a kick out of this mod con. No matter how much he anticipated the toast popping up, it still gave him a fright when it actually did.

After his breakfast and a smoke, he offered Joy a cup of tea. She was not having anything to do with it. "Bugger off. Go and bug Mom and Dad if you're so awake."

Giggling at his new wife, Gilley decided to walk outside the patio door to enjoy the morning and have his second smoke and the cup of tea meant for Joy. He contemplated the amount of cigarettes he had smoked in the last two days. He realized the amount he had smoked in that short period of time was greater than what he would have smoked in England for the whole month. Due to the cost, he had hoarded his smokes at home only allowing himself 4-5 a day. Sometimes he even saved the ends. Here in BC cigarettes were five times cheaper. He could smoke all he wanted without worrying about the cost. "Can this be good for my health," thought Gilley? "Oh well, it can't be that bad or they would ban them." With that thought he finished his tea and smoke and decided to investigate the aroma of bacon which had begun wafting through the air. Fairly convinced the smell was coming from upstairs, he followed his nose and came upon Jim cooking a large quantity.

"There you are, Gilley. Wake you up did I?" said Jim.

"No, I've been up for some time. I wanted to help clean up and I looked into the bar and it's all done. What happened, Jim? Did the good fairy come while we were asleep?"

Veron chimed in, "I'm the Good Fairy, Gilley." This startled Gilley. He hadn't noticed Veron sitting at the table as he'd been so focused on Jim cooking bacon. Grandma was sitting with her and they both had their tea cups in front of them. Grandma said, "I'm the Good Fairy's helper."

"You sure look sharp this time of the morning, Gilley," said Veron.

"It's that magical shower you have here in Canada, "Gilley replied.

Everyone in the room laughed, including Uncle Paul, Grace and Rosa. Gilley had not noticed them either as they were sitting around the corner waiting for breakfast. Paul asked, "What do you mean 'magical' shower, Gilley?'

Gilley explained, "We didn't have showers at home. We only had a bath tub which we were allowed to use twice a week if we were lucky, whether we needed it or not. The only showers available to us were at school or at various sports complexes when we played soccer. At the Welfare, there was one big shower head and a huge communal tub. All the guys would crowd into it after a soccer game to clean up before going home. There was no pressure like you have here. Here the shower invigorates my skin and seems to give me extra energy." Everyone laughed again and Grandma rolled her eyes.

Grace, confused, asked, "What's the Welfare? The Welfare here involves those who need extra assistance with their income and other things. These people are disadvantaged to a large degree. They wouldn't have a benefit no one else had."

"Oh no. The Welfare in England was actually like a social club for miners. The owners of the mines started these grounds as a benefit for their employees and families and these grounds had tennis courts, putting and bowling greens, quoits, which is horseshoes here, and a large football field (which is soccer here) and a playground for the children. There was a large pavilion which was used for meetings, parties, dances, weddings or whatever. My sister Iris had her wedding reception at the Throckley Miner's Welfare and it was a grand affair."

Jim responded, "The meaning of welfare is very different here in Canada. In England, it's called the Dole. This is for the people who can't get employment or have been laid off and need financial assistance."

At this point, Jim called them all to the table. "Breakfast is ready. Come and sit down and help yourselves to whatever you see here."

With that, the group sat at the table. Everyone began to load their plates. Gilley wasn't' sure where to start. He looked at the piles of toast, the platter filled with bacon, sausages and fried eggs. "Can I make a bacon sandwich," Gilley said?

"Do whatever you like," said Jim. "Would you like an egg with that?"

"Sure," said Gilley, wondering what he would do with it. Fortunately for Gilley he had a plan. He took two pieces of toast from the dwindling stack and placed several strips of bacon on one. He then took an egg and laid that on top, then placed the freshly buttered other piece on top of the pile. Everyone watched to see what he would do with this creation next. Gilley opened his mouth very wide and took a large bite. "Oh, this is a great sandwich. Why is everyone looking at me? Isn't this the country of sandwiches and burgers?"

"Would you like another one," Veron asked? By this time, the pile of toast was gone along with the bacon. This time, after Jim had supplied fresh toast, Gilley made a sausage and egg sandwich.

"Creative, aren't you," asked grandma? "You'd better enjoy it while it lasts." Everyone was amazed at the speed Gilley devoured the sandwiches. After breakfast was done almost everyone made their way to the deck for a cigarette and to enjoy the beautiful fall day. "Boy, you sure put those sandwiches back in a hurry," commented Grandma.

"Well, Grandma, in England we only had twenty six minutes for lunch where I worked. Fifteen of that was taken up by playing soccer. One had to eat as fast as one could in order to make the most of the time available. I suppose it's a carryover from that."

Gilley and Jim had an errand to run. It was off to the bootleggers for them. By this time, it was about 11:00 AM and Jim knew beer would be in demand very soon and if they didn't hurry they'd be out of luck. "You can drive, Gilley," said Jim, tossing the keys in his direction. "You have to get used to driving on the left hand side of the road sooner or later."

"Thanks, Gov. Where to," said Gilley, catching the keys?

Jim directed Gilley to Mickey's house in New Westminster. "Park here in the back lane, Gilley. I've called ahead so Mickey is expecting us. We have to be discreet."

Mickey met them at the door as Jim opened the trunk of the Duster. "You wanted four cases, right, Jim," asked Mickey? With that, he handed Gilley two cases covered in burlap. "Put those in the trunk and hand the burlap back to me for the other two. We have some nosey neighbours and I don't want a visit from the local constabulary, if you know what I mean." They loaded the other cases and closed the trunk lid.

"That's six cases for these four that I owe you, right, Mickey? Did you want to come over to our place this afternoon? The party is continuing."

"That's right, Jim. As for the invitation, no, thanks very much anyhow. Elaine's got some plans for us this afternoon. Would you like to come in for a quick one before heading home? Have to sample the wares, you know."

"Sure, that would be good, Mickey," replied Jim.

On the way home, Jim explained how things worked for a bootlegger like Mickey. "He's not a true bootlegger. Here in BC a true bootlegger started out during Prohibition and made hard liquor and sold it on the black market. We have many wealthy families in the lower mainland who are respectable now, that had this kind of shady background.

As for Mickey, he does it more for his friends and doesn't take money for his beer. In BC it's illegal for anyone but the government to sell alcohol, so what Mickey does is trade one case for a case and a half. That way, no money changes hands and he's not doing anything illegal. If he gets reported for selling by his neighbours, he won't have unexplained cash on hand. He does have an unordinary amount of beer in his garage, but there's no law against that."

Arriving back home, the duo were met by Paul, ready to give them a hand with the beer. "It smells like you two have started before the rest of us."

"That's what happens when you're the provider," said Jim, opening the trunk and handing out the cases. "There has to be some rewards for knowing where to get beer on a Sunday. Take them and put them into the fridge straight away as they are a little warm. Where is everyone?"

Paul responded, "The women are upstairs talking about the old days. Gilley you should to upstairs and listen. You might learn something about our family. It'll come in handy one day, believe me."

Gilley supposed that Paul wanted a private word with Jim or maybe he just wanted a beer, warm or not. With that, he followed Paul's suggestion as he had wondered about how the Smiths, Veron' family, had come to immigrate to Canada. No sooner had Gilley arrived in the kitchen when Grandma said, "Gilley it's about time you learned how we came to live in Canada. Come and sit down and listen."

Gilley was taken aback. "Has she read my mind? Or did she and Paul plot together for me to hear this?" He sat down as directed and smiled. "Funny you should bring this up. Paul was just telling me I might be able to hear a story or two."

Grace jumped in at this point, "You bought some beer, didn't you. I think it's time for a drink. This is a long story and I've heard it before."

"What time is it," interjected Grandma?

"It's quarter to Twelve," answered Joy.

"It's too early for a drink," said Grandma. "Wait until I tell Gilley the story. You can wait that long, can't you?" With that she launched into it. "It was 1947. England was in turmoil after the war. Bombed buildings, very little work, everyone was on rations. Making a living was hell. Along with that, our home had been bombed and all my fine belongings had gone with it. We were fed up with living in temporary housing and living hand to mouth. My husband Frank was quite happy driving his bus for the city. Together with that, he had all his friends and hangers-on in the pubs. But I knew it was time for a change. I didn't think there was any future here in England for my family.

I just happened to be reading the newspaper and saw an advert for Canada. They were welcoming us to come to this new country where there was lots of opportunity. I had a little money set aside and decided this was the place for us. Frank didn't want to leave his work and friends, but my sister Rita was already there. She had written several times as well, telling me about this new land and the opportunities she had in Winnipeg. Winnipeg was going through a building boom and she told me there would be lots of work for all of us.

I started to do some research in the library and decided that British Columbia would be where I would want to end up. I especially liked

Victoria as it was reported to be so much like England, with the Empress Hotel and all the British style building. I saw a book with pictures and it just looked like where I wanted to be. I could see a future for us all. My husband, Frank decided he would stay behind and said he would join us later. Peter my second son and third child decided he would stay behind as well. He already had a good job with an insurance company. Even though he was just nineteen, he had established himself in this field and I thought it best for him to stay as well.

We came to Canada—Frank, my oldest son and his father's name-sake, Veron, Rosa, Paul and myself. We came by boat. It took us three weeks and we were sea sick most of the time. We landed in New York on Ellis Island and took the train to Toronto and then onto Winnipeg. We did stay in Toronto for a couple of days while Frank went for an interview with Imperial Oil as an Engineer. He was hired right away and of course had to stay. We carried onto Winnipeg where Rita met us. I wasn't much impressed with Winnipeg. It was a dusty city and very crowded. All roads and trains from Eastern Canada and the United States had to come through Winnipeg in order to go to the Western Canada and vice versa. I didn't like it as there were too many transients. It wasn't long before we were on the train to British Columbia.

We stopped in Vancouver overnight and took the ferry to Victoria. Once we had an opportunity to look around, I knew I had made the right decision—this was the place for us. First off, we had to get Veron and Rosa a job. After all, they were twenty-one and eighteen and there was no excuse for them not to find a job. Paul was only nine and I had to find a home for us all to live. The girls got work at the Empress Hotel and I was successful in getting Paul into school. I was able to find a nice little place above a store for us to live. Eventually, I rented the store and started a second hand business. There are always those who can't pay the original price for things and those who want to sell their excess. I provided the perfect place."

Grace, who was impatiently waiting, jumped in, "I've heard all this before. It's time for a beer." It seemed everyone agreed with her as there was a rush for the stairs down to the bar. Paul and Jim enjoying a nice quiet beer looked up in surprise at the crowd coming down the stairs with Grace leading the way. "Must be nice for you two down here having a drink. I want a beer before we get going to Vernon. Don't forget we have to be there by 6:00 PM tonight for supper with my parents and to relieve them of Kenny and Gwen, our kids." Turning to the rest of the family, she informed them, "We have to be in Prince George in time for me to start my shift at 3:00 Monday afternoon at the hospital."

"We have to catch the bus in New Westminster at 4:00 PM in order for us to be on the 5:00 PM ferry back to Victoria," declared Grandma.

"Let's have a drink and I'll get lunch ready for us all," said Veron. "Where are Sally and Anne, when I need them the most?"

"Still in bed, probably. After all, it's only 12:30 PM," said Jim. "Cheers"

After two sips, Veron rushed up the stairs and shouted loudly, "Get up, you lazy heads. What are you doing lying, stinking in bed at this time of day? You have family that will be leaving shortly. Get down here and help with lunch."

Even from the basement, the girls could be heard running for the shower. With a satisfied look on her face, Veron returned to the bar and finished her drink.

CHAPTER 5

THE PRESSURE'S OFF

THAT NIGHT, AS GILLEY was getting ready for bed, he was contemplating his situation. "Tomorrow's Monday again. I know Veron is going to be on my case about getting a job. Going to Trail to be a draughtsman is not really what I had in mind and Joy's not thrilled about leaving New Westminster and her family either. I knew this country was big, but I had no idea how big. It seems a long way to go just to say 'no'. BC Hydro might be a possibility as I could eventually work my way into the engineering department. However, there's nothing to guarantee I'll be staying in the lower mainland. BC Hydro covers all of BC and, as I'm finding out, that's a lot of country. It's seven times that of all of Great Britain. This country is going to kill me just trying to figure out where I'm supposed to go."

In order to avoid Veron that morning, Gilley decided to spend it catching up on his letter writing to England. There was so much to tell in such a short period of time already. Before he knew it, Veron was calling him to lunch from the top of the stairs. As Gilley entered the kitchen, Jim greeted him with, "Gilley, I have good news for you. A temporary job has just come open at the School Board. They are looking for someone to help with the fall clean-up and other fall projects. The job is yours. You can start tomorrow. There's about five to six weeks worth of work. It should see you through until November. By then surely something will have come along. The job pays $1.85 an hour which is not bad for starting out. In addition to this, you will get your social insurance number. This is a must if you are going to work anywhere in Canada."

Right away, Gilley thought it was a great idea and he said as much, "Anything to get working and start bringing in some money. That's great. I will get my social insurance number and be productive while I'm waiting for other things to happen." He also thought, 'Whew that will get the pressure off. It will also keep Joy and her mother happy because I'm finally making money'.

The only problem presenting itself was the clothes he would need for the job. "I don't have any clothes for this type of work as I've been anticipating something altogether different." Bringing this up to Veron, of course she found a solution and found some old clothes belonging to Jim. These, she thought, were suitable for the type of work Gilley would be doing around the grounds the School Board were responsible for.

The next problem, Jim was quite a bit smaller than Gilley. After some searching, though, Veron found a pair of pants, an old shirt, a worn coat and some shoes. All were a bit short in the arms and legs and a bit tight around the middle, but would do for the time being. Veron said, "That is until your first pay cheque and then you'd better get clothes of your own. The Salvation Army is a good place to start. They have all types of clothes at very reasonable prices and along with that you'll be helping their cause. Besides, by the time you pay some bills, that'll be all you can afford."

Gilley could hardly wait until Joy came home from work to share the good news. She was pleased he would be making money until something in his field came along. She did get a bit of a chuckle when she saw the clothes he would be wearing for this job. That night, Jim had one final instruction to give Gilley as they drank beer at the bar, "Just remember, we have to keep this low key. This means you have to find your own way to the grounds and not let anyone know you are my son-in-law. The exception is the grounds crew, they know you're coming. They can be trusted."

Six thirty AM found Gilley walking along Eighth Avenue heading east to New Westminster High School. Gilley felt like a true DP or displaced person in his ill fitting clothes going to a job provided by his father-in-law.

Right on the dot of 7:00 AM, Gilley found Mickey MacRorie exactly where Jim had said he would be, in the equipment shed. Mickey was pleased to see Gilley again, "Good morning, Gilley. I understand you're going to join our crew for a bit. Jim says you're a hard worker. Come with me to meet the man you'll be working with today."

With that, they found, much to Gilley's surprise, Harry Marsh. "Hello Gilley. Good to see you again so soon. I hope your looking after that pretty wife of yours? Jim tells me you're going to be our seasonal helper this year. First job—we gotta line the fields."

Harry, in his late fifties, was a fellow Englishman from Devon. He took Gilley into the shed and directed him, "Hide your lunch back there, son, and come with me." On the way, Harry explained he was a gentleman dairy farmer in England and then had bought a farm in the United States. He eventually sold that and moved to Canada. He did not elaborate on why he moved to Canada, but Gilley felt something strange had happened. Gilley's first job was re-lining the soccer pitches. This was good as he knew what was needed. In England, he had had to help line the fields before his team could play. Harry informed him he would be back later on.

"Well," thought Gilley, "This is easy. I could do this with my eyes closed, except I don't want to get wiggly lines. I may do that anyway if I keep watching those lovely girls running around the track." There were two pitches to be lined out and, given Gilley's knowledge this didn't take him too long. He was finished and waiting for Harry. In the mean time, he was enjoying the scenery.

Eventually Harry came back, "Oh my goodness, Gilley, I forgot all about you. You've missed your coffee break. Well, the next thing needed is cleaning out the lining equipment. If we don't do that, the next time we go to line the fields, it'll be all gunked up. Come along, I'll show where the water is and the brush you'll need and then where to place the machines. By then it should be lunch time. This, I won't forget". So off they went to the bleachers where the lining equipment was normally stored.

At twelve o'clock sharp, Harry was there as promised. They walked across the field, past the equipment shed and into the carpenter's shop where everyone was already gathered, having their lunch. There were a lot more men than Gilley had met in the morning. They were all sitting around eating and amused themselves by watching Gilley search for his lunch bag. He knew where he had hidden it. After all, he took Harry's directions seriously. He couldn't find it anywhere. There were silver boxes, brown boxes, and this great big red box. Right next to the red box was a brown paper bag. Gilley thought, "Right, there it is. I'm starving."

Just as he was going to pick his bag up this big, deep voice said, "Hey, that's my lunch there." And Gilley turned around and there was this bloody giant towering over him. "Holy God, he must be seven foot," Gilley gaped.

"Whoa! Well", Gilley, stammered, hunger driving him on, "I think the brown bag is mine, sir".

"I don't know about that," said the giant. With that, he walked towards Gilley and much to Gilley's relief, opened the huge red box. Inside there, Gilley couldn't believe it. There was a full chicken, bread, fruit, biscuits plus a large thermos. It appeared there was enough food for everyone. He didn't take a lunchbox, he took a bloody hamper.

"Whoa, man, I tell you,' thought Gilley and he seized the opportunity to grab his lunch bag and sit next to Harry who was laughing loudly along with the other guys.

"You don't know who you just took on. That's Mike Cacic. He played with the BC Lions football team," declared Harry. Gilley decided to take a bite of his sandwich. If he was going to fight, it wouldn't be on an empty stomach.

Before he could complete his plan, Mike boomed, "I'll get you for that, Lad. If I'm still hungry, I'll have you for lunch."

Gilley thought, "You might be big, but I move fast. And the door's right here". With that he wolfed the rest down as quickly as he could, positioning himself at the exit for a fast get -away.

After everyone had eaten lunch, Harry took the opportunity to introduce Gilley to everyone. "Can I have your attention, everyone? This is Gilley. As you can tell from his accent, he's from England and he's the temporary fall help for the next few weeks to help us get prepared for the winter." At that juncture, he turned to Gilley and said,

"Ok, son, off we go. I've another job for you this afternoon. You'll be working with me."

Gilley said to Harry, "Is Big Mike for real?"

"Oh, he's harmless. He does that to all new starters. He just loves intimidating everyone for a bit."

"Intimidating, whoa! Just his shadow would scare the living daylights out of anyone," said Gilley. He soon found that Harry was a real comedian, joking with all the kids and teachers and whoever else he could get on with. He had Gilley in stitches for the rest of the day as they snipped and trimmed the grounds around the school getting things ready for winter. Gilley couldn't believe the weather because, even in October, it was so warm and dry—a lot different from what he was used to in the northeast of England.

At 3:30 it was time to pack up. Gilley couldn't believe how fast the day had gone. As he walked back home, he decided to stop at the bank where Joy worked and surprise her. Looking through the window, as the bank was closed by this time, seeing Joy at a desk, he waved. Joy, seeing him in all dirty and unkempt, motioned for him to hurry along. She'd never seen him in that state. She was used to the collar and tie image from England. "Is Canada really the place for him," she wondered after he'd made a face at her and left? "It would be a shame to have him working as a laborer with all his education and experience he has to offer".

Gilley continued home and had another magical shower. As he went through his routine, he thought, "I really like Canada. I could do this kind of work forever it's so easy and so much fun. One is outside all day, joking with one's mates. Well, I guess until something else comes along. Hmm, in England I was making 29 Pounds per week. What would I be making here? A $1.85 per hour times 40 hours a week. That equals about $74.00 a week. The exchange rate is $2.55 to one Pound. That's 29 Pound a week just for laboring. That's incredible especially given that the cost of things here are so much less. I can make the same wage as a laborer as I was making as a draughtsman in England. How can that be?

The cost of living is so much less. For example a pack of cigarettes only costs $.35 a pack of 20. At home they would cost $1.53 Canadian for the same amount. Wow!" Getting excited, Gilley took his thoughts further, "At home a pint of beer costs 1 Shilling and 10 Pence and a case of 12 here costs $2.25. That translates into almost $6.00 a case in England. I really can do this until something better comes along."

By this time, Joy had arrived home and Gilley was dressed.

"That's better, Gilley. Don't ever come by my work again looking like a tramp. If the manager had seen you, I would have been so embarrassed."

"Ok, sorry. I didn't know. I just finished work and was looking forward to sharing my day with you. I thought I could walk you home," Gilley then excitedly informed her of his good news and reiterated his thoughts.

Joy responded, finishing up dinner preparations, "Just think of how much you'll be making when you get a draughtsman's job." With this, Gilley groaned inwardly and they sat down to supper.

Of course, they had hardly finished dinner when a knock came to their suite door, "Are you two finished dinner? Gilley, I want to hear all about your day. Come to the bar for a drink," Veron demanded.

Joy rolled her eyes and Gilley responded, "Coming, Veron. We're just going to clear up here. See you in a titch." With knowing looks exchanged, Joy and Gilley did the washing up and went to the bar with a half case of beer to finish the day by discussing the events thereof.

The following day was Wednesday. Gilley could hardly wait to start the day. As he hurried over to the grounds shack to hide his lunch, Mickey called Gilley, "You need to take your lunch with you today. I'm sending you and Mike over to Queensborough School."

Gilley thought, "Oh, oh, there goes half my lunch." Out loud he said, "Hey Mike, did you want my lunch now or later?" Mike and the others laughed.

"Come on", said Mike, "I'll take care of you and our lunch, no problem." Harry was in the background laughing his head off. This gave Gilley a little bit of comfort. "After all how bad could he be?"

They got to the Queensborough School grounds about 9:30 and Mike said, "We'd better have coffee break as Harry said you'd missed yesterday's". So off they went to this little café. Mike was well known there. As he walked through the door, he asked Gilley what he wanted. Not sure, Gilley asked for a fried egg sandwich. Mike ordered his usual. Soon the meal came and Gilley couldn't believe what he saw-three fried eggs, four sausages, four rashers of bacon and six slices of toast. At that juncture, Gilley thought, "He mustn't have brought his lunch today. I guess mine is safe now." Comparing his sandwich to Mike's breakfast, Gilley began to think about how he was going to pay for at least his portion. He knew he had $2.00 in his pocket, but how far would that go for a breakfast that would serve four. Well, at least coffee refills were free, it said so on the wall sign. Good job, the amount Mike was drinking.

Gilley continued wondering, "Should I just pay for my own or do I offer to pay for the whole works? What is the custom here? I've only got $2.00 on me", he began to worry at this point. He had never had any need for money up till now.

Much to Gilley's relief, Mike picked up the tab and said, "I'll pay for our coffee break and lunch is on you, Gilley." As they left the café, Gilley checked the amount rung up on the till. It said $2.65. He could not believe it. On top of that, Mike had left three one dollar bills. He shuttered to think what the bill would have been at home. Suddenly he remembered that now lunch was up to him to pay for. "Shit, if Mike ate all that just for coffee break, what would he eat for lunch? I've only got this $2.00 on me. Well, nothing to do for it, but see what happens."

Back at the school, Gilley saw that the grounds had been prepared for the fall seeding already. The only thing left to do was to rake all the stones off these areas thus finishing the preparations for the seeding with an additional layer of topsoil. Mike instructed, "We'll take the stones from here back to the school board area as Mickey said he needed them for another job tomorrow." Mike filled the wheel barrow, wheeled it over to the truck and said, "Hey, Gilley, give me a hand with this." Gilley stooped to get the wheel end of the wheelbarrow. Mike, having the handle end, began lifting the entire wheel barrow off the ground. Astounded at this feat of strength, Gilley hurriedly lifted his end to keep up with Mike. He didn't want Mike to think he couldn't do his part. "Good team work, Gilley", said Mike. "You understand this kind of job requires good team work." Finishing up, Mike said "Where's that lunch, Gilley. It's 2:00 PM. We've worked right through. That's what a good breakfast does for you."

They return to the truck and Gilley was prepared to hand his lunch over. After all, Mike had paid for breakfast. However, it was not to be his turn to provide. Mike pulled out a huge red "hamper" and Gilley's little brown bag from behind the cab. Mike said, "Lunch is on you

Gilley" as he opened the brown bag and ate Gilley's two sandwiches. Then he opened the hamper. To Gilley's amazement, it was half empty. Mike said, "I got hungry on the way to work this morning." To Gilley's relief, he laughed and said, "You didn't think I'd let you starve did you?" With that, he shared the remainder of his lunch with Gilley. This was the start of their friendship.

After lunch, they finish off the landscaping, loaded the truck with the tools and remaining stones and returned to the school board grounds. They pulled up in the truck as the rest of the workers were arriving at the shack. Mike jumped out of the truck, "Come on Gilley, let's unload these rocks for Mickey." With that, they lifted the wheel barrow from the bed of the truck onto the ground. "Hey, Harry, wheel this over to the tool area, will you," shouted Mike. Harry, not wanting to be outdone, attempted to do so. Much to the great amusement of his co-workers, he could not get the load off the ground. He turned around to both Mike and Gilley, "OK, clever buggers, you come and wheel it over there."

Mike looked at Gilley and grinned, "You show them, Gilley."

Now, unknown to Mike and the others, Gilley had sold coal in his youth. He had loaded up many a wheel barrow full of coal and then put two large sacks on top of the pile. He'd developed a technique for lifting this heavy load. So, he casually walked over to the wheel barrow and used his method to accomplish the task. Well, no one could believe what they saw. They had all assumed it had been Mike who had done the major lifting. Mike looked at Gilley and said, "You are a bit of a sleeper, aren't you? Can you play football?"

"Depends on what type of football you want to play," responded Gilley. Everyone had a good laugh as they went home.

Thursday, Mickey informed Mike and Gilley that he wanted them to wash the stones they had brought back the day before and lay them around the borders of certain gardens. Then after that, they were to return to Queensborough and finish the raking job and clean up.

About 1:00 PM, Mike and Gilley returned to Queensborough to complete their assignment. They had done all they could and it was only 2:30 PM. Mike declared, "Time for a beer." So off they went to the Queens Pub. Gilley, now knowing the price of beer and the custom, quickly dropped his two dollars onto the table. No sooner had the money landed on the table than the waiter dropped eight beers and the change and snatched the two-dollar bill and moved on. Gilley felt like a native.

The place was packed, with all eyes were staring at Mike. Gilley remarked, "Everyone's looking at us, Mike."

"Watch this" Mike said and moved his head slowly around staring at all the people. How quickly they turned their heads about, as Mike said, "They're not used to seeing me in this place. Do you know what they're thinking? They're wondering, 'Is that Mike Cacic of the BC Lions?' I've been through this quite a bit. We won't tell them." With that, he drank five of the beer as Gilley downed three, thinking "What an experience!"

Finally, Mike stood up and bellowed, "Time to get back, Gilley before we get fired." Thankfully, Gilley had enough money to cover the bill and a tip. By the time they arrived back at the school board, it was 3:30 and everyone else was arriving back to pick their things up and leave.

Harry jokingly said to Mike, "You two have been drinking".

"So what's that to you?" said Mike.

Harry retorted back, "You could have invited me." It was the end of another workday. Tomorrow was Friday, the end of the work week and pay day.

On Friday, Gilley was put on leaf raking around the immediate grounds. At coffee break in the shed, Mike turned to Gilley and said, "I forgot my lunch today."

Gilley shouted out, "Everyone, take note, our illustrious friend has forgotten his lunch. I think it would be very smart of us if we all offered him a portion of ours, or else, he'll just take whatever he wants."

Harry piped up, "He hasn't forgotten his lunch. I saw him devouring it in his truck this morning."

Mike said, "Big Mouth, Harry." With that, he jumped off the countertop and chased Harry out of the hut. Harry couldn't move fast enough, poor bugger. Mike's hand just stretched out like an endless telescope and grabbed the back of Harry's jacket. All everyone could hear was a loud, tearing sound. To everyone's amazement, the whole back of Harry's jacket came off in Mike's hand and Harry was still running. Everyone started to laugh and, hearing this, Harry turned round and saw Mike with the back of his jacket hanging in his huge paw. All Harry was left with was the front and the sleeves.

"What am I going to tell Gwen?"

Mike said, "Don't tell her it was me. She'll kill me. I'll get you a new jacket," He went over to his truck and pulled out a jacket of his. He handed it over to Harry. Harry discarded the remains of his jacket and put on the new one. As it was one of Mike's, it hung down to his knees. Everyone had another good round of laughter. Just then, Jim arrived to distribute the pay checks.

Noticing Harry swimming in his jacket, Jim said, "Lost some weight, Harry?"

Harry's response was, "If you had a big bugger like Mike chasing you, you'd lose weight too."

Jim looked to the ground and saw the remains of a jacket and picked it up. Guessing what had gone on, said, "I'll take this to Home Economics for repair. I don't know what to tell them though. I bet you they've never seen this before. What *should* I tell them?"

Harry said, "You'll come up with a good story, Jim. I would like to be there when you tell them, though."

With that, everyone left for home. Gilley arrived before Jim and went directly to have another magical shower and get changed. He was about to exit the suite when a knock came to the door. It was Jim, "Here you go. This is what you've been waiting for. Came in the mail today. Come on open it while I get us a beer." It was from BC Hydro requesting Gilley to call them to confirm the appointment for an interview at their Boundary and Lougheed office at 2:00 PM the following Tuesday afternoon.

"Don't give you much notice in Canada, do they?" said Gilley as he took his first drink.

"Don't worry about it Gilley, I'll pick you up at 12:00 PM on Tuesday and bring you home so you can have a shower and get cleaned up. I'll drive you to the office in time for the appointment. I have business I can do in that area anyway. Oh, here comes Joy and Veron. Let's tell them the good news."

Veron said, "Well, it's about time you got an interview."

"Yes and it'll be much better when you have a proper job", added Joy. "I have heard BC Hydro has excellent benefits."

"Yes. These days any type of government job is good to have because you have job security as well as benefits. There's lots of room to move up the ladder too. They promote from within before they hire someone from outside the organization." Everyone had a celebratory drink. For once, since Gilley had arrived at his in-laws, everyone called it an early night.

Saturday morning they rose later than usual. Joy was off for her hair appointment, Veron had gone to her spa and Jim had gone to the school board for a special meeting. Gilley thought, "This is a good time for me to read my letters from England and hopefully reply to some of them." But most of all, Gilley was looking forward to reading the Football Pink. This was a local sports paper his parents sent him from England and was put out every Saturday. It focused on Newcastle United and the other local teams in the area. It brought Gilley back home again. There were often articles that talked about people he knew and friends he'd gone to school and played football with.

After his first read through the Pink this morning, Gilley decided a cup of tea was in order. While he waited for the kettle to boil he reflected on the previous two weeks. He was a bit shell shocked. His life felt like it was one of those nonstop trains that traveled across the Prairies until it reached the Port of Vancouver. And yet, contrary to this feeling, it was a much more relaxed lifestyle. Living in Canada was much better than he had bargained for and he felt this was the place for him. The remainder of the day was remarkably quiet compared to previous days. This was a welcome change and Gilley took full advantage of the unusual fall weather by spending the majority of his time in the sun on the balcony. This was quite a new experience for Gilley. To his knowledge only the rich could afford to do things like this but here in Canada it seemed to be the norm.

That night they all had been invited to Anne and Eric Godden's home for dinner. Anne and Eric were long time friends of Jim and Veron's and lived in Langley which was about 30 miles east of Vancouver. Eric had been a pilot in England in the Fleet Air Arm with Jim who was a recognizance officer during WW II. They happened to meet each other again at an auction in Victoria in 1948. Eric was out of work and Jim, working for the provincial government at the time was able to get Eric a job as a land appraiser.

Anne had been born in Ashington, which was a small mining village in the north east of England. It was famous for the footballers it produced such as Jackie Millburn (Newcastle United) and Bobby (Manchester United) and Jack Charlton (Leeds United) and all three had also played for England. Anne had been sent by her parents to live with her uncle and aunt during WWII for her safety. Later her younger sister, Jean followed her a few years later when she too was able to travel alone. It had been Anne who had been responsible for Gilley and Joy meeting each other. Her youngest sister, Joyce had invited Joy to stay with them while she was in England.

Arriving at the Godden home, Gilley saw it was a different style of house compared to Jim and Veron's. It seemed most houses in Canada were different from each other. This house was on two acres of land next to Newlands Golf Club. Eric was standing in the driveway with this large German shepherd. Jim didn't like German shepherds or rather, it seemed that they didn't like him. Eric was a bit of a tease. "Jim, he won't hurt you. He's as gentle as a lamb," Eric said as a greeting. With that the dog growled. "It seems he thinks you're a trespasser, Jim. Well, you stay here and the rest of you follow me into the house."

"Just the same," said Jim ignoring Eric's comment, "with all of my experiences with those dogs, I'd rather you put him in the yard behind that locked gate, if you don't mind," replied Jim. As Eric did so, the dog growled again. "I told you the dog doesn't like me," said Jim.

At this point, Anne came out of the greenhouse and welcomed them to her home. "This is your first time here to our house Gilley, let me show you around. I'm very proud of our home as we took the original structure and renovated it to match our dreams."

"We built the greenhouse to connect the garage and house so that one has to go through the greenhouse to enter the back door. This is a unique feature. By doing this, it gives the people who visit us an idea of who we are and what we love. It also gives us an opportunity to give our guests a gift from our garden." From this point, Anne led them through a hallway, pointing left into the kitchen, and right to the eating area which featured a bay window. Then she led them up three stairs to a nice spacious lounge with a deck overlooking their orchard-type yard. A high hedge of cedar trees circled the perimeters of the yard and made it totally private.

It was a beautiful late October day. The leaves on the apple and pear trees had turned their fall colours and with the backdrop of the deep green cedar trees, it looked like a painter's dream. Eric came in with a tray full of drinks for everyone. He obviously knew what most of the party drank, and Gilley was surprised he knew Joy drank beer like the rest of the men. After drinks were served, Eric, said, "Come on, Jim, Gilley, let me show you the rest of the house while the girls get caught up." With that, he led them downstairs to his office. Contrary to the rest of the home, this area was very cluttered. Eric said, "I keep it untidy intentionally as it keeps Anne out of here, right? A man has to have his own private space." He then showed them his own private stash. "Here, have another beer, boys before we go back upstairs."

Standing around with a beer in his hand, Gilley took in this room. He was impressed by the sheer volume of books on the shelves and the floor. At the same time, he also observed there was no real warmth or sense of welcoming in the room as there was only one solitary chair. He understood, this room was for Eric alone to enjoy.

Returning upstairs, Eric played the good host and replenished drinks all around. Soon Anne announced that dinner was ready. She led the way into the dining room set for six. Again, this room was open to the beauty of nature with large picture windows overlooking the gardens. This meal was to be yet another Canadian experience. After the salad, Anne brought out the entrée. It was quite the opposite of what Gilley had come to expect at Veron's. Each plate served contained a very small bird, lying on its back surrounded by all variety of vegetables with an ample serving of roasted potatoes.

At first, Gilley thought he was being served pigeon which was a popular northern dish in England. Anne, seeing the expression on Gilley's face jumped in, "This isn't a pigeon, Gilley. This is called a Cornish Game Hen and is considered a delicacy here."

"Ah, thank you Anne. I do appreciate you letting me know that. I thought you were trying to serve a northern dish to help me feel at home. This is a nice touch. I thought they were bloody big pigeons."

As dinner progressed, the conversation flowed. Anne explained she owned a dress shop in Langley and she had two other sisters besides Joyce whom Gilley and Joy knew already. Jean who was next in line to Anne, lived in Langley and had one son called Alistair who was a captain in the Merchant Navy. Then there was Mary. She lived in a small place called Wark in Northumberland. "Here's a story I love," said Anne, "Mary told us she met a nice looking man one time when she was visiting us here in Canada. They were getting on quite well when he asked her where she was from. She said, 'Wark'. With that, he got up and left. As he walked away, she realized he thought she meant,

"Walk—telling him to leave." By the time she recovered herself, he was long gone. "Too bad he misunderstood me so readily. He showed promise,' she said, "But now I know how to get rid of undesirable suitors."

"That's the trouble with the English language. It depends on whose saying what in order to be understood," said Joy. "John, you remember, there's a place in Northumberland you showed me that's called Ulgham and you pronounce it "Uffum"? It sounds so odd."

"Aaah! Those bloody Geordies. They've got their own way of saying things. Isn't that right, Jim?"

"I have to agree Eric. I had to spend some time and effort learning the dialect so I could understand what my daughter was getting herself into. But, all things considered, Gilley's not too bad. That is until you get him drunk. Then I don't even think he understands what he's saying."

By this time, dinner was finished. Anne said, "It's time for dessert. Let's clear the table. I've got a real treat for you." The women following Anne, left the men to themselves so Eric turned to Gilley, "I understand you have an interview with BC Hydro soon. What you must remember is that no one here understands the British education system. You have to bullshit your way through an interview and tell them the truth at the same time, but in a manner that they want to hear it. Jim and I've done the same thing, haven't we, Jim? So whatever they ask you, you answer with embellishment. I've learned that's the only way to get on here."

Gilley was about to reply when Anne appeared with her dessert, "Gilley, this is my special apple pie. I used apples from our trees and I my mother's recipe from Ashington. She was a good old Geordie. We didn't use whipping cream, but here, this is an added bonus. Here," she said as she handed Gilley what looked like a quarter of a pie piled high with whipped cream, "Enjoy."

"Well, now we know who Anne's favourite is, don't we. I've never seen her serve such a huge piece to a guest before," said Eric. "He's just another magpie isn't he? After all, they flock together, don't they?"

"You've always been jealous of Newcastle United, you Southerners, because you didn't have a Jackie Millburn," retorted Anne.

Jim and Eric together said, "Whose Jackie Millburn?"

Gilley came right back, "He's the Messiah of the north, don't you know?"

With that, the men laughed and everyone lapsed into silence as they ate the piled high pies and drank the coffee enhanced with liquors.

"Gilley, I understand you play golf. Why don't you and Jim come and play golf next Saturday with me? Don't worry about bringing golf balls. I have enough for all of us. Did I tell you about Max and how he contributes to my game? Max is my guard dog and I've trained him to protect my property. He doesn't take kindly to things (or Jim) coming into the backyard. I've trained him to fetch golf balls. My yard borders the 10th Tee. Well, often golfers hit their balls out of bounds into my property. Max fetches them. Of course, no one would dare challenge Max. This keeps my supply up at no cost. Clever, eh?"

"I'm sure you have at least a dozen of my balls in your storage area. About bloody time you gave them back," said Jim.

"Jim, I've never seen you hit a ball that far," teased Eric.

Soon it was time to leave and Anne said to Veron, "Please take a whole bunch of vegetables back with you. There's too much for us. This year has been a bumper crop. There's so much, I'm afraid it will rot before it's used. That won't do, now will it?" Veron was waiting for just such an offer so with that, Anne and she filled a large paper bag with produce from the greenhouse and garden. "You might as well take some of these apples and pears for the kids, too. That includes you, Gilley."

"I love apples. You know what they say, an apple a day keeps the doctor away."

Driving home, Veron commented on the amount of fruit and vegetables they had been given. "Anne's right, she has a bumper crop this year. I've never seen so much. You'd better take Eric up on his golf invitation next Saturday. You can get more fruit and vegetables then. I can always can some if we find we have more than we can eat fresh."

Joy spoke up at that point, "Gilley doesn't have any clubs or shoes. How can he play golf?"

"Well," said Veron, "He can use my clubs. Your dad has an old pair of shoes that should fit Gilley. Also, Jim, if you go early enough, you could let Gilley drive out there. He needs the experience." Jim looked at Gilley and winked. Suddenly it all came together for Gilley, Jim and Eric had planned this. He understood now what Jim meant when he had mentioned 'the Veron Operation' in the bar just before they left for the dinner.

It was late when they arrived home and Anne and Sally were in the bar playing pool with two male friends, Al and Nicky. Al was Sally's new boyfriend whom no one had met before. Nicky was Anne's friend who was around the house often. He was useful as he liked fixing electrical gadgets.

Jim eyed the boys, "You haven't been into my stock without my permission, have you boys?"

Sally piped up, "Well, Dad, Al is 19, so I gave him a beer. I knew you would have if you'd been home."

Nicky joined in, "Can I have a beer, Mr. Wilson? I'm almost there and you're home now. Mom and Dad let me have one once in awhile."

"OK, everyone can have one beer for the road and then off with you, boys. It's late and we have a busy day tomorrow, "replied Jim.

It wasn't long before the kids left. Veron turned to Jim and said, "I don't like that Al. There's something about him I can't trust and I don't like the way he looks at Sally."

Jim retorted, "Every boy of his age has only one thing on his mind and Sally is a good looking girl. Why wouldn't he be attracted to her?"

"It's not just that, and the way he's always touching her. There's something scheming about him. What do you think, Joy?"

"Well, he seems to be a nice guy but there is something sleazy about him. Time will tell," Joy said.

Gilley and Joy retired to their suite. Settling into bed, Joy said, "Did you know Nicky offered to lend us his parents' old TV? The Springates are a well known family in New Westminster, you know. According to Anne, they had a fire in their home recently and have replaced most of the contents. He brought a stereo over to Anne last week. Now he says they have this old extra TV that they don't use. Come to think of it, his father has a large engineering company. Maybe you could get a job with him, Gilley."

With that comment, Joy was asleep. Gilley lay there in bed thinking about his latest experiences. What no one here seemed to grasp was there were so many different types of disciplines and jobs available in engineering. "My field is mechanical design. That's where my talents and interests are especially in manufacturing. So far nothing in that area has come up." Then Neil's words came to his mind, "No matter what you do, Gilley, always give 100% to whatever comes your way.

Remember, experience is in what you've accomplished. The challenges you've overcome will be what you are measured by, not in the years you have worked."

The next morning Gilley made breakfast for them both, bringing Joy hers in bed. She said, "Thank you, Gilley. Remember today is when we're going to celebrate Thanksgiving. You know the day is really tomorrow, but it's more convenient for our family to have our dinner on Sunday this year. Monday will be a day to rest, if Mother lets us. She told me we were going to have roast beef this year in your honour. Usually we have turkey. That's traditional for Thanksgiving. But she wants to make Yorkshire Puddings for you and you need roast beef for that. I can hardly wait. I love Yorkshire Pudding with gravy."

The day passed with everyone being assigned tasks by Veron, the Sergeant Major, as she was called. "Anne, bathrooms, Sally floors, Jim bar, Joy kitchen and potatoes, Gilley sweep off the deck. When you're done, come and see me for more."

Dinner time came and we were all seated around the dining room table. Dinner was served. There were potatoes, carrots, peas, turnips and of course the Yorkshire puddings. Then came the heart of the entire dining experience a baron of beef. Gilley was amazed at the size of this piece of meat. He explained; "I've never seen a roast that big in my life. The biggest piece of beef my Mother served was about a quarter of the size. Another thing I can't understand is that you just started to cook this a few hours ago. My mother would start on Saturday cooking the meat for Sunday."

Joy said, "No wonder it was well done and the portions were so small. When I asked for more, Gilley's father, Jack looked at me and said, 'I'll give you one more piece because some is for my Sunday night snack at the club and the rest is for Monday night's Cold Done Up." Smiling, Jim started to carve the meat and the blood was just pouring out. Gilley had never seen this before. "I can't eat this," he said, "I like my meat well done." Everyone laughed and Veron came to Gilley's assistance. "In the North of England, they're not used to having the meat rare. When he talks about it being well done, it's like shoe leather."

She turned to Jim, "Just cut off the ends for him and I will pour the hot gravy on it so he can't see the blood." It was still a lot rarer than he would normally eat and the amount was way beyond his normal serving but Gilley was grateful for Veron's thoughtfulness.

"You'll get used to it, Gilley," Jim said. "We did." With that, everyone tucked in and while eyes were down on their plates, Gilley was trying to find a way to reduce his helping of beef without anyone seeing him as there was no way he could eat all that had been piled onto his plate.

Tinker the dog was under the table, quietly waiting for morsels to be dropped. Gilley thought, "Ah ha, there's my way out. How can I get some of this to the dog?" Bringing his napkin up to his mouth, he grabbed a large piece of meat and carefully lowered it to his lap under the napkin. Tinker immediately seized the opportunity and grabbed the meat munching away to his delight; he realized he had a new friend. After a few morsels, Tinker started to beg at Gilley's lap.

Veron said, "What's the matter with Tinker? He's never bothered people before."

"Tinker, get out of here," shouted Jim. This left Gilley with his dilemma as his plate was still heaped high with meat. By cutting the meat into small pieces and mixing it into his other food, Gilley was able to camouflage the rare beef especially with the roasted potatoes which were done to perfection. Joy realized that Gilley was struggling and kept giving him more Yorkshire puddings and potatoes so he could complete this ordeal successfully. Jim, standing up, started to cut more meat. Gilley remarked, quoting one of his father's sayings, "With my gracious respects, I must decline. I have partaken of ample sufficiency."

For dessert, pastries and cake from Woodward's bakery came next. "You can't beat Woodward's for quality and price and even though these are day old, you could never tell." Sally, who had a sweet tooth, took a large piece of cake and excused herself from the table. Just as she had sneaked in right after dinner was served, she sneaked out just before the end. Clever girl, she knew how to avoid a confrontation and the work of cleaning up afterwards.

Gilley, knowing that Veron had prepared this meal for him, thought he should say something, "Veron, this was a wonderful meal. I had never seen such a piece of meat before and I appreciate all the work you put into making this come together. I realize this was for me, especially the Yorkshire Puddings and I have to say the potatoes were superb, roasted to perfection. Over time, I will adjust to not having my meat well done. This is truly a good Thanksgiving. How could anyone not like this wonderful country? In the short time I've been here, I've experienced more than I could ever have imagined. What will tomorrow bring?"

Down to the bar—playing pool and darts were becoming part of life. Every night was like a night at the pub in England except one did not have to leave home. Gilley was introduced to a new game—Cribbage. Jim was astounded that Gilley had never heard of the game before.

"This is amazing, my lad. Why, the game was invented in England in the 1600's. I think the man's name was Suckling. He was knighted by the King. Eventually he fell from grace as he was a waster and a womanizer. I thought the game was played everywhere in England. I guess not in the North, eh? It's popular here. The original game was called 'Noddy'? That's because the Jack or Knave was called Noddy in the old days. Also, if the dealer turned up a Jack, he automatically scored 2 points. That's how it still is today. Don't really know how they came to name it Cribbage. But one thing I do know for sure is you're going to have to learn how to play it before we play golf with Eric as he'll insist we also play Cribbage afterwards. One more thing you need to know is it's legal to cheat in Cribbage. So if you don't count your point correctly or call your opponent on his count, that count becomes legal."

Monday came around quickly. Gilley was salivating. What they had in England at supper on Monday was called 'Sunday Cold Done Up.' He approached Veron and asked her if this was her plan for Monday night's dinner. When she said not, he asked if he could be privileged enough to make Monday's dinner. He said his plan was to do Sunday Cold Done Up. To his amazement, Veron said, "Great, I hadn't thought about that for a long time. Let's you and I cook together. You do the vegetables and I'll do the meat. Is that OK?"

With that, they proceeded-Gilley dicing all the vegetables and Veron doing the meat. To Gilley's amazement, Veron had an English grinder, like his mother's and just like Mother, she attached it to the table and ground the meat, rare as it was. Gilley thought, "Well, when I finish cooking, it'll finally be well done."

Mixing everything together in Veron's largest bowl—cabbage, peas, potatoes, carrots, turnips along with the ground meat-adding several eggs making a gooey mess, Gilley poured it all into her largest frying pan. The aroma attracted attention. "What are you cooking, Mom," asked the girls?

"It's not me, its Gilley. He's making "Sunday Cold Done Up," said Veron.

Jim, overhearing this, "Veron, what on earth is Gilley doing?'

"Like I just told the girls, he's making Sunday Cold Done Up," replied Veron.

"Must be a Northern dish. I hope it tastes as good as it smells," said Jim.

Time to serve dinner. Everyone was seated in the dining room. Gilley brought in his masterpiece and served it out. All sat looking at this mess on their plate. Veron, Joy and Gilley looked quite pleased. Gilley produced the HP sauce. "This will help those who are new to this dish as well as us veterans." With that he began to eat his portion attempting to catch up to Veron and Joy. Jim Sally and Anne decided to give it a try.

After a moment or two, Jim came up from his plate, "This is really good, Gilley, especially with the HP sauce. There's only one thing missing and that's the Yorkshire Puddings. And we know who ate all those. By the way, Gilley, where did you learn how to cook?"

"Monday in England was wash day and because the women were so busy with that, often, I'd help Mother prepare this dish. When I was young, we didn't have the mod cons that are available today. Mother would wash the clothes in a manual washer and mangle then hang them outside to dry weather permitting. However, it was often raining, so she had to hang them all over the house on clothes horses. It started with her asking me to get the left over Sunday night dinner out and chop the vegetables. Eventually, I was doing it all as she changed the clothes around getting them to warmer places so they dried faster. Father really enjoyed this meal. He often said it was the best one of the week after Sunday."

Tuesday was back to work. Everyone was surprised at how the weather was holding. It would be a bit chilly in the mornings but wouldn't take long to warm up. By noon it was quite balmy. Gilley learned this type of weather was called "Indian Summer". No one knew why, but everyone was quite happy about it.

This was the day Gilley had been waiting for. He had the appointment with BC Hydro. Jim had arranged work at the School Board so that Gilley could be off early, get home, shower and change and be ready for the appointment at 2:00 PM. They had to go into Burnaby to the corner of Lougheed and Boundary. Jim drove.

The interview went fairly smoothly with the conclusion Gilley was a suitable candidate for further testing. He was to go into Vancouver next week, to the main building, and take an IQ and an aptitude test. As he came out of the building, Jim asked, "How did you do?"

"Well, I think they liked me and they enjoyed my resume. I embellished things just like you and Eric told me to. They told me I may be over-qualified for the types of jobs they normally start people at such as a meter reader. They gave me an appointment in Vancouver next Wednesday for an IQ and aptitude test. I know what an IQ test is, but I don't know what the hell an aptitude test is. Tell me Jim, do you know?

"I sort of know a little bit about it, Gilley. The government has strange ways of working. They apparently hired this company from California and they can tell if you're mentally stable and fit to work for Hydro. They can tell if you have any odd tendencies, such as homosexual or criminal inclinations."

The rest of the week flew by with work at the school board and learning the game of cribbage with Jim. This was as important as golf was on Saturday. Gilley had figured out by this time Jim and Eric had a bit of a competition going on and it was up to Gilley to tip the tables Jim's way.

Saturday came quickly. Jim handed Gilley the keys, "It's time for you to learn to drive on the other side of the road." Now Gilley had his chance to drive the Duster. He did find it a bit odd to be driving on the right side of the road, but because he'd been a passenger for so long, he adapted quickly. Before he knew it, they were pulling into Eric's driveway. As they pulled in, it was just gone quarter past seven. Eric greeted them at the door, "Breakfast is just about ready. Come on in." As soon as they got into the door, they were given a cup of tea and pushed into the breakfast nook, Anne promptly served them with fried eggs, bacon, sausage and toast.

"I thought there were going to be four of you," asked Anne. "Who else is supposed to come?"

"Brian Turner is our fourth and he will be meeting us at the club house about 7:50," responded Eric. "You remember Brian and Marva, Gilley? They came to the party. They have the corner store across from Jim's place. Marva runs the store and Brian works for Seagram's Distillery. That's the largest in Canada."

"What am I going to do with all of this breakfast? I've cooked for four, "said Anne.

"Give it to Gilley," Eric and Jim responded in unison.

Gilley responded, "Maybe I should take a bacon sandwich for Brian."

"That's a nice thought," agreed Anne. "Maybe we should make it a bacon and egg sandwich. I can keep it warm over here until you boys are ready to leave."

After breakfast was finished, Eric instructed Jim and Gilley to drive down to the clubhouse. "I'll walk down seeing as how it's so close and I leave my clubs at the pro shop anyhow."

As they jumped into the car, Gilley with Brian's sandwich, Jim said, "It's a shame we have to give this to Brian, we could have this ourselves later on. Eric, of course, would let the cat out of the bag though, so I guess we have to give it to him after all."

Brian was waiting patiently, with his golf cart and bag, adorned with these beautiful knitted club covers. Jim and Eric didn't have club covers and they commented to Brian, "How do you know which club you've got underneath those covers."

"Do you see how they have rings around them? Well, one ring means the driver, the one with two rings is a number two wood. The one . . . ." Eric cuts him off, "We get the idea. You don't have to go through the whole set. Give him that sandwich and let's get going before we miss our tee off time." Jim was busy getting the clubs out of the trunk of the car. He took his out first and then went for Gilley's which was Veron's old set. He saw immediately they had club covers. "Gilley, get rid of those before anyone sees them. You're going to get enough stick about the colour of your bag without adding to it with colored club covers. Women!"

They walked to the Pro Shop, Gilley carrying his bright yellow golf bag. So far he hadn't been teased about his bag. He knew it was coming at some point, though.

At the pro house, which was just a wooden shack, the golf pro was a guy called Ken Green. How appropriate to pay your green fees to a guy with this name. "That'll be $8.00 each," he said.

"No it won't," replied Eric, "because I'm a member. It'll be $6.00."

"You never miss a beat, Eric," Ken said. "See you in the coffee shop after the eighteenth. Who's the cute guy with the yellow bag?"

Eric turned around and saw Gilley with his bright yellow golf bag for the first time. "Jim, what's he doing with a yellow bag? Is he a trend setter or just trying to outdo Brian with the covers?"

"We needed a fourth and I found one, didn't I? It doesn't matter what colour his bag is, does it," retorted Jim. "Veron was kind enough to lend him her clubs."

"Well, I wouldn't be seen dead with a bloody yellow golf bag. He'll use that as an excuse when we beat the two of you."

On the first tee, Eric explained the rules to Gilley. "You're playing with Jim and Brian's my partner and this is how it goes—first team on the green gets a nickel from the other team, closest team to the pin gets a nickel each, first down gets a nickel each, lowest score, gets a nickel each. After nine holes, the scores of the partners are combined and whichever team has the lowest score pays the other two a quarter each on top of their other winnings. Then on the back nine, the scores are tallied again and whoever has the lowest combined score on the back nine pays the other team a quarter. On the overall eighteen holes, whoever gets the lowest score, receives 50 cents from each of the other players. Got that, Gilley?"

"Right," thought Gilley. He knew he'd have to pay attention in the beginning to learn just how Eric was really keeping score. Jim had warned him about Eric and he was going to heed the warning.

They tossed a coin for the first tee off. Eric to go first, followed by Brian then Jim, then Gilley was last. First hole was a par four for all. On their second shots, Eric got first on the green. A nickel for him. And Jim said to Gilley, "Now, hit short of the green and we will get the best chance to get closest to the pin."

Jim's game was a short game, so when it came time for his third shot, he missed the green again, but just on the fringe. It was apparent that he knew what he was doing. As both Brian and Gilley were close to the pin, it was left to be seen what Jim would do. Jim took his putter from his bag. He stood very still, reading the green and judging the distance. He stroked the ball very positively and lo and behold, it went right in the hole. He got closest to and first down—two nickels to Gilley and him.

Now it's up to Eric. He's going for the lowest score, that being a birdie. Lo and behold, if he didn't get it. This continued seesaw, seesaw on the first nine holes. The nickels added a certain flavor of competition to the game. One did not have to be a good golfer in order to get one of those nickels.

After the first nine holes a cup of tea was in order. Into the coffee shop, they went. The scores were added up and lo and behold Gilley and Jim won the first nine. "Now onto the tenth tee," was Brian's comment," We'll get them on the back nine right, Eric?"

Now the tenth green was facing Eric's back garden. It was right there in front of them approximately ninety-five yards from the tee. This was a par three with a dogleg, slightly to the right. Eric liked the layout of the hole as many people misjudged the distance and their balls landed into his yard—private property—out of bounds. As he was explaining this to Gilley, he finished with, "Remember, I haven't bought a golf ball in years. You're first up, Gilley"

Sure enough, Gilley's first shot shanked and over-hit and landed right in Eric's back yard. "Thanks, Gilley put another one down." Bang. Same thing happened again. "Anything to help the cause, Eric," said Gilley. Fortunately, Gilley's third shot went more to the right and fell just short of the green. Jim's shot was also just short of the green. Brian shanked one into Eric's yard. The total now was three balls for Eric. Brain's second shot was OK. Of course Eric banged one right onto the green. "Do partners get their balls back, Eric," asked Brian?

"No, because then everyone would want to be my partner, wouldn't they, retorted Eric, "Especially on this hole."

Much the same thing happened on the back nine. Eric and Brian got their quarter back each and of course Eric had the lowest score—home turf advantage. Into the coffee shop they all trotted. This time we can have a beer" said Jim. "How about a game of crib," said Eric?

"Well, the only guy who's never played crib is Gilley," said Jim, winking at Gilley.

Playing along with Jim, he asked for a practice round so he could learn the rules and get a feel for the game. That was acceptable for everyone. The partners were the same as for golf. It didn't take long before the game was over in spite of Gilley's practice with Jim the previous week. This game took more skill than Gilley first thought, especially with a master like Eric. "Good job we didn't play for money on this one," said Jim.

Over by the side wall there was this long, white table with a trough all around it. It had red and blue round discs about one inch high sitting on it. Gilley asked, "What is that game over there?"

"Shuffle board," answered all three.

Eric, the Conqueror, said, "I'll show Gilley this game. First you have to put a quarter in for the lights"

"Here we go again, thought Gilley, "You're the only one with quarters, Eric, as you've taken them all off us."

Eric said, "Let's keep the same teams again. Gilley and Brian at one end, Jim and me at the other end." The idea of the game was to outshoot your opponent. The game is a similar version of curling. Instead of ice, though, a fine sand is sprinkled on the surface to allow the "rocks" to slide smoothly. This was another experience for Gilley. As Eric outmatched everyone again. It seemed as if there wasn't a game in the coffee shop he couldn't win.

"Spoiled youth he had," thought Gilley.

Well, Eric said, "In the back room there is a full size snooker table for members."

"Oh, good, thought Gilley, "this is one game I know how to play." In Gilley's youth, he was shown how to play snooker and billiards in the Institute at Walbottle. Walbottle was a small, converted church hall that housed two full sized billiard tables, two dart boards and books upon books. It was a place for the retired men of the village to go and spend time with one another. They encouraged the young kids to participate in the game of billiards. The older men delighted in teaching the young the tricks of this great game of skill. Gilley had taken advantage of this opportunity and learned from the best of the area how to utilize those tricks and skills to his advantage.

Unfortunately, Gilley's glimpse of redemption was short lived as they discovered the box receiving the money for the lights was out of order. Since the lights wouldn't go on, there was no game. This meant back to the lounge and another round of beers. Over this round, the conversation turned to Gilley's coming interview with BC Hydro. Jim explained Gilley had to go for an IQ and an aptitude test. "Eric, what do you know about this kind of interview, being associated with the government?"

"That's an interesting question. Gilley, I don't think you'll have a problem with the IQ test. You're a pretty smart young man. However," said Eric with a gleam in his eye, "you might have problems with the Aptitude test. It's a screening for abnormal behaviors like Homosexuality, criminal tendencies, deceitfulness and so on. The papers I've seen say things like, "Complete the following sentence". They don't look terribly difficult and one just has to answer honestly. Since you want to work as a Public Servant the government finds it necessary to make sure their employees are on the up and up. Even a meter reader which is what you will be starting as, has to be respectable. They need to rely on you as you will be sent to people's homes sometimes in remote areas. The government doesn't take too kindly to any scandals, I'm sure you know that by now."

Soon it was time to go home and the foursome made their way to the parking lot where they said goodbye to Eric, who only had to walk a few paces to home. A parting shot from him, "Gilley, for heaven's sakes, get rid of that yellow bag. It looks bad for all of us. It could even improve your game."

Arriving back home, they were no sooner out of the car and Veron was at Jim, "Did you remember the vegetables because I'm planning on canning tomorrow."

Jim, quick on the draw replies, "There wasn't a lot of time also I didn't ask as there wasn't much lying around like there was last week."

No sooner had he said that and Veron was on the phone to Anne. As they came into the kitchen, they overheard Veron diplomatically speaking about the vegetables they were given last week. She was thanking Anne for them and wondering if there was enough left for her to can in the coming week. "I was looking forward to canning some, if there was anything left. They were so good." They saw the disappointment on her face and heard her saying that was very enterprising." Eventually, Veron hung up and said, "Can you imagine that? Anne and her sister Jean have canned the whole lot already. She offered to give you boys some when you play golf again. I think you should go out next Saturday so she doesn't have to store her surplus for too long."

Jim, grinning at Gilley, said, "Let's go downstairs and have a drink before dinner." As they entered the bar and were out of earshot, Jim continued, "That worked out well. We have permission to play golf next week and we don't have to help out with the canning. All you have to do is get rid of that yellow bag. I'll work on that."

Tuesday arrived too soon for Gilley. It turned out Jim wasn't able to drive Gilley to the appointment, but could drop him off at the Greyhound Bus Depot on 6th Street. He had explained to Gilley that it was time to learn about the public transportation system in the lower mainland anyway. "It's nothing like what you're used to in England. Here are directions for getting home. You can take the Greyhound directly into Vancouver and get off at Burrard Street. However, after your appointment, you will have to take the city buses home as the Greyhound doesn't come back this way until later in the day."

Gilley arrived at his destination without difficulty. It was a beautiful day yet again. Everyone had remarked on the weather and how lovely it was. The walk from the bus stop to BC Hydro was quite enjoyable. Upon arriving at the building Gilley took a closer look at the address and his appointment instructions. "Mezzanine, Hmmm, "I wonder what that means," thought Gilley. He looked around, spotted a man in uniform sitting at a desk. He asked where the Mezzanine floor was. "Take the elevator to the second floor," was the man's reply.

Gilley thought the man said "escalator" and looking around, couldn't spot one. "Now what do I do? Mmmm, in England there were three ways to get to upper floors: using the stairs, using the lift and using the escalator. "Where was the escalator?" thought Gilley. He wandered down the lobby area searching for his way upstairs. No escalator. But he could see people coming and going out of what he called the lift. "Ah, that may be a way to the second floor," thought Gilley as he entered the lift and pushed the button for what he thought was the second floor. The doors opened and a large sign read, "3rd Floor". "Oops, I must have missed the second floor." Back into the elevator, Gilley looked at the buttons more closely. The button below "3rd Floor" was marked "M". "Could that be for Main where I was or would that stand for Mezzanine?" Always ready for an adventure, Gilley pushed the "M" button. Low and behold, the doors opened onto a floor displaying a sign "Mezzanine" "Whatever that means. In England this would be the 1st floor because we have a Ground Floor. How confusing?" With that he headed towards the "BC Hydro Reception Area."

"Hello, I'm here for a 10:30 appointment to write some exams, "said Gilley as he presented himself to the receptionist.

The receptionist checked a list and acknowledged he was indeed scheduled for the exam and handed him a large brown envelope. "Here are the test papers and the instructions for writing both of them. You will find a vacant desk over there in that area. Just pick any seat that suites you, Sir."

Gilley took his brown envelope and found a desk to his liking. There were quite a few people sitting at desks in this area and Gilley assumed they were writing IQ and Aptitude tests, just like him. Sitting down, he took the pencil he was given and read the instructions. Then he began to scan the test questions. As he was about to start, he heard the scraping of a chair. A man came and sat near him. Gilley returned to his exam. After approximately fifteen minutes, he heard the chair scrape again and saw the man stand up to leave. He indeed had the same test Gilley was working on. He had finished already.

The man walked to the desk, handed in his paper and was given another one. He returned and sat down again. Gilley remembered why he was here and applied himself again to his paper. After about 15 more minutes, the chair scraped again. The man was finished again. This time, Gilley could not contain himself, "Excuse me, Sir. I couldn't help but notice you've finished both tests so quickly."

The man looked over and said, "Oh, don't mind me. We take these all the time at university and I've been doing these through all the courses I've taken. Once you know how to fill them out, it comes very easily. I must have done twenty so far."

"That's a relief," said Gilley. "What are you taking?"

"I'm almost finished my degree in Languages. Very interesting course."

"Oh" was all Gilley could muster. Remembering his manners, Gilley added, "Thank you." After the man left the area, Gilley thought, "Oh my. He's taken a degree in Languages to be a meter reader? I can't believe it." Finishing up his paper, he turned it in and received the Aptitude paper, now thinking about what Eric had told him on Saturday, not quite believing his story.

He read it over. "Eric was right. These are ridiculous. How can one be judged on these. Questions like,

My favourite pastime is ______________.
I love to ______________.
In my spare time I ______________.
Most of my friends ______________.
My parents were ______________.
When I get home ______________.
______________ I love ______________.
What excites me is ______________.
Etc.

Gilley looked through the questions again. He thought about the man he had just spoken to and about it taking up to two years meter reading before moving on in the company and he decided he didn't want it. This was not for him but he had promised Jim and Veron he would take the tests. "Be honest in your answers." Time was pressing on. He had fifteen minutes left before they closed for lunch. If he didn't get this done by then, he would have to come back at 1:00 PM. He did his best to comply.

My favourite pastime is drinking beer, playing pool and darts.

I love to have a beer with my wife.

In my spare time, I play pool, drink beer and play darts.

Most of my friends live in England and love drinking beer.

My parents were very old and live in England and don't drink much beer.

When I get home *I have a beer.*

My wife and I love to have fun in my in-laws bar, drinking beer, playing pool and darts.

What excites me is *having a shower every day.* Etc

Gilley finished with only a minute to spare. "Here you are, Miss."

She replied, "You will only hear from us if you are successful."

"When you read this paper, "Gilley responded, "I know I won't hear from you again and I don't really care. This is Hydro's loss not mine. Being a meter reader for up to two years would take me back to my young teen days, going from house to house delivering papers. I'm far from that."

Walking down Burrard Street in Vancouver, he eventually found Hastings Street and headed west. He passed many beer parlors, but none appealed to him until he came to the Waldorf. It was the friendly appearance of the place that attracted Gilley. He entered and found a table to his liking. "Time for a beer," he thought. "There's no hurry to get home, its only 1:30 PM. Besides, it's nice to be on my own and savor the Canadian life in my own fashion." He wasn't sure what was in store, but he was up for adventure. He was thinking everyone in the place were loggers, the way they were dressed. All eyes were on him as well with his odd dress. Finally, Gilley spotted the waiter and realized he was dressed like the waiter with a suit and tie. "Well, at least I'm not the only one in a suit." With that he dropped a dollar bill onto the table. Quick as lightening, the waiter came over and dropped four beer and twenty cents change.

Gilley sipped on his beer and began to secretly study the men, wondering what so many were doing here at this time of day. In England, this would be unusual. After a short time, Gilley realized he was a bit hungry. He looked around to see what the parlor was offering to eat and spotted some potato crisps hanging behind the bar. Picking up his glass, Gilley made his way over to the bar and asked the bartender how much the crisps were. The bartender glanced at him and then turned away, waving to the waiter. The waiter hurried over and took the glass right from Gilley's hand. "Sir, you cannot walk around here holding your drink. That is illegal here. Please to come and sit at your table, "declared the waiter.

"But" said Gilley, "I would like a bag of crisps if they aren't too expensive."

"Crisps??? Oh, you mean potato chips? Yes, yes, come back to your table and I will get you some." With that, the waiter headed back to Gilley's table. Gilley had no choice but to follow him if he was to finish his drink.

The waiter motioned Gilley to sit down and walked away. In a moment he returned with a full glass of beer and two bags of chips (or crisps as Gilley thought about them.)

"Sir, you are from England, no?" inquired the waiter.

"Yes, I am, "replied Gilley. "I've just come to Canada with my new wife. I'm here in Vancouver looking for a job. You don't sound like you're from Canada either. Where do you come from?"

'Ah, you are very perceptive, Sir. I am from Italy. My name is Louie. I've been here four years. My English is still not good. But you don't need much English when you're serving beer."

Curious, Gilley asked Louie who seemed quite knowledgeable in spite of his declared lack of English, "What are all these people doing here, this time of day."

Oh, these men are longshoremen. They load and unload the many boats that come into the harbor. You must know Vancouver is a very big port. Today, there were only two boats and the men finished early. Some days there are many more to work at and some days there are no boats at all. That is when we are the busiest as the men pass their time here until they go home."

"What sort of product comes in and out of here," asked Gilley?

"That is a very good question, sir. There is grain, mainly wheat from the prairies and then there is potash and coal from Manitoba. The local mills send paper and lumber to countries as well. It is a busy port. Also many goods come into Vancouver through here. It is the largest port in Western Canada. Many men find work."

By this time, Gilley was feeling a bit guilty for occupying Louie's time, "Oh, sorry man. I hope you don't get into trouble for talking to me. I've taken a lot of your time."

"Smiling, Louie replied, "Don't worry my friend. If the glasses are full, there's no problem. But I see I will have to leave now as refills will be wanted now."

"You're very good at what you do, Louie. Could you bring me two more beers and another bag of crisps, I mean chips, at some point?"

Gilley finished his beers and crisps. Now it was about 3:00 PM and time to go home. "Louie, can you tell me how to get back to New Westminster?"

"No, Gilley. I'm afraid I don't know. I think the bus stop is one block east from here, but if that bus goes to New Westminster, I don't know."

"That's OK. How hard can it be? I took one bus here. I just have to find that one bus to get back home. I'll see you again, Louie. Thanks for the beers and the conversation."

With that, Gilley headed east and found the bus stop Louie had referred to. A bigger test than that at Hydro now awaited Gilley. He had to get from downtown Vancouver to New Westminster by bus. Having been told that there was no direct bus to New Westminster and that he would have to transfer busses, he was prepared a for long ride home. He sat down at a bench under a sign that said "Bus Stop" and lit a cigarette. About ten minutes later, a bus came along and stopped. Gilley approached the driver to ask if this was the bus that would take him to New Westminster. "You won't get to New Westminster on this side of the road. You should be over there at that bus stop and catch a bus that will take you to Kootenay Loop."

"Kootenay Loop? Are you sure? That's a strange name."

Looking at Gilley in his English styled suit and tie, he said, "You're not from around here are you? You'll find quite a few strange words around here, my lad." He closed the door and left Gilley to ponder "Kootenay Loop".

So, Gilley crossing to the other side of the road, remembered he had to cross at a cross walk which was at an intersection. He certainly didn't want the same embarrassment he experienced with his mother-in-law when he crossed the road as he would have in England and drew the ire of a policeman. He found the bus stop the driver had referred to and immediately saw the bus going to Kootenay Loop pulling to the stop. "What luck" he thought and jumped aboard, "I want to go to Kootenay Loop and eventually onto New Westminster. Am I on the right bus?"

"You are, lad. Pay your fare and here's a transfer for the next bus. Neither this bus nor the next one goes directly to New Westminster. You'll have to take another from the Kootenay Loop to the Brentwood Exchange in Burnaby. Then you change busses again there and the driver will tell you where to catch the one to New Westminster. The next bus to Brentwood will be in half an hour. You'll be there in lots of time."

"Thanks very much," said Gilley as he made his way to a vacant seat. "This is quite complicated here. In England, you could get a bus in five minutes to anywhere you needed to go. But, Canada is quite young compared to England, and it's so big. That's probably why things are so chaotic. No wonder everyone wants to drive their own car. It's much more convenient and efficient." Just at that time, the bus pulled into the Kootenay Loop.

Gilley got off and looked around but before he left the bus he thanked the driver. "No problem," he said, mimicking the English accent. "Good luck. Remember to take the bus going to the Brentwood Exchange. There you will get the one going into New Westminster."

"Thanks again," said Gilley as he looked around. There were lots of bench seats and few busses visible at the moment so he chose a seat, lit a cigarette and checked his pocket for change. "Jim said it would be a challenge getting home from Vancouver and he's right. Since I have this transfer, I won't have to pay bus fare again. That's handy. I wonder if I'll get another transfer ticket when I get to Brentwood." Just then a bus labeled Brentwood Exchange pulled up near to Gilley's bench. All the passengers poured off and others queued to enter. Gilley joined this line and as he gave the driver the transfer, he asked if the driver would tell him when he was at Brentwood. "You see, Sir, I'm trying to get from Vancouver to New Westminster on me own and I've never done this before."

"I'll make sure you get off at Brentwood as the next stop will be back into Vancouver again. Here's another transfer to take your next ride."

They arrived at Brentwood, and the bus driver pointed in a general direction. "You'll catch your bus over there." And he was gone before Gilley could confirm where was 'over there'. As Gilley stood by the bus stop, not having developed his sense of direction for his new homeland yet, was once again unknowingly standing on the wrong side of the road.

It was a good thing he was observant for he noticed a bus saying "New Westminster" going the other way. "Whoops, on the wrong side again. I guess I missed that one. One of these days I'll get it right." Laughing at himself, waited for the green light, crossed the road and stood at the correct bus stop waiting for the next bus.

He also noticed that it was beginning to get dark now. Looking at his watch, he realized that it was going on 4:30 and he also noticed the temperature was starting to drop. "Well, it is October." In England, it would be the rainy season and very cold and damp. Everyone was telling him here that this was a beautiful fall. They haven't had a warm sunny fall like this in a long time. In Gilley's mind, before coming here, Canada was always covered in snow. "What will the winter bring," he thought?

It was getting close to 4:45. Another fag and getting chillier. No one else was standing at the bus stop. Maybe there isn't another bus coming here. Maybe that was the last one. Just at this time, a bus came over the brow of the hill and stopped in front of Gilley. People got off and Gilley asked the driver, "When is the next bus to New Westminster?"

"It's not coming till 5:30. Jump on and I'll take you to Lougheed Mall. You can get a New Westminster bus earlier there." "Whoa, another bloody bus. The quicker I get a car the better off I'll be. Course I have to get a job first before I can get a car." Just as they pulled into Lougheed Mall, the bus to New Westminster pulled up too. Taking no chances, he jumped onto that bus. No transfer this time. He had to pay another twenty five cents. "Well worth it."

At last he arrived in New Westminster and got off at the Woodward's store. Finally, somewhere he recognized. The time was close to 6:00 PM. Gilley had to walk the rest of way home. Arriving home finally, he headed straight for the bar. As he came into the room all eyes were on him. "Where the hell have you been," said Jim. "It wasn't that big a test was it? It's after 6:30 PM."

"The biggest test today was getting back home from Vancouver. It took me over three hours to get home on the busses. I have to say I did stop at a place called the Waldorf. Very nice."

"I knew you wouldn't miss a bar and you found the Waldorf, did you," asked Veron? "That's my old stomping ground when I worked at BC Sugar. How did you find your way down there? Never mind, tell us about the exam."

"Well, the exam was a bit of a laugh. I know by the way I answered they won't call me. I don't want to be a meter reader for BC Hydro. Veron, I smell your great cooking. That wouldn't be your Minestrone soup would it, that you served for dinner?"

"You're a sly devil, you! You're just trying to butter me up. But I did save some for you. Have your supper before the MacRories come round. They're coming for drinks and to see how your interview went today. Mickey has an idea for a job for you and he wants to tell you about it."

"Thanks, Veron. I've only had two bags of crisps today or chips as you call them here. I'm starving."

No sooner had Gilley finished his supper than the door bell rang announcing the MacRories. He met them as they descended to the bar. "Big day for you, Gilley, I understand," said Mickey as he reached for the beer Jim handed him. "How was your interview? Was it as strange as the rumor says it is?"

"Well, Mickey, I'm not too sure about the rumor but if you've heard they want to know what your mother likes best, then yes, it was quite interesting. I decided to just tell them the truth. That's what Jim told me to do. I told them my favourite pastime was drinking beer. I also said my wife's favourite pastime was also drinking beer. Then they wanted to know what excites me."

"They wanted to know what excites you? What did you tell them," asked Joy?

"I told them that the shower excites me every day. Who could ever live without the shower? I don't think they'll be calling me."

"Oh, you've told me enough" laughed Mickey. "You're right. I wouldn't call you. However, I have a friend that may be able to give you a lead. Let's play some pool and I'll give you the details."

As they played pool, Mickey told Gilley about his friend John Manly who operated a small shipyard at the bottom of Rumble Street on the Fraser River. "I've told him about you and your experience as a mechanical engineer. He has time to see you on Thursday morning if you're interested. He may not have a position open, but he has contacts in the business and may be able to connect you with someone who does."

"I really appreciate you doing this for me, Mickey. Of course I'm interested. Please let him know."

"Well, Gilley, here's his number. All you have to do is call his secretary and tell her and she'll give you an appointment."

"I'll take care of that," interjected Veron. "You're working so I have time to make the call." With that she snatched the number out of Gilley's hand and walked away.

Elaine, observing the transaction, jumped in "That's my girl, Veron. Don't let the men get ahead of us."

Gilley and Mickey looked at each other and shrugged. Jim added, "That's that taken care of, Gilley. Let's finish the game."

Wednesday morning came and it was back to the school board working with Mike and Harry, cleaning up the summer debris and preparing all school grounds for the winter. Mickey said, "I don't know if you're aware of this, Gilley, but there's an ongoing competition between the school board and the city. They want to see who has the best kept grounds and your father-in-law is adamant we will keep the winner's title. He believes preparation is the number one key to keep ahead of them. You may wonder why he insists on so many details and that's the reason."

"Oh, thanks for that information, Mickey," replied Gilley. "I just thought that's the way the man was. You've seen his own garden and how well manicured it is."

At the end of the day, Mike said to Gilley, "Harry's been bugging me to show you how Canadian football is played. He's a BC Lions fan and wants everyone to join in. Since you know about soccer, he thought you were a good candidate. Let's go out to the field and I'll give you a few pointers."

"That would be great, Mike. I've been curious myself as to what the differences are. In England, our football is what you call soccer. We are always kicking the ball and the only person to handle it is the goalie or when we take a throw in. Jim and I have caught a few games on TV and I've noticed that your football is very different. It's more like what we call rugby in England. It seems to me the only time the ball is kicked is when you want to score a field goal. I can't understand why it's called football. It's handled and thrown most of the time to get it to the opponent's goal."

"You're on the right track, Gilley. Let's go and toss the ball around. Harry will meet us down there."

Gilley noted that the football for this game was shaped like a rugby ball, but smaller as it was thrown from the hand. Mike who was a defenseman (his size indicated that—350 pounds, 6 foot 5 inches) threw a few balls into the air so Gilley could get a feel for catching them. Just when Gilley thought he had it down, he threw one directly at Gilley. Gilley caught it, but wow, it was like catching a bullet in his chest. "Wow that was a hard throw, man."

"Good catch, Gilley. Not many men would have been able to catch that. Maybe you could have been a good receiver."

"Is that as hard as the quarter back has to throw it?"

"The quarterback, Gilley, has a different type of throw. He has to be able to throw it a long or a short distance with great accuracy. On top of that he has to be agile, alert and fast. He's the main player in the game. He has to also watch carefully because there's big buggers like me who will come down on him given the chance. It's getting dark now. Let's call it a day. I'll take you to a live game and explain the full rules. It's easier if you can watch how it's played."

"That would be great, Mike. I'd like that." With that they each headed home. Gilley arrived home to find Veron waiting on the front steps.

"Where the hell have you been? You're usually home by 5:00 PM at the latest. John Manly's secretary is waiting for you to call. I told her you would call before 5:30 PM. Now it's 5:25 PM. You'd better call right away. Here's the number." With that she shoved the paper into Gilley's hand and left.

"Thanks, Veron," said Gilley as he made his way to the telephone. Once he was done, he knew he had to report immediately to Veron and he found her in the kitchen preparing dinner. Just then Jim and Joy arrived home.

"Well, tell us the news, Gilley. Don't keep us in suspense."

Gilley said, "I have an appointment at 10:30 AM with John Manly. Jim, how's that going to work out with me having to go to the school board? I've already taken so much time off looking for work. You've been so good in helping me get to my appointments."

"Don't worry about that Gilley. You were hired as a part time worker and paid by the hour. When you're not there, you don't get paid. But I do have to tell you Friday will be your last day, though."

Joy exclaimed, "What do you mean his last day?"

"You know what the school board is like. There are a lot of politics going on. Even though I checked with the Board of Directors before I hired Gilley and they approved it, there have been some complaints. Some people think I've used my position inappropriately by hiring my son-in-law. Now the Board agrees so I have to lay him off."

"That's a load of bull shit," Veron said. "You have so many problems in the fall hiring temporary workers to keep their grounds up better than the city's and they're tying your hands now."

"Yes, I know all about that, Veron. Let's hope this interview with John Manly works out. Gilley, it's just at the bottom of Rumble. You can walk there. I think it will take you about half an hour. I can pick you up about 11:30 AM and take you back to work. We have a lot of clean up still to do and I want to use you to the fullest while I have you. I'll take your work clothes with me in the morning so you can change at the site."

Not wanting to be left out, Veron said, "I'll take Gilley down to make sure he doesn't get lost. Besides, the market is open and I can do some shopping at the same time.

The following day, Veron dropped Gilley at the shipyard. It turned out he was fifteen minutes early, so he took his time looking around and taking in the scenery. It was a beautiful sunny day and the area was bustling with activity. A tugboat was pulling a large log boom directly ahead in the river. Two others were pulling huge barges upstream. He hadn't seen them close up before. They were a very short and squat boat, almost comical looking, but when Gilley saw them at work, he realized that they contained very powerful engines.

Looking around the shipyard, he could see one of the tugs being overhauled. There was a lot more boat below the water than was seen above. Sort of like one of those powerful icebergs, innocent looking, but not to be tangled with. Entering the office, it was close on 10:30 and Gilley could see there wasn't the usual receptionist waiting to greet visitors, not like Hydro. This appeared to be an all male establishment where people seemed to come and go as they pleased. Because everyone was dressed alike, Gilley didn't know who was important and who wasn't.

As he stood there looking for the opportunity to ask someone, a man approached him. Seizing the moment, Gilley asked, "Could you tell me where I could find John Manly?"

"You're talking to him," came the reply. "Who are you?"

"I'm the chap who had a meeting with you at 10:30. I'm Mickey MacRories friend, Gilley"

"Good, grab yourself a coffee and come on through," said John as he headed away.

"Great, where the hell do you grab a coffee from?" thought Gilley. So looking around, he saw a big urn in the corner, much like the one at A & I Engineering, so he went over and grabbed a Styrofoam cup from a silver sleeve dispenser. The urn had a long glass tube that indicated the level of coffee left in it. There was a can of grimy evaporated cream and some lumps of sugar beside this device. Gilley, ever willing to go along with his hosts, took a cup from the sleeve and tried to get the coffee from the urn. He knew that it came out somehow, but at the moment, the urn was winning the contest. Feeling a little self-conscious, as this was again a totally new experience, he finally figured out how the urn worked and was able to add the cream and sugar.

By now, of course, he had lost Mr. Manly, so he wandered down the obvious hallway towards what seemed to be the most likely place for an office. Yes, there he was sitting behind his desk talking on the telephone. Looking up he motioned Gilley to sit down in the only other chair in the office. The office too was grimy and beat up.

For such a young, vibrant country, these shipyards couldn't be much older than seventy or eighty years old, yet they looked much older. They looked like they had been erected as a temporary measure and had been extended past its intended life expectancy. Behind Gilley, from Mr. Manly's viewpoint, was a large window that looked out over the Fraser River. The river looked very congested in this one area with log booms, saw mills, and related businesses, along with various other riverboats.

John Manly hung up the phone and said to Gilley, "So what can you do? No, before you answer that question, let me take you for a quick walk around the shipyard to give you an idea of what we do here." Never having visited a shipyard before, but having been born in an area where shipbuilding was a common industry, Gilley felt somewhat at home, but nonetheless, very out of place.

John Manly said, "I hear you come from Newcastle-Upon-Tyne. That's a great shipbuilding area. What you see here is totally different." He was right. Gilley had never seen anything like this in his life before. Men were just working all over the yard, fixing and carrying and welding with no real protection for visitors. As they walked through the yard, Manly took Gilley over to the tugboat getting repaired. On the back of that tug, was a large towing winch getting new cable rolled onto its drum. As Manly was talking, he said, "Do you know anything about winches?"

"Not a lot." Gilley said. "It's just like another piece of handling equipment such as yard cranes etc. My brother worked for a company called Clark Chapman's who are a large deck equipment company from Tyneside."

John Manly said, "Oh, I know them very well. The reason why I ask is that I may be able to get you a job with a company called Swann Winches and what you're looking at is a Swann Towing Winch. Do you feel comfortable designing this type of equipment and do you know much about hydraulics?"

"I feel OK about designing the hydraulics, but I don't have any practical experience other than brake systems in mobile cranes, but I did take basic hydraulics in college while I was serving my apprenticeship as a machinist."

"Good", Manly replied, "I'll make a call then. Come with me."

As they walked through the machine shop, which was something out of a war zone, Gilley mentioned, "You have some old machines in here. That lathe in the corner must be a hundred years old."

"How come you know so much about a machine shop?"

"Well in England," Gilley said, "Before you can become a mechanical draughtsman, you had to serve an apprenticeship on the shop floor learning how to operate all the various machines."

Manly said, "That's another bonus you've got."

Back to his office, Manly grabbed another coffee and sat at his desk to make that important call. He got off the phone and declared, "Looks like everybody's at lunch. The receptionist will pass my message on when they return. I have a lunch appointment too. Give me a phone number where I can reach you this afternoon."

The only number Gilley could remember was his mother-in-law's number. It began to look like he would have to spend the afternoon with her. Manly asked Gilley where he lived and offered to give him a lift back home. "That would be nice," Gilley said, "But my father-in-law is picking me up. I had planned on going back to work with him at the school board. I'll tell him the developments and make sure I'm by the phone to get your call. Thank you very much for a most interesting tour and for your help. I really do appreciate it all."

"That's fine, Gilley. I'll do anything for Mickey MacRorie. He and I go a long way back. We used to play lacrosse together and we also made our own sticks. We'd even sell a few when we could. Glad to help a friend of a friend."

Jim arrived and Gilley brought him up to date on the latest developments. "We'll go home and have lunch. Don't worry about the job today. I only hope this works out to a full time job for you. It will get Veron off our backs."

The afternoon dragged on, sitting with Veron on the deck looking over the Fraser, having a cup of tea, and smoking cigarettes one after the other, waiting for this call. 2:00 PM went by, then 2:15 PM then 2:30 PM. Gilley was about to jump over the railing with impatience when the phone rang. Veron jumped up, "Hello?" and handed the phone to Gilley. "It's John Manly."

"John Manly here, Gilley. Phone this chap at Swann Winches. His name is Dennis Shears and do it now. Here's the number. Best of luck! Tell me how it comes out."

"Can I use your phone, Veron? I have to give this guy a call right now."

"Sure you can, Luv." And she drew her chair closer to the phone.

In England, phones were more of a luxury than an everyday affair and Gilley didn't have much experience making telephone calls. In England every call had to be paid for individually and having a phone was an indication of importance. Given this and making this call Gilley was doubly nervous. Not only was he making a telephone call but a call that could be life-changing.

"Dennis Shears here," came a voice at the other end. Gilley explained who he was and how he came to make this call. Without hesitation, Dennis stated "You don't have to tell me your background. Wait until tomorrow morning. You have an appointment with me at 10:00 AM here at the office."

"I'll be there, Sir. Thank you," stammered Gilley and hung up.

"Well," Veron says, "What's happening?"

"I've got an appointment at 10:00 AM tomorrow morning with Dennis Shears of Swann Winches."

"Good, I'll get Jim to drive you. What's the address?"

"He said it was just behind the Waldorf on Franklin. Do you know where that is?"

"Back in my old hunting grounds, you bugger. Remember, I used to work at BC Sugar. You've already sampled the beer at the Waldorf, so you've already acquainted yourself with the area."

The next morning, Jim drove Gilley to the interview. When he dropped him off, Jim said, "Don't worry about getting home from this interview. I have some people to see in this area and will be back about 11:00 AM to pick you up." Before Gilley got out of the car, he asked Jim what he thought would be the going rate for this type of job. Jim's reply was, "About $400.00 to $450.00 per month. That would be a good start. Best of luck. See you in an hour."

Entering Swann Winches, again another old tattered affair of a building, he followed the arrows upstairs to an open reception area.

There was a conglomeration of men sitting at desks, working at whatever was their task. Picking the closest man he asked where he could find Dennis Shears. "Just one minute. Dennis said to expect someone. That must be you."

At that point, a man of medium build who was leaning over talking to someone looked up, "Come in Gilley, I've been watching for you. I'm Dennis Shears. Come with me. I'd like you to meet the general manager Art Burgess." Following Dennis, he picked his way across the room and entered a smallish office near the far side.

"Art, here's the young man John Manly called about yesterday. Gilley, this is Art Burgess, the general manager."

Art stood up and shook Gilley's hand. "Pleased to meet you, Gilley. I have several questions to ask you, so please have a seat." He had a strong Birmingham accent and continued, "Can you tell me what your background is?"

Gilley responded, "I've served my apprenticeship as a fitter and turner and when I finished that, I spent four years as a junior draughtsman. During that period, I went to day release college where I got my final City and Guilds in product design."

"Oh," said Art, "I've been away from England for twelve years. I didn't know they offered City and Guilds product design at day release college. When I was there, City and Guilds only offered extensions for the machinists."

"Yes, that's right. What they've done is blended the National course and the City and Guilds trades and started a new course which the call a technical program. This gives you the theory and practical in three stages. Once you've completed the third one, you become a technologist."

"It's about bloody time they did something right. That's good. You have the skills we're looking for. What do you think Dennis?"

"I think it's time to take him down to see Barry Freeke, the Chief Engineer." With that, Art and Dennis stood up and Gilley once again followed Dennis, his head in a whirl.

Entering the engineering office, Gilley said to Dennis, "What part of England are you from," as he had detected a bit of an accent?

"West Hartlepool."

Gilley's remark was, "isn't that where they hung the monkey?"

"You're right and it's not everyone who can claim that fame, is it? And one day I'll tell you the full story as only West Hartlepool folks know it," he grinned as he introduced him to Barry Freeke, the chief engineer.

"Pleased to meet you, Gilley. Where are you from? I detect an English accent," said Barry in his Yorkshire accent.

"I'm from Newcastle," replied Gilley.

"Oh, a bloody Geordie, are you?"

"That's right and proud of it. What part of Yorkshire are you from?

"Very good ear. I'm from Leeds. You are the young man Dennis told me about. Can you tell me what your qualifications are?" Without another word, Gilley produced his certificate and his indentures. "Ah, not often you see those things," said Barry. "I recognize the City and Guilds Product Design and the indentures. I see you served your apprenticeship as a fitter and turner. It's nice to have someone who has had the technical as well as the practical experience. I think you'll fit in here well." Barry asked Gilley a few more questions and, satisfied with his answers, he said, "Now I'd like to introduce you to the team." With that, he led Gilley into the drawing office and introduced him to the team.

There was John Pendry, chief draughtsman from London, David Mosley, designer, from London, Graham Hyatt, detail draughtsman, from Birmingham England, Cecil Harcourt, hydraulic systems designer from Lancashire and Allan Pickering, design draughtsman, the token Canadian.

Barry said to Gilley, "As you see, Gilley, we are tight for room in this office. But there is a spare drawing board here. Let's go upstairs and talk to Art and Dennis and discuss your future." With that they left the office and arrived in Art's office.

"Well, Barry what do you think?" said Art,

"He not only has the technical ability, but comes with the practical side which we lack at the moment. I think we can use him," replied Barry.

"That's what I think too. Dennis is in favor of hiring him also for the same reasons," Turning to Gilley, Art continued, "Gilley, when can you start and what sort of wage are you looking for?"

Gilley's remark was, "I can start as soon as you'd like me to too. But, I haven't been here in Canada long enough to know what the normal salary would be."

"Well, we normally start draughtsman at $550.00 per month, but designers like you with those credentials, we start at $700.00. Why don't we start you off at 650.00 for three months and see how you do? Then after that, we can put you on our medical and dental program. If things work out we can add a $50.00 increase. You get two weeks holiday after the first year. You get paid for all statutory holidays. Would that do? We'd like you to start on Monday."

Gilley said, "Monday is fine with me and the starting salary is good too. Thank you very much."

"Good. We need someone like you as our workload has been increasing steadily. We'll look forward to seeing you then."

Leaving Swann's with energy in his step, Gilley met Jim in the parking lot, a little later than the agreed upon time. "Well, Jim, you are now looking at Swann's newest employee."

"That took quite some time, so I'd gathered you'd gotten the job. When do you start?"

"Monday, at $650.00 a month!"

"With that sort of money, you can buy me to lunch. I'll take you to a special place. It's just around the corner, so let's walk there and get some fresh air."

"Sounds good to me, Jim, as long as they have beer. I've only got $20.00. Will that do?"

"If it doesn't, I can handle it."

As they turned the corner, Gilley realized Jim was taking him to the Waldorf. "This should be interesting," he thought to himself."

However, instead of entering into the beer parlour, Jim opened an elaborate door that let into a dark foyer. There were steps which led up to the main room. As his eyes adjusted to the light, Gilley saw the entire place was done up in a Polynesian theme. There were bamboo chairs and tables, bamboo canes decorated the walls and the ceiling was unbelievable. It was a dark blue with very small lights. It looked like a clear night sky. Gilley had never seen anything like it. Seating themselves at a nice table, Jim said, "This is the best place for curry." No sooner said, than the waiter dropped four beers.

"I hope this is what you're drinking, Sir as we have a full compliment bar."

Looking up, Gilley saw his friend Louis. "Louis, how are you? You bet we're drinking beer.

"So soon we meet again. I hope this time you have good news," grinned Louis.

"Yes I have. I just got a job at Swann's across the road there. I start Monday."

"That is good news. I hope to see more of you, Sir. Remember, this is my usual location. I was just helping out in the beer parlour that day. I recommend the curry shrimp today. It's our Chef's specialty."

"Let's have two of those, "Jim interjected. "Make mine hot. How about you Gilley?"

"Same, Thanks, Louis"

With that Louis, walked away. "How did you come to know Louis? Have you been here before?"

"Don't you remember, Jim, I stopped in here the day I went to the BC Hydro interview. Nice fellow, Louis. He's Italian and working hard to stay in Canada. He became quite friendly with me as I looked like a fish out of water. I didn't know you weren't allowed to wander around carrying your own beer in Canada. Made quite a point of it, they did. Louis came to my assistance and took care of me."

As they waited for their meal, Gilley looked around, taking in more of the décor. There were several large paintings in particular that took his eye. These were all paintings of various people from the Islands and were quite well done.

Jim said, "Have you ever had a real curry before?" Being English, he realized most English dishes are not very spicy and are generally meat and potato dishes. They were very tasty, but not hot at all (in the way of "hot").

"Yes, your mother cooked one for Joy and me when we visited her in London before we left for Canada."

Jim said, "That would be real curry. My mother was brought up in the West Indies. My great grandfather had been a governor to the Queen in Ceylon. Therefore the whole family had been exposed to the hot dishes of the East. How did you like my mother's curry?"

"It was a challenge Jim, because I had never had any hot, spicy hot that is, food like that before, so I thought when I was told it would be spicy, I would have a beer with the meal. And your mother said, "Beer is one of the best things you can drink when you are having a curry." But she did explain that it wouldn't be as hot as she would normally make it. I found out that bananas have a real cooling effect when your mouth is on fire from the spice as well. It was a lamb curry with chutney, rice and pomatums which she told us to crush all over our curry dish. It was a splendid meal. It was hot, but I don't know what it would be like if it was really hot. I could see that Joy was struggling a bit with it too."

Well, Jim said, "For my mother to cook somebody curry and serve beer, it had to be someone very special. My mother was brought up with servants. She was not the type to put herself out to cook for anyone other than herself or her immediate family. But she did know how to run a good household and how a good meal was prepared. Maybe she was just showing off for you. I've never had the privilege of my mother making curry for me. She didn't care much for men. I was the only boy out of four. I was sent off to boarding school at an early age. My great like for curry developed when I was in the fleet Air Arm (this is the Navy's Air Force). I happened to be stationed in Ceylon along with Eric Godden. He was a pilot and I was a recognizance and navigator. That's where we first met."

Shortly Louis brought the food along as well as four more beer. "Here you are, Gentlemen. And I saw your drinks needed refreshing."

"Oh, that looks good. Smells good too. Say, Louis, what can you tell us about those paintings? Quite striking, aren't they," asked Gilley.

"Well, Sir, they are a gift from a famous Polynesian painter to the owner of this hotel. He received them as a Thank You gift for services he did for the people. They are to remain here for all time."

"Interesting. Mmmm, This is what I call a good curry. Not many places around Vancouver can make my mouth burn, but this one sure is. Good thing we have our beer," said Jim.

Gilley nodded in agreement and took another swallow of his beer. He was very glad there were bananas on the plate as well. These helped cool the burn of the spices. "We can't stay too long or Veron will get jealous, especially if we tell here we've been here, her old watering hole."

As they drove slowly back to New Westminster, Gilley said, "I can't believe we got that wonderful lunch for under $20.00 and that included the tip. Canada certainly is the place to be. Something similar in England would have cost me at least $50.00."

It was approaching 2:00 PM in the afternoon and Gilley was feeling more than a bit guilty that Jim had taken so much time off work, helping him to find a job and all. "Well Jim, I guess you are glad that I finally have a full time job. Now you can get back to your regular responsibilities."

"Well", Jim said, "Nobody really knows what I do, but they do know I do a good job of it. Many other school boards have asked me to go and work for them for a better salary. But I like my freedom. Here, at this job, they know I get the job done efficiently, within budget and on time, so they don't ask me to account for my time. I've just got to stop at the office to pick up my messages and see what else is going on. Then we'll go on home, share the good news and celebrate with a beer."

By the time they got home, it was 5:00 PM. Veron, standing at the top of the stairs to the bar, arms crossed, barring the way. "What's the news? No beer until I know."

"Can't tell you until Joy's here. After all, it wouldn't be fair to her to hear the news second hand," replied Gilley with a grin.

"I won't tell her. You can tell me! I can keep a secret."

Just then the front door opened and Joy walked in, saving them all from further argument. "What's the news, Gilley?" She said, getting to the point.

Jim finally announced, "We must go downstairs, pour the beer before we announce the news. After all, we need to be civilized about the whole thing."

Jim could hardly pour the beer for the begging that went on. Finally, beers poured, he lifted his glass, "Congratulations to Gilley. He starts his new job on Monday morning for Swann Winches. Cheers."

After the first swallow, both women said at once, "For how much?"

Jim, playing the role, said "He did quite well. I thought he would come out of there with between $300.00 and $400.00 a month. But our Gilley knows his worth. He starts at $650.00 a month."

"Ooh," said Veron, "That calls for a big celebration. Let's go to the Royal Towers for drinks."

Joy says, "Who's paying for this then? He hasn't got his first pay cheque yet."

"I will pay this time. But when that cheque comes in, it will be his turn."

Off they went, down to the Royal Towers. Jim had a Martini, Veron had her Vodka and seven, Joy had a bloody Mary and of course, Gilley had his beer. After three more rounds, Veron said, "We should go home and have supper, not that I feel like cooking."

Joy said, "Why don't we stop at the White Spot for supper?"

Veron replied, "I'm not having any of that quick food."

"It's not like McDonald's", said Joy. "You can get chicken pot pie, meat loaf, steak, fish and chips and of course, I'll pay."

Jim said, "That's a good idea. Let's do that."

Veron immediately chimed in, "Don't think this will get you off buying us a real dinner when that first pay cheque comes in."

In the car, Joy leaned over and whispered to Gilley, "Where's that Twenty dollars I gave you this morning?"

"Oh, I spent it. I took Jim for lunch at the Waldorf."

"What!" Then turning to the others, "You know these two have been out celebrating by themselves already today. The Waldorf of all places!!"

"The Waldorf," commented Veron, "That's my old stomping ground when I worked at BC Sugar. The girls and I would often go Thursday nights for Girls Night in the Polynesian Room. Do they still have that wonderful curry? I would order that dish most often."

"It was a well done curry today, Veron. You would have really enjoyed it. And Louis is still working there. He served us."

"Well, it seems like everyone else, including Gilley who hasn't been here for more than six weeks, has been to the Waldorf. When do I get my chance," complained Joy?

It was decided they would eat in the restaurant at the White Spot instead of at the drive-in. This sounded very strange to Gilley. "Of course, you would eat in the restaurant. What did they mean?" He said this out loud.

"Gilley, the White Spot is famous for its drive-in service," explained Joy. "You go to the back lot and leave your car lights on. The car-hop comes and takes your order. You have to make sure you turn your lights off then because he will come back and ask what you want. Then the meal comes on a tray that fits across the car and hooks into the windows. You get to eat in the comfort of your car. It's quite nice."

"Oh, we'll have to do that one day. It sounds very interesting," replied Gilley as he caught a look at the parking lot and the cars with their lights flashing on and off.

Sitting down in the restaurant, everyone seemed to know what they wanted even before they looked at the menu. Jim was having the Chicken Pot Pie, Joy, her Triple "O" (whatever that was?) and Veron, her Fish and Chips. Not wanting to hold up the order, Gilley had Fish and Chips. It was the only item he recognized. Everyone talked about the new job, but fell silent when the food arrived. As the plates were being cleared away, Joy said, "Gilley, you might as well go and buy yourself a new set of golf clubs so you can play golf on Saturdays with Jim."

Gilley replied, "It seems like everyone wants to spend my money for me and I haven't even got it yet."

Veron piped in, "We'll go up to our friend's sports shop. It's *'Rumbles'* on 12th street and I'll see if I can get you a deal."

The following day, Veron was anxious to get going. "Come on let's get those golf clubs. Then I'll take you to downtown Vancouver to the Bay. I've got to do some shopping and maybe we'll get a chance to pop into the Waldorf. Besides, you need to know how to get to and from work, now that you have it. I can't have you getting lost again and again, getting on the wrong buses and the only way for you to travel is by bus."

Joy was a bit miffed that she had to miss yet another adventure to the Waldorf as she had to work. She decided to warn Gilley that Mom was an arduous shopper and never paid the ticket price. "Don't be surprised when you see Mom switch price tags. She never pays regular price for anything."

At the sports shop, Veron demonstrated her friendship with the owner by asking, "Doug, how are you today? What good deals can you give us? My son-in-law here wants a set of golf clubs and doesn't have a lot of money. What have you got? He's been using mine since he's come here and I don't want them ruined. But I have to keep Jim happy as he needs Gilley as a golfing partner."

"I have some half sets of old stock here which I'm trying to get rid of. They are about $225.00 new, including the bag of course, "replied Doug.

"Let's have a look at them and see. Come on, Gilley, try them out." The set consisted of a #1 wood, a #3 wood, #3, 5, 7 & 9 irons and a putter. The bag was slightly damaged." They felt good in Gilley's hand and he said, "I'll take these, how much?"

"I can let you have them for 199.00."

"199.00?? Doug, I'll give you a cheque for no more than $160.00 and that will include a dozen golf balls." Turning to Gilley, she said, "And you can pay me back in installments with interest."

Doug, knowing he couldn't win, looked at Gilley and said, "Ok, you have a deal, Gilley. But I will only throw in a half dozen balls. I assume this is to your satisfaction? By the way," continued Doug, hoping to distract Veron, "Did you know the golf balls here in North America are 1/16 of an inch bigger than those in England?"

"Oh, no wonder I can hit the ball better since I've come here,' replied Gilley catching on quickly, "Well, thanks everybody," With that he loaded the set in car trunk. "You've had very good weather for golf and it seems its going to go right through to the end of November, according to the weather man. It seems like we are having a real Indian Summer."

Veron said, "Yeah, but we'll pay for it though, by probably getting a great dump of snow this year. Doug, you haven't fooled me with that golf ball story. I'll let it go this time, but remember, I live next door to your brother."

"Yeah, we normally have to pay the price for good weather eventually" agreed Doug, "Make the best of it while you can. Veron, when was the last time you were golfing? I'm sure you could use three of these Ladies golf balls I've just gotten in. I understand they will be all the rage soon."

Gilley, trying to keep up with the hidden agenda as well as the conversation offered, "I thought the weather was always like this in Canada. In the beginning of this year, around about February, Veron sent us a photograph of her sunbathing on their deck."

"Come on Gilley, we have to get to Vancouver now," interrupted Veron. Into the car they got and Veron said, "I'm going to take you on the route that the bus will take you on Monday so you will feel at ease and know where you are and where you have to get off. We don't want you getting lost again on your first day of work. Doesn't make a very good impression, does it?"

As they passed the stop on Hastings and Victoria where Gilley would have to get off the bus for work, Veron said, "Don't go passed this stop because it's a long walk back. The next stop is quite a ways away. And to catch a bus at nighttime, you should check with the people at work. I think it would just be the bus going in the opposite direction, but I'm not too sure."

As they drove down Hastings Street, coming into the downtown area, Veron pointed out some sights for Gilley. "This here is called Skid Row. This is not a place where you want to be especially at night." By the state of everyone staggering around, Gilley said, "You're right; I don't want to be here in the day time. But all large cities have these areas."

Finally they arrived at their final destination, The Bay. They parked underground and Veron said, "I've got some shopping to do for the girls. Why don't you go and amuse yourself in the Sports Department and I'll catch up with you in about half an hour?" So off to the Sports Department Gilley went. This isn't too bad. He thought he'd have to tag along with Veron, carrying her purchases and such. After pricing the clubs, etc, Gilley realized that he did get a good deal at Doug's. He probably saved about $100.00. After browsing for awhile, he saw Veron coming down the aisle, her arms full of shopping bags. She ordered Gilley, "Grab these bags, it's good to do your Christmas shopping now. Let go to the Waldorf now. I don't want to be outdone by Jim."

At the Waldorf, Veron remembered how it was inside from her days working at BC Sugar. The girls used to have a couple of drinks there once a week, "It was the only safe place in this area that a woman would feel comfortable having a drink without a male escort."

They sat there discussing Gilley's new clubs. "I really appreciate the fact that you've let me use your clubs, Veron. I know my game will improve now that I've got my own clubs and everyone will appreciate me not turning up with the yellow bag, especially Eric."

"Don't be so silly. Eric's a male chauvinist, "she said without thinking, "The bag doesn't make the golfer. The clubs might help. Men's clubs are longer and heavier, so maybe you will have a better game once you get used to them. But don't expect immediate results."

At this juncture, Louis appeared, recognizing Gilley, "Back here again? And who's the young lady? Didn't you used to come in here with some girls from BC Sugar a few years ago?' said Louis to Veron. "Scotch and Ginger, wasn't it?"

"Louis, I can't believe you remember me from those years back and that you remember my drink," said Veron, obviously flattered.

"Oh, my dear, you would be surprised what I remember. For example, I remember this young man came in by himself to the beer parlour and we chatted for awhile. Then with another man to this part of the hotel. They sat at that table over there and enjoyed the curry of the day. You drink beer—Labatt's Blue, yes?"

"You'll probably be seeing more of this young man. He starts at Swann's On Monday."

"Yes, I know," smiled Louis as he left to fetch the order.

"It hasn't taken you long to get to know people,' declared Veron.

"Remember I told you I came here after the interview with BC Hydro? It was Louis who educated me to the rules of a beer parlour. Then you know I came here with Jim. I can't believe he remembers all these things. And he remembered you from what you told me was a few years ago. He's quite extraordinary," replied Gilley.

At this time, Louis appeared with their drinks. "A Scotch and Ginger for you, Ma'am and for you Sir, a Labatt's Blue. Now, we have an appetizer on special today. Hand peeled shrimp for only $2.00. It will be a nice compliment to your drinks."

"I'd rather have a packet of crisps with my beer," said Gilley.

"Sir, I think you mean potato chips, not crisps. Sorry, Sir, they are only served in the beer parlor. I'll bring you an order of shrimp. I think you'll find them more than satisfactory." With that Louis left their table.

Veron was quite enthralled. "He really knows his customers, doesn't he? I love shrimp and I was just thinking of them before we came here. We often had them with the girls after work. I can't believe he remembered."

Arriving home before everyone else, Veron shooed Gilley downstairs, "You go down and play with your clubs. I have to hide these gifts before anyone comes home."

Down in the suite, Gilley looking at his clubs was anxious to play golf on Saturday. Hearing a noise, he looked up to see Joy enter. "I see you got your new clubs. How much did you pay for them?"

"I didn't. Your mom wrote him a cheque for $160.00."

"You let mom pay for them? You've got to be kidding?"

"What do you expect? I don't have any money. She said I could pay her back on three monthly payments of $55.00 each."

"So that means she makes $5.00 off us. Well, I guess, considering Mom, that's not too bad. The bank rate would have been $167.50 at today's rate. You must be in Mom's good books to get off that lightly. I will make sure we pay her back or we'll be in even bigger trouble. And, don't forget that now that you have a job, next month we have to start paying rent at $95.00 a month. Living here isn't a free ride now."

CHAPTER 6

STARTING WORK

MONDAY ARRIVED QUICKER THAN anyone wanted it to and it marked the end of Gilley's extended holiday. Even though the bus trip into the first day of work was uneventful largely due to Veron's thoughtfulness in showing Gilley the route, it was not what Gilley expected. Most of the people were either reading books or sleeping. This was not at all like home. In Newcastle, bus trips were marked by lots of conversation as friends exchanged the news of their various weekends.

The bus Gilley took got him to work half an hour earlier than his start time of 8:00 AM. Arriving at the front counter of Swann's he discovered others were in early as well. He asked directions to the drawing office. One of the tradesmen said, "Just go to the back of the shop and you'll see a green door. That's where you cartoon characters work."

Recognizing a Scottish accent, Gilley's reply was, "Coming from your part, that's all I thought you could read was comic books."

"Oh we do have a clever bugger here," said the Scot attempting to ignore Gilley.

However, Gilley, recognizing an opportunity, said, "Yes, clever and about to start my first day," holding out his hand, he continued, "I'm Gilley."

"Jim Rogers. Pleased to meet you."

"With that accent are you a Rangers or a Celtic supporter" asked Gilley?

"Hmmm, you should know better. Now isn't that a Geordie accent YOU have?"

"Yes it is."

"Then you should know there are more teams in Scotland than just Celtics and Rangers."

"I do agree. However, there are only two real teams in Scotland—the Celtics and the Rangers. Who do you support?"

"Neither one," retorted Jim.

"So which part of Scotland are you from?"

At that moment a buzzer sounded. "Oh, gotta start work. See you later," stated Jim.

Following Jim's directions, Gilley found the green door and entered the office behind it. As he entered, a man turned and greeted him. "I'm Allan Pickering, the token Canadian here in this office. Come over here and have a coffee," invited Allan. "What do you take?"

"Cream and sugar," replied Gilley.

"You Limeys are all the same. You don't know what good coffee really is. Good coffee is meant to be black."

Gilley thought, "Oh, not black coffee." Aloud he said, "I've never drank black coffee and first thing Monday morning I don't really want to try. How about if I try one next time.

"The coffee pot is always on," said Allan. "You can have as many cups as you want. There are three rules, though. One, the person who takes the last cup has to make the next pot. Two, the first one in makes the first pot and three; the last one out cleans everything up ready for the morning."

Gilley took his coffee and found an area in which to await his boss. As he sipped his coffee, the first one through the door was a joyful character who boomed, "Good Morning Everyone. Well done Allan, I see you have the coffee ready." Allan introduced this man as Dave Mosley. He was a thin Englishman, with dark hair, a tweed jacket and tie and dark rimmed glasses sitting upon a huge nose.

Allan offered, "Pour yourself a coffee and come and meet Gilley."

Next one to arrive spotted Gilley immediately and introduced himself as John Pendry. He was the chief draughtsman and had blonde hair, a stocky build and a southern English accent. He was a very friendly chap and chatted as he got his first coffee of the day.

The next one through, Allan introduced as Graham Hyatt. Graham was average build with frizzy hair and a jovial greeting for all. Gilley thought he could detect a Birmingham accent. Sel Greenwood arrived next. He was much older than the rest and came to the coffee pot straight away. He was in his late fifties, of average height and on the stocky side, but his "Good morning" was definitely from Yorkshire. They all congregated around the coffee pot area, welcoming Gilley aboard.

Next came Barry Freeke, the chief engineer—a familiar face. Gilley knew from the interview he was from Yorkshire as well. He was very reserved, especially in comparison to the rest. He was thin and sported a red goatee that matched his neatly combed hair. He said, "Well you've all been introduced to Gilley. It's now my turn. Gilley, I'll just get my coffee and we'll meet in my office." He went onto give instructions to most of the men for the day's work. Gilley noticed that Sel went about doing his own thing. Surrounded by so many Limeys, Gilley felt somewhat at home.

Barry and Gilley retired to Barry's office where Barry made him feel very welcome. After some time of pleasantries, Barry explained that Gilley's task for the day was to go from man to man and observe how things ran. "Before you do that, though, I'll take you on a tour of the place and introduce you to the rest of the staff." Walking through the plant, Gilley said to Barry, "I'm noticing this machinery is older than I've been used to seeing in England."

"Don't worry about the machinery, Gilley. It's the skill of the men making the parts that count."

"It's true, Barry. I'm just curious that such a young country would have machinery as old as these appear to be. Especially living with my in-laws, I've seen all the mod-cons available here in Canada."

"Good observation, Gilley. Since we are so close to the United States, we have all the new conveniences for our homes yet industry has to make do with what it has," replied Barry.

Returning to the office, Gilley noticed the blueprinting machine in the far corner. Above it was a large stainless steel hood that reminded

Gilley of a fish and chip shop. Turning to Barry and pointing to the hood, he asked, "When are the fish and chips going to be served?"

Barry, laughing and knowing what Gilley meant said, "That wouldn't be a bad idea. We might be able to make more money at fish and chips than with blueprints. Actually the reason for the hood, which has a fan inside, is we use ammonia to develop the prints. If we don't have the fan on, we'd all be choking with the fumes."

"Isn't that strange, because the last drawing office I worked in used a wet process that didn't smell. The only disadvantage was the infrared drying section. If the paper rolled up on the belts, it would set on fire. That caused quite a stir as you could imagine. It needed the full attention of the operator."

As he was looking at it, Allan, needing some copies from the originals, took the opportunity to show Gilley how the machine worked. Gilley offered to help. Allan's first instruction was to put the fan on. Then start the machine up and give it five minutes to warm up. The next phase was to turn the ammonia tap on.

Once this was done, Gilley realized why there was this huge fan and hood. The ammonia fumes were overpowering. Gilley coughed and stepped away with his eyes running. Everyone started laughing as Allan explained, "Next time you turn the ammonia bottle on, you have to get away quickly. After it settles down, then you come back to do the printing." Gilley proceeded to do the printing, as operating printing machines was familiar to him. Even though the ones in England were far more modern, the principles were the same. After completing the task, Barry took Gilley to introduce him to the rest of the staff.

These included John Clark, a Scottish lad, who was head of estimating. Dave McLuckie, another Scot was John's assistant. "How apt having two Scots working together," Gilley thought? Jim Hunter came next. Surprisingly, he was a Canadian lad and the purchasing agent for the company. Bill Robins, another Canadian, was the Works Manager. George Strutt from Manchester, England was the Special Projects Manager. Harry Truzzel, the bookkeeper had his own corner. Gilley saw where Dennis Shears worked. He had his own area as did Art Burgess, the general manager. It was amazing how many people were jammed into this small space and none of them seemed to mind.

Next they walked down a flight of stairs to what appeared to be a half floor. Here there was another office. Barry opened the door, stuck his head in and said, “Lorne, here’s Gilley our new draughtsman. Gilley, this is Lorne Hughes. He’s the machine shop foreman.” At that point, Lorne took over and toured Gilley through the machine shop. Gilley met Mac Harrison whom Gilley would come to think of as the hydraulic guru. Then, there was Ken Diamond, the assembly shop foreman. A surprising staff member was Bill Swann. He had a nice, small office close to the front entrance and was introduced to Gilley as one of the owners. His job was customer relations. Next to Bill was an open area where Gilley was introduced to Danny Ellis, another Canadian. He was the illustrator for advertising and marketing. Last but not least, were the general shop personnel who were a mixture of Englishmen, Germans, Italians, Scots and Canadians.

Gilley had never met such a variety of different nationalities working together in one place. Generally, everyone in the office seemed to get on well. Right away, Gilley could feel the good rapport that existed throughout the company. This went far in making Gilley feel at ease. By the time Gilley returned to the drawing office, it was lunchtime. Everyone sort of sat around the office, eating their lunch and chatting. Gilley realized he had forgotten his lunch. Allen Pickering saw Gilley standing there and realized what was happening. “Gilley, it looks like you don’t have lunch with you today. Neither do I. Let’s go to the coffee truck. It’s due now.”

“Oh, Thanks. What’s a coffee truck?

“Come on and you’ll see.” With that, Allen headed out the door. Suddenly a loud horn sounded and in zoomed this truck with a large silver box on the back where the bed would have been.

Out jumped an attractive woman yelling, “Hurry up boys, I’m running late.” With that she opened the back door. It swung upward to reveal a shelf loaded with sandwiches, fruit, donuts and pop. There was a coffee urn to the side and a price list prominently displayed. This, obviously, was the coffee truck. Men from all over swarmed out to greet Rita.

It was Gilley’s turn. He had been so busy watching the proceedings, he hadn’t thought of what he wanted. Rita said, “What’ll you have, Hon?”

Gilley said, “Ummm.”

“Oh a new one, eh? Where’re ya from, Big Boy?”

Allen jumped in, "Rita, this is Gilley. He's new here to Swann's and he's just come from England to boot. He'll have a deviled egg sandwich."

"From England? Do you know the Beatles? Probably not. Too bad I don't have any cookies left or as you'd say in England, biscuits. By the way, I come by here at 7:30 every morning with fresh coffee and donuts too. I'll look for you, you're cute. Maybe I'll see if I can save some biscuits for you. Ta ta, as they say in Limey Land." With that she slammed the door shut, jumped into the truck and roared away, leaving Gilley standing there with sandwich in hand and mouth gaping.

"Shut your mouth, Gilley and eat your lunch. That's your introduction to Rita's coffee truck. She services all the businesses in this area, is always on time and flirts with everyone. Great fun! Let's go for a walk and I'll show you the docks. Mosley will join us soon." With that they strolled down to the docks to have a look round.

Gilley saw the working port for the first time. Many of the ships that had come in were filling up with grain from the towering silos standing on the water's edge. He saw trains labeled from Alberta, Saskatchewan, and Manitoba and was told they had transported most of the grain here from those provinces. Allen explained this was Burrard Inlet and it went many miles inland to the east and was a natural harbour, with accommodation for deep sea vessels. The water was crowded with tug boats and freighters.

The mountains around the inlet were spectacular with some being snow capped which was normal for this time of year. Allen pointed out the peaks of interest to Gilley. "Those are the Lions. They're called that as they look like two lion heads. Then there is Cypress, Grouse, and Seymour Mountains. These are popular ski mountains and get the most snow in the area. See that bridge to the west? That's called the Lions Gate Bridge, obviously named after the mountains and it leads through that green space called Stanley Park to West Vancouver and the British Properties. These properties were given to the Guinness Family by the Crown. The family built the bridge in order to access their lands as the only other way was by boat. This is one of the richest areas in Vancouver. You'll have to drive around there to see it, or maybe you'll get an invitation to Dennis Shears place. He lives there."

"Does he now? Well, I wonder what one has to do to get such an invite?" asked Gilley. Grinning, Allen said, "Let's get back to work. We don't want to be late on your first day."

Returning to the office, Barry gave Gilley his first task. He was to check a pile of drawings for errors. Gilley knew exactly what to do and set about this easy introduction to their system. He found a free table and sat down to study the drawings. As he found the errors, he circled them in red as he had been taught in England. After he completed this task, he showed Barry. Barry then handed him the original drawings and instructed him to make the necessary corrections.

Taking the originals back to his desk, Gilley began to look around for the appropriate tool with which to begin this job. Not finding it, he looked up and shouted, "Does anyone have a rubber I could borrow?" Everyone in the office stopped what they were doing and stared at him. "What were they staring at," thought Gilley? So he asked again, "Does anyone have a rubber I could borrow."

By now everyone was laughing very hard. Gilley was more than a little confused by the response he was getting. Finally, Allen Pickering, wiping his eyes, said, "Is it an eraser you are looking for?"

Gilley thinking he said a razor, which, in drafting was used to scrape the ink off the linen drawings which were done by tracers. Gilley said, "It's not ink drawings I'm correcting, its pencil drawings, so I need a rubber." Again everyone started laughing especially the English guys who knew what he meant. It took Allen to explain that here in Canada a condom was called a rubber and what Gilley was really wanting was called an eraser.

"Oh," said Gilley, finally getting what the laughing was about, "We would call them Wellies in England." This sent everyone into laughter again. "Only in Gilley land" somebody said. Coming back with a good defense, Gilley pointed to the English guys, and said, "From the south, you lads would call them Durex or French Letters."

The laughter continued and Sel interjected, "And some call them skins." There was more laughter as someone showed up with an eraser for Gilley and pointed to where all of the supplies were kept so that in the future, Gilley could help himself. With some effort, Gilley returned to his task, thinking, "I think I'm going to like this place. It's just like back home."

At the end of the day Gilley was still working on his assignment when Allen said, "Its five o'clock and time to finish up. It's a tradition to take a new employee out for a beer." So back to the Waldorf Gilley went with his new workmates. This time, they went into the beer parlor. Gilley, quite familiar now with the Waldorf, looked around for his friend Louis as Allen and the boys moved tables and chairs together. Just as everyone threw 50 cents each into the center of the table, Louis swept from the bar carrying a large tray loaded with glasses of beer. "Gentlemen, I have been waiting for you. Here are your refreshments." With that, Louis dropped twelve glasses of beer onto the table and picked up the money. He was about to make change, when Allen leaned over and gave him another quarter and said, "Keep the dime too, Louis."

Louis thanked Allen and then turned to Gilley, "Gilley, you are back again now with another set of friends, your new work mates. You are a becoming a regular here."

Everyone looked at him, surprised that he was known here. With this, Gilley told them of his visits to the Waldorf and how he thought it was the best establishment in Vancouver. As drinks were finished up, everyone threw another 50 cents into the center of the table. Gilley, only having a twenty dollar bill, threw it in too, thinking he would buy the entire round. "No, Gilley, take your money back," said Allen. "We buy you your first drinks here. After today, you can take your turn. Besides, you have to go to the bar to get a Twenty changed here. Waiters don't carry enough change for that large a denomination."

After about four or five beers, Gilley was starting to think about getting his bus and heading home. "Thanks everybody. I have to catch my bus now."

Allen said, "Don't worry, Gilley, I'll give you a lift home. I'm going into New Westminster tonight. Let's just finish these beers off and we can get going."

They left the bar and headed for Allen's car. It was a dark green Ford Falcon. Now a Falcon was a very powerful car with a V8 motor. Allen sure knew how to drive it. He held nothing back. They were in New Westminster in less than half an hour.

Gilley asked him into the suite for a beer, wanting to introduce him to Joy and to thank him for the lift home. It turned out Joy was in the bar with Jim and Veron. Of course everyone wanted to know how

Gilley's first day at work went and to meet his first workmate. Allen was very impressed with Jim's bar and enjoyed a game of pool. He excused himself after one beer as he had other commitments and left. As he left, Allen said, "I could get used to this Gilley. You might end up having a lift home most nights."

After Allen left, Veron said to Gilley, "Nice man, Allen. I just hope you don't think you can make a habit of bringing him or any of your other workmates back here every night after work for drinks. After all, beer costs money and money doesn't grow on trees. Once in a while is OK. But remember, it is our bar and there are a lot of freeloaders around."

"Don't worry, Veron, now that I'm working, I'll contribute my fair share to the bar," retorted Gilley.

Later that night, Joy said to Gilley, "I'm beginning to think we should look for our own place. Then we can be free to do what whatever we want. Mother means well, but she likes to be involved with everything that goes on in this house. We need our own space where we can be independent. We should look for a place in the New Year. We need a place that's close to where I work and to your bus route. Eventually we'll need a car because buses aren't always convenient or reliable for that matter."

When they arrived home Tuesday evening, they discovered the crate they had been waiting for had arrived from England with their rest of their belongings. Gilley was quite excited as he would now have his own instruments and books for work. Borrowing Jim's crowbar to pry off the lid, Gilley was surprised at how easily the lid popped off. Quickly, they delved through the contents, looking for certain long awaited items. The clock given to Joy and Gilley as a wedding gift from Joy's Grandma in England was missing.

Looking further, they discovered a couple of antique plates, and several old classic books were also missing. It was hard to believe this could happen as they had packaged everything up themselves and had seen the shipper nail down the lid. They checked the contents received against the manifest and discovered these items were indeed missing. Gilley discovered another side of his new bride. "I can't believe someone would have the nerve to open our crate and pick through it like they did," Joy ranted loudly. "You remember, we carefully packed the clock Grandma gave us in its original box and surrounded it with softer things so it wouldn't break in shipping? We did that with the antique plates too. Those bloody thieves must have looked through the manifest and taken their time stealing the most valuable items. I can't believe their nerve. That's why the lid came off so easily. I won't rest until I get to the bottom of this." Just then Veron, not being able to wait any longer to see what was in the crate, knocked on the door and came in. "What's all the yelling about?"

"That bloody shipping company has stolen some of our things. The beautiful clock Grandma gave us for a Wedding gift and those antique plates she also gave us are missing. They took two of the antique books as well that Gilley's dad gave him. Can you believe their nerve?"

"The world is getting more and more corrupt. We'll have to act immediately so they know we're serious. You can't make many calls from work so do you want me to call for you?"

"No. I can do it from work. I can do it on my breaks and I'm sure Mr. Onions will allow me more time once I tell him what happened."

"Well, will he allow you to make long distance calls on the bank telephone? You'll have to call England, you know. And it's not cheap."

"I don't think it will be a problem. I've already decided I'm going to call them collect so they have to pay for the calls. And if they don't accept that, well, I'll have to pay the bank back. I think we get a corporate rate."

Gilley slipped out of the suite and headed for the bar as the two women were planning their strategy. He knew the shipping company was in for a fight. Joy had become like a dog with a bone and over the next three weeks the battle raged on. Jim was at the bar already having a beer. "What's the problem Gilley? I can hear that Joy is quite angry?" Taking the beer Jim handed him, Gilley explained the situation. "It's best to leave it to them Gilley and not get involved. You know too many cooks spoil the broth. Take it from me, just be sympathetic and nod at the right times. Otherwise, you won't get any peace."

It started the following day. The shipping company declared that they would not be held responsible for any shortages. One should read the small print. The company claimed that besides not having the proper insurance, Gilley and Joy had been there when it was sealed in England and had been there when it was opened in Canada. The company had not been present at the opening. Joy and Gilley could claim anything was missing. The company claimed that they were only responsible for the entire container, not for anything missing inside. This really got Joy's back up. Her argument was they had packed these items into the crate and the manifest listed these items and these were now missing. Joy believed that since the company had the crate in their possession for almost two months they should be responsible for making sure it was not tampered with. Each evening after returning from work Joy updated Gilley on the developments that had occurred. It was a fight to the finish and she meant to be the winner.

Finally it was Friday. This wouldn't be a very good weekend. All week Gilley had been able to stay on the sidelines and do what Jim had advised. On the weekend, it would be harder to get away from Joy and Veron's wrath. Just then, Allen came to Gilley's drawing board and asked, "Would you and Joy like to come to my belated Halloween party tomorrow night? I'm having people over to my apartment on Pender Street."

"Oh, I thought Halloween was just for children. They were so cute coming to the door asking "Trick or Treat".

"Yes, it is over, but I had something else come up that prevented the party. Since its tradition for me to have a Halloween Party I thought I'd do it this weekend. My friends have been pressuring me to have one after all. They're saying "A party is a party."

Dave Mosley piped up, "You don't want to go to any of Allen's parties, Gilley. They're wild especially Halloween. And this one is going be particularly so as its also our Guy Fawkes Night."

"What's Guy Fawkes Night?" asked Allen.

"Guy Fawkes Night is held on November 5th where the English remember the man who tried to blow up the Houses of Parliament. This event occurred in the early 1600's during the reign of James the 1st. We build bonfires and have a big fireworks display. It takes weeks to collect the wood for the bonfire and the entire village participates in this collection. Eventually, the pile of wood can reach 12 to 16 feet tall. The week prior the kids with their faces blackened, go knocking on doors pulling an effigy of Guy Fawkes in a small cart. They ask for "a penny for the guy" which is supposed to be spent on fire crackers.

When the 5th finally arrives, the elders bury potatoes in the center of the bonfire under the ground. There is a large opening left in the pile so he can do this. Also, people bring newspapers, cardboard, old boxes and garbage to add inside. When it's all done, an elder lights the fire.

Kids throw their crackers in there and it's a hell of a celebration. You can see the fires from the surrounding villages for miles in each direction. Everyone stays until the embers have cooled. The elder then digs out the potatoes and passes them around with gobs of butter supplied by the women of the village. It was bigger than Christmas.

"Well, Gilley," said Allen, "That does add a bit more excitement to my party."

"I would like to come, Allen but Joy's parents have people coming over tomorrow night for a bit of a get together and we have to be there. Thanks anyway. Keep me in mind for another time. I like nothing better than a good party," replied Gilley. "It's interesting how many of our customs are similar."

Saturday came and the men went golfing as usual and were home in time to do the chores Veron had lined up for them in preparation for their guests and by 8:30 they began to arrive.

The party started with lots of Veron's delicious appetizers. People played pool, threw darts and told lots of jokes. It was a fun evening and quite loud. Many of the jokes were what Jim referred to as 'colorful'. Many of the people were Jim and Veron's age or older and many were school trustees and members of the school board. This did not stop them from having a good time. Gilley was a bit surprised at how they let their hair down. It was 2:00 AM by the time the last guest departed, leaving the bar in a bit of a mess. "Thank goodness for that magical shower tomorrow morning. I know I'll be the one cleaning up after this lot."

November remained very mild. During the week, everyone went about their work schedule but on Saturdays, the men golfed and the women got their hair done. Saturday evenings became more and more interesting as Jim and Veron went out with their own friends allowing Gilley and Joy the freedom to use the bar to entertain their friends. The battle with the shipping company continued and, much to the men's relief, Joy and Veron left them out of it for the most part.

As couples, Linda and Howie Gale were becoming good friends with Joy and Gilley. Linda was born in New Westminster and went to school with Joy. Part of their friendship entailed playing hooky together. There was a group of friends that did this. They would often go to Lorraine Lamont's place to hide as her parents were away working for the day. Many times Brian Peterson who was Lorraine's boyfriend at that time entertained them. (He later became her husband.) With Gilley's first introduction to Brian (to Whistler), he could see why Brian was so popular. He had that winning personality—a bit of a rebel, yet quite charming and wouldn't have discouraged them from this habit of hooky. One of Joy's biggest mistakes was that her father was the grounds superintendent for the School Board and the teachers would be very quick to tell him of Joy's absenteeism. Jim was also a bit of a detective and always succeeded in finding her hiding places.

Jim was quite upset with this behavior of Joy's because all of her life until Grade 10 when this hooky-playing began as she was an "A" student and showed her ability academically. She was definitely university material with her musical ability being an asset. He couldn't understand this dramatic change in her behavior. Her grades started to suffer as she missed more and more classes. What he didn't understand was that Joy was feeling the pressure from her parents to succeed and be good role-model for her two sisters.

Howie was born in and grew up in Port Alberni, which was on Vancouver Island. He never would speak a lot about the area and Gilley could never understand why. Joy explained that Port Alberni was a pulp and paper and lumber town. It was what Canadians called a mill town and the general opinion of people was it was just a place to get away from, like most mill towns. The production of pulp and paper was a smelly affair and not popular with tourists.

As these Saturday nights progressed, Gilley came to enjoy them as he learned quite a bit about his new bride from the conversations that flowed. One evening, Linda and Howie couldn't get a sitter for the children. Veron told them they could use her car to get to their place, so off they went to Millardville, which was the French Quarter of New Westminster. Gilley was introduced to two new things—Ripple Chips and French Onion Dip and a game called Rummoli. This game is a board game based on the hands of poker with eight sections representing different hands. Generally, players come with a jar of pennies for betting. Cards are dealt and each player places a penny in each category as well as in the middle portion called the "pot".

Joy and Gilley had come unprepared for this by not bringing their own jars of pennies. Linda, who played the game often, had lots in supply and sold a dollar's worth to both Gilley and Joy. Gilley, who usually picked up games quickly, was soon out of pennies. Linda again, sold him another dollar's worth. His luck wasn't in the cards tonight and his penny level dropped again. Loosing gracefully wasn't easy for him. Joy, who was winning, saw a new side to her groom. To be polite, Gilley got very quiet, muttering to himself instead of out loud as was his usual habit in this case. Only when he did win a hand did a big grin spread across his face. Otherwise, he was silent. "Oh, Gilley for heaven's sake! It's only a game. You're taking this far too seriously. It's only because you usually win that your pouting now," chided Joy.

"I never win at money games. If we weren't playing for money, that would be different," growled Gilley.

Joy grinned to herself. "Ah hah! A weakness!"

As the evening wore on, with everyone drinking and smoking, the game ended with no pennies left in Gilley's pot. He was hard put to smile at this fact. Joy was having a great time as she had won quite a bit. She insisted Gilley drive home. The normally good natured Gilley was glad to get out of the house so he didn't have to keep up the pretence of being a good loser. While driving home, Joy fell asleep. Gilley thought he knew where he was going but ended up in Vancouver, quite irate as midnight was long passed. On top of losing, now he's lost.

At this point Joy woke up. "Where the hell are we?"

Gilley, not wanting to admit his error, said, "Vancouver."

"Why Vancouver," she asked?

"Well, you were having yourself such a nice little nap and I thought I would just drive around and get myself familiarized with the area some more. But I've got just one question-how do I get back to New Westminster?"

"You're bloody hopeless. You're on Kingsway, heading towards New Westminster."

"That's what I thought. At one time I was on Marine Drive heading to New Westminster. I just wanted to check I was on the right track this time because New Westminster keeps avoiding me."

"What time is it anyway?" groaned Joy.

"It's two o'clock."

"Well, we left Linda's at eleven. Where else have you been?"

Gilley replied, "Oh, I don't know. I went over two different bridges. After the last bridge there was a park called Stanley Park that I went through several times. It was a nice drive as Allen Pickering had pointed it out to me when we were walking on the docks at lunch time."

By now Joy was feeling a mixture of exasperation and wonder, "God, did you stop anywhere for gas? I hope we have enough to get home because they're all closed by now. If we do run out of gas, you will be pushing us all the way home." Thankfully, with Joy's direction they went straight to New Westminster, this time and arrived home safely. Joy mumbled a comment about driving on fumes as she stormed into the suite for the night.

The following morning, Joy gave Gilley a kick, "Get out of bed and get that car filled up before Mom finds out she has no gas in the tank."

Wanting to stay in Veron's good books, Gilley jumped out of bed, "Right-O". He jumped into that magical shower and came out feeling fresh and sprightly and dashed off to the nearest gas station. There was another adventure waiting for the unknowing Gilley. He arrived at the station, pulled up to the pump labeled "REGULAR" and sat waiting for the attendant. He sat and sat. "Where is that blasted attendant?" Finally he got out of the car. He saw the lady in the paying booth waving at him. His first thought was she was in trouble; therefore he dashed over to see what the problem was. She ungraciously informed him that this was a "Self-Serve" station.

"What the hell is 'Self-Serve' when it comes to gas stations," thought Gilley? This wasn't the case in England. Who'd ever heard of such of thing? Well, not to be daunted, Gilley returned to the pump to do his duty. "Now where to from here? I have never pumped gas before in my life. It can't be that difficult. Probably a good idea. In England, you'd have to wait for bloody ever for an attendant to fill the car. Ah-hah! Instructions! 'Remove the nozzle from the pump; press lever down, press nozzle in tank and pull the trigger to begin filling.' "That's easy." With that, Gilley began to fill the tank.

He realized this was not too bad at all. Keeping a steady eye on the counter for the number of gallons entering the tank, and, also watching the cost of this, Gilley was amazed that already at ten gallons, he hasn't spend $3.00 yet. "How much does this tank hold?" Just as this question finished flashing through his mind, the nozzle shut off. Full! Some even splashed out onto his trousers. He struggled with disbelief, but remembering this new world he had entered, he obediently walked over to the woman in the booth to pay.

Upon getting change back, he also asked for a package of "MacDonald's" filter tips. Not bad coming out of there. "A full tank of gas and a packet of smokes including a free book of matches cost under $5.00. This would have been at least five pounds in England, which would convert to about Fifteen dollars. This is not a bad land. Nothing wrong with this country, eh? My friends would be quite jealous," thought Gilley as he headed home.

Driving back home, he decided he would cook bacon and fried eggs for breakfast as making breakfast was becoming a Sunday tradition for him. Upon arriving home, Jim and Veron were in the back lane behind the house. They were standing there with quite puzzled looks as Gilley drove in. "Where the hell have you been? We were just about to call the police as we thought the car had been stolen."

"Gilley replied, "I just went to fill the car up as you were so kind to loan it to us yesterday."

"What are you talking about, Gilley? I just filled up on Friday. A full tank normally lasts me all week, sometimes two. Where the hell did you and Joy go last night? I just thought you were going to Linda and Howie's for drinks."

"Well," Gilley hummed and hawed," Um, we got lost. Well, I got lost."

"Lost?" she says, "You must have driven all over Vancouver."

"How about North and West Vancouver also," Gilley replied.

Jim said, "Oh my God, Joy should know better than to let you drive since you don't know the area."

Gilley didn't want Joy's secret to be known to her parents-that she fell asleep, so he said, "Since it was such a nice night, Joy thought she would let me drive around Vancouver and Stanley Park so I could begin to get familiar with the expanse of the lower mainland. Anyone could get lost with the size of this place."

Jim said, "Well, you gave us a bit of a fright. We thought someone might have stolen the car. We heard you come back late last night, around 3:00 AM I believe, and when we looked out of the window this morning the car was gone. I was just going to knock on the suite door, not that anyone would want to wake Joy up this early especially on a Sunday morning. Let's go and have breakfast. I was just going to make bacon and fried eggs."

"Oh, just what I was going to cook for Joy myself," replied Gilley.

"Well come on and help me," said Jim. "We'll send some down for Joy. I remember she likes breakfast in bed." Soon, breakfast was ready and Gilley took Joy her breakfast with a large glass of orange juice, the bacon and eggs, etc.

"How kind of you Gilley, this is my favourite treat. How did you know? I'm starved!" declared Joy.

"I thought this was everyone's favourite. Also, your dad told me we're invited to go to visit the Godden's this afternoon with them. Did you want to go?"

"Yes, that would be fun."

"I think your mom said we have to leave about 1:00 PM. I'm off to get my breakfast now. Enjoy, see you in a bit."

At 12:30 PM, everyone piled into Jim's car. Jim insisted Gilley drive as he thought it would be good experience for him to continue to 'get the lay of the land'. Arriving at Anne and Eric's, the topic of conversation was the weather. It was exceptional for November. As a matter of fact, it was warm enough for the group to have their first drink on the porch. As everyone was enjoying their drink and a cigarette, Jim told them of Gilley's driving adventure the night before.

"Tell Eric how many times you went around Stanley Park?" Jim chuckled.

"Stanley Park," Eric exclaimed, "you dirty bugger. It's not how many times you went around the park, it's how many times you stopped in the park? That's the question. What time did you get home?"

"3:00 PM." Jim said.

Anne said, "Quiet you guys, you're embarrassing Joy." Just at this time, Anne's sister Jean appeared with a platter full of sandwiches.

Anne, realizing Gilley had never met Jean before, said, "Gilley, this is my other sister Jean. You met Joyce in England. Jean lives in Langley as well and she immigrated to Canada a couple of years after I did. She just lives down the road." With that, Jean joined the group and the two of them regaled the others with stories of the early days in Langley. They told of their uncle, who had since passed away and had been one of the first mayors of the city. He had pioneered quite a bit in the district and created the infrastructure for much of the area.

Anne told of how she had owned a small dress shop, which catered to the more affluent part of the population. She had developed quite a good reputation for carrying the latest fashions and she reported people would come to her shop even after they had moved away. "Many of my customers could count on me having "just the right thing" for the occasion they were shopping for.

Jean told Joy and Gilley how proud she was of her son Alistair. "He's now in the Merchant Navy, you know. He's worked his way up to Captain. He comes home whenever he can and often brings me little gifts from places he's been to. The next time he comes home, you'll be sure to meet him." Another round of liqueurs and it was time to bid farewell.

CHAPTER 7

GILLEY'S FIRST CHRISTMAS

DECEMBER CAME AND WITH it came the cold weather. Gilley had to get warmer clothes as the things he brought from England didn't do the trick. To correct this, Joy took Gilley to Eaton's for their winter sales event and found just the right overcoat to protect him on his way to and from work.

Work was progressing quite well and Gilley realized he was the good fit Barry Freak and Dennis Shears predicted he would become. All of the training and studying he had gone through was finally bearing fruit for him in a manner he never expected. He was able to keep up with other draughtsmen and his machining background contributed to the overall team effort. He became to be very friendly with his co-workers and the rest of the personnel at Swann Winches.

As the month advanced and as Christmas came closer, people were quite excited about what they called the four day weekend over Christmas. They explained to Gilley that because Christmas Day fell on a Friday and Boxing Day on a Saturday, the Monday following would be a holiday as well. Then with New Years day on the Friday, the workers would have a three day weekend. What a holiday. Often, it was explained, these days fell in the middle of the week and one had to come in for a day here and a day there, but this year it all worked out into days off in a row. "That's how it is in England. I'm glad some things have stayed the same," thought Gilley. In addition to this, Gilley was looking forward to Swann's Dinner Dance party which was open to all of the employees. The most Gilley had come to expect from his employers in England was a round or two at the local pub to wish one another a Happy Christmas.

Gilley noticed many of the houses sprouted strings of colored lights. There were even some places that went all out with cardboard figures of Santa Claus or the Nativity Scene. This was another new thing for Gilley as in England, Christmas was a more sedate affair. At the Wilson's this was Jim's big event. He spent hours decorating the outside of the house in blue and green lights that trimmed the roof line as well as the windows and front doorway. No one was allowed to help him as every light had to be perfect. The inside of the house, with the exception of the Christmas tree, belonged to Veron and the girls. They were as particular as Jim. Now, as far as the tree went, Jim scoured all the Christmas tree lots for 'just the perfect one'.

This year he took Gilley with him and this again, was an amazing sight for Gilley. He could not believe the number of lots devoted to housing cut, live trees for sale. Jim explained that every house would put up a tree and decorate it with ornaments, lights and tinsel. It was often a family affair and a bit of a competition between neighbours and friends to see how nicely a tree was done up. On top of that, the aroma of the fresh pine tree in the house added to the spirit of Christmas.

Getting the tree home was quite easy because the Duster had such a large trunk, or in England, the boot, that this six foot tree could easily fit in with only two feet sticking out. This, Jim tied a yellow flag so the drivers behind him knew when to stop. "You can't be too careful, Gilley, and it took a long time to get this tree. We don't want to have to find another one."

"You're right, Jim this took us quite the long time to find. I reckon three hours at least. I didn't realize how many trees are not quite perfect for the discerning tree buyer. It's a good job you didn't ask me to fetch one for you. I'd have bought the first one I saw.'

"That's nothing, Gilley. When I bring Veron with me, it can take all night and once, even two nights. Now, you do realize buying the tree is only the first step. Once we get home we have to decide just where the perfect place in the living room to put it."

"Oh, you're kidding, right Jim?"

"Oh no! If the tree isn't placed just right and in harmony with the fireplace and the furniture, there will be hell to pay. Not only that, the people who visit over the holidays will not appreciate the beauty of it and the effort it took to make it a work of art." Once they arrived home with the tree and had displayed it to the women, who, to Jim's relief and Gilley's surprise, approved of the selection, the next step was to set it up so that it was kept fresh for at least two weeks. "Since we put lights on it and these give off heat, we have to make sure the tree is kept watered. Otherwise it might catch fire. Every year, we hear of a tree or two doing so because it's dried out and burned the family home to the ground. We certainly don't want that to happen to us."

Jim showed Gilley a special five gallon bucket which had several screws which, when tightened into the trunk, prevented the tree from toppling. It also contained the necessary water to keep the tree alive. "Fascinating," said Gilley, as he helped Jim saw the tree trunk at an angle so it could absorb the maximum amount of water. "Then we need to saw off the lower branches. These take up extra water and don't allow space for the presents."

The next step to the perfect tree was balancing it so it stood straight. This was imperative. Jim had all the gear, wooden wedges that he placed around the tree and adjusting the screws so the tree would cooperate. Veron was the judge of the straightness while Gilley got the honour of holding the tree while Jim did his bit. Eventually, around midnight the deed was done. "Tomorrow night we decorate." Gilley could hardly wait.

On top of this excitement at home, Gilley was anticipating December 19th. This was the date of the Swann's Christmas Dinner Dance party. It was to be held in a small banquet hall not far from Swann's. He was told by his co-workers this was one party not to be missed as Swann's went all out in appreciation for the hard work its employees contributed all year round. They would pay for the dinner, the music and even two drinks for each employee and spouse. There were also to be games and spot prizes to spice things up.

The anticipated "Wilson Tree Decorating" evening arrived. Everyone had to be home in time for dinner and all had to help with the clearing up afterwards, all except Jim and Gilley. Their task was to take the decorations out of storage and bring them up to the living room. Each box was carefully labeled and had to be placed exactly where Jim ordered. The lights were the first thing to be strung onto the tree. Only he could do this job as no two colours could be close together. Gilley was instructed to watch and learn and hand him the next string when needed. This was something Gilley had never seen in England before. He had never seen coloured lights like this before. The family tree in England stood maybe two feet tall with a few coloured ornaments and the decorations in the house consisted of a variety of coloured crepe paper streamers twisted and hung from the ceiling. Now, after Jim finished placing the lights it was the girls' turn. They placed various ornaments spaced perfectly throughout the tree. Next came the garland looped over the branches symmetrically draped as to highlight the ornaments and lights. Finally, string by string the tinsel was hung. Veron's job was to put the tree skirt over the base of the tree. The finished product looked like something out of a fairy tale. The final touches in the living room were the stockings. They were hung on the mantel of the fireplace. Then some presents appeared and were carefully placed under the tree. Gilley stood, watching the entire production with awe, saying to himself, "Boy, my mother and father would be impressed with the Canadian way of celebrating Christmas. I've got to take a photograph and send it to them. Otherwise, they won't believe me. I also have to include a shot of Eighth Avenue with all the lights on the houses. Amazing!"

Saturday December 19th arrived and Gilley and Joy, dressed in their very best arrived at the company party in a cab as Gilley didn't want to chance driving Veron's car. Entering the hall, everyone greeted one another and the hostess directed Gilley and Joy to the table designated for them. First order was to get a drink of course with their free tickets. Getting beers was not easy as there was a long lineup. This gave Gilley the opportunity to introduce Joy to his colleagues as they all waited in line. The Disc Jockey was playing soft background music and Gilley spotted the first round of food being brought to the buffet table. Gilley saw that everyone was dressed in his or her very best clothes. A sound at the microphone drew their attention to the stage. There, Allen Pickering was tapping on the mike to make sure the sound was turned up. "Ladies and Gentlemen, please take your drinks to your seats. We will be eating dinner shortly. As you can see, there are numbers on each table. We're going to draw numbers out of this hat so you don't think I'm playing favorites. Dennis, come and pick the first two numbers. When the number of your table is called come and get your dinner. Please don't try to jump the cue. Your turn will come. There's enough food for everyone." Gilley's table was drawn fourth. Again he could not believe the feast set out. Pasta, cold cuts, salads, baron of beef, chicken, salmon, various styles of potatoes and other vegetables. The line up went quickly and no sooner had Gilley and Joy finished their plates, then Allen said, "All those who would like seconds, just help yourself. But I warn you to save some room for the fabulous desserts which will be put out shortly." Gilley just had to get more of what Joy told him were scalloped potatoes.

Then came the desserts-trifles, cakes, pastries, cheeses and fruit and chocolates. So much to eat and so little room to enjoy them all. "Don't worry Gilley," said Dave Mosley. "They leave the desserts out for most of the evening. They know most of us are too full to really enjoy them until later after we've danced off some of the dinner."

"You read my mind, Dave. This is something else." Before the dancing started, there was a short program of speeches where the managers got up and spoke highly of staff in their areas and thanked everyone for their hard work. Allen got up next and told everyone to pay attention. He called out a number and instructed everyone to look under their seats. Whoever had number 10 was the winner and it went on with other games. The idea was for everyone to get a prize. Dancing started and then the spot prizes were given out. Gilley won a figurine of Cupid that he knew would fit into Jim's bar nicely as it was a self-contained water dispenser which would bring a few laughs. Draws for door prizes came and Joy won a bottle of wine. Suppliers had given most of these presents to the company. There was so much fun and goings on the evening was over before they knew it. Allen called it to a close at 2:00AM. He said the company had asked the Yellow Cab Company to stand by for those who would take advantage of this service.

The following morning, Gilley was pleased it was a Sunday as his head this day was feeling rather heavy. Would the magical shower do its trick? After a much longer period of time in the shower, it began to work its magic for Gilley. Hopping happily out of the shower, Gilley began to celebrate the gifts and prizes that they had received the night before. He was overwhelmed. Nothing like this happened in England to his knowledge. Joy was not too happy about this noise and his excitement. "If you're so excited about everything, go and tell mom and dad about last night. I just want to lay here in peace."

So, off he went, with the Cupid water dispenser, a bottle of rum and Joy's bottle of wine. The candies were left downstairs for another time. As Gilley got upstairs, Jim and Veron, having a cup of tea, said, "It's about time you were out of bed. Do you know what time you got home last night? I think it was 3:00AM."

"It was closer to 4:00 AM," Jim said. "Do you know what time it is now? It's 10:30 AM. You've missed breakfast." Veron, relenting, offered a cup of tea and put some toast on.

"So what offerings have you got there, Gilley," Jim asked?

"These are the prizes we won last night. I thought they would look good in your bar."

"Oh, that's a nice thought," smiled Veron now, "Would you like some bacon and eggs with this toast?"

"No, just jam is fine, thank you," answered Gilley. Turning to Jim, Gilley explained that his company's suppliers had donated all of these prizes.

Jim said, "That's a normal tradition here in Canada. I will be able to stock my bar with the donations given to me by my suppliers. That's why we will be holding a few parties ourselves for School Board staff. Of course, you and Joy are welcome to come. Your contribution will help. By the way, I have to decorate the bar this afternoon. You can help me with this and tell me how Cupid works."

Jim had pulled out his bar decorations. He had a small imitation tree about four feet high. He repeated the same ritual with the lights, making sure each was placed just so. The difference was beers accompanied this process. Then came the ornaments and garland. "No tinsel on this tree. People get drinking and end up tossing it at each other. Makes a bloody mess. I think I can figure Cupid out. Its battery operated and once water is put in, it dispenses it through the little hole in his front. It should bring some laughs. Thanks for contributing it to the bar."

Gilley was amazed at the effort made for the Christmas season. All the stores and other public places were decorated throughout. The streets were a maze of lights as the city councils took great pride in decorating their cities. Even the government buildings such as the city halls and the municipal buildings were decorated with a hundreds of lights and figurines. Generally in each city, there was a large tree in a prominent place which was decorated with a mass of different colored lights and was the focal point of the town's display.

Jim and Veron's house was done in a two-color variety—green and blue—which did look really sharp. As Jim said, "Trying to keep all of the coloured lights in order was difficult enough, but trying to keep four or five colours ordered was more trouble than it was worth."

Their house had between one hundred and fifty to two hundred lights at least. And this was quite typical for most houses. As a matter of fact, Gilley could see that many of the neighbors had a bit of completion going on to see which had the best array of lights. It was a part of the Christmas activities for people to drive around the various neighborhoods to see who had the best house on the block.

Jim, a very particular man, wanted to show his house off, but it was against his nature to be flamboyant about it. Yet he felt very proud of the star he had on his chimney. As far as going overboard on the whole thing, such as reindeer on the roof and Santas in the gardens—that wasn't for him. Gilley noted that the blue and green Jim had chosen reflected his character. It subtly set the house apart from the neighbours' and was a welcome relief from the blaring multi-coloured lights.

Not only did people in Canada go all out on decorating the outside of their homes, but they carried it on into the inside as well. Everyone had a Christmas tree fully decorated with strings of lights, tinsel and small glittery decorations. Each family had a tradition to decorating their particular tree. Part of many traditions included the entire family going to pick the best tree either from a tree farm or a corner lot where cut trees were sold.

As Christmas drew closer, a package from England appeared from Gilley's parents. Along with this came a letter from the shipping company acknowledging some responsibility that the crate had been tampered with. This was a great victory for Joy and she immediately deposited the cheque into their account and said, "Perseverance got us this cheque. Good job I didn't leave it to you Gilley. I'm still not pleased with the amount, but at least we got some satisfaction."

Gilley said, "It is better than a poke in the eye with a proggie stick."

"Is this one of Gilley's famous sayings," asked Anne, "or is it just your strange accent that I can't understand what you're saying?" Joy explained that it was the same as saying "Don't look a gift horse in the Mouth."

It was tradition in this house that all presents could only be opened on Christmas day. As a matter of fact in this home Christmas day itself had its own rules. There was a special ritual to everything. In the morning, there was none of the usual push to get up. One arose at one's leisure. The day began with exploring the contents of one's stocking 'that hung by the chimney with care' as well as enjoying everyone else's stocking surprises.

These particular stockings were specifically made for each person having their names on them. Gilley was amazed at who had gone to all of this trouble and he asked Joy, "Who did all of this?" Joy confessed that it was tradition for her grandmother, her mother, herself etc to do these stockings for each other. She then explained that generally he would have to fill her stocking and she would do his, but because this was his first Christmas in Canada, he was exempted from this part.

Once the final stocking was opened, Jim cooked breakfast—bacon, eggs, sausages, toast, tea, and tomatoes—a wonderful fare. Jim said, "It's going to be a long day and you need a good solid grounding for this special occasion."

After the dishes were cleaned up, it was up to the youngest, which was Anne, to hand out the presents in any method she felt appropriate. During this time, Jim passed around small glasses of sherry to the elders. Veron's mother, who had arrived on Christmas Eve, enjoyed a glass or two of sherry expressed that this was the best part of Christmas. She toddled off to the kitchen to begin the preparation of the turkey. Even though she was out of sight, she was not out of mind or out of the action. She and Veron would jostle from present opening to turkey preparation, as it was important to get the bird in oven by noon.

Gilley was amazed at the amount of presents. He was especially surprised when the present from England was handed to him. His mother and father had sent him a high fashion pink non-wrinkle nylon shirt. This was one of the in things in England at the time and Gilley had always wanted a pink shirt. Much to his surprise though, everyone laughed. They couldn't believe that any one would wear a pink shirt. Even Joy, who understood the fashions in England, explained that this was not part of the Canadian scene. Along with this, Joy had given Gilley a three tone brown cardigan with a cable stitch design. Jim and Veron had bought Gilley a pair of waterproof golf shoes, which was a must in the rainy weather. They were black and white, which was the same colour as the soccer team he supported in England, Newcastle United. Jim commented as Gilley opened this gift, "Just think, Gilley, every time you take a shot, your magpie is with you."

For Christmas Day, the weather was nice, not white, as everyone had hoped. As the day preceded many people dropped in to have a Christmas drink and wish everyone the best of the season. Gilley became the official bartender for the day. Jim was right that good breakfast was important on a day like today as more and more of the visitors made their way down to the bar for the traditional Christmas drink at the Wilson's.

By about five o'clock, the guests began leaving for their own special Christmas festivities (which included the huge Canadian turkey dinner for most part). They wished all well as they left, full of Christmas cheer. Of course, they reciprocated with their own invitations for Gilley and the rest of the family to come over to their homes for Boxing Day drinks.

At last the Wilson's Christmas dinner was ready. Of course, there was a traditional way to begin this special occasion too. As soon as everyone sat down, Jim carved the turkey. Then came the Christmas crackers. These were full of surprises, jokes and hats, which everyone had to wear throughout dinner. Then the main course began to be consumed. There were mashed potatoes and the very best roasted potatoes (which was Gilley's and everyone else's favorite). The vegetables were carrots and turnips mashed together, Brussels sprouts and Veron's special baked onion dish.

Of course there was cranberry sauce and stuffing and to top everything off was the most fabulous turkey gravy, which disappeared very quickly on Sally's plate. She had no consideration for anyone else when it came to gravy. She would hoard as much as she could without her plate overflowing. It was a known fact in the family not to give Sally the gravy boat first or else there wouldn't be enough to go around for everyone. On the other hand, Anne would fill her plate full of turkey if she had the chance and leave out the vegetables.

There was a lot of wine as Jim had collected a fair bit from his suppliers. Gilley, not being a connoisseur of wine as of yet, still preferred his beer. As far as he was concerned, it went very well with this turkey dinner. However, it was traditional to have a glass of wine in order to toast the turkey. Joy had a pallet for wine and appreciated its flavour with her turkey dinner instead of her usual beer at this time of the year.

At the end of dinner was the finishing touch. It was a special surprise for Gilley—the flaming Christmas pudding. This was a very traditional part of the English Christmas dinners and he didn't expect it here. Part of the surprise was that the pudding was flamed with brandy. In his own home in England, the pudding was never flamed. Gilley's father often said it was a dangerous practice to flame the pudding. (However, everyone knew that it was the brandy he didn't want to waste on such a frivolous affair.) To top off the pudding Veron had made her delicious custard sauce.

Following this course, came the liqueurs. There was Tia Maria, Brandy which was Grandma's favourite, Drambuie and Crème de Menthe. At the sight of the Crème de Menthe, Jim turned a similar shade of green and said, "Yuk, keep that stuff away from me. Gilley, go and get me a beer and I'll tell you the story about Crème de Menthe and the honor of England." After the beer came he proceeded with this story.

"During the war, I was stationed in Ceylon along with Eric Godden. This day had been a hot and tiresome day and everyone had tumbled into the bar at the end of it. An Australian chap was already there. He turned around and eyed all of the English chaps throwing out the challenge, 'Who's up for the challenge of defending his country at this bar?' Eric had had enough of the Aussies and their bravado. He said, "My friend Jim here can rise to your challenge and drink you under the table in the name of England and the King."

"Of course, being very loyal, I could not refuse this challenge, thanks to Eric. To my amazement, the only alcohol available at this bar was what they called Sticky Greens—that being Crème de Menthe and lots of it."

After a few hours, the Aussie slithered off of his chair, having clearly lost the bet. I was declared the winner. I got slowly up from my seat, turned around and walked slowly out of the bar. I was shouting 'England, England, England'. I made it all the way to my bunk at the barracks and I was told I was not seen for two days. However, when

I did emerge, I knew I had taken one for my country and I declared, "The honour of England is still intact. Eric, being the prick he was, declared, "Right my friend, you've made us all proud. 'How about a Sticky Green?' When he said that, I could have gotten sick right there and then. Lucky someone handed me a beer instead and it did the trick at keeping my dignity."

Finishing the story, Jim said, "I will never drink another Sticky Green again as long as I live. But this beer is going down nicely." Gilley appreciated Jim's story. He caught an insight into Jim that had eluded him until now. After this, the dishes were cleared away and the leftover food put into the refrigerator. The family retired to the bar and spent a rare quiet time together, playing games and telling stories.

Saturday was Boxing Day and it arrived very early as Veron never slept in. Breakfast was served and everyone was instructed to get ready for the day. Things were back to normal. It was time to follow through on the invitations given by friends yesterday. Anne and Sally were excused from these social obligations.

First port of call was at Gwen and Harry's, who lived up in Burnaby. It was always a laugh at Harry's. He was full of energy, continuously making jokes and laughing at the same time. He was just a party boy, chasing the women.

Next stop was at Mickey and Elaine's. Mickey was the bootlegger. This was a much quieter visit than the previous one. Yet it was very hospitable and enjoyable. Elaine had a deep strong voice which drew the attention of all when she spoke. While Mickey had a higher pitched voice he always had to be the center of attention. And he knew lots about sports, especially hockey.

Terry and Marilyn Parsons were next on the list. Since Terry was a dentist, their home was very up-scale. This was the first time Gilley had been there for a visit. One could look down to the swimming pool from the kitchen. It was a beautiful home, but the smell of chlorine was everywhere. But after a few more drinks, cigarettes and Terry's pipe, the smell didn't matter anymore.

This visit went differently than the others as Veron used this opportunity to consult with Terry about Gilley's recent visit to her dentist. After he had inspected Gilley's teeth, and taken x-rays, (the only x-ray Gilley had ever experienced was when he had broken bones), he was amazed at the poor condition of Gilley's teeth with respect to the workmanship of the fillings. There was so much work to be done in order to bring his teeth up to snuff and this dentist didn't have enough time to take on Gilley's case. Veron wanted Terry's advice as to a good dentist who was taking on new patients.

Terry mentioned that there was a new dentist that had just started up at the West End Medical building. His name was Michael Foster. Terry said he would get Gilley into see this new dentist. Gilley was a bit miffed at this diagnosis, as he had just gotten all of his teeth done before coming to Canada. Terry was in agreement with this dentist as he had seen shoddy dental work in his newly landed English patients too.

Most of the English dentists didn't really care about properly finishing the fills, often leaving rough edges and bits hanging out. This caused gum irritations and discomfort for the patients. Yet when most of the English dentists came to Canada, they adopted the Canadian style of dentistry. They blamed the English National Health System as it didn't allow enough time for the proper finishing touches and care. Terry explained to Gilley that he was not into normal dentistry anymore. He had specialized in reconstruction of people's jaws and tooth alignment.

After a few more drinks and hors d'oeuvres, Terry and Marilyn invited Joy and Gilley to come over one night for a swim, in the not too distant future. Terry also wanted to show Gilley his plane and his Rolls Royce that he had stored in the back yard.

At this point, the group got up to go onto the next stop, that being the Donaldson's. Bill and Marg Donaldson lived next door to Jim and Veron's with their two children, Billy and Cathy. Cathy was about the same age as Anne and Billy was slightly younger than Joy. It was handy, them being next door as driving was getting beyond any one of the adults by this time of the day. Gilley was quite relieved, as he had been chosen as the driver and he still hadn't had a chance to go for his driver's license. The British license was OK, but only for so long and Gilley, remembering his run in at the border didn't want to chance it.

The spread at Bill and Marg's was huge as well as was the bar. As a matter of fact, there were a few drinks Gilley had never had before. Bill also had a fine selection of Scotch, which he offered in great abundance to Gilley. Gilley didn't want to hurt his feelings by saying "no", but no matter how much Gilley was enjoying Bill's hospitality, he couldn't take his eyes off of Marg's boobs for long. They did look like a bloody shelf and you could probably get two pints in them. Jim didn't help matters much as he kept teasing Marg about them and Marg, very much enjoying the attention, kept saying, "You dirty Bugger, you. Keep your eyes to yourself or I'll tell Veron."

Marg was a nurse, but she never seemed to get to work as she always seemed to be suffering from some sort of ailment or other. Bill who was the local pharmacist, reminded Gilley of his doctor back in England, Dr. Robson. He was a heavy smoker. Even when he was examining you, he had a cigarette on the go. Often, when one saw Bill, he had one going too.

This got Gilley to comparing the differences between the pharmacies here in Canada and the chemists back in England. Here, these stores were more like general stores, selling everything from candy to stamps to cards to toys as well as medicines, while back in England, the chemists only sold medications and medical supplies such as band aids and creams.

Things just seemed to be getting underway when Jim came over to Gilley and said, "That's enough, lad. We've got an eight o'clock tee off tomorrow Sunday morning and Joy and Veron have their own plans. Lets' go." At first Gilley was more than a little disappointed, but as he thought about it, he realized that it had been a long day and Jim was right. Excusing themselves from the party, they weaved their way home on foot. Thank God, they weren't driving.

The next morning, it was cold and damp and Gilley's first opportunity to wear his new black and white shoes. He had been wearing a pair of Jim's old shoes and they leaked like hell. Not much fun in the wet grounds as it seemed to rain throughout the week and be fine for golf on Saturdays. Everyone kept commenting on the weather. It was so unusual for British Columbia this time of the year.

The fresh air did well to revive the lagging spirits of the four lonely golfers. The new golf shoes were great and kept his feet dry as promised. However, Eric could not resist teasing Gilley about his magpie shoes. It was a ploy on Eric's behalf to try to distract Gilley and be the cash winner. And sure enough it worked. Even though Gilley's score was good his cash winnings were not. It was a pleasure to finally throw back a few beers after the game.

Then, as they didn't have time for breakfast that morning, Eric asked them all back for lunch, in particular to taste Anne's traditional mince pies and for more Christmas Cheer. Much to Gilley's delight, this included a generous glass of Nu-Plus Ultra Scotch, Eric's favorite (and now Gilley's). Jim and Brian preferred Canadian Club Rye. Eric really enjoyed having a Scotch-drinking partner and said to Gilley, "Make the most of this as it doesn't come very often."

Jim whispered, "Tight bugger is Eric."

"I heard that, Jim. Just for that, you have to stay and have another drink. I'll show you who's a tight bugger." Brian excused himself, saying he had promised Marva he'd be home to help set up their open house.

It was time they went home as it was almost six o'clock and they realized they were later than usual. As they approached home, they began to feel a bit apprehensive about the type of reception they would receive upon arrival as they were late and they were feeling no pain. They walked cautiously into the bar. Joy, Veron and Grandmother were having a great old chinwag laughing and talking as women do. As Joy was behind the bar, she offered the two of them a beer. Jim whispered back to Gilley, "What the hell's going on here, Gilley?"

"Shut up Jim, just be thankful for our good fortune," replied Gilley as he took his first sip of beer.

Well, it seemed as if the good fortune evaporated as soon as it came as Grandmother asked, "Where the hell have you been all day?"

"Yeah, where have you been? You couldn't have been playing golf this length of time," chimed in Veron. "Brian, your golfing buddy, just called about a half an hour ago and we are invited to their place for snacks and drinks."

"You're correct, we're later than we'd planned. We stopped at Anne and Eric's. He invited us to come over and taste Anne's minced pies. As a matter of fact, Anne sent some with us for you ladies," said Jim. "Go to the car and get the pies Gilley. They're on the back seat."

Gilley thought, "Here we go again, another bloody party. It's a good thing this Monday is a holiday so we can recover enough to make it to work Tuesday morning." The gift of meat pies seemed to ease the tension and make the women forget about the men's errors. Everyone changed and went to Brian and Marva's for drinks and snacks. It was about midnight when they returned home. Gilley was glad to roll into bed.

Monday, Gilley woke up about 9:00 AM. He was rather tired and thought about his wonderful shower. He listened and didn't hear any noises upstairs. "It's very quiet," he thought. He slowly gathered his thoughts and drifted into the shower with some pounding in his head. After a long shower the magic worked and he thought again how wonderful it was to be in Canada. "You couldn't ever imagine having a shower like this in England."

After his shower, he made himself a cup of tea and thought of the last few days. They had been very busy, but also very nice. It seemed that everyone in Canada was happy. He wandered from the suite into the bar area to make sure that nobody was up. He was amazed that it was all cleaned up. No one was around, no noises. Could it be that Veron and Jim have actually slept in? He crept upstairs.

To his amazement, when he looked through to the kitchen, there was grandma having a cup of tea and a smoke. "Come in, Pet" she said. "Join me for a cup of tea and have a slice of toast with this exceptional marmalade I got in my stocking."

"Don't mind if I do," said Gilley. "Where have Jim and Veron gone? Surely, they are not still in bed are they?"

"No Me-lad, poor old Jim got dragged out of bed to help clean up the place and then she decided it was her turn to play golf. So off they went. They should be back here by around 12:00 PM. I bet Joy is still in bed. She's one that does like her beauty sleep."

"Well, I wouldn't dare wake her up. If you want to wake her up, Grandma, you can," replied Gilley.

"No," Grandma said, "Let her sleep and we'll have a little chinwag, just you and me, about England."

Much to Gilley's surprise, Grandma said, "Tell me, Gilley, what do you think about Canada?"

"Well, since I've been here, I haven't had that much time to think, let alone think about Canada or England. Time has gone by so fast. The novelty and the newness still haven't worn off. I'm in awe about actually being here. It's like a dream you know. Jim and Veron have gone out of their way to make me feel at home and I will never be out of their debt. I have had a nice place to live, plus the fact I've got a magical shower downstairs," said Gilley.

"You've talked about his "magical shower" before. What's with this anyhow?"

"Grandma, in England, we were lucky to get a bath twice a week, let alone a shower."

"I remember that" interjected Grandma, "whether we needed it or not, we were lucky to get one a week. I was the oldest in my family and my poor sisters got to use my bath tub water after I did, and last but not least, the dog got thrown into it if he was dirty. I think, here in Canada, they use too much water. Mind you, they do have lots of it. I still like my bath once a week. I've tried having a shower, but couldn't get used to the water pounding onto my body."

"I don't know how can I explain it to you if you don't like it pounding on your body?" Gilley asked. "That's just what I like. It feels so invigorating. It also seems to wash away the night before. I love that I can use all the hot water I want and no one questions the amount. It just revives me and seems the right way to start a day. I've also heard that a shower takes a lot less water than a bath."

"I don't know about that. How do you know for sure? Maybe you should have a shower upstairs in the bathroom and plug the tub. Then we can check out the water and see if you're lying or not. We can get Jim in on this too," teased Grandma. "So would you go back to England?" Grandma asked.

"I have no intention of leaving this land till I've seen most of it and there is a lot to see. Plus the fact, financially, we are much better off here. Gas is cheaper and so are cigarettes. In general, I think most things are cheaper, except rent, which seems to be much higher. However, the amount of money you can earn is much more than what it would be in England. I can see life being very good here."

"But I do miss my family and friends, the beer and going to the football games. Mom and Dad send me the Football Pink once in awhile and it's great to catch up on all the news and scores. With all the channels you have here in Canada, not one broadcasts any results or shows any highlights from England. What they pass off as football over here is a combination of soccer and rugby. It's nothing like what we have in England."

Grandma said, "There are a lot of things for you to find out in this country as I did. I immigrated when I was forty-seven with four kids. I had a rude awakening. But you shall overcome as I did. I got what I wanted and that was my secondhand store. Joy used to help me many a time while her mother was out working. Remember it's important to never lose your sense of humour. One more bit of advice, my dear, buy land when you are able. It will always go up. Don't worry about developed property, OK? Developed property comes with many other problems."

At that moment, Joy arrived upstairs. "I thought I could hear your voice thundering through the house. So it was you and Grandma having all that fun eh? Where are Mom and Dad," asked Joy?

"Playing golf," both Gilley and Grandma responded together.

"What? Playing golf? They must be sick." Just at that time, in came the two golfers as the clock struck 12:00 PM.

And guess what Jim's response was, "Who's ready for a beer?"

"Well, the suns over the yard arm", said Gilley.

Jim's response was, "That's one thing about being part of the British Empire, the sun never sets on it, so it's always the right time to have a beer."

"While you boys have a beer," said Veron, "I'll stir up some lunch. Its turkey soup made fresh from the left over Christmas dinner."

"I've been taking care of it, Veron", said grandma, "while you were out gallivanting' on the golf course."

The two younger girls finally appeared from their long lie in. "Not turkey soup again," they said in unison. "How about having a turkey sandwich? Is there any of the turkey breast left?"

As Jim and Gilley descend to the bar, Jim retorted, "There goes my lunch and probably yours too, Gilley." Joy, not wanting to be left out of the basement refreshments, followed the men downstairs. Anne and Sally, hoping to sneak a beer in and perhaps play some pool too till lunch followed behind.

After lunch, compliments went to Veron on the wonderful turkey soup. It had everything in it, even the kitchen sink. It seemed to taste even better than the batch she made from the Thanksgiving turkey. He couldn't believe that after the size of the sandwiches the girls put away there could be any turkey left, but he was soon informed tonight's dinner was going to be the famed Turkey Crunch. On one hand Gilley was pleased, yet on the other, he felt a little more than "turkeyed out". Not wanting to complain, though, Gilley replied to the others' groans, "You sure get your money's worth out of that big old bird you have here in Canada."

Monday turned out to be as relaxing as Gilley had hoped. Everyone turned in early, as Tuesday was back to work. Grandma's parting remark just before everyone turned in was "Well, everybody, I'll see you in the New Year. Jim is taking me down to the bus tomorrow. I'm going to ring in the New Year with Rosalyn and her kids in Victoria."

Arriving at work Tuesday morning no one was in the mood for working as they were all talking about Christmas and the parties they attended. Eventually, they settled down and got some work done. The next day the main topic of conversation was what everyone planned to do for New Years Eve. This for once was not a new thing for Gilley. In England, they partied and partied big. He was looking forward to a Canadian New Years.

December 31st arrived and strangely enough everyone seemed to be back in working mode till round about 3:00 PM. At this time the mood shifted in the department. Suddenly, everyone started to put their gear away. Gilley was a bit puzzled by this as it was not normally quitting time and continued to work. Upon seeing this, his mates said, "Come on Gilley, knock it off, you don't get any brownie points for working into party time. There's a big spread down in the shop area. Lots to eat and drink. It's time to start bringing in the New Year."

"Great, more parties," thought Gilley. "Does it ever stop in Canada?" Off he went, to join the gang. Drinks and jokes and smoking—it was soon 6:00 PM. "Oops, I've got to go. It's almost time before the last bus into New Westminster leaves."

"Don't worry"' said Sel Greenwood, "I'll give you a lift into New West tonight since Al is not going that way tonight. You do know I live in there too, don't you?" Also, an offer came from Ken Diamond who also lived in New West. Relieved that he didn't have to take the bus and that he didn't have to miss any of this great party, Gilley took Sel up on his offer, as Ken Diamond was leaving right then. The party wound down around 7:00 PM and Sel and Gilley made their way out to Sel's car which was an Envoy. It turned out to be the same as the English Vauxhall Viva. Gilley's friend, Ray Cowie, had one just like it, but in white. Sel's was sky blue.

Their discussion on the drive home was about these cars. It was unusual for Gilley to be driven in an English car with the steering on the left hand side. Sel liked his car because it was easy to work on and, as his background was in controls with the Lucas Company in England, he was familiar with the English electrical system which was in many of these type of cars. This system seemed to drive Canadian mechanics nuts, as they couldn't figure it out. The two found lots in common and before they knew it they arrived at the intersection of 8th Street and 8th Avenue.

As they stopped, Sel told Gilley he drove past this intersection every day on his way to work. It would be no inconvenience to pick Gilley up on the way. It would save Gilley a bus trip and provide company for Sel. If Gilley wasn't there, Sel would just continue on. If Sel had other arrangements, then Gilley could still catch his bus on time. This seemed like a good arrangement to both men, as it didn't impose any restrictions on either of them. Wishing each other a Happy New Year, they parted company.

Walking home, Gilley began to reminisce about New Year's Eve in England. By this time of the night, things would be in full swing as England was eight hours ahead (and possibly coming to an end in some cases.) He began to wonder where his friends would be by this time. What mischief would Ray and Margaret be getting into? Who would be at John and Val's by now? They always had large parties, not only at New Year's but throughout the year. The only two single men left were Bill Wakefield and Dave Wright. Would his friends be carrying on the tradition which was set many years ago when they were all single? Going from pub to pub starting with the Wagon Inn and ending back at their local pub, the Centurion. Then came the pleasure of visiting everyone's parents for a New Year's drink. After all, with the pub closing at 10:30 PM and New Years happening at 12:00 AM, one had to carry on.

Gilley thought about his parents and how the gang used to stop in at their house too. "Father would dole out the brandy drop by drop as he thought the boys did not appreciate the finer taste of this type of luxury. But Mother would always tip the bottle and fill their glasses as she enjoyed having the boys around." After the visit there, the group moved on to Bill Humble's place. Bill was the manager of their soccer (football) club—Newburn Associated Football Club or the AFC.

Often this was where they welcomed the New Year in. Just after the strike of twelve it was traditional for a tall dark man bearing a lump of coal to knock on the door. He was what was called The First Foot and his crossing the threshold brought all in the house good luck. He would place the coal on the fire to bring the home warmth for the rest of the year. He would be served the first drink of the New Year and would offer a toast to all. Everyone would break into chorus of Auld Lang Sang.

The next stop which was absolutely essential was Aunt Phyll's home in Lemington. It had been tradition for as long as Gilley could remember that all members of the family and their friends stopped at Aunt Phyll's for a New Year's drink. (If you didn't you'd be in her bad books for a long time.) She was quite the character and her parties were not to be missed. The last party Gilley had attended included Joy and Liz who had been boarding with Aunt Phyll since September. That was some party. This year is already so different. What will happen at 1806 8th Avenue the house of the Wilson's?

Getting home, Gilley found Joy and Veron at the bar and Jim nowhere to be found. "Happy New Year, Ladies. Where's Jim," asked Gilley?

"He's still partying at the school board. He should be home soon."

"I was just telling Mom about last New Year's Eve in England. We went from pub to pub and then ended up at Aunt Phyll's. I'll never forget her and how she took us in when we decided to stay in Newcastle. That was a lot of fun. I wish I was still in England. I wish I had never left. You left all of those friends you were so close to. They always made me feel like I had been there from day one. When Liz and I boarded with your Aunt Phyll, there was never a dull moment. I miss your aunt. She was really good to me. I bet you Liz didn't have a dull moment tonight either as she is still living there. Do you wish you hadn't left England, Gilley?"

"No" Gilley said, "I'm pleased I've left England. Often when you're away from things, you appreciate them much better. It seems things have been happening so fast since I got here, I haven't had much time to think about it. As I was walking here tonight memories just seemed to come. They were good times, but I but I think there's a better future in Canada for us."

Jim arrived home then and shortly after that, the bar was filled with guests. At first Jim tended bar but he soon stepped down and insisted Gilley fill in as he said he had to mingle with his guests. There were many people Gilley had never seen before and he was glad to be tending bar. One by one, they introduced themselves as they came to replenish their drinks. One character who stood out was a fellow named Bill McKinley. He was one of the School Board Trustees. He was a tall man, about 6'4", had a tremendous sense of humor and handed over a bottle of his homemade wine. He called it El Collapse-so.

Veron said, "I don't think Gilley should try that stuff. He's not a wine drinker and we know why Bill calls it El Collapse-so. I'd better get some food down here before our guests get El Collapse-so without drinking his brew." With that she rounded up Joy and a few other ladies and disappeared upstairs.

At this time, Big Mike Cacic arrived with his wife who was blonde, very pretty and very tall. Gilley called over, "What would you and your wife like to drink, Mike?"

Mike replied "Rye and a Vodka and orange, Please."

Gilley picked up the bottle of Rye to pour the drink. Mike took the bottle, which was half full and said, "Thanks, Gilley. No point in dirtying a glass as this bottle's just about finished anyhow. This is just fine." With that he finished it off.

"Do you want a fresh bottle" asked Gilley?

"As long as it is Canadian Club, I don't care," said Mike, "And another Vodka and orange for my lady, please".

Jim gave Gilley the nod and Gilley passed a whole bottle of Canadian Club to Mike. He then turned to his wife, "Here's your Vodka and orange, Babe."

Mike said, "We can't stay long, Jim. But we just had to pop in to wish you a Happy New Year." To everyone's amazement, having said that, he downed the second bottle."

Out of the crowd, Harry shouted, "Drinking like that is part of their training. It's meant to deaden the pain."

Jim said, "I'm pleased he's not staying long as I'd run out of Rye, with him drinking like that. After all, some of us like Rye by the glass."

Mike grinning, "Thanks, Jim. I'll have a bottle to go."

"Bugger off and a Happy New Year to you both," quipped Jim.

With that, Mike shouted, "Happy New Year, Everyone." Just then Veron arrived with the food. "Oh, now you're talking. Here comes the food. Thanks Veron." With that, he took a whole tray of food from her and ambled out the door. "Must eat so I don't get too intoxicated," was his parting remark.

It was five minutes to twelve and Veron said to Gilley, "Gilley, you have to be the Tall Dark Stranger. Go out to the front door. I've left a piece of coal there in a paper bag. Get it and knock at twelve o'clock sharp. We'll do the English First Footing tradition."

"OK" said Gilley. With that, he went round to the front door, found the bag as described and waited. He knew Jim had already set the fire in the living room. At twelve o'clock sharp he rang the bell and waited and waited and waited. He couldn't enter on his own as this would break the luck. He had to be invited in by someone of the house. He rang again, still no answer. By this time, he was bloody cold. The alcohol didn't help now. He could hear them singing Auld Lang Sang downstairs, "Bloody hell. They've forgotten about me already."

He was about to leave when the door opened and there stood Joy, "Sorry, Gilley we forgot about you."

"Nice, bloody nice."

"Well come in. You'll catch your death out there."

"No, I can't come in until the owner invites me in otherwise, it's bad luck for an entire year."

"Don't be silly. I'm their daughter. I give you permission to enter."

"OK, I guess that would work," with that, Gilley entered the living room where the fire was burning and recited, 'As I place this piece of coal into your fire, it will bring you warmth, health and prosperity for the coming year. Thank you for inviting me into your home." With that, the couple went downstairs.

Everyone turned to them as they entered, "There you are," Jim said. "I didn't realize where you were until I was missing my barman.

Then Veron said, "Oops, in all the excitement, we've left that poor bugger outside." That's when Joy said, 'He'll be freezing out there. His Aunt Phyll wouldn't like that.' I see between the two of you, the problem is solved. Come and get yourselves a drink. Gilley, get me one too."

The party rocked on for many hours. Gilley was in his glory-a drink for this person, a drink for him, drink for that person, a drink for him. Gilley couldn't remember the end of that night, and the following morning, that magic shower didn't work—it helped, but it didn't completely do the job. With his head still throbbing and his stomach a bit iffy, Gilley remembered his father's tried and true remedy. "That's it." he thought, and with that he plugged in the kettle and made a nice hot pot of tea.

That was the easy part—the hard part was getting the second and most important ingredient for this remedy—the whiskey. For this,

Gilley had to quietly skulk out of the suite to the bar and obtain two shots of scotch. The skulking was very important, as he did not want Jim and Veron to know that he had a hangover. He also did not want them to think he had a drinking problem either, right? Having accomplished this, and having put it in his tea, he walked carefully so as not to disturb anyone in the house (especially Joy) and retired to the downstairs patio. There he had a deep drink of this medicine and a couple of cigarettes. Right away, he could feel the effects of the medication. The throbbing began to subside and his stomach felt back to normal. So effective was this remedy that another one was called for. By this time, to Gilley's surprise, he noticed that Jim's car was gone. Had Jim parked at the front of the house? Gilley walked around to the front. "No, it was definitely gone," thought Gilley. "Where would they go New Year's Day especially this early in the morning? How did these people do this?"

It was definitely time to get another dose of the remedy. As Gilley had become convinced that his In-laws were out, he strode into the bar this time to top up on the second and most important ingredient. Just as he was lowering the bottle, he heard a distinct clearing of a voice. Looking up, there stood Veron, with her arms crossed over her chest. "Hang-over, Gilley? I'm not surprised considering the way things went last night. Or perhaps you don't remember much after Big Mike left. So you're having the hair of the dog are you? Would you like to hear some of the stories about your antics?"

"No, no," said Gilley, "I don't know what you're on about. I remember most things that went on last night. You seemed to be having a good time too, Veron."

"I'm not down here getting a bit of the hair of the dog that bit me like you are."

"Would you like one anyway, Veron?"

"What is it you're having there," asked Veron?

"A cup of tea with a shot of scotch."

"Why not? Go ahead, you go and get the tea. I like cream and sugar in it. Can that be part of the remedy?"

"Yep, that's what I'm having in mine." As Gilley returned with a piping hot, fresh cup of tea for Veron, he saw that she was looking at the scotch bottle. "Nu Plus Ultra, that's a very fine scotch. Isn't this the one that Eric gave to you and Joy for Christmas? Fancy you putting in the bar."

After her cup of medication, she said, "That's not a bad drop of tea. Have you had any breakfast yet? Come on, I'll make you some fried eggs. By the time its ready, Jim should be back. He had to go down to the school. There was a problem with someone trying to break in."

As Veron was in the middle of frying up the eggs, Jim appeared, full of life and with no sign of hangover. That really didn't seem fair. Jim said, "I didn't think you'd be up this early, Gilley."

"Well, obviously his magic shower didn't work this morning. I caught him in the bar making this special remedy he claims he got from his father. Apparently, he was brought up on it or so he claims."

"What is this concoction you're going on about," asked Jim?

Gilley explained, "Well, Jim, I think you just might like this concoction. It's a hot cup of tea with a couple a shots of scotch in it. It works just great."

"I don't like scotch," said Jim. "What would it taste like with Rye?"

"Let's try it." Gilley poured a cup of tea for Jim. "Cream and sugar Jim?"

"Yes please," said Jim.

Gilley nipped downstairs and came right back with the Rye bottle. He poured approximately two shots into Jim's tea and handed it over. "See what that tastes like."

"That's very nice Gilley. You could be a bad influence."

"Not could," stated Veron, "he IS a bad influence. I tried his Scotch tea mix. It has good possibilities."

After finishing the eggs and toast, a lonely, dragged out figure appeared at the door. "I thought you'd be up here. How come you all look so refreshed?"

"Its Gilley remedy mix," Veron answered.

"Oh no, it's not his father's favorite remedy is it? For anything that ails you, he takes it. When I was in England, if he didn't have whiskey, brandy would do, whether you had a cold, a little bit of flu or any ailment. He tried to get me on it and I detest the taste of scotch or brandy."

Jim joined the conversation; "Maybe you should try it with Rye. I did."

"Oh no, not Rye. I hate rye even more than scotch."

"Well, Joy, "Gilley jumped in, "my other fix just for you is a beer. How about that?"

"Gilley, your fix in England was fish and chips, then a beer."

"I can't get you the fish and chips, but I can get you the beer."

"I don't fancy any right now. I've got a headache and all I need is a cup of tea and a slice of toast." This day turned out to be a long day especially for Joy who wouldn't take the medicine.

Chapter 8

Snowy Beginnings

THAT FOLLOWING WEEK WINTER arrived with generous fall of snow and of course cooler temperatures. Gilley had left all of his winter togs in England as Joy had assured him he wouldn't need them in Canada, not realizing Gilley would be out in the elements in order to get to work and back, whether it was riding with Sel or riding on the bus. Jim gladly donated his overcoat to the cause; "I never use it here as we are generally driving back and forth in a car, going door to door so to speak. An overcoat just becomes a problem"

Gilley was glad for the comfort of the lined coat and gloves even though both were a bit tight and the coat was short in the sleeves. It made walking to the corner of 8th and 8th was much more comfortable now. Added to this was Gilley's idea of wearing his all weather golf shoes. The spikes gave him the grip he needed on these icy mornings as he trooped to the bus or to catch a lift with Sel. This one morning was different. He knew Sel wasn't coming this morning so he had to catch the bus for the first time since he had to wear his golf shoes. As he clamored onto the bus, his spiked shoes made a loud metallic sound. Everyone, in their amazement looked down at Gilley's black and white golf shoes. In his embarrassment, he declared, "Can you believe how versatile these shoes are? Not only are they waterproof, but with the spikes, they give me grip in the icy patches." Everyone giggled.

Then one of the regular riders shouted out with a Manchester accent, "Anyone for golf? We could expect anything from a Geordie, especially with those black and white shoes. Are you trying to make a statement?"

"I am. I'm proud to be a Magpie fan. After all, we did win the Inter-city Fair Cup last year. Hopefully this year it will be FA Cup."

"In your dreams," replied the rider. "Your magpie luck has run out. You'll never see another cup in Newcastle." With that remark, the two bantered back and forth till Gilley's stop arrived as to who had the best team. The other passengers enjoyed the entertainment provided by the two Englishmen who continued to give each other verbal abuse.

That week the snow hung around for a few days. Jim was very busy organizing his crew to remove the snow from the most suspect roofs in the school district. He explained to Gilley the snow was not especially hazardous, but if things happened as per usual, there would be warming and considerable rainfall weighting down the snow. This is what presented the danger to all of the school roofs. They could possibly collapse under the weight of the wet snow and this was of particular concern regarding the flat roofs. At dinner that night, Gilley offered to help Jim clear the affected roofs. Veron interjected, "You shouldn't offer your services free of charge. The school board has allocated funds for this type of emergency and they pay well."

"If there's money in it, all the better. But then again as being part of the family, the board doesn't like family working for each other. Isn't that why I had to quit the School Board before? The offer still stands, Jim. If there's an emergency, I'll help free of charge. After all, I would do that for any family member."

That Saturday brought another set of problems—no golf. Eric had called on the Friday to say Newlands Golf Course had a foot of snow on it and was subsequently closed. As everyone sat around the kitchen table for breakfast the phone rang. It was Eric, "Guess what I found out? No snow in Tsawwassen. The golf course is open for business.

"Book a tee off time for 10:00 AM. We're on our way," replied Jim. "I'll call Brian and we'll meet you there."

Brian was full of agreement and said he would meet them there. To their amazement, there was no snow to be found in Tsawwassen and the course was very quiet. As they met in the parking lot, Eric declared, "we must keep up the tradition of golf every Saturday wherever it may be."

The game was uneventful through the first nine holes. On the tenth hole came the challenge. There were two strips of water between the tee and the green. The second strip of water was approximately one hundred and seventy yards from the tee to clear. Everyone else shot safely to the middle of the two waters. Gilley said, "I'm going for it, Jim." With a mighty hit, his ball sailed into the air veering slightly to the right. It looked good until, plunk, into the second water hazard.

"I'll try another. There's no one behind me and I'm sure to make it this time." With that Gilley hit another ball that landed directly into the same hazard. "OK, let me try one more. I think I've corrected my swing now." The shot cleared the second hazard landed on the bank and promptly bounced into the drink.

"OK. This is the last one. Nobody's coming. I can do it. I've practiced enough." Sure enough, this stroke cleared the water and landed nicely on the fairway just short of the green. "I told you I could do it."

"Oh sure," said Eric. "You are now laying seven and you are two golf balls short." As they walked over the second bridge, Eric continued, "You're laying seven. I'm on the green in two and a nickel in my pocket." Gilley took his eighth shot. It bounced onto the green, only to roll off the other side. "Ah, hah" said Eric. "Getting cocky are we?"

Brian chipped onto the green and was lying closest to. Jim's turn came and he was closest to. Gilley was lying just on the fringe of the green, was up next. He took his putter and drilled the ball right into the hole. This gave him closest to and first down. "What do you think of that, Eric," spouted Gilley as Eric three putted.

"Well, Gilley", Eric explained, "We have eight holes left to play. You are a nickel ahead of me but my score is five better than yours. You have a lot of catching up to me if you want to collect for the lowest score today."

The remaining holes on this course were quite difficult. Added to this was the amount of water laying in puddles. Gilley's game seemed to favour him. If he missed the puddles, his ball skimmed off the water and found favorable lie to the green. At the end of the day, they calculated the scores. Eric had shot an eighty-five, Jim a ninety-six,

Brian a ninety-seven and Gilley an eighty-three. Eric shouted, "Not only did Gilley get the lowest score, his team also got the lowest score. Eric tabulated the cash payouts and he concluded Jim was owed $1.50, Brian was owed $.50 and Gilley was owed $3.50. Nothing for Eric. He was not a happy camper. He was so used to winning, he had to recalculate the results four times before he was convinced they had been right the first time. "Gilley, you're buying the beer today. With all those lucky bounces and chipping in on the tenth, you'll never be able to do that again. You should be pleased to buy the beers, you lucky bugger."

On the way home, Jim chuckled, "You took a gamble on the tenth, but you did beat Eric for the first time. He will be after your blood the next time.

Gilley laughed, "It feels good to beat him. If I never beat him again, it'll still be a day to remember. He won't be so keen to play in Tsawwassen when it's snowing in Langley."

The following week Gilley received a letter from his parents saying they were planning a trip to come to BC to see the couple and they were coming this year. "Father says, 'Mother and I are looking forward to coming to Canada for the first time. Can you let us know what time of the year suits you both? We would like to come for three weeks. Your mother has already applied for our passports. She's ecstatic as this will be her first time in an airplane and her first time away from the shore of Britain.'"

They both looked at each other. "That means we have to make some type of arrangements for them," said Joy. "First we need to find a place to live that has two bedrooms. It's a good excuse for us to get out on our own as its time we had our own place. It also means we have to get our own car, some new furniture and you have to get your BC driver's license. On top of all this you have to continue your dental work. Oh how did your visit to the dentist go today?"

Feeling more than a bit snowed under by the sudden onset of the volume of tasks to be done in order to prepare for his parents' visit, Gilley replied, "Um, oh, right! Well, um, it's going to cost me about four hundred dollars to get all of the necessary work done and it will take about ten to twelve appointments. I can pay as I go. He's a nice dentist and his assistants are great. It's very different than in England where there are no assistants and just the dentist. These girls actually clean your teeth and get you all ready for the dentist. You never get that back home. The dentist just pops in, does what he needs to do and then the girls finish up. Nice that. It makes one feel really special and attended to."

Just then there was a knock on the suite door. It was Veron, "I see you got a letter today. Do you want to come and have a drink with Jim and me and let us know what it says?" Gilley and Joy took up the offer and over drinks told them of Gilley's parents' intentions. Joy concluded, "I think we'll have to find our own place. It would be nice to get a two bedroom apartment as we are getting cramped in the suite. That way we'd not only have more room for ourselves, but we'd have a guest room for company. If we didn't have the bar here to escape to, we'd go crazy in that little suite."

"It's done its job for you, hasn't it? It was only meant to be a temporary measure. But, funny thing you've said that, "said Veron. "I was just walking down Eighth Avenue on my way to Woodward's and saw there was a sign advertising a two bedroom suite available at the Bermuda House. I enquired on the off chance and it will be available starting the first of March. I made an appointment for you and me, Joy, to take a preliminary look at it tomorrow on your lunch break. It would be so handy as it's just across from your bank and not too far from us. Besides that, it's closer to the bus for Gilley."

Jim butted in, "Once you get set up in the apartment, you'll need a car. Plus you'll need more furniture. The furniture in the suite is part of our wedding gift to you but it's just a start on furnishing your own place. Let's see what tomorrow brings once you've taken a look at the apartment.

Gilley looked at Jim with raised eyebrows. Jim returned the look with a shrug and quietly said, "Just go along. It'll be for the best."

Veron, hearing some whispering, turned and said, "What was that, Jim?'

"Oh, I was telling Gilley the Duster's lease with the School Board is up in March and it will be for sale," rebounded Jim. "Gilley, I was about to tell you I know I can get you a good deal on it. It'll only be about twenty-five hundred dollars and the bank will not have a problem given that Joy works there and you having a steady job. It is also the bank the School Board deals with and I know the manager very well."

"Gilley, now you've really got to focus on getting your driver's license," said Veron. "You can't drive here without one after six months."

At that point, the couple retired to their suite. "Gilley, what's the matter," asked Joy?

"Well, I'm feeling a bit overwhelmed what with all these changes. After all, an apartment of our own, furniture, a car, my dental work and getting my driver's license, it's a bit much. How can we afford all of that at once? On top of that, I don't know if I can get time from work to attend to all these things as well as taking time to be with my parents when they come for their visit."

"Everyone usually gets two weeks' vacation after six months working for their employer," Joy informed. "You need to ask if that applies to you. I'm sure it does. And for getting furniture, many stores and the bank are open later on Fridays to accommodate people who work normal hours. We've been given some furniture as a wedding gift which we can take with us. But we'll need a bed for the second bedroom and a new TV."

"What do you mean 'the second bedroom, Joy?"

"Gilley with all our out of town relatives, we have to have a second bedroom to provide a place for them to stay. Besides, apartments with a second bedroom are bigger than those with only one bedroom. We can use the space when we don't have guests to entertain."

"Oh."

"The apartment Mom found for us sounds just right. We'll go and have a look at it on my lunch hour. Can you give me a call at the bank about 2:00 PM? I can let you know what I think and then we can make an appointment for after work."

That night lying in bed, Gilley asked Joy what the best time would be for his parents to come over from England. "Well, it's up to you. I have two weeks off at the end of August. However, normally one has to be at a job for six months before being entitled to take holidays."

"I think I'll write a letter to my parents for you to post tomorrow and tell them they can come at the end of August, as I know I can get the time off already. I can work extra hours and bank the time. That way it will cover my dental work as well. There's so much work to be done, I'm sure there won't be any objections."

"What! You're going to write them tonight?"

"Of course, then it will be done. I'll have it finished by midnight."

As planned, Gilley called Joy at 2:00 PM and not to his surprise, she gave him a positive report. "I've made an appointment with the manager for us to come at 6:00 PM so you can see it. I've already put a deposit down on it. That's how sure I am that you will like it."

"OK, Joy, I'll be there. I'll meet you in front of the bank and we'll go and take a look."

As planned, Gilley met Joy and the building manager. He showed them the suite and Gilley was amazed. The place was so huge-bigger than he ever imagined an apartment to be. There were two big bedrooms, a large bathroom with a tub for Joy and a shower for Gilley, which he immediately turned on and after watching the water pressure knew it would provide what he needed. There was a small balcony that overlooked the Fraser River. "You can see your Mount Baker in the day time, Gilley", Joy informed him.

The living room was big also with its own dining room and was just off the kitchen. The kitchen was small and well laid out. It included a fridge and stove. "They're included in the price of the rent, Gilley," said Joy. "The washer and dryer are in the basement. We share them with other residents and the cost is minimal. Its twenty-five cents a load each for washing and drying. We have a set time to use them, but there is also ample time called "free time" later on at night when its first come, first serve. The bit of furniture we do have will look very sparse in here. I think we'll have to make that trip to Wosk's."

"Wosk's?!?"

"Yes, they're the best place in New Westminster to get furniture. We could go to Woodward's, but Wosk's has a better selection according to my mom."

"Oh. What's the deposit for," asked Gilley?

"It's normal to pay a month's rent up front. They keep it until you move out. This is to insure they have money to repair any damage we may cause. If there isn't a problem, we get it back. It's like a savings account," answered Joy.

"In what way would we damage the apartment," this was foreign to Gilley?

"You'd be surprised at what people do when the place isn't theirs. I've heard of people removing doors, damaging walls and floors and even stealing the appliances."

"People would do that?"

"Yes, they do here, anyway. Doesn't that happen in England?"

"Well, it probably could, but I've never heard of it before. Mind you, most rentals are at the discretion of the local council and people usually rent the place for life. If someone does moves out, the council always comes in and repairs and repaints anyhow. But, I've never heard of the kind of mess you've described."

"They rent for life? Wow, here most renters are transients who move every six months or so or else they are like us and are saving to own their own home. Then when they have a down payment for what they want, they move out. These people are generally the most reliable."

"I just can't get over how different our two cultures are," replied Gilley. "Even with something as basic as renting, there is a different way of doing things. Joy, this apartment is great. We could never get something like this in England, not to mention the price of the rent. Let's take it. We can do well for ourselves here. It's time we had our own place." With that, they signed the rental agreement.

March 1st came quickly. Jim borrowed the school's flat bed truck to help them move the large furniture along with the piano Veron insisted Joy should buy. "You must continue building your musical abilities. You have a gift and it would be a shame to waste it. In addition, when you have children, you can pass it onto them. You never know, you may eventually want to teach piano. There's lots of money to be had for a good piano teacher. I should know as I paid a lot for your lessons."

Along with the truck came Mickey and Harry. Most of the furniture was moved easily. But eventually, they could not avoid the tricky part—moving the antique piano which was heavy and awkward. Everyone had their own idea of how to best get it up three stories. After struggling it into the first floor lobby area and placing it at the elevator door, they realized it would not be an easy fit. After some discussion, it was decided it had to be turned on its end. Well, Joy was not happy about this. However, it was the only way. Harry, Mickey, Jim and Gilley heaved and pushed it into the elevator. Gilley, trapped at the back, shouted, "Where is Big Mike when we really need him?"

The elevator took a sudden drop as the other three squeezed in. Slowly the elevator made it to the third floor. The level of the elevator turned out to be about an inch lower than the floor due to the added weight. Lifting the piano up over the drop was grueling as it was difficult to get a position and a grip at the same time. Eventually it was out into the hall. The next step was easy. They flipped it back and wheeled it down the hall.

The real challenge then came when they reached the entrance to the apartment. Now, the only way into Gilley and Joy's apartment was through a door that led onto a small balcony. There was a second door at right angles to the left that lead into the apartment proper. Of course all the doorways had sills on them which added to the difficulty. How to get this huge, heavy, awkward piece of furniture around each corner without damaging it was the real challenge. To make this happen, both doors had to be removed. Then they wheeled it carefully at an angle up over the sill and through the first doorway positioning it at another angle in order to get it through the second doorway. As they maneuvered the piano through the first doorway, and onto the balcony, they had to tilt it up in order to get it over the second sill and through the second doorway. As they did this, one of the castors went through the balcony floor. "Oh, no, there goes the deposit," thought Gilley.

Now once the piano was in the apartment, the moving was done and the men wanted to relax. But Joy was upset that the entrance balcony was torn up and wanted her dad to fix it right away. "No, that's not going to happen today," Jim said. "We're going to have a beer and we'll fix it tomorrow."

"What if the landlord sees it and complains," said Joy.

Jim immediately said, "The floor is rotten. That's why it gave way. If he complains he won't get it fixed free of charge. It should never have gotten that bad to begin with." Joy gave in as she knew the men were tired and hungry and she wouldn't win the argument anyhow.

Veron had made sandwiches and of course the new fridge was stocked with beer. Mickey and Harry sat on the chesterfield, Jim sat in the comfortable arm chair and Gilley sat on one of the dining room chairs. Joy and Veron had set out the sandwiches on the coffee table. Beers were handed around and Gilley sat in his new apartment.

As soon as Harry finished his first beer he said, "Joy, now that we've got your piano in place, how about giving us a tune on that Old Joanna."

"Right now, I'm not too sure that 'Old Joanna' would play a good tune any more. I purposely didn't have it tuned before the move as I knew it would have to be done afterwards."

"I've never heard you play the piano and your mom says it's been a long time since, so any note out of tune can be blamed on the piano."

Joy glared at Gilley, "I don't know where my music is packed."

Harry retorted, "Just play by ear and we'll sing along."

Joy, knowing she's lost the contest, sat down and played a boogie woogie tune that rivaled any artist. Gilley couldn't believe his ears. He had no idea his wife was so talented. "Joy, we don't need to get a record player for all those LP's we have. You can just play every night."

"In your dreams." Harry and the rest were full of encouragement. Joy played a few more songs and Veron relished in her music. Just then Anne and Sally arrived, much to Joy's relief. "Typical," said Joy. "Show up when all the work was completed."

Just then, Gilley noticed a small doorway in the wall right beside the main door about a foot square. "What's that for, can anyone tell me?"

Veron replied, "It's for deliveries—things like parcels and milk. Many people have their milk delivered by Dairyland. It's very convenient as people don't have to be home when the deliveries arrive, yet they are safe from theft." Just then the little doorway opened and Tinker appeared. He had followed Anne and Sally from home without them knowing it, much to Veron's disgust.

"Oh and it's good for pets too," said Sally.

"No pets allowed," said Veron. "No apartments allow pets. They can cause too much damage and you'd lose your damage deposit."

By this time, it was 1:00 PM and it was time for Mickey and Harry to take the truck back. There was only one load left which was clothing. This could be done with Jim's Duster. Everyone retreated to the elevator and Tinker decided to go on another scout about. He wanted to investigate the apartments along the hallway and went in and out of the little doors causing shouts from the residents. At this everyone scrambled into the elevator along with Tinker. Mickey turned to Gilley, "You see, the "P" on the elevator. This stands for "Penthouse". That's where John Manley and his wife live. You'll be in good company once he knows you're here."

After the boys left, everyone returned to Jim and Veron's for the final stage of the move. By supper time the Duster was packed with the remaining articles and the suite was cleaned. Veron called everyone to supper. She had made her wonderful beef stew. Again, Gilley could not get over the amount of meat in comparison to his mother's stew which in BC might have been called vegetable stew instead. A few beers and homemade bread later, Jim, Joy and Gilley set off with the last load destined for the apartment. They unloaded everything and Gilley and Joy settled down to enjoy their first night by themselves in their new home.

Sitting down with a beer in one hand and a cigarette in the other, they viewed their sparse surroundings. "Now it's time to get the telephone and BC Hydro set up. Its lucky for us the heat is included in our rent," said Joy. "Our bill for Hydro will be for our electricity, so we had better make sure we turn out our lights when we're not using them. This first month is free courtesy of our landlord, but we had better make sure we do our budget right away so our finances don't get out of hand. Of course we have to make that visit to Wosk's now. We need a new bedroom suite and TV. Lucky for us the fridge and stove are included with our apartment. How about we go down there on Thursday night as they are open until 9:00 PM?"

Thursday night came and Joy and Gilley set off on their first shopping spree of their marriage. After wandering around the store for some time, they decided what they wanted. It was just like magic when all of a sudden this salesman appeared and offered to help them out. They explained they were looking for a Queen sized bedroom suite with two side tables, a chest of drawers and a dresser. They liked the European design which was a light walnut color and had a heavier look to it.

The salesman took all of this information down. Then he said, "Are you looking for a TV by any chance? We have them on special right now. I could roll a TV and this bedroom, plus a mattress and a table for the TV all into one price. $1600.00, not including taxes of course. Gilley just about died. He was about to say, "No way, man. We can't afford that." But he turned and looked at Joy and saw this was what she really wanted. How could he say "No"? She turned to him and said, "A good bedroom suite is a good investment and it will last us a long time."

Gilley, realizing they didn't need this until June, talked to the salesman and suggested he could put $200.00 down today and he would pay the rest off within three months (working overtime of course) and still have money for the other things they needed.

The salesman, realizing that Gilley didn't understand about credit, asked, "How long have you been in Canada?"

"Six months."

"Do you realize the Canadian way of life is to have good credit," the salesman replied?

Gilley asked, "How do you get good credit?"

"You buy something and charge it to an account. Then pay it off according to the contract, usually on monthly installments. Once they know you are reliable, you can purchase other things on credit. That way you can have what you need right away."

"What sort of account," asked Gilley?

The salesman, recognizing Gilley's accent said, "This is what they call HP in England—Hire-Purchase. I'm sure you've heard of that."

"Oh, the never, never plan, as my father used to say. Once you subscribe to it you never leave as you keep adding more and more things to it," said Gilley.

Joy, understanding the Canadian way of life and credit said, "Gilley, let me handle it. I know the system, since I work at a bank."

Gilley was used to having someone handle his financial affairs and was quite happy to hear this, "No problem, Joy. You deal with it and I'll bring in the money, just like back in England with my mother."

The salesman took down all of the details such as where they lived and worked and of course their income and said he would call them in a few days to inform them of their approval for credit, "I don't see any reason for you not to be approved so don't worry until you hear from me.

Gilley was not too sure about all of this "credit stuff", but he had confidence in Joy's ability to handle the situation. After all, she worked at a bank and she looked after all of the bills anyhow. "OK. Is there anything else you need from us?"

"No, and thank you for your business. You'll be hearing from me soon and don't worry. Once I hear about your approval we can talk about delivery which is free by the way."

"Oh, that's a good thing, isn't it," thought Gilley remembering their recent move and trying to get the piano up to their apartment. With that they walked the long climb back home to their suite, (New Westminster was built on a hill and one either walked up hill or downhill) Joy and Gilley discussed their current furniture situation. They decided that they could live with the furniture from the suite they had been given as a "Starting Off" gift by Veron and Jim. This was a double bed, a dining room suite, chesterfield and chair and two occasional chairs along with a coffee table. Gilley couldn't believe all this had been given to them by Veron and Jim. How fortunate! The double bed would go into the second bedroom as guest furniture of course once the new bedroom suite arrived but the rest would be quite suitable until they could afford to replace it.

Next, Joy reminded Gilley he had an appointment tomorrow with the bank manager at her bank to see about a loan for the Duster. The bank manager was a friend of Jim's and he also was the banker for the School Board. Joy did not think there would be any problems with their obtaining the loan. Gilley was feeling more than overwhelmed, but decided not to say anything. After all, this was Joy's country and his new way of life. Being quite practical, he didn't think Joy would allow them to get in over their heads.

The following day, Gilley could hardly wait to get to the bank. He had gotten his six month raise earlier than expected as he had already demonstrated his ability to all those concerned. This had increased his salary by $100.00 gross. This netted him over $30.00 a pay cheque twice a month. What good news! After giving Joy the cheque, she was quite pleased.

In the meeting with the bank manager, Gilley discovered that the manager had already arranged for a loan for him to the amount of $2800.00. This was $2500.00 for the car and $300.00 for the insurance. Things seemed to be going smoothly for Gilley until the bank manager informed him he couldn't get the loan for the car without the insurance and couldn't get the insurance without the car. What a predicament! This was definitely a new rule, but it sure seemed crazy.

The bank manager had the solution, "Go to the insurance company with your father-in-law and he will explain things to them. He will give them the authorization they will need to precede in order for the bank to buy the car. They will then issue you the temporary insurance papers. Once you bring these to the bank, we will call the car company. They will then turn the ownership over to the bank. We can then proceed with the loan. The car becomes collateral for the loan. You will have the loan for three years at $95.66 a month. At the end of the three years, you own the car outright. You also get a special rate on the interest as Joy works here for the bank."

Since Joy worked late on Friday nights, Gilley had the opportunity to sit in his new home alone and examine his thoughts about all of the different transactions that had occurred in the last few days. All of these recent events were way beyond his basic life experience in England. Working in England he was paid every week, in cash. Basically, he lived from week to week and when the money was gone, it was gone. A certain amount of his money was taken, under Gilley's direction by his employer, and placed in a savings account for him. Another portion, he paid to his mother for room and board and clothing. Finally, he made payments to his father who had loaned him the money to buy his car at no interest. The only stipulation he'd made was Gilley would drive them wherever they wanted to go on Sundays. This left Gilley with what he thought of as his pocket money.

To have to arrange to pay bills and have credit and look after all of these different things, Gilley decided it was far better if Joy had full control of all of the financial affairs of the family. After all, she worked at the bank and had a far greater understanding of all of these things. Besides, Gilley realized that he was quite happy with just pocket money.

Suddenly Gilley remembered he was to meet Jim and Veron at Godfather's Pizza for dinner. Joy would come once she finished work. He hurried off and made it just in time to see them sit down at their chosen table. Joining them, he explained his recent thoughts. Veron seized the opportunity and said, "You've made a good decision, Gilley. You should let Joy look after all of the money. Jim used to look after paying the bills and it was a disaster. He would pay some, he would forget some, he would lose some. Now he's quite happy with pocket money."

Just at this juncture, Joy entered, dying for a beer. "It has been one hell of a week what with buying furniture, a car and getting our apartment. But did Gilley tell you he got a raise today? How about that? He wasn't supposed to get it yet, but he has proved himself at his new job so well they gave it to him earlier than expected".

Veron immediately said, "How much?"

"$100.00 a month," Joy responded.

"Well, you can buy supper tonight," said Veron.

"And you can buy the beer at golf tomorrow," said Jim.

"Well, if every time I get a raise, I have to buy you dinner and beers, I won't tell anyone about my raises again."

"Joy won't be able to contain herself, Gilley. We'll know all about your raises before you do—almost," said Veron.

When Gilley got home Saturday after golf, Joy informed him Wosk's had approved their credit and would deliver the furniture whenever they needed it. Things were happening more and more quickly. To top it all off, as if things weren't complicated enough what with the new purchases, the dentist appointments and all the overtime Gilley was working, he had to fit driving lessons into his schedule. The best solution was to do it all at once. Book the lessons and driver's test and get it done all in the one week. He wasn't too sure how many new tricks and rules were involved in the driving world in Canada but he already had discovered a few. Given what he had experienced so far he figured there were more to come.

The lessons went quite smoothly and Friday morning the test was scheduled for 9:30 in morning. He was standing in line with his little red English driver's license in his hand, wondering which would be first, the written or the practical. His thoughts drifted back to England and the procedure there. There was no written exam. The examiner would verbally ask the questions and then ask you to wait in the car while he scored the exam."

Gilley was jolted out of his thoughts by a gruff "Next." He passed his license over to the official on the other side of the counter. This man sat back and flicked through it.

Much to Gilley's surprise, he said, "Do you know Harry Clark?"

Gilley replied, "Do you mean Harry Clark with the cart and horse?"

"Yes" said the guy, "He's my cousin and I used to live in Lemington which isn't too far from Throckley."

Gilley was very excited to meet someone who knew the same people as he did. "Harry Clark drinks with my father, Ned Brown, Bill Coish, and others at the Bank Top Working Man's Club"

"I've been here for six years and never ever met someone from my neck of the woods. Once you've finished the practical part of the exam, make sure you come back and see me."

"Ok, I will," promised Gilley, hoping he could pull it off. As soon as he turned from the counter, the driving instructor approached him and directed him through a door and to the driving school car. As he started off, Gilley was very conscious of making sure he stayed on the right hand side of the road. All of a sudden he encountered a four way stop! Stopping and observing there was no one else at a corner, he proceeded through the intersection. The inspector said, "Turn right here. I'd like you to parallel-park along this curb. Then I'd like you to move out of the parking space and proceed down Sixth Street." Gilley did what he was instructed to do without any problem. Next the instructor said, "Turn left." All of a sudden an orange flashing light appeared.

"Shit," thought Gilley, "what do I do with this?" So he stopped. He proceeded very slowly, not too sure of what to do.

"Please do another parallel park here," said the instructor. Gilley followed his instructions. "Now proceed left and when you see the flashing green turn right and back into the motor vehicle branch." Stopping at the flashing green to allow the pedestrians to walk across, Gilley carried on to the branch and parked in the spot where the car had been before. "Thank you. Now go into the office to take your written test. Once you've finished that, take this paper and your test to an open wicket and present everything to the clerk. It will be scored and you will be told if you passed or not. If you passed you will be issued a temporary license until your permanent one arrives in the mail." With that, he left the car.

Fortunately for Gilley the clerk that first came available was the one he wanted to see. Gilley handed over his paper work and the man said, "My name is Joe Cousins. Here is my telephone number. Make sure you phone me. Here is your British driver's license back." He then stamped the license "NOT VALID" in front of Gilley. By now Gilley was sure he'd failed. Not only that but now he didn't have his English license to fall back on. "Wait, Gilley, I'll be right back." With that he left and disappeared for several minutes. To Gilley, it seemed like an eternity and as if everyone was watching him. Joe returned looking serious. "Well," he said in a deep solemn voice, looking into Gilley's eyes, "You are now legal to drive in British Columbia. Congratulations! Make sure you call me. I'd like to catch up on what's been happening up in our neck of the woods."

Beaming, Gilley replied, "I'll do that and thank you, Joe. I'd give you my number, but I don't have a telephone yet. My wife will be pleased that I passed." Leaving the building, his instructor congratulated him on his success and drove him to the closest bus station so he could get back to the Bank of Montreal.

As he entered the bank, he walked up to the counter looking for Joy. As he spotted her, he shouted, "I've passed." Joy, embarrassed, hurried to the counter and said, "Shhhhh, you're embarrassing me." Everyone turned around and stared clapping. Just at that time, Jim came into the bank and said to Gilley, "Good, glad to hear you passed. I can take you down to the insurance office now. I just have to get some pocket money out of the account."

After the insurance office, Jim gave Gilley a lift back to work. "What a lucky bugger I am," thought Gilley as he watched the scenery go by. I've passed my driver's test, gotten my car insurance and now have a ride to work." He was grateful for this ride as it would have meant taking more time from work.

Everyone was working overtime to catch up so the boys decided Gilley should buy them all a drink at the Waldorf in celebration of his new license. Well, after a few rounds there, he realized he missed the last bus, which left at 8:00 PM. Gilley said, "Al, since you're going my way and I can't drive, how about I tag along for a ride tonight. Is that going to be OK?"

"Of course, Gilley. The only thing you have to do is invite me over to your new place for dinner sometime soon so I can see it for myself," replied Al.

"You're on."

Arriving home with a few under his belt, he sat down with Joy and explained how good the day was and how well it had ended for him. She wasn't too happy. "I am still a bit upset that you embarrassed me at the bank and now you come home smelling of drink. Now that you've got your driver's license and you are also the owner of the Duster, you had better watch your drinking. I don't want to get a call that you've wrapped yourself around a pole or something. Plus did you not remember you were to drive Dad down to the dealership so he could pick up his new car?"

"Well, I could still do that."

"Too late, I've done that already."

"So I'm really in trouble now, eh?"

"You really don't get the car until April 1st which is next week."

"Is that my penalty for getting home late?" Gilley asked.

"Well the car dad had ordered won't be ready till then, so he's going to use the Duster until it comes in next week."

"So, really, I didn't have to be home after all. Well, I don't have a problem with that," Gilley responded, walking to the fridge. "Want a beer, Sweetheart?"

Joy's sullen mood began to lift, as she knew he was utterly incorrigible and accepted the truce offering. They sat in their living room discussing their future. Life in Canada was now taking shape. They were now really stepping out on their own beginning to feel as if they were really married. The honeymoon was over and life in earnest was beginning. They had rented an apartment, bought a car on time payments, purchased furniture on credit and were about to take on the responsibility of monthly payments for phone, electricity, and insurance.

This was quite unique for this Northern Englishman as he had left behind a debt free way of life in England, existing basically from one pay day to another. Now he was becoming Canadianized, much to his wife's displeasure. Joy had her heart set on returning to live in England and they had agreed to give Canada two years before returning. Gilley was determined to experience every adventure or misadventure that came his way while he had the chance.

CHAPTER 9

APARTMENT LIVING

WOSK'S DELIVERED THE NEW bedroom suite which consisted of a queen sized bed, side tables, a mirrored dresser, and a high boy set of drawers. Joy was well prepared for the queen sized bed. She had gone and purchased queen sized sheets and blankets as well as a bedspread. This was the first time Gilley had ever seen a queen sized bed and now he had the chance to sleep in one. What a luxury! Then there was the new TV with a stand (this was a black and white version. The couple had debated on a colour TV, but as they were just coming in, they thought they'd wait until the prices were more reasonable).

The next morning, Gilley jumped out of bed after the luxurious sleep on the queen sized bed. There was so much room that he thought at times, he was sleeping alone. As Gilley hopped into the shower he took the time to compare his new shower with the one at Jim and Veron's. And, hard to believe, it was better as it had more pressure. It gave a deep massaging effect and this increased the revitalizing effect giving an even better magical shower. On top of this benefit, at the end of the bathtub, there was a small window which opened up so one could see the Lions. These were all the way over behind North

Vancouver, which was over twenty miles away. These were part of the coastal range of mountains that gave Vancouver its spectacular setting. Gilley was so excited about this added feature he called Joy in to see it. "Come on into the bathroom and see this, Joy. It's magnificent."

"I'm not coming in there, you dirty old sod. It's too early in the morning for that," Joy called from under her covers.

Giggling to himself, Gilley got dressed and wondered around his new home. Drawing the drapes covering the balcony door, he looked out and was even more awestruck. He could see the snow covered peak of Mount Baker, which was well over one hundred miles away and was more than 11,000 feet high. Stepping out onto the balcony, Gilley stood there in the presence of this brilliant view. Once again he thanked his lucky stars which had brought him to Canada and this beautiful province of British Columbia. It was virtually impossible to express his experience in words. "Not only words," Gilley thought, "but in a photo as well for even that would not do justice to these vistas. Perhaps only an artist of great skill could convey the magnificence of these mountain vistas."

As Gilley and Joy settled into their new life as true newlyweds, Gilley was in for a big surprise. In England, the tradition was to have roast beef with all of the trimmings on Sundays, leftovers on Mondays, egg and chips on Tuesdays. On Wednesdays there would be a stew of some sort, Thursdays would be something like a soup and Fridays traditionally was fish and chips or Cornish pasties and chips and Saturdays was a free for all—lots of times it was Spam and chips. Everyone got what he or she could prepare. Now, Gilley was all prepared for the Canadian version of the English cuisine.

What a shock when he came home on Tuesday night to Chinese food, cooked by Joy none the less (not ordered in.) So much for tradition! It turned out that on Fridays, they would go to Shakey's Pizza Hut. This was convenient for Joy because on Fridays she worked later than she did during the week. The banks were open later in order to give their customers extra time to cash their pay cheques. This extended time allowed Gilley to have a couple of beers after work with the boys. By the time he arrived in New Westminster, Joy would almost be finished work then they and others from the bank would go out for pizza and their famous mojos (these were mashed potato patties, spiced and deep fried). This was also the first time Gilley had seen beer served in pitchers at the table. They would start off with at least two and go from there. On the odd time, Jim and Veron would pop in and join the crowd.

Saturday, when Joy had more time, Gilley never knew what to expect upon his arrival home from golf. Sometimes there would be Italian food, sometimes, Hungarian food, and at times a mixture of cultures that baffled him.

Sundays were more traditional, but most often this was because they ate at Jim and Veron's. Gilley was discovering that Joy was not only very versatile in her cooking talents but very good at whatever she prepared. What a pleasant surprise! Now also as a further surprise, Joy bought a deep frying pan so that Gilley could have his eggs and chips. This was by far his most favourite English dish aside from Chip Butties. (Now, Chip Butties were a delight for only the English.) They consisted of two slices of fresh bread, slathered with a good portion of real butter. The chips were then placed side by side on one slice of the bread. Then the fun began. Some people would put ketchup on them, others would add salt, pepper and vinegar-whatever came to mind. It was one's own creation and they were dangerously addictive.

Joy never ever really embraced this food, but secretly Gilley knew she could become a convert, but with her strong personality she would never let that weakness show. The other traditional dish Joy would cook was a corned beef casserole. Now this was one of Gilley's mother's favourite dishes and it consisted of canned corned beef layered with raw onions, sliced potatoes, and topped with a thin gravy that absorbed the delectable flavours of the ingredients underneath. The entire dish was then put in an oven and cooked until ready. This dish, standing alone was another huge favourite of his, however, if Joy had allowed him to, he would have made Butties out of this as he did in England.

Joy was starting to realize that Gilley was a Butties freak. He was known in England for placing anything that he found on his plate between two slices of bread. After he finished the broth from his soup he would even put the remainders in a sandwich. For some reason, Gilley could never figure out, this annoyed her tremendously. She could not understand why someone would place her delicious cooking between two slices of heavily buttered bread. Gilley tried to get around this habit of his by explaining when he was brought up, his parents taught him he could eat whatever he wanted to. They told him this was his body expressing its needs for nutrition. If he wanted a chocolate bar, then have one, if he wanted chips and eggs, go ahead, if he made Butties out of his meal, then all the better. He was following his body's lead.

Of course this concept was very foreign to the Canadian way of life and Joy, knowing fair well he would do this, tried her best to convert him to what she believed was a healthier way of eating. Joy would remove the temptation by cooking dishes where no bread was served. She even went to the extreme of not having bread in the house other than that meant for lunches (this being planned out carefully for the week, no extra slices were to be had.)

To top off her attempts, she used to serve different flavours of Jell-O. She would make Gilley guess what the flavour was or else he wouldn't be allowed to finish his bowl. This turned out to be quite the challenge for Gilley as there were many flavours of Jell-O that he was not familiar with. In addition to this; Joy would add some of her own flavour ideas. The whole idea was to teach Gilley to eat better. However, Gilley, used to getting his own way in this matter, resisted all attempts for reform for years to come but, in the end, Joy succeeded to some degree (or was it Gilley adapting to the Canadian way of life)?

Adding to their new lifestyle, Gilley and Joy decided to start entertaining their friends. Gilley invited Al and his girlfriend Sandy for dinner. It turned out Sandy was from Kent, England. She worked in Port Moody for an interior decorator. She was responsible for the drapes and other paraphernalia that went with window dressing.

Joy was anxious to show off her cooking talents along with the fact that it was the first time she was able to show off her dining room set. "This was a present from Aunt Mary, my Aunt," explained Gilley as they sat around with their drinks. "Aunt Mary lives in Northeast England in a place called Peterlee with her husband, Ernie. Ernie was a steam engineer working for the local colliery. One of the benefits was free coal so they always had a roaring fire. As most of the houses in England were not centrally heated, the main heat source was from the fire. They also had an Old English sheepdog. It would let you in the house but would not let you out. Different type of dog as Uncle Ernie used to say, 'The burglars will get in but they won't get out.'"

"Uncle Ernie enjoyed his beer and took us to the local workingman's club whenever we visited. This is where Aunt Mary introduced Joy to

Brandy and Baby Cham. Bloody hell, this was a very expensive drink and Joy seemed to enjoy it. It cost quite a bit more than our traditional "pint for Gilley and ½ a pint for Joy". Thank God Aunt Mary paid for it because I certainly wasn't going to. The cost for one Brandy and Baby Cham was more that the three beers together."

"Back at their house Uncle Ernie would always pour what he called "his favourite plonk" This was sherry in a chilled glass. He had come up with this idea after several visits to Eastern Canada where he swore that all of the drinks served there were served in chilled glasses, even the beer. He had been a Merchant Seaman in his younger years. Originally born in Australia, he had traveled the oceans extensively, but made his home in England. He spoke fondly of Canada and hoped one day he and Mary could come and visit. He had only been in Vancouver once and wasn't allowed shore leave. He couldn't get over the scenery and beautiful mountains. He remembered sailing under the Lion's Gate Bridge, seeing the large park called Stanley Park to the starboard side."

After a few drinks, dinner was served on their splendid set of china, first time in use. Joy had outdone herself as she served up the roast chicken, roast potatoes, peas, carrots, with a salad to begin with. The dessert was homemade apple pie with vanilla ice cream. The conversation centered on England and the experiences they remembered from their respective lives there.

Shortly after supper was finished, Veron phoned and invited them all over for a game of pool and of course more drinks. She had met Al before, but she was intrigued as to who Sandy was and could not wait to meet her. The foursome walked up to Jim and Veron's and enjoyed their hospitality. Upon leaving, Al said, "Gilley you certainly have taken to the Canadian way of life like a duck takes to water. By this time next week, you'll be joining the thousands of commuters by driving yourself to and from work."

Gilley was also settling into the different working environment. In Canada most of the Canadians could go to college for nine months and come out as a Draughtsman (Draftsman). In England one had to have five years recognized apprenticeship before one would be offered a junior draughtsman's position. Further education while being a junior was imperative and even this would not make him a senior Draughtsman in England. It would take an additional five years of practicing so that by the age of thirty, he would automatically become a senior draftsman and receive the corresponding wage.

In BC, the process of becoming a draughtsman was not as clear cut. Often it would take ten years for a person to obtain the necessary hours needed to become a Journeyman. This was because the work was often seasonal or sporadic. There were many things to take into consideration and Gilley struggled to make sense of it all. But one thing he found out was the Canadian was very versatile in all Engineering aspects, if not as well groomed as the English. Survival here was the name of the game. You took any job to make it through.

In addition, there was no time for training in the finer aspects of Engineering as finding work was the important thing. Vancouver was not a big industrial center. Most of the industries were either in or associated with mining, forestry (logging, sawmills and pulp and paper) and of course fishing. As part of the marine activity, ship building and repair made up a small part of the market. Many tradesmen had to travel far afield if they wanted to complete their apprenticeship in a short span of time. Many of them found other occupations on the way which gave them great experience and a variety of skills. No wonder, some of these Canadian men were well into their twenties or even older before completing the necessary requirements for obtaining their Journeyman ship.

Swann Winches was one of the few companies who could offer continuous employment and apprenticeships. This was due to the fact they were a well established and versatile winch company serving a growing part of the fishing industry as well as serving other marine and industrial areas.

Gilley was absolutely amazed at the number of different nationalities employed by Swann's. He had never met the huge variety of people one company would actually employ. There were Germans, Italians, Scots, Greek, Spanish, Englishmen and of course Canadians. How could all of these people get along so well, speaking all of the different languages and having all of the different cultural backgrounds? Gilley discovered the bridge between all of these men was the common language of Engineering and the trades that went with it. This brought everyone together as all over the world, drawings and numbers were the same. This was absolutely incredible. He would not have believed it if he hadn't seen it for himself.

These varied cultures brought another challenge to Gilley. Not only did he have to adapt to Joy's culinary explorations around the world for dinner, but he came to experience the many different foods these various cultures offered at lunchtime as well. He tasted sauerkraut, goulash, a variety of pastas and sauces and Souvlaki. Of course, Gilley's favourite was sausages whatever nationality! Then there were the many, many different breads from around the world. What a cultural shift! At Swann's everyone took all this in stride and adopted what worked without any friction. This too amazed Gilley.

There was a good sense of humor and harmony between everyone. Drawing offices were well known for playing pranks and Swann's was no different For example, there was the time when one of the winches had the shape of a tank. The drawing office designed a turret cut from cardboard and found a long, cardboard tube which looked like a gun barrel. After all of the employees had left that night, this devious lot put the plan into action. They changed the winch into a German Panzer with the corresponding markings.

The following morning all hell broke loose in the assembly shop. One of the Germans took offense to the other German and that other took offense to him. The whole shop was in uproar and as Gilley entered the drawing office he found everyone laughing aloud and it was contagious. Gilley said, "There's no one laughing in the shop, Lads. I think it's gone past funny. All hell is popping loose in the shop."

Suddenly, the door sprung open and in came Bill Robbins, the works manager. "I think you boys have some answering to do here today." He made them all march out and apologize to the two Germans and all of the others. The drawing department was quite humiliated; as they had no idea what damage this prank would cause. In their defense, Bill Robbins indicated the other department had it coming as often the drawing department took a lot of ribbing and ridicule. The comment, "Whose responsible for this cartoon drawing?" was leveled at them. Because this department was under a lot of pressure, their creative thinking often led them to bizarre humor. In a few days things settled down and returned to normal. However, within the department, a pact was made. "Next time no one would know who did it."

The world was expanding its search for oil in the North Sea and other seas. There was a great demand for off shore supply vessels as these ships were needed to move the oil rigs into position and supply them with the necessary machinery and equipment. The Canadian government saw this opportunity to entice foreign investments to the shipbuilding yards within the Vancouver area that were experienced in building similar vessels for the tug boat industry. This came in the form of a federally assisted shipbuilding fund directed at creating work opportunities in this area.

Swann's was seen as a vital part of this endeavor as they specialized in marine deck equipment. They had offices in Singapore and Halifax and would need to expand to take advantage of this opportunity. At the same time a company in Sidney, Australia called Beck and Jonas wanted to represent Swann's in Australia.

With all of this happening, the Vancouver operation needed to expand their premises. The Canadian Wire Company next door was moving and this building was up for sale or lease. It was the perfect solution. This building would more than suit the needs of Swann's, however Swann's would have to move fast in order to take advantage of these opportunities. An investor was needed. One of the potential partners was a company called ABC Packaging. They were heavily into salmon fishing for their canning operations with their fleets working out of Vancouver. They were also looking to expand and diversify so the joining of these two companies seemed to be a natural next step.

Gilley realized that he would need to do some homework on the winch industry and on hydraulics as most of the winches were driven hydraulically, (and hydraulics was not his strongest point). One of the supply companies to Swann's was a company called Avis engineering. There was an English salesman called Brian Shoesmith (he was from Liverpool) who supplied Sunstrand hydraulic pumps. Brian took a bit of a liking to Gilley and presented him with three practical books on hydraulics as a gift along with many other hydraulic references to help Gilley in his homework.

Eventually, Gilley became quite conversant with the hydraulic business of that time period. He read a lot about gear design, welding techniques, pneumatics—he would study anything that pertained to that field. He saw an opportunity in Swann's to go around the world to places such as Singapore and Australia and he also saw the potential of becoming an Overseas Sales representative like he had dreamed of being. This could be his opportunity.

The job future looked very bright. This would please Gilley's parents who were soon to arrive to assess their son's new life in Canada. Time was approaching a little bit faster than he had expected. Joy and Gilley had decided a trip around BC would combine the need for catching up on their relationship along with the opportunity for his parents to see the province. Joy, typically, was ahead of schedule. Long before they arrived, she had the trip around BC all planned out. First they would go up to Williams Lake, stopping there to break up the long journey and then carrying onto Prince George to visit Joy's Uncle Paul and stay overnight. On the way back south they would stop at Barkerville (this was a ghost town from the gold rush days). From there, they would go into Kamloops and stay overnight. From Kamloops, they would head to Penticton to a place where Joy, her sisters and parents had spent many a summer holiday. This place was called El Rancho and because it was so beautiful, the travelers would stay over a couple of nights before heading to home base through the Hope-Princeton Highway. This trip was approximately 1300 miles. This was unheard of in Gilley's world. In England, Gilley wouldn't travel that far in a year let alone in just a week.

Gilley was a bit anxious, remembering English cars, in particular his Vauxhall Victor. He decided to talk to Jim and he was glad he did. Anxiety was removed when Jim explained to Gilley that most North American cars are designed to travel many, many miles safely and soundly. Gilley explained to Jim that if you got from Newcastle to London and back without a hiccup or a hitch, it was a bit of a miracle. Gilley reminded Jim of the time they all first met and when he drove Jim and Veron all over the north east of England in his 1964 Victor. This included the Lake District, the Cheviots, Bamborough and the coastline down to Tynemouth. This was a trip of approximately 200 miles.

"Your car went the entire trip without one hiccup", said Jim.

"Well," said Gilley, "I have to admit I did some minor tune-ups at nighttime so things would run smoothly during the day. The time we came to see you off to Canada at your sister's place in Teddington, near London, I did a full tune-up before I left and by the time I got back to Newcastle, with a little bit tinkering here and there, we managed to get back with only a few minor hiccups. I'll tell you all about them one day as Joy won't let me forget."

Jim said, "You'll have no problem with that Duster. When I was working for the government in the early fifties, I did many, many miles around the province where most roads were just gravel and I didn't have any problems. Cars built in North America are built to handle long journeys and they stand up well to the challenges presented by the roads here. I want to stress that you have to do the normal tune-ups, keep brakes and tires regularly maintained and your oil changed. Doing this maintenance along with your mechanical knowledge and the skills you have shown us around here, you should have no problems wherever you go."

Gilley, thinking back to his trip to Whistler with Brian, acknowledged that one wouldn't want to break down just anywhere. One never knew what animals one could encounter. Answering this question, Jim said, "Yes, in my many years of driving, I have encountered a number of animals especially at night or first thing in the morning. They are usually grazing or looking for the nearest watering hole. You'll really enjoy this trip Gilley and your parents will be quite entertained."

Along with Gilley's parents, Jim's sister, Eunice and her husband Edmond would be arriving in August, just before Gilley's parents would be leaving. Eunice was a very interesting woman. She should have been on the stage. She was always bubbling with happiness and never frightened to tell a good joke, no matter what company she was in. This might have been accounted for by the fact that their father was an actor. She was also very hospitable and generous. Nothing was ever too much for her. There were four of them in the family-Jim, Peggy, Eunice and Lillibet (who had died at a young age). Eunice just loved Jim, who was her older brother (and the only male in the family).

Edmond was Polish and had immigrated to England just after the Second World War. He told a very interesting story about apples. He just loved apples because he claimed one had saved his life. Apparently, during the war, his unit was staying overnight in a barn on the Polish-German border. He spotted this delicious looking apple that was still left on the tree. Of course, he didn't want anyone else to know about it or he may lose it or have to share, so he snuck out and ate it not knowing it was bad. During the night, he had to leave the barn as he had a bad stomachache. While attending to business, a bomb flew through the air and blew up the barn and unfortunately, all of the company. He had great difficulty telling this story, but it was easy for him to love apples, as an apple saved his life. Unfortunately, that situation devastated him for the rest of the war and still had power over him even till today.

Eunice and Edmond lived in a place called Ashington in Sussex. It was quaint little house, called Tetra, and built by Edmond. The house included a hairdressing salon from which Eunice plied her trade and downstairs was a suite ready for Jim' and Eunice's mother to move into when she sold her property in Teddington. Including these rooms was no small feat as the property upon which Edmond could build was quite small. He had managed to lay the entire house out so that every square inch of space was utilized to its fullest. This even included a well-manicured back yard, overlooking Edmond's favourite place where he spent most of his spare time concocting all sorts of drinks along with a fine selection of wine. They also had a small little dog called Pepe, which was spoiled to ribbons, as they had no children. Pepe was their substitute child.

Before Gilley immigrated to Canada, Joy and he stayed with Eunice and Edmond for a few days before flying out from Stansted to Canada. It was one of the handiest places to have as it was just a stone's throw away from the neighborhood pub called the Red Lion.

Given all of this company what with his parents first and then Eunice and Edmond, Gilley was anticipating a very busy summer playing tour guide. He was really looking forward to seeing his parents as he'd been a bit homesick and he certainly wanted to see Eunice and Edmond as they were lots of fun. However, Gilley still had to juggle working and studying for future potential opportunities. He knew he could do it, but wasn't sure exactly how.

Sitting in their apartment, Gilley and Joy appreciated their own place and Gilley often said to Joy, "You know, this is the only place that I've ever really had that's truly my own and where you and I can have a little privacy surrounded with our own possessions. We can truly just sit and relax and appreciate what we've achieved."

The six weeks that were left before Mom and Dad arrived just flew by. Both Joy and Gilley were working hard and saving up for these visits. They were also painting, cleaning, decorating, shopping and stocking the bar in anticipation. Then "Boom"—guests were here.

CHAPTER 10

THEY FINALLY ARRIVE

THE DAY OF HIS parents' arrival finally came. Gilley was a bit concerned as his mother, Nellie who was 66, had never flow before and his father who was 72, (even though he considered himself a seasoned flyer, having flown back and forth from Newcastle to Ireland) were on the longest flight of their lives. It was nine hours from Prestwick to Vancouver. Having just accomplished this feat not long ago, Gilley knew the strain they would be under. (Thank God they were coming into Canada and not the United States of America). Gilley's brother Neil had driven them to the airport to support them as far as possible and now it would be up to him, at this end, to pick them up and make sure they were cared for during their big adventure.

Gilley and Joy were at the airport with time to spare. They were standing at the Arrivals Area and were able to watch Mother and Father, through the television monitor, as they cleared Customs. Gilley could see they were very tired as Father struggled with the baggage cart full to the brim. They spotted their son and daughter in law and the British reserve crumbled as tears ran down their cheeks. Father said, "Take over this bloody cart. I hope we aren't going home with as much as we came with."

Nellie's first words were, "I could do with a good cup of tea. The stuff they call tea on the airlines is like dishwater. Nothing to it and it makes me want to throw up." However, Dad didn't have any disagreement with the free drinks.

Gilley said, "Well, Mother, you'll have to wait until we get to Jim and Veron's. Then you'll have a bracing cup of tea. It's about 40 minutes. I'm going to get the car and load up the luggage." No sooner had they set off for New Westminster, than Nellie was asleep as normal. She was the best forty-winker that Gilley had ever known. In England, she could get on the bus at one stop, be asleep before the next stop and be awake again for her stop. Jack, on the other hand couldn't stop asking questions.

Arriving at Jim and Veron's, it didn't take Veron long to have a good English cup of tea made for Gilley's parents. She served this down in the bar as Jim served up beers and drinks for the rest. Veron also provided a light snack as well for all. Jack, seeing the drinks served, took Jim aside and asked, "Could I have a wee nip of Scotch in here. It's been a long flight and tea at this time of day, needs a bite."

Veron, noticing this, said, "Ah hah, now I know where Gilley gets his drinking habits from."

After a short visit, the four of them headed for the apartment. Arriving there, it didn't take Nellie and Jack long to get settled in. They were quite impressed with the apartment and their bedroom. After another cup of tea, Nellie declared she had to distribute the presents before anything else took place. First of all, there were duty free cigarettes and whiskey, at which Nellie exclaimed that, since she was a tea-totaler and non-smoker, there were more cigarettes and whiskey for everyone else. (Joy and Gilley suspected Nellie had her bottle of port hidden somewhere). Then there came the presents from the rest of the family. They filled the coffee table.

With the gift giving out of the way, Gilley knew it was important to tell his parents some of the differences they would encounter during their first days in British Columbia as they would be spending the next few days alone, what with Joy and Gilley having to work. There were things to explain, like the many stations on the TV that were free; the telephone that was free to use anytime; the electrical outlets that didn't have switches on them like in England; the different door locks that locked themselves if you weren't careful and many other small things.

Gilley's father found another difference immediately. The toilet water was blue here when you flushed. Gilley, having his father on, said, "The reason why the water is blue, is so that you can distinguish it between drinking water and toilet water." Jack, being tired, thought that was a hell of an idea. It made sense to him. Why have good water just to flush things away? Gilley realized that Jack had bought into the joke. He called his friends the next day and got everyone to add the sanitizing pellets into their toilet tank so that everywhere was on the same page. Jim and Veron were especially delighted to participate in the joke.

The next few days provided quite a lot of amusements as Gilley's parents were intrigued with the new country's electrical gadgets especially the little plugs. In England, they had these huge plugs with a switch at the receptacle. This is an on-off switch for safety as in Europe the voltage is twice of that of Canada and the US. Also there was a lot of intrigue with the door lock system.

The one that was the most fascinating was the door handle that could be pushed in and locked and to release, one just had to turn the handle back. Some of the old ones, of course got a bit tricky, providing some frustration and much hilarity. It took Gilley himself quite a while to get onto the different methods of locking through the door handle. There were the little turnkey door handles, such as was common for bathroom doors, which became rather interesting as they were the most difficult to figure out. They also could be locked unintentionally. This created no end of frustration, confusion and eventually, humor, as the parents could not figure out how to get a key to work with these. When they finally were able to lock the damn thing, they could not get them open. It was fascinating to find out how many different ways people have invented to lock one in or out of one's' home (or bath room). The saving thing with the bathroom was there was often a small hole in the outside door handle that one could poke with a pin and unlock the door in the event of an emergency.

Another fascinating thing was the TV. There were so many stations available. There were not these many at home. England, at that time only had two stations. There was ITV, which had the commercials strategically placed between segments of shows and then there was the BBC, which was commercial free. That was all there was for entertainment. Plus the fact that English TV finished at 12:00 AM.

Often, neither channel began broadcasting until 9:00 AM and then shut down during the afternoons for a few hours.

Here in Canada, there were at least 12 different stations available to those in British Columbia. There were three that were Canadian based and the rest originated in the USA. Most of them would broadcast from 6:00 AM until at least 12:00 AM and a few went on until 4:00 AM. The only station that did not have commercials and advertisements was the one out of Seattle called PBS or the Public Broadcasting Station. This was supported by business sponsors, public funding and donations from the viewers raised through telethons.

Both parents were amazed at the variety that could be watched, but were infuriated by the breaks for advertising that came so frequently they found it hard to follow the storyline. They hardly had time to make a cup of tea before the show started again. These commercials were of varying lengths and unpredictable in their timing.

The other one thing was the telephone. It was amazing at how frequently it would ring and how frequently it was used. As a matter of fact, both parents commented that the telephone seemed to take precedence over most things and they felt it was an intrusion on their privacy. Of course, they didn't have a telephone in their flat (apartment). As a matter of fact in England, only about one in twenty families had a phone. In the event of an emergency, the people who were friends of the family with the telephone were allowed incoming and outgoing calls. (Of course, all outgoing calls cost the users money.)

Gilley and Joy explained there was just one small flat fee per month here in BC for the use of the telephone for all local calls and there was a charge for long distance. Once Gilley's parents understood this, one couldn't get them off the phone. It was such a novelty they called everyone even if there wasn't much to chat about. They called Joy, Jim, and Gilley at work and Veron at home. Then there also was whoever else would give out their phone number. It got so bad the phone was always busy no matter what time of day it was.

Just when Gilley and Joy thought Nellie and Jack had gotten the hang of everything, Jack said to Gilley, "You must be a dirty bugger."

Gilley, taken aback said, "Why is that?"

Jack replied, "I've noticed that every morning you get up and have a shower. You wouldn't have a bath in England like that every day."

"Ah", said Gilley finally understanding, "Dad, this is a magical shower."

"What do you mean a 'magical shower'"?

"I wrote to you about this. You get up in the morning feeling groggy and tired, then have a shower and suddenly you feel alive again."

"No wonder with all the bloody beer you two drink," interrupted Jack.

"Once you step into this shower," continued Gilley, "You feel so alive and invigorated. It's irresistible. You have to try one dad."

"I don't know about that," hesitated Jack.

Gilley's mom piped up, "I'd like to have a go at that right now."

"Nah, nah, I'll have one first," demanded Jack. "I have to make sure it's safe for you."

Gilley had to instruct his father how to take a shower in Canada. Of course it was very important that one set the temperature correctly as one did not want to peel one's skin off with the hot water. Then the next step was the proper way to stand so that one did not slip and fall on the suds from the soap. After this experience was over for Jack, he came out properly dressed, tie and everything on, and expressed great pleasure and approval of the new experience. At this point, Nellie wanted to try this new experience. This time Joy gave the instructions to Nellie and also contributed a bathrobe for her to don after the experience. (It was time to settle down to watch a bit of telly). Joy's greatest contribution to Nellie's experience was the use of a shower cap to protect her hair.

Much to Gilley's surprise, telly did not follow that evening. Instead a vigorous dialogue on the pros and cons of shower versus bathing took over the evening entertainment. Showering had the advantage of washing away the grime while bathing actually caused one to sit in it for a period of time. Showering took less time, but did not provide the relaxation of bathing which was to Joy's liking, as she preferred to bath instead of shower. Even though his parents enjoyed the showering experience, they decided to stay with their one bath per week, needed or not. It just did not make sense to become used to a convenience one could not transfer home to England.

At this point in the discussion, a knock came at the door and in came Jim and Veron for a drink. After drinks were served, the bath/ shower discussion continued. Of course, Jim was an advocate for the bathing experience as he read his book every night for at least half an hour (or so) as he bathed. Veron was also a bathing advocate, but she admitted that when she was in a hurry, she would have a quick shower. They all agreed that it was more efficient for time and cleansing of one's self as well as a great water saver (showering took about one third of the water). "Yeah," said Gilley, "That's why showering is great for the man on the move."

The reason Jim and Veron had come round was to wish the four of them a good journey as tomorrow was the start of the big trip through British Columbia. Jim told the new comers that during this trip, they would only see a small part of this vast province. It would be an important part, but not close to the extent of what could be seen. He had traveled the province in the days he had worked for the government, going to the smallest towns and outposts. And he just wanted to reassure them that today's traveling was a hell of a lot better and safer than the gravel roads he had traveled in his days.

Jim decided to loan Gilley his famous Pentax camera as he was a fanatical photographer and wanted some good photographs of their trip. Gilley was flattered to have this loan and at the same time he was concerned. He knew the value Jim placed on this piece of equipment and he wasn't sure he wanted the responsibility. Jim insisted as they were going to undertake a similar trip to the one planned for Eunice and Edmond once they arrived from England. It would be nice for them to have photos of where they were traveling to.

Near the end of the evening, the discussion turned to the length of the trip. Nellie was concerned about Jack as he was a diabetic whose condition was controlled by diet alone. She informed them it was important he not go longer than two hours without something to eat or drink. Nellie, being the responsible caretaker she was and being in charge of his eating schedule had planned to take snacks and refreshments with them in the car. Joy informed her that this was not necessary as in spite of the vastness of the country, there would be ample opportunity to stop for refreshments along the way to meet this need. Having said this, Joy also said it was convenient to have some refreshing drinks for the in between spots along the journey. With this in mind, Joy packed a cooler with snacks and chilled beverages, including beer for those who wanted some.

The following day the party started off on Trans Canada Highway Number 1 heading east. Their first stop was Hope at about 11:00 AM. It was a great place for an early lunch. The salad Jack ordered was so big, he thought he'd become a rabbit if he ate it all. Nellie and Jack couldn't get over the size of the portions which were served and the small price charged for this huge amount.

They continued up the Fraser Canyon Highway with their planned destination of Williams Lake. This was at least five hours from Hope without stopping. However, there was a planned stop at Hell's Gate.

As they set out from Hope, along the Fraser Canyon Highway, Gilley, Jack and Nellie couldn't get over the way the mountains encased the Fraser River as it came out of the Fraser Canyon. This was old hat to Joy as she and her parents had traveled this way several times on their summer vacations. The party from England had been told the Fraser Canyon was a tremendous drive with spectacular views and was also a tremendous feat of engineering. How the roads and railway lines were developed with the obvious challenges the terrain presented to the pioneers in bygone days had been overcome in ingenious ways.

Hell's Gate was a "must stop". This was another feat of engineering to allow the salmon to get back to their spawning grounds as the turbulent waters of that area were beyond anyone's imagination. The turbulent waters were not a natural occurrence, but were caused by the construction of the railway line. The explosions used to clear the way for the lines had fallen into the Fraser River creating this narrow passageway and preventing the salmon from migrating to their spawning grounds. The railway companies, recognizing the importance of salmon as a natural resource for all concerned, focused their energies on building a method for the salmon to continue their migration. They built a fish ladder which took many years to construct due to the water flowing through this narrow gap at such a great velocity. During this time period, while the gate was being built, many of the salmon were manually transported around the construction to the other side so that they could continue onto their destination.

The cable ride down to the Gate was a great adventure for all. At first, Joy was very apprehensive about going in the cable car, but wasn't to be outdone by Gilley's Mother as this was a first experience for them all. After they got to the bottom, a cup of tea was in order. (A beer would have been better.) After spending an hour looking at all of the different views of the rapids as well as the construction of the fish ladders, they got back onto the cable car. Going up did have everyone a little concerned, as it looked steeper from that angle than it did going down. It felt as if they were going upwards vertically.

The next portion of the drive was more fascinating than previous to Hell's Gate, as they twisted and wound along the mighty Fraser, going through tunnels and along the edges of the cliffs. There were times that no one, including the driver, Gilley, could look over the edge as it was so steep. The views were astronomical and the vastness of this part of the country was something they had never seen before. Added to this was the sight of miles of railway that traveled on the other side of the river together with trains longer than they had seen before. The length of each train amazed everyone. The railway bed was even narrower than the roadbed and at times, it looked as if the train, speeding along the track, might tumble into the churning river. This had actually happened many times in the past. One could see the snow sheds which were built to protect the railway lines during the winter. The entire sight appeared very hazardous.

Cache Creek was the next stop. Not paying attention to the time, they had to stop for gas and another cup of tea. As soon as they pulled up to the station, an attendant ran out and began filling up the tank. Not only did he do that, but he cleaned the windows, front and back, checked the oil and the window washing fluid and also cleaned the headlights. This was amazing. One would never get this type of service in England. Gilley's response was, "The only time I haven't gotten this type of service was at the Econo Station in New Westminster, waiting like a dummy for someone to serve me. I didn't realize they had changed to self-serve. And it's the only one I've ever run into it here. Maybe we'll find some more on our journey." Right next to the gas station was a little café. Inside, the English travelers enjoyed their cup of tea with crackers and cheese, while their hosts enjoyed a well deserved beer with their snack.

The next stop was Williams Lake where supper was to be had. William's Lake was known for its stampede and unfortunately, they arrived at just the wrong time and could not experience this cultural event. In spite of this, the town was busy and interesting for all concerned as they drove through the streets. There were many locals dressed in their traditional costumes and numbers of cowboys and cowgirls strutting down the streets in their finest western wear. The travelers wished they could spend more time here experiencing the Wild, Wild West.

As they were all tired and hungry, Joy suggested they stop at the A & W Drive-in as the meal would be served more quickly than in a restaurant. After all, they had to get to Prince George for the night. She explained they would be able to enjoy a truly North American experience—the drive-in meal consisting of the famous hamburger and French fries. Then there was the A&W legendary root beer. Since Nellie and Jack had never seen a drive-in they obviously didn't know what to do. Joy explained how to proceed. One of the highlights was watching the waiter carry trays, covered with food and drinks to the various cars. The next part of the entertainment was watching as he or she slid them onto the car windows. The idea was that the inhabitants of the car would roll the window down to about 4 inches above the frame. The waiter/waitress would hang the tray onto the window and collect the money. Once the meal was finished, the lights would go on and they would come and take the trays away. Gilley wondered how he was going to manage with the Duster as it only had windows that opened in the front of the car.

Fortunately, the windows that did open were big enough so the waiter could hang two trays onto them. This solved the problem. The next problem was passing the food to the back seat. The headrests on the front seats were permanently raised and the food had to go through a small space between the two headrests. Nellie and Jack were very good sports about it thoroughly enjoying their first Canadian hamburger and fries. Nellie said, "Well, I suppose, Joy, this is the real Canadian hamburger, not the one you were disgusted with at the Whimpy's Bar in England."

Joy exclaimed, "You'll find this type of food in Canada a lot more palatable than it is in England."

At that remark, Nellie immediately responded, "This is a good hamburger. I can understand now why you didn't like the ones you had in England. What do you think Jack?" Jack was buried up to his eyes in food and wrappers. As Joy and Gilley looked in the rear view mirror at his parents, all they could see was two tops of heads and fingers holding the burgers. Once in a while, they could make out eyes and nodding of the heads as they thoroughly enjoyed this very Canadian custom.

Nellie was not to be out done though. She had conceded to the food, but she was not about to concede to the tea. "The food here in Canada is very good, but I've yet to have a good cup of tea other than you and Veron served to us." As they ate their meal, it was just like watching a Punch and Judy show as they devoured their food and drink, bobbing up and down.

Finding the washrooms was another treat. It was a good job Joy was around to assist Nellie. One had to obtain the key from the carhop and then go around to the back of the building. Of course in England, they weren't called washrooms. They were generally called toilets with the words indicating "Gentlemen" and "Ladies" under their corresponding entrances.

By now it was getting close to eight o'clock and they were running behind schedule and the reservation for the motel would not be held much longer. Joy decided the best course of action was to call Uncle Paul and advise him of the delay, asking his advice. It would be approximately an hour and a half to Prince George having the travelers arrive at approximately ten thirty. "Don't worry", said Uncle Paul, "We don't go to bed early as a rule, so you'll not be keeping us up, so the best thing would be to stay with us instead and cancel the motel."

As they traveled north, it seemed to get lighter instead of darker as they expected. This had been discussed but never experienced by the English travelers. So, in essence it never seemed to get dark as they neared Uncle Paul's. Another very noticeable thing happened as they approached Prince George. The smell! It was the vilest smell they had ever encountered. Joy said, "I told you, Prince George is a stinky town. It's due to the pulp mills here. I think it's something to do with the chemicals they use to make paper."

Jack said, "Well, in Newcastle they say 'Where there's muck there's money' and I bet here in Prince George, they say "Where's there's smell there's money." Eventually, they arrived at Paul's and were welcomed by Grace and the two children, Kenny and Gwen. As this was happening, Paul opened four beers and Joy asked, "Do you have a kettle, Grace, I have brought tea bags for Nellie and Jack. They are just dying for a good cup of tea."

"Good job you did, Joy, as we don't drink tea," replied Grace. While everybody sat down and enjoyed a visit, tea and beer, Grace had prepared the rooms for her guests. The privacy of one bedroom was given to Nellie and Jack, while in the basement Gilley and Joy were shown to the hide-away bed. That night everyone slept like logs.

The next morning dawned early and Gilley was in demand right away. Kenny and Gwen wanted to play with him right off the bat. Kids just seemed drawn to him. Kenny decided cowboys and Indians was the name of the game. So Gilley with his toy gun charged around the house chasing the kids. He was in his element. The adults sat drinking their tea, and coffee. They were not in the mood to join in the fun (if that was what it was called so early in the morning.) Gilley's Mom and Dad knew that Gilley always played with the kids. This was a new side of her husband for Joy and she wasn't sure what to make of it. She decided that it might not be proper. "Don't excite those kids, get up here and have some breakfast, "she ordered to which Gilley gratefully acquiesced as, even though he didn't want to admit it, was longing for his first cup of tea too.

The plan for the day was to visit some more and rest a bit, then to be on the road again by about 11:00 AM as the next stop was Barkerville. This was about a three-hour drive away. Paul advised Gilley that the road from the main town, Quesnel to Barkerville was nothing but a dirt road and that it could be very bumpy and slow. As a matter of fact, the time spent in Barkerville would be shorter than the drive into it. "Make sure you stop at the Chinese graveyard on your way in. This is a very interesting part of the sightseeing tour. It's difficult to see it on your way out as the angle of the road prevents one from seeing the turn off to it and its not well signed."

By 11:00 AM, they were on the road again. The drive between Prince George to Quesnel was rather boring as tall trees on either side bordered the highway. What amazed the Brits was the shear abundance of trees no matter where they looked. They couldn't believe the wealth of this province just in trees alone. Entering the road to Barkerville—it was just as bumpy as Paul had predicted. Potholes were numerous. Gilley had to slow right down to a crawl in many places so as to not damage his new car.

Amazingly, they did not encounter any other vehicles on the road. Joy wondered if they had taken the wrong road. As they rounded a bend, they came to the Chinese graveyard (confirming that Gilley was on track after all). Everyone got out of the car and inspected the graves. They were amazed at how young the people were when they had passed away. Some of the graves had been opened up and the remains had been removed by the relatives—perhaps back to their ancestral home. There weren't any signs or other bits of information available to let the group know much more than their eyes could see. In many ways, it was a little melancholy. Hopefully, in the main part of Barkerville, there would be more information about the people who had inhabited this land.

At the main gate into Barkerville, there was a nominal charge of a dollar per person. They were given a small flyer with a bit of the background on the town. There was a bit of history on Billy Barker himself and the great fire that was there. Most of the buildings were still boarded up. The church was open, as was the theatre and a few shops plus the Chinese laundry. The shaft of where the great mother lode was discovered was open for viewing as well. At that time, there were still few residents of Barkerville. These people were caretakers of the remnants of the town during the wintertime as the town was only open to the public from May through to September.

It was now time for Gilley to take some more photographs with his Father-in-law's Pentax. As he snapped away, there was a peculiar sound and he discovered that the picture counter was not advancing. "Oh—oh," he thought, "Should I tell everyone that something is wrong, or should I keep it a secret? Joy would be very upset that I might have broken her father's camera." Gilley decided that discretion was the better part of valor. He shot away as though nothing was wrong. Time was getting on and the rest of the drive to Kamloops would take about three to four hours including the stops for tea etc. But before leaving Barkerville a cup of tea is definitely needed. There was no beer to be had so it was tea for all, how refreshing.

As they left Barkerville, Nellie and Jack were all conversation. They were quite impressed at the wildness of the town and how people had lived in this country. It became clear why people had died early as they lived under extreme conditions like living in tents even during the winter and the very difficult working conditions. This is not to mention the lack of a balanced diet and proper hygiene along with the medical care available in more civilized, populated cities of that time. They were amazed how, this far from civilization, people could come up to the wilderness and actually find gold. At one time, Barkerville had four and five thousand people. And just outside Barkerville was a place called Wells which was another mining community. There just wasn't time to stop and see other sights. It was apparent this whole area had been full of gold and silver mines. Gilley would be back.

After about two hours, it was time to leave if they were to make their next destination before dark. They passed markers labeled 112 Mile House, 110 Mile House, 103 Mile House etc. These marked the distances between Yale and Quesnel and were rest stops for the miners. There was a 100 Mile House, which was largest in comparison to the other stops. This was a must stop for tea place. Time was proceeding so the stop was short. They had to push on in order to get to Kamloops before 8:00 PM. The motel they had booked would be waiting for them.

Driving south towards Kamloops, they experienced the opposite effect of the drive north. It became darker more quickly as the sun lowered in the sky. It showered wonderful red and pink streaks in the skies and across the road. It coated the trees with little flickers of light and touching the few clouds with orange.

Arriving in Kamloops at about 8:30 PM, the night's air was still hot and humid. This was the place where the two rivers met, the Thompson and the Fraser. The landscape was very different from what they had left. The scenery was like arriving in some place where Indians and Cowboys roamed in the movies. Gilley and his parents were amazed at how, in such a short space of time, the countryside had changed so dramatically. And Nellie kept saying, "I'm sure I'm going to see an Indian and a cowboy soon." Gilley felt the same way too. As they arrived at the motel, Gilley began to realize what Joy had meant when she kept saying in England, "You don't have any Motels here, just hotels?" Of course a motel was a new experience for Jack and Nellie also.

Joy explained that motels could have originated from what were called station houses, which had been bunkhouses. These bunkhouses were places where the stagecoach drivers would rest themselves while the operator of the station would feed and rest the horses (or perhaps supply fresh horses) for the continuing journey. The drivers would stay overnight in the bunkhouse with their coaches parked out front so that they could watch them or work on any minor repairs that might be needed. The passengers would go into the big comfortable, station house for the night.

At a motel, people just paid at the office for the privilege of sleeping and washing as people would start early in the morning creating no inconvenience to any of the other tenants. Joy had booked this motel ahead of time. She had chosen this one as it featured two rooms that had an adjoining door just for families. It didn't look like the best accommodation on the outside, yet when they opened the door, it was huge inside and Nellie and Jack commented, "This is bigger than our house in England."

Gilley added, "There is a huge bath and a shower. It's time for a shower after this day and then we'll go out and have something to eat." Everyone happily agreed with this plan.

The following day brought another climate and geographical change as they headed towards the Okanagan. Kamloops was very dry and arid and as they headed south east the landscape became greener and more treed. As they approached the Vernon area, they could see countless orchards. Nellie asked what type of fruit was grown in this area. Joy responded, "You name it, they grow it: peaches, apricots, cherries of many varieties, apples and many types of vegetables. Tomatoes are especially good in this area. We'll stop at a road side stand and buy some fruit so you can sample fruit directly from the trees."

The next dramatic sight was Lake Okanagan. Joy, explaining this lake to the newcomers told them the lake stretches for miles and is a huge contrast with the semi arid country-side. It also has similar characteristics to Lock Ness, as it is famous for the Ogopogo monster whereas Lock Ness has Nessy. The Ogopogo supposedly lives on the bottom on the lake. Ogopogo dates back to the First Nations people arriving in this area. This snake like creature has been around for hundreds of years, and the sightings still continue. Ogopogo has become part of BC folklore and is a protected species under the provincial wildlife act.

This creature is spotted once or twice a season at least. As Jack said, "This Lake must be ten times the size of Loch Ness. I sure hope the monster isn't ten times the size of Nessy." The colour of Okanagan Lake is the beautiful bluey-green. For a long time, the road wound alongside the lake and the tourists were captivated by the numerous watercraft they saw plying the waters. It was interesting as the countryside was often dry, even dessert like, but the lake was blue, clear and refreshing to look at.

Eventually, the troupe came to the city of Kelowna. This city is build at a narrowing of the lake with a floating bridge linking both sides of the town. A floating bridge was another new sight for the Brits. As there was a lot of traffic on the east bank of Kelowna, the party decided to stop further along to their customary cup of tea. They came to a quaint town called Peachland and nice looking roadside restaurant. This did the trick. Again, it was tea all around as the restaurant wasn't licensed to serve alcohol. Before heading out again, they stopped at a roadside fruit stand. This fascinated Nellie, Jack and Gilley. The fruit and vegetables were laid out in boxes and on shelves with signs indicating the price per pound as well as the price per box. They had never seen such a variety of produce in one place.

Refreshed again, the party carried on travelling along Highway 97 which continued beside the lake. Eventually the road climbed up and began to drop dramatically down into Penticton. Joy explained this town was between two large lakes and was a popular place for the teenagers to come for summer vacation to camp and swim. Lake Okanagan is on one side and Skaha Lake borders the other side. This lake was much smaller and its claim to fame was its wonderful beaches and camping resorts. Camping, Joy explained, is a wide-spread and favourite activity for many families. Coming to a place like Skaha Lake where the beaches offered safe swimming for the children and nice shaded campsites was very popular.

The plan for this leg of the journey was to stop in Penticton and stay at the El Rancho Motel. This was a beautiful spot. Joy had picked this motel as this was where her family had stayed many a summer. This time they had a two bedroom suite with a kitchenette, dining room and living room. It also had a balcony that overlooked the swimming pool. Nellie was so pleased she could finally make a good cup of tea. Before anything else, that was what everyone did. Tea as it should be-finally.

At this juncture, Jack said, "Right, time to cool off some." He then proceeded to remove his jacket and his shirt. He then removed his undershirt. Nellie screamed, "What are you doing?"

"Well if it works for Gilley, it'll work for me. I just want to cool off by removing some layers."

Gilley offered, "Now that you're half naked, would you like to go for a dip, Dad?"

"Nobody wants to see a skinny, old, white guy like me in that pool." Jack was about 5'8" and about 150 lbs.

"That's OK, Dad, they don't have vultures flying around here."

"What's that supposed to mean? Do you think I look half dead?"

"No but you do look bloody thin."

"Well I used to look better than this until I got that darn Diabetes, Eh. Too much direct sunlight isn't good for you anyhow, especially this bloody temperature. You can't expect me to get a tan at my age."

They decided to take a stroll down the lakeshore. This was just like going down to the seaside in England but much hotter. The problem they ran into was it was very difficult to find anywhere to have a beer as Penticton prided itself on being family oriented. Thank God, Joy had put some in the fridge back at the room. The next few days were spent just lazing and stretching and walking around. Joy and Gilley went swimming as Nellie and Jack sat by the pool under brightly coloured umbrellas that attached to the back of the seats. "Thank God, we brought those with us." Joy said.

Nellie and Jack fell in love with this area. Jack kept saying, "If I was twenty years younger, I would come out here to live." The desert air seemed to agree with them. As a matter of fact, everyone, including the white skinny guy began to get golden tans. (Gilley kept thinking, "I'm glad the old man's getting some colour. His skin would make white socks look gray.")

Unfortunately, all too soon, it was time to leave Penticton and it was going to be about a five to six hour drive back to New Westminster, (not including tea breaks). Bidding farewell to the El Rancho and Penticton, the group headed for Keremeos which was known for its fruit stands. Peaches, pears, cherries and every kind of vegetable were to be had at these stands. Everyone was ecstatic to see this delight because back in England, the ordinary person did not have the opportunity to see such abundance unless they were fortunate enough to live close enough to the bigger cities which had large markets. Newcastle was one of these. Here there were fruit stands all along both sides of the highway and each one was filled with the abundance the area was famous for.

Gilley, Jack and Nellie filled up the empty spaces in the car with cherries, peaches and plums, while Joy selected the finest tomatoes she could get. Everyone was happy with the knowledge they had gotten a bargain.

The next stop was Hedley which was a famous gold mining town. The town was made famous by the discovery of gold in 1897, and became one of the great names in Canadian gold mining history. Named after Robert R. Hedley, manager of the Hall Smelter in Nelson, who had grubstaked many of the early prospectors, Hedley grew quickly and by 1900 boasted a population of over 1,000 with 5 hotels and a large stamp mill. One could look up the sheer cliff where one could see the remnants of the gold mine. Gilley was in raptures. "Another place I'll have to come back to and inspect more closely." The Hedley of today was a sleepy, little town much like what one would imagine they would find in the Wild West days. The foursome had lunch in a little truck stop along the road. They had come to realize truck stops were renowned for having very good food for a very good price as well as, for once a good cup of tea.

"That's all we like in England. We don't like any fancy food," Nellie said finishing her meal.

The next juncture in this episode was the drive between Hedley and Manning Park Lodge with Princeton in between. Now, between Hedley and Princeton, the drive was quite tame with a gentle rolling countryside. It was after Princeton where the excitement began. The rolling hills changed to steep mountain terrain. To their left was a sheer drop and to the right was a steep mountain wall. The road was very winding and narrow in areas. It also went up steep grades and dropped down almost as quickly. This was an exhilarating experience for Gilley and Nellie (Jack was oblivious to all of this as he was focused on eating cherries in the back seat.) "Joy kept saying to him, "You've got to go slow down. There're often radar traps around here." And Nellie, much to Joy's surprise, kept saying, "Go faster Gilley. This is great."

Coming closer to Manning Park, the road opened up into four lanes and Gilley thought he'd give it a boot. No sooner had he done this than the sirens began to wail and he was pulled over by an officer of the law. As the officer walked up to the car, Gilley wound down his window. With this, the officer could hear Gilley getting static from two women. He was to discover these were Gilley's wife and mother. Immediately, he felt sorry for the poor bugger. He, nevertheless carried on with procedure and asked for Gilley's license, "Do you know what the speed limit is here?"

"No sir, I didn't see a speed sign," replied Gilley.

"Well, do you know what speed you were doing?"

"About eighty miles an hour?"

"Well, it was closer to ninety," replied the officer.

Nellie piped up, "I'll make sure my son never speeds again, Officer. I'll watch that speedometer for him." With this comment, she gave Gilley a slap across the back of the head. The officer walked away with Gilley's license and insurance papers. Gilley wasn't certain, but he thought the officer was giggling slightly.

Joy glared at Gilley and said, "I told you there are radar traps around here. Now we're going to get a ticket. You know that, don't you," she said, pointing a finger in his direction. The officer walked back and could still hear Gilley getting hell from the women.

"Well, sir," he said, "I don't want to be the first one to blemish your record, so this is just a warning. Drive your parents carefully, stop off at the lodge for a cup of tea and if you drive slowly to Hope, there's a good chance you'll see some black bear. Have nice trip." Gilley could not believe his luck.

"Thank you, Officer. I won't speed again."

"You lucky bugger," said Jack. "Joy warned you about speeding here but you wouldn't listen. I'm sure if it had been someone else, they would have received the full force of the law. It's a good job your mother was in the back seat here or she would have hauled you out of the car by your ear."

"But, Dad, she's the one who encouraged me to go faster."

"Yes I did, but I didn't mean for you to break the law. You should know that by now," retorted Nellie.

Finally they arrived at the Manning Park Lodge and for once Gilley was looking forward to that cup of tea. After all, he had to do something to break the tension. As they went into the cafeteria section, Joy said, "I think we should have something light as we'll be stopping at Hope for dinner."

Of course the united remark from Nellie and Jack was, "A cup of tea and a biscuit would hit the spot."

As everyone settled down, Nellie was still giving Gilley hell for speeding. By this time, Gilley was getting a bit fed up and decided to defend himself somewhat. "I only did it for you, Mom so that you could see a Mountie."

Nellie's remark was, "I thought your Mounties in Canada had Red coats, Navy pants with a yellow stripe down the side, and riding boots along with a broad brimmed cowboy styled hat. The one that stopped us was dressed rather drab. He didn't look like a Mountie at all. Next time if you decide to do something stupid like that, just make sure you make it worth my while."

Sighing and changing the subject, Gilley decided to tell the truth about the camera. After all, if he was in trouble for speeding he may as well be in trouble for the camera as well. Get it all done and over with. He began by explaining to his father that the mechanism didn't seem to advance the film. It didn't seem as if there was any pressure there. Joy's reaction at this confession was, "That's really nice, eh. Borrow my father's prize possession and break it straight away. When did you find out it wasn't working?"

"In Barkerville", was Gilley's reply.

"So you've gone all of this time not telling us that the camera was broken and you missed all those shots. Now we don't have a single picture of our trip." Joy said angrily.

Gilley responded, "We do have a few from the early part and I just thought the camera was malfunctioning and it would correct itself. I tried to get it to work without opening it up, but nothing would do the trick. I've never had a camera like this before so the inner workings of it are a mystery to me."

Gilley's father, not to be left out, jumped in and said, "What sort of engineer are you, can't even fix a bloody camera."

Gilley shot back, "Photography was not my engineering specialty." Gilley was feeling a bit upset with himself by this time as he realized he should have admitted the problem earlier. He didn't tell anyone that he had secretly looked for a camera repair shop but had no success as these were not the sort of shop to be found in the outlying towns.

Everyone got back into the car and continued onto to Hope. While driving through Manning Park they did actually spot the black bear with her cubs. Gilley slowed down for all to see, feeling very bad he could not take a picture. Jack rubbed it in by remarking, "It sure would be nice to take a photo of these bears back to England. I wonder if they will believe us when we tell them of this experience."

"I'll buy you a bloody postcard to take back with you." Gilley responded. "No one will know the difference."

"Aw, but we will," said Nellie.

"Can't win," thought Gilley.

Once reaching Hope, they decided to stop at the same restaurant they had eaten in on their way up to Prince George. Jack had liked the BC Salad so much he wanted to have it again. "It's good for my diet and for once, I'm full on this lettuce stuff. Most salads are nothing but lettuce and I feel like a bloody rabbit."

"Well, you're skinny enough to be a rabbit." Gilley retorted.

"He's being a cheeky bugger again. Take care of your son, Nellie. He doesn't pay no mind to me."

While they were eating, Gilley gave some history of Hope. "Hope was the starting off point for the Gold Rush days even though Yale was considered Mile Zero. The Fraser River takes on another dimension as it torrents through Hell's Gate and rushes its way towards the Pacific. Here at Hope, it widens out and slows down, allowing the gold to be deposited on the sandbars. The Chinese settlers, experts at panning the gold from these sandbars, had the patience and the knowledge to extract the fine gold and silver." (As he said this, Gilley decided to make note of this knowledge for future exploits for himself.)

After dinner, they started on the last leg of their journey. No more stops. Eventually, they came to a place called Bridal Falls and started going downhill or what Gilley would eventually come to refer to as the "long driveway to home". This was where the traffic would start to build up on its way to the lower mainland and in the process, slow down to a dreary crawl. In addition to this, the scenery never seemed to change as one drove through the flatlands of Chilliwack. The rest of the trip was uneventful.

As they got towards Langley, Joy mentioned there was a place called Fort Langley, which had been an original fort on the Fraser River during the gold rush days. She also told everyone Jim had been commissioned to reconstruct the buildings as they had been in the original fort as it stood on the Fraser River. He was to use the building techniques of the early pioneer days. This required quite a bit of research on his part. The goal was to make Fort Langley an actual working fort as it would have been those many years ago. Joy also told Nellie and Jack that Jim and Veron planned to take them to visit the fort on a day when it was functioning as it did in the old days. They thought it would interest Nellie and Jack to see people dressed in period costumes and going about their business as they would have done over 100 years earlier.

Soon they approached the Port Mann Bridge and the panoramic view of the valley opened before them. Colony Farms was to the right and they could see the saw mills, fishing boats, log booms and manufacturing plants below them from the bridge deck. On the hillside, houses upon houses overlooked the Mighty Fraser. To the left one could see the increasing development of the area. Again, log booms, tug boats and even sail boats could be seen and New Westminster was visible in the distance. The backdrop for all of this was the blue Coastal Mountains adding their magnificence to the picture. This was a favorite scene for Gilley and a sign he was almost home.

Arriving back at the apartment in New Westminster they were welcomed by the house budgies, five in all. While they had been gone for the week, Veron had come in every day to make sure they had enough food and water. However, they were overjoyed when the party arrived. They had lacked company and so proceeded to welcome them with a chorus chirping and other melodious sounds. Promptly Nellie put the kettle on and declared that it was time for a cup of tea before unloading the car. Joy and Gilley decided to have a beer and Jack added a little whiskey in his tea. They needed to recuperate before tacking the unpleasant task of unpacking.

By the time they were having their tea, Nellie, feeling a bit more comfortable with her new daughter-in law and ventured to ask, "Why do you have so many budgies? Don't you find that they make quite a mess and a good bit of noise during the day? Do your neighbors not complain about them?"

Joy explained how it happened that they had acquired so many. Firstly, they had been given a white pagoda cage. It was a beautiful cage and it had sat empty for some time. Both she and Gilley decided having some sort of living presence in the house would be nice and went out to buy one budgie. They went to the local pet store and chose one they both thought would be perfect. Joy then spotted the little albino bird with a crippled foot. Once the decision was made, Joy realized there was only one bird left in that cage. It was a little albino with a crippled foot. It just didn't seem fair to leave him alone. In addition to this, the first bird would need a friend, she reasoned. It also helped that the albino budgie was half price.

The second thing that happened was, not knowing Gilley and Joy had already bought two budgies, Jim and Veron showed up one evening with two more for the "empty" cage. Then, the third event happened. Another budgie found its way to Jim and Veron's. It seemed lost and hung around the patio. This was a much older bird and keeping it was just a temporary measure until they could find the owner. They had advertised in the paper and put signs up in the markets. No one had claimed the bird and rather than keeping it for themselves, Veron reasoned it would be happier with others of its kind, so brought it to Joy and Gilley's. That's how five budgies came to live in the beautiful white cage and become part of the family.

"You asked about the noise they make. Well, if you put a cover over them, they go to sleep," explained Joy. "When you take the cover off, that's when the racket begins because they wake up. Sometimes, we forget to put the cover on at night time, as its dark and they just go to sleep. However, when the sun comes up, they begin their racket and Gilley doesn't need an alarm clock to get up then. Yet the noise doesn't seem to bother any of the neighbors. The mess is an easy matter of the vacuum cleaner and that shuts them up too."

Turning to Gilley, Joy ordered, "Gilley, go and get the cases now as I've got to get the washing started. Saturday is a free day for laundry."

Nellie's curiosity was pricked. "What do you mean, 'Saturday is a free day?"

"Oh, here in BC when one lives in an apartment, there are laundry facilities in the basement. Everyone is assigned a particular day and time in which to do their washing, However, Saturdays are open to whoever gets there first. Now's a good time as most other tenants have completed any washing they have. Besides, there are four washing machines and if they're not being used, we can use them all and get the laundry done more quickly. There are also four big dryers to complete the task. We can have everything washed, dried and folded in less than two hours."

Gilley, doing as he was told, brought in the suitcases and the women sorted out the dirty clothes and hurried downstairs while Gilley and Jack enjoyed another drink. Nellie was fascinated by the size of the washing machines and dryers. She also couldn't get over the fact that they operated by coins. It took about 45 minutes for the automatic washer to go through all of the cycles and perhaps an hour for the drying time (depending on the weight of the clothes to be dried). After

45 minutes, Joy went down to transfer the clothes into the dryers, with Nellie close behind. Nellie was not about to miss this new experience.

Since Nellie and Joy were making dinner by the time the drying was completed, Joy sent Gilley down to get the clothes. Jack, not wanting to be left out, came close behind. He wanted to see this setup for himself after hearing Nellie go on about it all. On the way down, Jack wondered what the little doorways were that were beside all of the other apartment front doors.

Gilley explained, "They are like delivery doors. If people order milk or the newspaper, the delivery people put the items inside the doorway, then close the door. When the tenant wants to retrieve their deliveries, they open the door from the inside of the apartment. This proves to be a secure arrangement, except for in the summertime. Some of the tenants will leave both of the doors open in order to get a through draught instead of leaving the main door open. Jim and Veron's dog, Tinker, loves the summer because when he comes visiting he uses these little doorways to explore people's apartments, frightening them out of their wits. Then he scurries back out before they know what's happened. As no pets are allowed in these apartments people are not sure where the animal has gone. Tinker is not one to be left out of anything."

At the laundry area, there were four big dryers all going at the same time. "Which one was ours?" Jack said, "You'd better go back upstairs and ask Joy which one is yours."

Gilley replied, "Now, if we go about this logically, Joy would have told me if there had been anyone washing ahead of us. I think others began their laundry after she did. The machines that stop first will be ours." Just as he said this, one of the dryers stopped and then another one did. Opening them up, he saw that indeed, these were their garments.

"Lo and behold, you bugger, that was clever thinking," declared Jack.

"Nothing to it Dad, You've always said I should use my noggin."

Back up to the apartment, Jack couldn't hold himself back. He just had to explain to Nellie how his son had deduced the right dryers and also he had to tell her about these little doors and about Tinker. Joy laughed at that. She had forgotten, temporarily about the exploits of Tinker.

The next day after breakfast everyone strolled down to Jim and Veron's house for the day. Gilley knew he had to break the news to Jim about the camera and was not looking forward to the aftermath. It seemed everyone, except Gilley, was looking forward to seeing Jim and Veron again and telling them about their vacation. Gilley was not looking forward to this meeting at all. He felt more than apprehensive. After all, the camera was Jim's pride and joy and to have to return it broken could put a big damper on their growing relationship. How would he begin the explanation? He decided the best strategy was the straightforward one. Rehearsing his lines in his mind, he was glad the walk between his apartment and Jim's house was about half an hour long.

Of course there were pleasant greetings all around when they arrived. Jim and Veron were most anxious to hear about the trip, about how the English visitors enjoyed the beautiful scenery of British Columbia and about how the car functioned. "Did you have any trouble with the car," was the first question Jim asked.

Jim was particularly was interested to hear if they got any good shots of wildlife they could take back to their friends in England. With that question asked, everyone fell silent and turned towards Gilley. No one was going to own up to the camera fiasco. That was Gilley's job.

Of course Gilley knew he would be the one having to do the explaining, but things were not going as he had planned. There was no taking Jim to one side and quietly explaining the problem. No, he had to give it straight out, right in front of everyone. This was almost too much for him, but, our boy rose to the occasion (as is his wont). He cleared his throat and began, "Well, Jim, it's like this. We were taking great pictures up until we reached Barkerville and, well, I don't know any other way to say this, but the camera just stopped working. It was as if it wouldn't catch the film or something and would not advance. The picture counter would not move forward. Also when you would try to forward the film, there was no tension in the lever and it would not advance. I promise you I did not drop it, or mistreat it in any manner." With this explanation blurted out, Gilley fell silent. Everyone else was silent too. They were all waiting for Jim's wrath, or disapproval at any rate.

Surprisingly, Jim said, "Well, these things do happen. I've never had this happen to me before, but maybe what happened, was the mechanism was stiff and broke the film. Did you feel any extra tension as wound it ahead?"

"Not really," said Gilley, "It just functioned the way it did when you showed me how to use it. I'm not any great expert, but I don't think anything was out of the ordinary."

"Well, I'll take it into the camera shop tomorrow and have them take a look at it. I'm sure it'll be nothing much after all; it is a brand new Pentax camera. It might even still be on warranty."

"Whatever the cost," Gilley said, "I'll pay for it to be fixed."

Gilley felt uncomfortable vibes coming from across the table from Joy. They said, "Don't offer until we know what the problem is!"

At that stage, the doorbell rang (much to Gilley's relief) and Veron, realizing how Gilley must feel, (even though she relished the fact that he was in the hot seat, it wasn't fair for Gilley to go through his while his parents were there.) said, "Well, I wonder who that could be. Don't worry Gilley, there's no sense crying over spilled milk until we see how much has been spilled. Go and answer the door."

In came Harry and Gwen. "Harry helped us move the piano when we were moving into our apartment," explained Gilley as he introduced them to his parents. "He also works for Jim at the school board. Harry insisted he meet you both when you came to visit. After all, he's from Somerset and came over here via America. He was a dairy farmer in England and in the US as well. He eventually came to Canada to seek his fortunes. He and Gwen have been married for a long time." Gilley was grateful it was Harry because Harry could make any get together into a party. He flirted with the woman (didn't matter how old they were) and teased them mercilessly. He got on well with the men as well. The attention was now on Harry and Gwen and off Gilley.

Everyone went down to the back yard, as it was a beautiful afternoon. The cherries were dropping from the trees; they were so ripe and plentiful. This came as a great delight to Jack as he just loved cherries and these were great huge Bing cherries to boot. "Where in the world could one go and sit under a cherry tree and be fed with this delight" he proclaimed?

Harry intervened and explained, "Wonderful things that fall from trees don't always have to be cherries. It would be nice to have a tree full of beautiful young women, although, that might be asking for more trouble than it's worth. But, its one hell of an idea."

Jack replied back," I think cherries would be much easier to handle, they don't cost as much and you have no explaining to do."

Harry agreed and laughed. He thumped Jack on the shoulder and said, "Jack, my boy, you've got that right!"

At that moment in came Brian and Marva and Terry and Marilyn Parsons and the Donaldsons' from next door. Introductions were made all around and drinks were passed out. Now Jim noticed the fridge was beginning to run low on beer. Since it was such a hot day, everyone had taken to beer drinking. That meant a call to the neighborhood bootlegger, Mickey MacRorie. Mickey and Elaine were coming anyway, so Jim called them to ask them to bring supplies. Much to Jim's disappointment, they had already left home for the party. Just at that time, they arrived. Jim asked Gilley to go back with Mickey to get more beer. This was no problem for either man, as it meant getting out of the house and having a breather and a beer on their own.

It was nice and cool in the garage at Mickey's and they were in no hurry to return to the now hot July afternoon in Jim's back yard. By their second beer, Mickey, knowing Elaine would be on the phone if he was gone too long, said they had to get going. As they were finishing their last beer, sure enough the phone rang. Mickey ignored it and said, "Let's get going. Gilley, grab those two cases while I get the other two." Off they went, back to the house, feeling quite rewarded for this little errand.

As they arrived back a t Jim's, Elaine was somewhat upset at the length of time that it had taken for this errand. Mickey explained, "I had to get the very coldest beer for this hot day and that meant that I had to get the ones from the very back of the basement. Don't forget, I have to be very careful, especially on Sundays."

Jack, overhearing this conversation said, "What do you mean?" Jack, of course did not realize anything about the strange liquor laws in BC that limited the purchase of alcohol on Sundays."

"Oh, well, yes," said Jim, "Jack, on Sundays, the liquor stores are all closed and one cannot obtain any booze for parties etc. The only people who have access to booze are bootleggers and our good friend, Mickey here, helps us out from time to time," he explained. "This is very hush, hush as not everyone knows about this arrangement. We have to be careful not to be overheard by all the guests as not everyone is privy to Mickey's sideline business."

Jack replied, "Mum's the word, Jim."

Nearing the end of the afternoon, Joy and Veron went upstairs to prepare dinner. By around about 6:00 PM, all of the guests had left for their own Sunday dinners. Anne, Sally, Jim, Jack, Nellie, Joy and Gilley all sat down at the dining room table. Once again Veron brought out an enormous roast of beef for Jim to carve. Jack and Nellie couldn't believe the size of this thing. Gilley had not been exaggerating in his letters after all. Jim, obviously practiced at the art of carving, stood and asked how each person liked to have their meat. Knowing that Gilley liked his meat well done, he offered Nellie first choice. "Would you like the outside piece, Nellie? I know that in England, you prefer your meat well done. At least that's what I've been told by Gilley and Joy."

Jack's response was, "Well, I've always liked my meat sort of medium, just like the way it's being served here." At that point Nellie glared across the table at Jack, knowing fair well that the bugger was lying for some reason. Obviously, when in Rome, do as the Romans do. This was Jack's philosophy at times, anyhow.

The rest of the meal was served. It consisted of roast potatoes, carrots, peas, and cauliflower and of course Yorkshire puddings. These puddings were as unbelievable as the roast beef. They were perfect as well as huge. Nellie graciously admitted, "Veron, these are great looking Yorkshire puddings."

The amount of meat that was divvied up was unbelievable to Jack and Nellie. During the course of the meal, Nellie commented, "The amount of meat which has been served here tonight is more than I would buy in a month back home. It could even be two months. Do you always eat like this or is this a special dinner that you put on just for visitors?"

"No," came Veron's rely, "this is our typical Sunday dinner. Some Sundays we have chicken or salmon or ham. Of course, from the leftovers, I make stews, casseroles, soups and great sandwiches during the rest of the week."

"You eat exceptionally well here and Joy has taken over her mother's traits. She is a pretty good cook too," complimented Nellie.

With that, Jack chimed in, "Do you ever cook salmon, Joy? That's one of my favorite dishes. However, I have heard that the pacific salmon is different from the Atlantic salmon and we've only ever had the Atlantic version."

Veron, seizing the opportunity, stated, "I've a salmon dinner planned for next Saturday. I'm going to cook it on the hibachi, along with corn on the cob and salads. Joy will make the potato salad."

"What's an hibachi," queried Nellie?

"You'll have to come over next week and find out." Veron replied.

Next came the dessert. Veron carried out this huge watermelon. She had hollowed out the center after she had cut it lengthways. She had then taken the scooped out watermelon and mixed it with peaches, cherries, grapes, strawberries and honey dew melon. All of this was returned to the watermelon shell and served with vanilla ice-cream on the side. Everyone thought they would burst.

Nellie and Jack were totally awed by the meal. They thought this was a feast worthy of a king. Clearly, Gilley had not been exaggerating in letters when he had written of the meals in this household. It was a wonder they were not all terribly overweight.

Jack's final comment on the meal was, "I have partaken of ample sufficiency." This was one of his sayings and he reserved this particular one for extra special meals.

The walk back to the apartment on a nice warm evening gave everyone the chance to walk off the fabulous dinner. It was also reasonably early as Joy and Gilley had to go back to work the following day. The group talked about the itinerary Jim and Veron had worked out for the following week for Jack and Nellie and especially the trip to Fort Langley.

Of course, the evening was not complete without the last cup of tea. Nellie took this opportunity to confront Jack about his comment on the roast beef. Not known for her diplomacy, Nellie declared, "Jack, that wasn't a very good comment you made to Veron about the roast beef. You've always wanted your meat well done, that's why I cook it that way."

Jack, fast to reply, "The reason I like you to do the meat well, is so I can make scone sandwiches and take them to the club, enjoying them with my friends over a couple of pints. The dampness from the roast beef not being well done would ruin the taste of the delicious scones you are so well known for."

Joy was quite impressed by Jack's reply and thought to herself, "Now I know where Gilley gets his bullshit from."

Nellie, not to be overdone by this remark said, "If I cook the meat medium, then I don't have to cook anymore scones."

Jack, fast on the ball, remarked, "You know I take two or three scones with me so that I can share them with my pals, Ned Brown and Bill Coish. You know they love your cooking especially your scones. They would be very disappointed not to have them anymore or to have medium meat in bread instead of in scones. We are used to this and it goes down so well with the beer."

"Maybe you should get them to take the meat and you take the scones. That way I don't have to cook the meat and they can take part in the affair. You can make your own sandwiches at the club then."

"That won't do because the club doesn't like us bringing in our food. They want us to buy their crisps and nuts and maybe the odd pork pie. You know crisps and especially pork pies upset my stomach. Another big thing is I take the sandwiches and they buy the beer."

Nellie, triumphant at last remarks, "So you do like your meat medium well done then. I like mine that way too. Just the way Veron cooked it. Now I see why Joy was astounded in England by the size of the joint (meat) and why she asked for more. If we had only known."

Joy exclaimed, "It was a great learning experience. The food in England is quite boring even though it's wholesome. Here, we get so much variety from the United States and other countries yet, I would gladly give up the great food here in BC to live back in England."

Nellie jumped at the chance; "I promise you a joint cooked your way if you would move back to England. I don't care what Jack says—that he wants it well done so he can feed his friends." In the back of her mind she thought, "I would gladly have my boy back in England. Jack would also. Maybe the way to accomplish this would be to work on their new daughter-in-law."

Gilley, seeing what was going on decided to keep quiet, as he wasn't ready to go back to England. Joy indicated immediately, "We will be back next year." Looking at Gilley, "You said you would give it two years and at the end of next year, the two years will be up." She then looked around to everyone, making sure they all caught the meaning of her words.

"Time for bed," said Gilley. He knew when it was time to break up the momentum. Gilley was usually not one for bed very early; as a matter of fact he was always the last one to bed. This night he took the lead and walked into the bedroom. Joy was astounded that he was leaving her in the presence of his parents. What went on from there, Gilley would never know, as Joy did not follow as he thought she would. As a matter of fact, it was quite a while before she did finally come into bed, talking at great lengths with Jack and Nellie. Try as hard as he might, Gilley could only hear the faint buzz of low chatter coming from the living room. He knew that something was up, but he just could not stay awake and he couldn't loose face by returning to the living room. He was sound asleep the time she came to bed.

CHAPTER 11

BACK TO REALITY

THE FOLLOWING DAY WAS back to work for both Joy and Gilley. Gilley arrived early that day so while waiting for the eight o'clock start, he told a few of the tales from his holidays especially the one about the broken camera. Dave Mosley came to Gilley's aid explaining that there's nothing worse than having someone else's camera go "poof" on you. "What sort of camera was it Gilley?"

"It was the latest Pentax camera and Jim had just purchased it a few months prior to our trip," responded Gilley.

"Was it on special because I bought one a few months ago as well? What happened to mine was the mechanism that winds the film froze and consequently snapped the film. I think it's a manufacturer's problem. Its easily fixed but quite a nuisance as usually an entire film is ruined. They fix it for free and give you a roll of film as compensation, but that's little comfort when you lose all your pictures. I tell you what Gilley, I've got my old camera, my Taron. It takes great pictures even though it's a bit antiquated. The light meter is separate from the camera so you have to play around a bit to get the lighting right.

I bought this camera when I was in the RAF in Singapore. We were given cigarette rations and since I didn't smoke, I sold my portion to save up for the camera. How about if I bring it in tomorrow? I'll sell it to you for forty bucks."

"That would be great," Gilley exclaimed. "The only camera I've ever had was a Brownie and the pictures were just black and white. That bugger broke on me just before I came to Canada. Good job Joy had a cheap color camera, which we used to take pictures in England. But I dropped that one when we moved to the apartment and broke the whole thing."

"This sounds like a habit for you, Gilley." Dave replied. "I'll take the forty bucks before I give you the camera just in case."

Just as work was to begin, Gilley remembered he had to ask Dave something. Dave had been taking golf lessons and was dying to get out and play golf. Gilley had made the offer earlier to Dave to become the team spare on the Saturday morning foursome as often Brian was unable to make it due to his shift work at Seagram's and, with Dave standing in the wings, they wouldn't have to play with a stranger in order to make up the required number. This arrangement would suit both sides as Dave had already met Jim.

"By the way, Dave, would you be up for playing golf this Saturday with Jim, Eric and Brian? I have to take my parents to Victoria and they will need a fourth. And this is already OK with Jim as he asked me to ask you."

As they walked to the drawing office, Dave said, "That would be great, but how the hell do you get to Newlands from Richmond?"

"I'll show you on the map and I'll tell Jim you'll be there for 7:30. Meet them at the Pro shop."

That day the workload was stupendous as the illustrious salesman, Dennis Shears was outdoing himself selling winches not only locally but overseas as well. At lunch time Barry asked everybody if they could work overtime. At first Gilley was inclined to say no, but on second thought realized this was a great opportunity to make more money and prove his value.

Right now would be a good time to phone Joy as she would still be at home for lunch. Calling home, Nellie answered the phone, much to Gilley's surprise.

"Hello," came the shy, unsure voice.

"Hello, Mother," said Gilley, "How are you doing? I'm surprised to hear you answer the phone. Is Joy there?"

"She just left. She made us all lunch, but she has to do a bit of shopping. She'll be back within the half hour." Nellie was a little surer of herself, now that she knew who was on the other end.

"Tell her that I won't be home till 7:00 PM as we've been asked to work overtime tonight."

"Well, son, you can't look a gift horse in the mouth. If you've been asked to work overtime, you have to comply as you would in England. Don't worry about us. Joy is doing a fine job looking after us."

"That's great, Mother. Have a good day and I'll be home as soon as I can."

Gilley arrived home at 7:30, late as usual. Joy, annoyed as usual, was ready to give Gilley hell. "We have been waiting for you as it's your favourite tonight-egg, chips and baked beans. Before we eat, if you want a beer, you have to go to the liquor store."

"I don't have any money," Gilley replied

"You never have any money," Joy came back in a frustrated voice.

Jack joined in, "He never had money in England either. I just don't know what he does with his money. It seems as if it burns a hole in his pocket."

Nellie, nudging Jack, "Go down to the liquor store with Gilley and buy the beer."

Off the men went. It was the first time Jack had been in a Canadian liquor store. He couldn't believe the amount of beer stocked as well as the variety available. He was also awed by the great abundance of wine as well as Scotch, Gin, Rum, Vodka, Rye, Port, Sherry,-everything imaginable was here in one store and the prices were so low. Jack said, "Let's get two cases of beer, a bottle of Scotch and, look, we'll buy your mom a bottle of Port." Gilley couldn't believe what he was hearing. Back in England to get his father to spend a shilling was like pulling teeth.

On the way out of the liquor store, just inside the exit door, there was a small kiosk selling cigarettes, cigars and any kind of smoke accessories needed. Gilley explained to Jack, "This store is run by the blind. It amazes me how they can tell the different denominations on the bills."

Jack said, "Let's give him a ten see what happens. I'll buy two packs of cigarettes but you keep your eye on the ten." As he passed the ten over to the clerk, the blind man felt the bill by rubbing it between his fingers. He then put it under the counter. He waited a few seconds and said, "That was a ten you gave me, Sir." Both Gilley and Jack were so impressed they asked him about it. The blind man responded, with a laugh, "That's a trade secret. You'll have to find out another time."

"That's amazing. I'll be sure to be back to find out how you do that. Your mother would be impressed. We have to remember to tell her when we get back home."

"You're right, Dad," Gilley said, as they drove back to the apartment, Mother would be fascinated. As another point of interest, did you notice the large store beside the liquor store? It's called Safeway. That's where Joy had her first job at the age of sixteen. She worked there until she was eighteen and graduated from school. Then she went to work for the Bank of Montreal. Veron wouldn't allow any of her kids to have idle hands. Once they were old enough to work, they were put to the task."

Jack was very taken by Joy and he said to Gilley, "You made a good choice when you picked her. She looks after you very well, you lucky bugger."

Gilley's response was, "I think she chose me, you know."

Back at the apartment, Jack could hardly wait to tell Nellie about the kiosk with the blind man selling cigarettes and about how he saw the Safeway store Joy had worked in when she was only sixteen.

At that point Joy said, "If you didn't have a job at that point in time, you were put to work for Mother and working for her was like working for a sergeant major. In spite of having a full time job, though, she still expected us to do some chores around the house."

Nellie interjected, "Yes, I could see how your mother would be a task master and a half. Looking at Gilley said, "I'll bet you have to watch your p's and q's with her too."

"We have had a few run-ins, but I don't think the big one has happened yet. Just wait until you meet Joy's Grandmother. You'll see where Veron gets it. Yet for all of Veron's gusto, I think she has a warm heart."

Nellie was really impressed Jack had thought to buy her a bottle of Port, but with her Port, she liked to have lemonade. Now Lemonade, in England, is not what Canadians think of as lemonade. In England, it's like a soft drink, similar to 7-Up, but with a more lemony taste. To solve this little dilemma, Joy offered Nellie 7-up with a slice of fresh lemon. That went down very favorably. As a matter of fact she said, "That was as good as a cup of tea."

With this topic of conversation, Gilley reminisced about his cravings for some of the English pops or sodas such as Lemonade, Tizer, Dandelion and Burdock (which is very much like Root Beer) and Limeade. But most of all, he really missed Ginger Beer. Joy thought these comments were very encouraging, as she was hoping Gilley still missed England.

"Well," said Nellie, "This dinner—egg and chips and baked beans is very English. I'll bet you'll want to have your favorite—chip butties as well." She smiled secretly. To Gilley's surprise, when dinner was served, there were processed peas instead of beans and a mug of the juice of the peas just for him. It was just as if he was in England. This created a very nostalgic moment for him. After one chip butty, Gilley was up to get more bread.

Jack said, "It's like an addiction for him. He'll eat and eat until he explodes."

"No, he won't, he's allowed just two more slices of bread and then that's it," said Joy.

"Whew, you sound just like your mother, Joy," retorted Gilley as he spread the butter thickly on each slice. "The only way to eat a chip butty is to let the butter be melted into the bread by the hot chips. It's a culinary delight." Gilley was so wrapped up in his treat he didn't notice that no one else participated in his experience.

As dinner progressed, Nellie told Joy, "Don't let him embarrass you in a restaurant. He'll make chip butties there if you let him."

"Most of the restaurants here don't serve bread with chips," said Joy. "However, I'm sure if he insisted they would bring him a couple of slices, for an extra fee of course."

"That's right. He'd find a way no matter what," said Nellie, "He'd even go to the back and ask for it."

Joy expressed, "Most people would be as disgusted with that dish as I am." She noticed Nellie and Jack didn't have a chip butty. "Don't you participate in this Northern dish? He's told me it's a very popular dish and everyone eats them."

"It's the younger generation who likes these chip butties. It's only Gilley and his pals that eat them. I've seen them come home at night 1:00 AM - 2:00 AM, put a pile of chips on and go through a loaf of bread and a pound of butter and think nothing of it." Joy grimaced with disgust at the very thought.

"Don't think you're going to get into that sort of thing here with your pals. I won't put up with that," Joy stated emphatically.

Nellie continued, "As a matter of fact, just so you can be aware, Gilley will put anything between two slices of bread-beans, peas, cold done up, potatoes-mashed or baked—anything. I once caught him putting a slice of chocolate between two slices of bread."

"Mother," Gilley retorted, "That's not as bad as you putting sugar between two slices of heavily buttered bread."

Nellie' comeback was, "Your Dad likes sugar sandwiches too, but he can't have them anymore because of his diabetes."

Jack remarked, "Nellie will let Gilley eat anything he wants. He's the baby of the family, you know. And she does let him get away with murder, too. She used to pamper him at home. I'm glad to see he doesn't get pampered much here with you. That's good."

Nellie's response to all of that was, "He's a big man and that was the only way I could fill him. I had to let him eat as much bread as he wanted and it didn't seem to do him any harm."

Jack decided to change the subject real quick, "Well, my son, I see you're putting a bit of a belly on."

"I'm not playing football (soccer) any more. I haven't really searched out what's what here, but one of the trustees on the school board has a son-in-law who used to play for the Canadian International Team. He had indicated to Jim the fall would be a good time for me to see what's available. I did play in a game—office staff against the factory workers-back in May. It was different. Some people knew how to play, some didn't, but all had a good time. The final result was four-three to the factory workers. I also play golf every Saturday. Golf is very good exercise."

"Yeah, your bloody brother plays it all the time in England. He plays any time he can if he's not fishing." replied Jack. "If you go back to playing football, you'll have to quit smoking, loose a few pounds and do extra training also. Remember it'll probably take you a good half a season to get into match fitness. It'll take that long because you've been out of the game for awhile."

To change the subject again and get it off himself, Gilley asked. "What did you two do with Jim today? He said he was going to show you around New Westminster.

"Jim took us on a tour around the different schools in New Westminster. We were very impressed with the number of schools he is responsible for. He also took us to the school in Queensborough where you and Big Mike worked when you first came here. Then, he took us back to the School Board Office and introduced us to the staff there," answered Jack.

"We finally got to meet Big Mike. We could not believe the size of this guy. Again, we realized you had not been exaggerating in your letters home. Indeed, we now realize the enormous meals you described he ate were probably only close to the truth when you see his size."

They also were introduced to Harry again, who kept flirting with Nellie. Then there was Mike MacRorie, who regaled them with his great fishing stories. He was known as a steelhead expert and offered to take Jack on a fishing trip if time allowed.

"Tomorrow, Jim and Veron are taking us out to Fort Langley. After that we are going to visit Eric and Anne Godden who live right next to your golf course. I understand that Anne was from a place called Ashington, Northumberland," said Jack.

"I hope we're not taking too much of Jim's time up," continued Jack, "he seems to be involved in many things having to do with the city. For example, he told us he's one of the advisers on a project to build a new pool and recreation center. I think it's going to be called the Canada Games Pool. He briefly showed us the site where it's going to be built."

Gilley commented, "Jim is an artist at delegating responsibilities. He has the talent for picking the right person to do a job and he is generous in giving them the credit for a job well done. He can get people to do things no one else could and when they do things for him, they do it happily. He often says, 'I always believe the secret to delegating a job is allowing employees to think it's their own idea, yet they know the final decision is up to me.' No wonder he's well respected throughout the School Board in New Westminster and in other districts. You know, once a year all of the school boards all over British Columbia get together for a convention that focuses specifically on the maintenance side of the school buildings and grounds."

"Apparently, these conventions are full of fun, even though they are supposed to be an educational tool. There are distributors who show their wares during the days, giving demonstrations of how these work and why. There are things such as the latest fertilizers, grounds upkeep equipment, and even the newest sports equipment. They have the latest in paints, tiles, floor waxes, cleaners, heating, ventilating etc, etc. Jim made quite a name for himself last year as he and Veron were key organizers for the very successful convention which occurred here in New Westminster. Most of the Royal Towers Hotel was booked solid for that week. Jim held many parties in his bar in the basement of his home," Jack reported.

"It's a shame I missed that one," said Gilley.

A big sigh came from Joy, "It's a good job he did miss it, we don't know what would have happened."

The following day was full of busy for Gilley at work. The company had purchased the building next door and the team was figuring out how to move into it without disturbing the flow of work needing to be done. This purchase was quite timely, as they were rapidly outgrowing their present building.

These premises were built especially to produce wire rope and the attachments needed. It was a very beautiful, old building, mainly constructed of wood. Most buildings of that era were built of wood in British Columbia, as wood was abundant in the province. In England, Gilley had only ever seen these type of buildings made from steel and cement.

Gilley decided he would go to the newly acquired building on his lunch hour and upon seeing it, just couldn't get over how beautiful the wood was in the columns supporting the place. However, he noted there were many columns that had large vertical cracks in them. Gilley made a mental note to ask Jim about this. Gilley, continuing to inspect the building, discovered a network of steel pipes in the ceiling. Every so often there was a brass spinner inserted in the pipe. Further inspection, he also discovered there was a glass tube between the spinner and the pipe. He came to learn this was a method of fire control called a sprinkler system. When a fire occurred, the glass tubes broke, releasing the water, spinning it everywhere and soaking everything underneath.

Upon further inquiry, Gilley learned, in buildings with this system, the water damage was worse than the fire. Yet fire insurance was very difficult to get if a company didn't have a sprinkler system. As he was walking around the building, Gilley experienced firsthand the effects of this wonderful system. They were testing the system and he was in the wrong place at the wrong time. He got absolutely soaked.

This building would be much more practical than the old one, as now each department could be put together. In the old site, for example, draughtsmen were put anywhere a drawing board could fit. This held true for many departments. He could hardly wait to move in.

That night, Gilley was happy to make it home on time since they had planned to take Nellie and Jack to another North American phenomenon called a drive-in movie. As Gilley had only experienced this once before with Joy, it was left up to Joy to organize the outing. There were many of these drive-in movie places around the lower mainland, but Joy chose the one that was just south of the Pattullo Bridge as it was close by.

The in-laws had no idea what to expect. Joy and Gilley had done their best to describe what the experience would be like, but there is nothing like actually being there. Nellie could not understand until they arrived, how they were all going to be able to see the movie, especially along with about two hundred other people, and Jack could not believe they were going to watch the movie in daylight. He also couldn't figure out how he would be able to hear the dialogue in the movie.

When they drove in, seeing was believing. There was a giant screen at one end of a large asphalt parking lot. Interspersed at regular intervals were metal pipes which were about three feet in height. There were boxes hanging on these pipes with wires attached to them. Jack and Nellie could see there were many cars already parked beside these metal posts. Gilley, after much coaching from Joy, found just the right spot and put the Duster at the right distance from one of these poles. He rolled down the window and brought the box inside, hanging it on the inside edge of the door window. After adjusting the knob, he was able to get the interval music that the theatre had playing to entertain the guests as the time for the movie approached.

Of course, a drive-in movie could not be attended without beer in the trunk. This had to be carefully brought to the front of the vehicle as drinking was not allowed on the grounds. Nellie spotted the coffee stand and decided a cup of tea was more in order for her. Joy decided to accompany Nellie and Gilley had to juggle the speaker off the window, put it back onto the stand, get out of the car, and then just as carefully replace it in order to get out of the car in order to allow his mother and Joy access to the snack stand.

Waiting for the movie to begin was another experience. As they waited, Jack and Gilley had a cold beer and watched as people milled around waiting for the movie to begin. Generally speaking, they noticed, people are not very patient. Therefore, there was much horn blowing and light flashing that went one especially amongst the younger set. Then there were the latecomers, driving in. They had to jockey around to find the right spot for themselves, and often they would be blocking someone already settled in and would have to jockey around again. This, in and of itself, kept the men quite entertained. The women arrived back at the car on time and finally, as dusk approached, the movie finally began. The sound came in just perfectly and there was John Wayne in all of his glory. Joy had picked this particular movie, *True Grit*, as Nellie was infatuated with John Wayne.

Nellie's fondness for cowboys and their ways had come from her mother. Grandma Jackson just loved anything having to do with cowboys. She thought they were very romantic and when it came time to give her a gift, a cowboy novel was a sure hit. Nellie settled into the seat and sighed, "Grandma Jackson would have loved to have been here. The first time she went to a movie it was a silent movie. She and your Aunt Elsie went together. To be able to go was quite a treat at that time. It was playing at the Lyric Theater at Throckley. They were sitting in the theatre and the bad guy was hiding behind a big rock. Grandma Jackson jumped up out of her seat and shouted at the good guy, "He's hiding behind the rock. Careful or he'll get you." No sooner did she say that than the bad guy jumped out from behind the rock and smashed him on the head. She then shouted, "See, I told you he was there. Of course, I can't remember the name of the movie, but I'll never forget her reaction."

Once the movie had started and everyone had found a comfortable position in which to watch the movie (no small feat in the Duster), the fellow behind them gave a loud blast of his horn and then flashed his lights. This startled everyone out of his or her spots. "What the hell is he doing that for," retorted Gilley loudly?

Joy looked around and spotted the problem, "Get your bloody foot off the brake. You're spoiling their view with your break lights." Taking his foot off the brake, Gilley did feel a bit embarrassed, but decided not to pay too much attention to his error.

Settling back into the movie, Gilley poured beer for those who wanted it. Now, because alcohol was not allowed on the premises, they had to put their beer into coffee cups. Joy also warned they had to be careful as there was a man patrolling the lot looking for lawbreakers. If one did get found, he was forced to pour out the precious beverage on the ground in front of all who could see. Many times when this happened others would flash their lights and toot their horns. Fortunately, the foursome avoided detection and really go into the movie.

Half way through the movie, the screen when black and an announcement came on. It was intermission. Joy had already jumped out of the car. She knew if she didn't get to the refreshment stand ahead of the crowd, she'd miss the first part of the second half. When she returned, she had a giant cardboard tray brimming with hot dogs and French fries for everyone and two teas for mom and dad. This was great as they were beginning to feel nibbly.

Nellie and Jack were fascinated by yet another North American food experience. "What the hell are these and how is one supposed to eat them without a knife and fork," declared Jack.

Giggling, Joy instructed, "Well, you hold it like so and begin eating at one end. That's why they're wrapped in napkins. I added mustard, raw onions and ketchup to both of yours as that's how most people eat them. Of course, you know what to do with the fries. I brought extra ketchup if you want to dip them into it. Gilley and I wanted to give you the total drive-in experience."

Nellie said, "That's very thoughtful of you, Joy. I was just wondering if a nice young waiter was going to come by with a tray for the window. I'm not sure I can juggle all of this at one time and not spill my tea."

"You'll get the hang of it, Mother," replied Gilley. "If you like, I'll hold something for you as you get settled." Looking in his rear view mirror Gilley was just in time to see his father solve his problem. He shoved the entire hot dog into his mouth all at once, chewing frantically. He then had hands free to manage his tea and chips. Gilley never thought he'd see his father do something like that. How funny!

Joy began to tell about some of her other drive-in experiences. "Once, when I had a blue Austin Mini, Linda and I went to the drive-in by the Lougheed Mall. We had gotten out to go to the washrooms and to get a hotdog. When we returned my car was gone. Some guys who thought they were clever had picked it up and had moved it four stalls over. There was quite a lot of light flashing and horn honking that night as it took us some time to find the car. It was dark, the movie had started and the car was a dark blue. Add to that the fact the car was so small and the cars over here are so large, it was hard to spot. Let me tell you, people around us got a second show that night."

Now, Nellie decided that the two cups of tea had taken their toll and she had to go to the washroom. Of course, Jack had to go now, too. Gilley was OK—he could hold it forever. After much juggling and squirming about, they were out of the car. Joy took them over to the washroom leaving all of the French fries to Gilley or so he thought. Just as she was about to leave, she poked her head back in through the window. "Don't you dare eat all of those chips! We'll want some when we get back." Of course, getting back to the car was another adventure because now the movie had started. More juggling and squirming and finally everyone was settled again. Faithful and true, Gilley had left lots of chips for the returning trio, but by now, they were cold. Just before Joy sat down, Gilley said, "Oops, don't get in yet. You have to get more beer out of the trunk. I can't because I've got the speaker here." Huffing and glaring, Joy did the deed. Gilley realized she was not exactly happy with this arrangement.

Getting back into the car, she declared, "The least you could do was to get the beer while I was taking care of your mom and dad."

What could Gilley say? He'd blown it again. "Sorry"

His father leaned over and said to him very quietly, "You should put your thinking cap on under these conditions and you'd save yourself a lot of grief."

At the end of the show, Joy said, "Watch out for the guys who take off with their speakers. Even though you've heard the warning, there will be those who forget." Sure enough, someone a couple of stalls down did just the very thing.

"Oh, oh! Gilley, just sit here for a bit. Look at that guy. He'll try and run out of here now to avoid the fine." Sure enough, the car screeched around the lot and attempted to get ahead of the rush for the exit. He didn't get very far as everyone else was trying to get out as well. It was like a stampede for the exit. Security spotted the offender and took things under control. Gilley was glad they'd waited for the crowd to thin as it was like watching another movie, it was so entertaining for all.

It was the better half of thirty minutes before Gilley was able to make his way out of the theatre and get onto the road home. It was going on 12:00 AM by the time they arrived home. What an experience for Jack and Nellie. Not only did they get to see a show on the big screen, but also a show all around them. Even though it was well passed Jack & Nellie's bedtime, they had to tell Joy and Gilley about their day with Jim and Veron and their visit to Fort Langley. But first, a cup a cup of tea was in order. Jack started by telling Gilley Jim had gotten his camera back and it was discovered the camera mechanism had been faulty. Unfortunately only two pictures could be retrieved, but because the camera had gotten stuck, they were double exposed and so in reality, there were no pictures of the trip at all. But one good thing, there was no charge to fix the camera and they did give him a free film as it was under warranty.

Then Jack told about their day with Jim and Veron. "We couldn't believe how they presented the Fort. There were people dressed in clothes of that day. There was blacksmith with his forge and anvil, working away, hammering out horseshoes. There were women doing washing on the old scrub boards in metal tubs."

Nellie jumped in, "I can remember days when I used to do that. Thank God, they brought in those automatic washers we used in the basement the other day. I remember when I got my first manual washing machine just after the War. It had a manually operated agitator and a manually operated ringer set above the tub. This was great as it was so convenient and the water would run back into the washtub. It really saved on water and kept the floor dry. Our next machine was an electric spin washing machine. Many times it used to bounce around the kitchen when it was in the spin cycle and I would make Gilley sit on it to keep it still. I often thought it would be better to have my old mangle back."

Jack continued, "After we left Fort Langley, we went to Eric and Anne's for lunch. Her sister Jean joined us. We had lots of salad again and on top of that, lots of lettuce in the sandwiches. I can't believe the amount of vegetables that come with meals here. Anne's salad had lettuce, of course, and she also put in tomatoes, cucumbers, celery, radishes, scallions, and like a watercress type thing. There were also lots of different sauces to put on the salad. She had a great variety of cold cuts."

"It was a lovely spread, though and she did make a lovely cup of tea," said Nellie.

"And bloody well she should have, coming from Ashington," replied Jack. "Ashington is a well know place because of the good footballers it raised. For example, Jackie Millburn, Bobby Charlton and his brother Jack, just to mention a few. There was a lot more, but not so famous. Interesting it would do that since it was such a small mining village. It might have been the foot running competitions they ran. You must remember us telling you about the time your brother Neil ran against Jackie Millburn known in the North as Wor Jackie?

Joy asked, "What does Wor Jackie mean? I've never heard of that term?"

"It loosely means "ours", said Jack. "To have "Wor" in front of your name means people have taken you into their heart. For example, we would say, 'Our Joy's coming over', or 'Wor Joy is coming over'."

"Ah," said Joy.

"Anne then told us the story of when she left Northumberland to come to Canada. She came to help her Uncle who was Mayor of Langley at the time. Afterwards, she started a high-end dress shop, which apparently, no one thought would make a go of it. It turned out her instincts were correct as there is a lot of money in Langley and quite a few were willing to spend it to be well dressed and to stand out from the crowd."

"Then Jean joined Anne a few years later in Langley with her son Alistair. Apparently something had happened to Jean's husband. Anne's other sister Joyce still lives in England along with her husband John Lyons. It turns out John is the managing director of Shanks which is one of the largest manufacturers of toilets, bidets, bath tubs, basins, and the utensils that go with it".

"Anne was telling us when they moved from Fenham to Darras Hall, which is THE place to live in Northumberland that her husband, in their bathroom area, had all of the faucets gold plated." Jack turned to Joy, "Joy, these are the people you first visited when you came up north. Am I right?"

"Yes," agreed Joy, "I remember when I first came to Newcastle? I was standing in the Waggon Inn having a drink with Joyce and John. They were well known at the Waggon Inn. Fred and Muriel, who managed the pub, as you know, were very welcoming to me. I was told Muriel was well known for her delicious toasted sandwiches and also chicken in a basket. That night, Muriel invited us into the kitchen. Guess who was sitting in the kitchen eating a sandwich, but Gilley. And that's how I first met your son."

"Yes, said Gilley, "We used to go into the back and if we were lucky we would get one of her defective sandwiches. Muriel would never give anything away if she could sell it. Fred, on the other hand, was quite liberal with the beer, especially as the night went on and he got more into his bottle of scotch. Poor Fred, he couldn't get away with too much though, as they used to have this Mynah Bird who talked. As soon as Fred would leave to have a drink, it would begin saying, "Where's Fred, Where's Fred." Of course this alerted Muriel straight away and she would search him out and get him back tending the bar."

Joy chimed in, "After meeting him in the kitchen, Joyce and I returned to the bar. I turned around and discovered he had followed me. We started talking and before I knew it, he offered to take me around to see some castles in the area because I was leaving soon to return to London. He then arranged for the use of his friend David's car as his was having the engine re-built.

I thought this was great but I didn't realize this meant a date for three because David insisted he drive. They picked me up at Fenham the next day. Before we could set out, the boys had to come to Morning Tea, which included a little bit of sherry and scones. The purpose of course was to be vetted by Joyce and her friends. Once they found out Gilley was Draughtsman and his friend David was a School teacher, they relaxed and let us go our way. They felt safe there were two of them to escort me around the countryside. This is when my love affair with England began. Then, after I was hopelessly in love with England, Gilley decides he wants to go to Canada," Joy ended with a growl.

At this stage, Jack jumped in and said, "After lunch, Eric, Jim and I went to your golf club, Newlands for a beer or two and I didn't realize Eric's property runs parallel to the golf course. He told me he picks up lots of golf balls. He hasn't bought a ball in years. Jim introduced me to the game of Shuffleboard. It's similar to Push-Halfpenny. Anyway, it's getting late and time is getting on. You kids have got to go to work in the morning and I'm getting tired." Turning to Nellie, they all realized that she had nodded off in the chair.

Joy added, "Tomorrow is promising to be another big day as I understand Mom is taking you two shopping for gifts for England and then we have the barbeque on the hibachi tomorrow night for dinner. This is the salmon you've been waiting for, Jack."

The following day Veron drove Nellie and Jack into Vancouver for their shopping day. It was very tiring and confusing. Most of the items they chose to take home as souvenirs from Canada had "Made in Taiwan" on the bottom. Veron decided to take Nellie and Jack to a strictly Canadian store where they could purchase unique gifts for England. After a successful sortie into this shop, Nellie asked where she could find those wonderful T.V. tables.

"There is absolutely nothing in England like those tables," she declared. "I like how they come in a set of four and fold up so nicely against the wall on their own little stand. I really wanted to buy a set to take home as we have so little room around our flat, especially when friends come over." She was also thinking she could show them off to her family and friends in England.

Veron said, "I know just the place where they have them on sale right now. I read about it in our paper. The Hudson's Bay Company is a truly Canadian store. It began back in the days the pioneers traded with the Indians. You remember Fort Langley? They talked about the Hudson's Bay when we were in the general store."

Sure enough, they found the TV tables in the kitchen section, on sale as Veron promised. Nellie was so happy she bought a set for Gilley and Joy as well. She also purchased a bathroom set. This was another Canadian invention she just had to have. It came with a toilet seat lid cover, a tank cover, a contoured rug that fit around the toilet and a rug that could be put in front of the bath tub. As far as Nellie was concerned, it would give the bathroom a warmer feeling and add a touch of Canada to her home.

That night, after showing off all her acquisitions of the day to Joy and Gilley (Joy was over the moon with her gift from Nellie of the TV tables), they set out for Jim and Veron's and the long awaited salmon dinner. It was a big, beautiful salmon. Jack and Nellie had never seen a salmon of this proportion before. If they were going to have salmon at all, they could only get the much smaller Atlantic version. This was the king of all salmon—the sockeye. Nellie was thrilled as she had only seen sockeye salmon available in a can and it sold for a very dear price.

Nellie made a comment to this effect and Veron said, "You should take a few cans back with you. We'll go down to Safeway tomorrow and get enough for you to take back to England".

Jack's comment was, "We got the tables, we got the food and now we have the toilet cozy to take back with us. I hope we can get through customs."

The dinner was no disappointment to Nellie and Jack. Veron had really outdone herself this time. The salmon was cooked slowly over hot coals on this hibachi. There was corn on the cob, green salad with fresh tomatoes, cucumbers, multi-colored peppers and green onions, and homemade rolls. Joy complimented the dinner with her famous potato salad. All of this food was served outside on the patio. What a feast! Jack was stuck for words. He had never tasted salmon so tender and moist, with that beautiful flavour of being barbequed. To top off this splendid feast, Veron served fresh strawberry shortcake with whipped cream

The corn was the only thing that presented a bit of a challenge to Nellie and Jack. You see, they both had false teeth. In spite of this, they didn't say a word as it was so delicious and everything else was top drawer. Joy however couldn't let this opportunity go by. She said to Nellie, "Do you remember when I tried to make this in England and you couldn't believe people would eat such a thing? You indicated corn was only used for the pigeons, right? Well, this Canadian dish is what I was hoping to introduce you to. I now know that the corn in England couldn't equal this."

Both Nellie and Jack agreed that this corn was very good and nothing like that available in England. Gilley took his last bite on the spare cob that was left in the pot. (Everyone knew Veron always made extra for Gilley.) Often she would comment, "Boy Gilley, you're putting a bit of weight on." Then she would turn around and offer him another helping of food with a smile.

Jack's comment was, "No wonder he's putting bloody weight on, with all of the good cooking and the abundance of the varieties of food. I feel I'm even putting on the weight since I've been here. I've always been under ten stone (140lbs.) but this morning when I got onto the bathroom scales, it shot over 10 stone, but I'm not going to tell you how much. I've got to watch my bloody weight because I'm diabetic. I didn't think all of these salads would put that much weight on." Then he turned to Nellie, "Speaking of all of this good food, I hope, Nellie, you're not thinking of bringing an hibachi back to England with us. I've got enough to carry what with those tables and all."

Then Nellie said, "That hibachi would look nice on our little veranda. It would set the neighbors really talking if we were to take to cooking out there."

Gilley finally piped up, "And as soon as you lit it up, the first call the neighbours made would be to the fire department. That would set everybody talking then."

As they sat back relaxing, Jim, being a seafaring man and a student of history, mentioned the fact when he was over in England in 1970 for Joy and Gilley's wedding, he had taken it upon himself to find out where the grave of Captain George Vancouver was. He found it in the churchyard in Petersham, which is located in the outskirts of London. He discovered it was overgrown with weeds and not kept up at all.

"So, I took a photograph of it and wrote a letter to Vancouver City. I informed the Mayor of Vancouver that the grave of the city's namesake was in disrepair and needed attention. I felt for the inheritance of our future generations, the city of Vancouver, British Columbia should donate a sum of money to ensure its upkeep. I just received a photograph and a letter from Vancouver indicating this has been attended to and will be so for the ongoing future. The money is being sent to the church and a brigade of boy scouts called the Ham Sea Scout Group is doing the work. They ensure a wreath is laid on the grave every year on the anniversary of Captain Vancouver's death.

Captain George Vancouver sailed from England in 1791 to circumnavigate the coast of Vancouver Island and to map the west coast of BC also discovered that a strait separated Vancouver Island from the mainland. It is now Georgia Strait. He died in 1798."

Jack commented, "It's a shame a lot of our pioneers go unrecognized in England and it takes someone like you to take action. As often I think in England, we have so much history we take things for granted and forget the contributions these people made to the world. Yet most of these explorers were funded by the rich as they could see their investments would bring them large returns."

Jim, who was from a wealthy family and was aware of Jack's socialistic beliefs, continued the dialogue—the pros and cons of capitalism and socialism throughout the night. In the end, no one won or lost the debate and things ended on a friendly note.

After thanking everybody for supper, the walk back to the apartment was greatly appreciated by all, as there was time to walk off the dinner before bedtime. Tomorrow, Friday, brought another surprise for Nellie and Jack.

Traditionally, Joy worked late on a Friday night at the bank as it stayed open till 5:00 PM (normally 3:00 PM was the closing time and banks were not open on Saturday). This was because all transactions had to be completed and the customers needed money for the weekend. Joy never really got out of there until 6:30 PM while Gilley, typical of a Friday evening had a few beers with his working buddies at the Waldorf Hotel.

Friday night was a wind-down from the hectic workweek. In Canada the workweek seemed to be especially more demanding of one's time and energy, not like in England where the set routines of life made things simpler. For example in England everybody, no matter where they worked employees and employers alike, stopped at 10:00 AM for a ten-minute tea break. Everyone left their desk or workstation and went to the canteen and purchased some refreshment.

While in Canada, the company often provided the refreshments and there was no set time for a break for the office workers. Instead, the coffee pot was always on for the office workers, as many never took a break. In addition to this, there was often no place provided for staff to go to for their break. People just sat around near their work and took refreshment as they could. Swann's was especially guilty of this. They were so busy and there was quite a lot of pressure on the design and draughting staff and overtime was a necessity. Regular breaks could not be taken. Even lunch times suffered.

This seemed to take its toll by the end of the week. Friday was longed for and much anticipated by all employees and those that met at the Waldorf Hotel were no exception. Hotels were more accommodating than banks as they would cash the fellows pay cheques right there for them. What a convenience for both the clientele and the management.

This Friday was different. Gilley could only have a couple of drinks with his mates before he had to get home to meet his parents and he knew that if he was home by 6:15, he would beat Joy to the punch. This night was planned for Nellie and Jack to have another Canadian experience. It was to go to Shakey's Pizza Parlor for dinner. They were also to meet up with Joy's fellow bank employees, as most of them would also go there to celebrate the end of the workweek.

The Pizza Parlor was just around the corner from the bank and from the apartment (Stagger in and stagger out—no driving involved). What made this restaurant so unusual was that they had long picnic style tables and benches for the patrons to sit on. They had giant jugs of beer and enormous pizzas. Jack and Nellie had never experienced the likes of this in their lives. Pizza was not English and jugs of beer (about 2 liters in size) were unheard of in England and beer parlors in Canada as this was an American idea.

Shakey's had another unique menu feature. These were called Mojo's. This delight was a boiled potato that had been mashed up with a few spices added. Then this was formed into patties, deep fried and then baked in the oven to really crisp them up. Gilley really loved these, even better than French fries. If only he could find a way to put them into a sandwich. What a sandwich it would make! This could equal or even beat his favourite chip butties.

Joy had an experience in England of trying to make a pizza for Jack and Nellie and Gilley so that they could experience a Canadian dish. Unfortunately, due to the lack of the right ingredients, the pizza did not turn out to be what Joy had hoped for. The only takers were Jack and Gilley and that was only to be polite. Nellie couldn't accept the taste. Tonight could be tricky, given this experience.

Everyone arrived at about the same time and sat at one of the long tables. The plan for dinner was for everyone to order whichever pizza they wanted and then to share it around to others in the group. There were selections such as double cheese and salami, green peppers, pepperoni and mushrooms, Canadian back bacon with fresh tomatoes, shrimp, pineapple, and mozzarella cheese and the house special of the night. Of course there were several jugs of beer placed on the table for everyone to help themselves.

Nellie, not a drinker was choking for a cup of tea. At this rustic and boisterous place, the tea was undrinkable, even for Nellie. She had to settle for water. Jack was more used to a dark beer like Guinness, but he soldiered on in his task of consuming what he could. Luck for

Gilley his only competition was Joy with the jug of beer at his end of the table. Nellie picked the shrimp pizza; Joy picked the Canadian back bacon. Jack and Gilley didn't have any say in the matter. The only thing Gilley ordered was his plate of Mojo's.

To Gilley's disappointment, the pizzas came much before the Mojo's. It was so busy that evening that they were behind in serving them up. He had almost had his fill with pizza before his number was called out for him to go and pick up his order. On his way up to get his dish, he thought, "This is really lucky for me that it happened this way. Everyone is full of pizza and beer and I can have the entire helping to myself." This turned out to not be the case at all. To his dismay, both Nellie and Jack took a real liking to the Mojo's as the pizza was not much to their liking. They just weren't used to the strong taste and the spicy flavor.

Nellie and Jack quite enjoyed the rustic atmosphere of this restaurant and the company of Joy's co-workers. Walking back to the apartment, they chatted about their experience and Nellie said to Joy, "Now I know what you really meant to show us when you made that pizza in England. I feel with enough time I could develop a liking for these pizzas you are so fond of."

"Well," Joy said, "It's not my most favorite food, but your son has taken a really liking to it. Of course the Mojo's just finishes his dinner doesn't it?"

Back in the apartment, by this time it was about 11:00 PM and no sooner had they closed the front door, than Gilley cracked open a beer. Jack remarked, "Haven't you had enough bloody beer tonight?"

"You can never have enough beer," was Gilley's comeback.

Nellie jumped in, "A cup of tea would be a lot better."

"Yeah, a good cup a tea. Would you put the kettle on Joy," said Jack as Gilley opened a beer for Joy as well.

Both Nellie and Jack said in unison, "You two make a bloody good pair."

Chapter 12

The Victoria Visit!

TODAY WAS THE PROMISED trip to Victoria to visit British Columbia's Capital city and Joy's infamous Grandmother and Aunt. Normally, Saturdays were a golf day for Gilley and a lying in day for Joy. It was also her hair appointment day. Since this was to be a special day, Joy had moved her appointment to 10:00 AM from her normal 2:00 PM time and had added Nellie. Nellie had been feeling it was time to get her hair done and this would be a great time for mother and daughter in law to bond. Unfortunately for Gilley, since the plan was to take the 1:00 PM ferry from Tsawwassen to Schwartz Bay there was no golf game for him.

The trip to the ferry in itself showed Nellie and Jack different scenery yet again. The landscape became very flat and Vancouver Island could be seen on the far horizon. As they approached the ferry terminal causeway, Gilley remarked, "Mom, Dad, look behind you. That view is what I saw as I came through the border into Canada. It captured me in a way nothing else has. "What Nellie and Jack saw as the followed Gilley's directions, was a breathtaking panorama of the coastal mountains, rising up above the city of Vancouver.

"Oh Gilley, you tried to describe this to us in your letters, but nothing you said could have captured this view. It's spectacular. No wonder you fell in love with this part of the world."

Approaching the ferry parking lot, Jack commented on the word 'Tsawwassen' "How do you pronounce that word," he queried?

"As you just said, Jack," Joy responded.

"And why is it called this strange name?"

Joy replied, "It's a Native name for the band that originated in this area and still lives here on the reserve. That's about all I know about it, other than the town to our left has taken the band's name to honour the heritage of this area. You will notice we have a number of towns, cities and other areas with native names, such as Coquitlam. These all come from the bands of Aboriginal peoples who lived here before the white man settled."

As they were waiting in line to buy their tickets, Jack spotted a giant mountain of black to his right. "What the hell is that over there?"

Gilley said, "That's called Roberts Bank and it's one of the busiest coal terminals in North America. Remember when we were traveling through the interior and saw those long, everlasting trains pulling cars of coal? Well, this was their destination. Most of this coal is industrial coal and is shipped to Japan and Korea for the making of steel."

After purchasing their tickets, they were able to drive right onto the ferry. (This was unusual as often there was a one or two sailing wait.) As they pulled onto the ramp, the large trucks, the number of cars and the sheer volume of noise was overwhelming for Nellie and Jack. This was their first time sailing on a ferry and Gilley's first time driving onto one.

Once parked, Joy took over and told everyone it was OK to get out of the car, but they must watch their step as there might be raised steps and other low objects common to ferries. The next quest was have some lunch. The object was to get to the cafeteria as soon as possible as Joy told everyone that long lines developed within a few short minutes after the ferry was loaded. Fortunately for them, they had parked in an area that was the shortest distance to the cafeteria and Joy, being the knowledgeable ferry traveler that she was, got them to the front of the lunch queue.

The available fare was hamburgers and chips, salads and the ferry's famous clam chowder, as well as various cold sandwiches such as devilled egg, salmon, tuna, and ham and cheese. Of course there was a wide range of beverages to choose from including several varieties of tea. This choice delighted the foursome and they gave their orders, received their food and found a table was close to a window. Sitting down and tucking into their food, Jack looked up and said, "How come you're not having a beer, you two?"

Joy's immediate response was, "There is no alcohol allowed on these ferries as they are considered public places. This includes passengers bringing their own to drink, yet we know many do down one or two while they are traveling as they go down to their cars for a nip now and again before they arrive at the other side."

After lunch, it was time to go out on deck to watch the scenery. The size of the ferry amazed Nellie as they walked around the decks. She just couldn't believe how it could keep floating with the hundreds of cars and large number of trucks that were being carried along. Joy explained that there was a great deal of traffic between the mainland and the island and often there were long line-ups of cars waiting for the next available ferry. "However," she continued, "If one ever needed to make sure of not having to wait, one could just park their car at the terminal parking lot and catch the Greyhound bus across. It's always first on and first off the ferry and never has to wait in line. In addition to this, if, for some reason, the bus was late, the ferry would never load until it is in its place."

At this juncture, the ferry started to approach the Gulf Islands and Active Pass. This was another wonder for Nellie and Jack. The scenery was breathtaking. At certain points, the ferry came so close to the land, it seemed one could reach out and touch the trees.

Numerous cottages and cabins could be seen peeking out from the trees and lining the shore. These were all privately owned and were as individual in appearance as the owners themselves. Some were ramble down shacks and others were obviously built by the wealthy. This is incomprehensible for Nellie and Jack. The beauty, the remoteness and the vastness of this part of British Columbia overwhelmed them. "No wonder you fell in love with this vast and picturesque country. If I was twenty years younger, I would move out here and build a home on one of these islands. It could be a bit tricky getting to your home though. I imagine most of these people own their own boats," Jack said excitedly?

Just as he was speaking a much smaller ferry came into view. Joy explained, "Do you see that small ferry over there? It's called an Island Hopper and there are several that serve these islands, moving people from island to island. For example, this island on our right is Galliano and to our left is Mayne Island. As we come out of Active Pass here, you will see Pender Island and Salt Spring. It's like a sea bus for those who live here."

As everyone looked to where she was pointing, a large number of all kinds of crafts came into view. There were small motorboats, sailing boats and various fishing boats and several larger yachts. The view was absolutely stunning with houses, islands, boats, "This is a land of plenty," exclaimed Jack.

Approaching Swartz Bay, an announcement over the PA system asked that all passengers return to the bus. Shortly after this, an announcement came for all vehicle passengers to return to their cars. The ferry was full of busy as people went to their respective places. One had to be careful not to forget where one had parked their vehicle. Joy was the one who remembered where their vehicle was parked (not that Gilley would have admitted that he had forgotten) as she was used to traveling on this ferry. As the cars rumbled off the ferry, Nellie was a bit concerned. The ramps shook and the volume of noise and the exhaust fumes from the departing vehicles was very high. She wondered if this was normal or if something was wrong.

After all the excitement had died down and they were on their way, Jack asked, "Is Swartz Bay an Indian name too?"

"I don't think so, Dad, but that's a good guess. It was actually named after a friend of one of the early Premier's of British Columbia. His name was actually Swart and it was meant to be called Swart's Bay, but somehow over the years it became known as Swartz Bay."

As Gilley maneuvered the car out of the terminal and onto the highway leading to Victoria, he was thinking of his mother's age and how this was the first time she was able to experience these new things. She wasn't old really (only sixty-three) but this was the first time she had been away from England and experiencing a new part of the world. Here he was only twenty-six and he had seen more at his age than his mother had all her life. He thought of his friends in England, how they would enjoy what his parents were seeing today. Gilley had never seen anything outside of Great Britain. He had come six thousand miles to see how other people lived. He hoped one day his friends would come to visit so that they could see and experience this unique land.

During the drive into Victoria, Joy pointed out a red and pink house which, she said, used to be her Grandmother's. It sat on the left hand side of the highway as they approached the city. One could not miss it as it sat in an open lot and the color was so unusual. Joy claimed that she could feel Grandma's presence there even now many years later. Perhaps this was because Joy had spent her formative years in the Victoria area and this house of Grandma's figured largely in her memories.

At last they reached Grandma's house on Menzies Street which was just behind the government buildings. Nellie and Jack commented on the number of Government buildings in the area. Joy explained Victoria was British Columbia's capital city and that was why there were so many of these. As a matter of fact this was where Veron and Jim had met. "But that is a story for another time. Here we are at Grandma's."

Grandma watching for her guests, greeted everyone in her Birmingham accent before they finished parking, "Welcome, come on in ducks. I hope your ferry ride was enjoyable. I'll put the kettle on while these two youngsters will enjoy a beer. I bought two just for the both of you. If you want any more you better go to the liquor store now as they close at six o'clock here in Victoria. It's nice of the government to protect us from our sins. As far as I'm concerned all it creates is a bloody circus on Saturday night as everybody seems to wait till the last minute to get their booze in for the weekend. But come on in and make yourselves at home."

Nelly and Jack were in for a good visit with Grandma as she was a wealth of information on Victoria as well as a number of other things. Gilley and Joy decided to take her suggestion and go to the liquor store to stock up for the weekend. "Have bloody fun down there. It'll be like a stinking jungle. By the way, while you're down there you might as well pick me up a bottle of brandy. Here's $10.00. Don't get that expensive brandy, now. Do you hear?"

"Well, for $10.00 you're not likely to get that now are you?" retorted Gilley. As he said, this she went to the cupboard and brought out a bottle with a little bit left and she pointed out the four stars on it.

"Get the bottle with these on it and nothing else. If you don't have enough, you pay the difference because you're staying at my house, after all."

They went down to the liquor store which was just across from the Empress. It was just as bad as Grandma had said. After driving around and around, Gilley finally found a parking spot. The store was packed. "Is there not another store in this entire town?" Gilley complained as they collected their choices.

"Well, of course there is, but don't forget when I lived here these stores were not my main concern so I have no idea where they might be. Once we figure it out and get there, it'll be the same amount of time as if we just shopped here."

"Well, I'll be pleased when I'm out of this goddamned zoo. People here are crazy! I thought Victoria was a little bit more laid back than this. It seems when they get into the liquor store, all hell breaks loose," Gilley grumbled.

"Well, I guess it's because there's not a hell of a lot of things to do here on a Saturday night. It's not like when we were in England where we had many pubs to visit and friends to see. They seem so backwards here now I have England to compare things with. I so do wish I was back there," exclaimed Joy.

Gilley took a breath. "There it is again," he thought. "She wants to go back to England. Oh, oh, how can I distract her from this train of thought?" Out loud he declared, "That might be nice, but we did promise we would give life two years here. By the way, where did you go to school? Was it close to here?" He hoped his ploy worked to distract her from these thoughts of returning to England.

Before Joy could reply to this change of subject, it was their turn to pay for the liquor they wanted. By the time they got out to the car, Joy had forgotten the conversation as she had to remember how to get Gilley back to Grandma's.

Grandma was waiting at the front door. "What did I tell you? It was a circus down there, right? Well, I hope you are ready to go visit Aunt Rosa. Put the booze on the counter over there and the beer in the fridge. We're going to walk over. That way, Jack and Nellie will get to see more of Victoria." Joy and Gilley looked at each other. They had been looking forward to a thirst quenching beer as soon as they had run this errand. Hopefully, Aunt Rosa had beer at her place.

Aunt Rosa lived in a small house on the corner of Toronto Street. It wasn't too far from Grandma's and Gilley was glad he didn't have to try to find a parking space. Her youngest son, David greeted them at the door and invited them into the living room. Inside, it was very small and dark since most of the furnishings and walls were of dark colors. Sitting in the corner was Janice, Aunt Rosa's daughter who shyly greeted the guests. Aunt Rosa's oldest son Doug, who was close to Joy's age, said a quick hello as he was on his way out to his job at the drugstore. Rosa was full of busy and greeted her guests with enthusiasm.

"Come on in and sit down. Could I make you a cup of tea or would you like a little bit of the good stuff?"

Nellie replied, "Tea would be fine for me and Jack." Rosa had already cracked a beer for Gilley and Joy. It seemed as if their reputation had preceded them. Grandma and Rosa had their concoction of brandy and wine. Gilley shuddered at the very thought.

He chatted to Janice who was about thirteen and still in school. She was a shy girl with long dark hair and very thin. David, the youngest at about ten, was full of chat and quite the opposite. He declared loudly, "I don't like school. As far as I'm concerned it's a waste of time. I would rather be working full time. Right now, I have a paper route and that's good enough for me until I can work at something that pays better."

With that comment, Gilley turned to David and commented, "I had a paper route in England when I was your age. How big is your route and how many different types of papers do you carry?"

"What do you mean "how many types of papers"? We only deliver one paper which is the Victoria Times."

"So how many papers do you carry in total?"

"I deliver to about 40 houses in a ten block area."

"How long does it take you to do your route?

"About 45 minutes."

Gilley decided to tell about his experience delivering papers when he was a boy. "Let me tell you David, in England one has to be thirteen in order to get a paper route. This was due to the child labour laws. And I started out with an evening paper route which was included, the Evening Chronicle as well as all the comics, magazines and periodicals that people ordered."

"Sometimes it was a hell of a job, getting them to the right door. We used to have a book listing who got what. If they didn't get their order when they were supposed to they often ran down the bloody road after you yelling "Where's my bloody comic?" Then on Sundays there were so many papers, we had to do it in two rounds. We had to deliver the Sunday Sun, the Mirror, the People, the News of the World, The Observer, the Sunday Times, the Sunday Telegraph and the Sunday Post. I delivered to about 70 houses. The evening round used to take me about an hour and a quarter to do while the Sunday round took at least two and a half hours," continued Gilley.

"And to make a bit of extra cash, I had another Sunday round, which meant delivering to small farms outside of the village. There were eight in total. Thank God, I could take my bike on that round. It would take me about an hour and a half to do that one. It was quite funny. It was good pay, but on top of that you often got a dozen of eggs or some fruit or vegetables for your efforts. Some days, I could hardly carry the stuff home. When I was fifteen I took another route in the mornings, which comprised of about 30 houses and about five national newspapers.

David was anxious to find out how much money Gilley made delivering all of these papers. He imagined it would be hundreds of dollars and was wishing he could have the same opportunity here in Victoria.

Gilley explained he earned two pounds a week, which equaled about six Canadian dollars. David chuckled, "I get ten dollars for just what I do. So it wouldn't be worth my while to work so hard."

Grandma interrupted and explained to David how the cost of living in Canada was a lot different to the cost of living in England. Nellie interrupted here too as she had worked for the local newsagent in Throckley. "If Gilley was doing this today in England today, he would be earning approximately 10 pounds a week or thirty dollars Canadian."

Now this impressed young David. He quickly changed his view and said, "Would you like to go on my round with me tomorrow?"

"That would be a good idea if I get up in time. What time do you do it," asked Gilley?

Nellie piped up to explain how, when Gilley worked full time at Bren Manufacturing, she didn't know if it was worth his effort or not. "Believe it or not, he made less money as an apprentice than he did doing his paper route. As a paperboy, he made about 2 pounds a week.

As a pre-apprentice, by the time we got finished paying for his bus fare, his deductions and the like, he was bringing home less than a pound a week. That would be between two and three dollars a week as opposed to six dollars."

"To give himself some pocket money, he kept one of his paper jobs, which was the farm route on Sunday mornings. Jack Matthews, the local newsagent, knew how difficult it was for young apprentices and their families. So he gave Gilley the job of preparing all the papers for the newspaper boys. As well as that he trained Gilley on the cash register selling items such as cigarettes and candy etc in the newsagent shop. Gilley earned about 10 shilling or $1.50 for that job and then he still did the route to the farms. As the paper routes were getting bigger, Jack Matthews needed a younger body to bring in the papers dropped off from the various publishers and sort them out for the ten paperboys. This was hard work, but you know, hard work never killed anybody."

Jack, not to be outdone, commented about the time when the paperboys went on strike for equality with their counterparts in the village of Newburn. "They were getting approximately one and sixpence more than the Throckley boys. Yet if you had no errors, you would get a bonus of six pence in Throckley. Remember, most of these boys' families didn't have much money. They often had to buy their own bicycles and other sports equipment and help out at home too eh.

There was this upstart, Wally Wilson, who wasn't a paperboy to start with," continued Jack, "but had talked to Gilley and a couple of his friends about going on strike for equality. So this night, just about the time the boys were ready to leave with their newspapers, Wally went in and demanded equality with Newburn paperboys. After a time, Jack Matthews and Wally came out and Jack said he would forego the six-penny bonus and give them a raise to 10 shilling. He would think about a one-shilling bonus. He couldn't make this commitment right then, as he had to do some calculations.

Well, Wally Wilson wasn't happy with that and asked all the boys to hand in their paper bags. At that stage, Jack Matthews asked each and every one of the paperboys what they wanted to do. Did they want to have a job or did they want to follow the lead of Wally Wilson. Two boys did, that being Peter Muxworthy and Allan Phillips. The rest said, "Whatever Gilley does, we'll do. How about it Gilley?"

Gilley took up the story from here, "There I was, on the spot. I felt caught between some of my friends and my obligation to Jack Matthews. I also knew most of the boys, including myself, couldn't afford to lose even one day's pay. I also thought about them having to go home and tell their parents they didn't have a job anymore. That would be pretty brutal. I thought about the customers who were relying on us to get them their papers and how much trouble this would cause Jack. I had been quite surprised when Jack had offered us a raise to begin with and then had said he would think about an additional shilling on top of that.

I made up my mind. We would stick by Jack, keep our jobs and deliver the papers. I also said that, as a group, we would complete the rounds of the two boys who had joined Wally Wilson. Jack Matthews and the others were happy with this decision as they had been thinking along these same lines. We did as promised that night.

Unknown to me, Wally and the other two boys, decided to black list me, called me names and did everything possible to injure me. They threw stones and mud balls at me and at our front door. For days they chanted nasty remarks at me such as Yellow Belly, Traitor, Turn Coat with a few adjectives that went with the names of course."

Jack interjected here. "Remember, I was a strong Union man, still am. And for my son to be attacked for what he stood up for was something I could relate to. I'd been called many names as I walked those picket lines. I would slap Gilley on the back and say, "You were forced to make a decision affecting many people and their incomes against someone who didn't even have the right to speak on your behalf. Wally Wilson had nothing to lose. He was actually the bully and he had counted on you to side with him just for the power of it. You did the right thing. I was proud you stood up against him and those two other upstarts. Remember, I always said to you, 'Sticks and stones can break your bones, but calling names will never hurt you.'"

Grandma stood up. "Well, that's enough of that crap. It's time we went home to have some supper. My roast chicken will be charcoal if we stay longer." Saying their goodbyes to Rosa and the kids, everyone sauntered out into the summer evening. Walking back to the house, Grandma remarked it was good for her to hear about Gilley and the English way of life as she often missed it. She was curious about Nellie too. She asked, "What did you do for a living, Nellie?"

"I still work for the newsagent store once owned by Jack Matthews. When he died, his son, Gary, expanded the operation by opening another two stores in Throckley. He offered me the job at the Broomey Hill store as I had been working with the news agency for many years delivering morning papers."

Grandma said to Jack, "How could you allow your wife to deliver papers so early in the morning. What are you doing at that time of the day?"

Nellie jumped to Jack's defense, "This was my choice. When Gilley was eight, the doctor diagnosed me with a blood disorder and recommended I walk at least an hour a day. I thought if I was going to have to bloody well do this, I might as well earn some money doing it. Gilley got his start by helping me on some mornings."

"Well done Nellie. I would have done the same thing. You don't do something for nothing, if you can help it," Grandma said.

Arriving back at Grandma's, it didn't take her long to complete dinner preparations. After a few finishing touches, they all sat down to a good old-fashioned English dinner. There was chicken, roast potatoes done around the chicken, peas, turnips and carrots and of course Yorkshire puddings (even though Yorkshire puddings were more traditional with beef, Grandma knew how much Gilley really enjoyed Veron's version and Grandma wanted to show him how much better hers were.)

The dinner conversation picked up where it had left off upon arriving home. Grandma, wanting to find out more about these visitors asked, "Now Jack, Nellie has told me what she does for a living. What did you did before you retired?"

"I was the caretaker of the local council offices in Newburn," replied Jack after he'd swallowed his mouthful.

"What did that entail?"

"I would start at 7:00 AM in the morning and work until 9:00 AM. During that time, I had to make sure the boiler was stoked up for the day as hot water radiators heated all of the offices. It was a coke boiler and this was done by hand. This brought the building up to a nice warm temperature for the office workers. Even in the summer time, the boiler had to be stoked as the building was made of stone and the floors were made of marble. It was a cold building even in the hottest weather.

Between 9:00 AM and 9:30 AM, I would come back home. Then my day would start again at 4:00 PM and go until 9:00 PM or 10:00 PM, depending on what mess was left from that day because as well as making sure the boiler was up to standard, I did all the janitorial work for the building after the workers went home."

Nellie jumped in at this point, "Tell her about your other job, Jack."

"Well, most people don't want to hear about that, Nellie."

Of course, this interested Grandma even more, now. "Come on Jack, have you got something spicy that you're hiding from me?"

"No, I don't think you'd call this job spicy. But if you really want to know, one of my jobs was to clean the mortuary out once the coroner had completed his exam. The ambulance department and the coroner's office were part of the council offices in those days. I would often be asked by the ambulance department to prepare the body for the coroner. This entailed washing the body down and preparing it on the slab. There were many disturbing times for me as numerous bodies were from industrial or car accidents, which left them dismembered or injured in some other horrible manner. But my biggest problem was when young children had drowned or been killed."

"Oh, that was a horrible job for anybody to do, Jack. Why did you do it?"

"Well, someone had to do it and in those days five shillings per body came in very useful."

"I bet you have a few stories to tell," responded Grandma.

Nellie, encouraging Jack on, "Tell them about the one that returned to life right before your eyes."

Just at this time, Rosa appeared at the door. "Here I am ready to join the party. Doug's going to look after the kids. They're all sitting down watching TV. I just thought I'd come around for a visit with Gilley's parents as this might be the last time I get a chance to see them." Her timing was perfect. Everyone had just finished dinner and were ready for an after dinner drink. Joy and Gilley jumped up and cleared the table in preparation for the washing up."

"Before the washing up, let's sit down and have a drink," said Rosa. "I'll have what your having, Mom."

Grandma said grumpily, "Do you have any wine? I don't have much left to mix with the brandy. I only have enough for two drinks."

"Well," Rosa said, "If someone runs me over to the liquor store in Esquimalt, I'll pick up a bottle of wine there. It's the only store open at this time."

Gilley jumped up with his keys, ready to go. Of course Joy decided to join them.

"What the matter, Joy? You don't trust me alone with your new husband," Rosa jived?

Grandma mumbled, "Bloody liquor store rules. It's so antiquated. Not what you're used to in England is it, Jack? By the way, Rosa, I don't blame Joy for coming along with you two. Someone needs to make sure you get back sharp because we've got stories to tell. Nellie and I will do the dishes while Jack catches up on the news."

After the trio left on their mission, Grandma commented to Nellie and Jack, "That Rosa is a bit of a wild one at times."

The three of them reached the liquor store, which was as crowded as hell and as they got up to the till to pay for the wine, a man accidentally bumped Rosa. Well, Rosa was not going to let this go. "What the hell do you think you're doing? Are you trying to make a pass at me? If so, you're going to have to do a hell of a lot better than that. And who's to say I'd be interested in you anyhow?"

The man was embarrassed and he immediately responded, "What the hell are you talking about, Lady? Are you crazy?"

"Don't you call me crazy," yelled Rosa, her voice escalating.

At this stage, Gilley felt he needed to step in as it looked like it was going to get ugly. He motioned for Joy to go and pay for the wine before she got involved. It was too late. Joy jumped to Rosa's defense, "You shouldn't pick on my aunt."

Gilley said, "Listen man, why don't you just go and pay for your booze. The counter is open. It's yours. I'll look after this situation."

The man cooperated fully with this suggestion, but Rosa wasn't finished. By this time, Joy realized Rosa had had a few too many drinks. What was really needed was to quiet her down before she could cause any more trouble. Eventually they got back in the car. Rosa continued to yap on all the way back to Grandma's house. Even as they came into the house, Rosa was carrying on. As a matter of fact she was out of the car almost before it stopped and up the stairs to tell Grandma, Jack and Nellie of her ordeal.

As Joy and Gilley came into the house and gave the wine to Grandma, she said, "So, you enjoyed your little outing with Rosa did you? Stay a while and you'll have a few more stories to tell."

Drinks were served all around and Grandma, settling into her favorite chair said, "OK, Jack, I've been waiting for over an hour now to find out about this bloke coming alive on you."

After filling Rosa in on the job at the mortuary, he picked up on the story. "It went like this. It was a cold winter night and I was at home listening to the radio, sitting by the fire. It was about 11:00 PM, just about bedtime. A knock came to the door. It was the ambulance driver. "Jack, sorry to inconvenience you on a night like this, but we have a dead one for you and we need to get into the mortuary."

"Into the ambulance and down to the offices we went—about a 15-minute drive. The mortuary was always cold, but tonight it was colder than hell. I opened the door and let the boys with the body into the building. After undressing the body, they helped me place him on the cold slab for washing. As they left to go to get a hot cup of tea for me, I started to just clean up the place and wait for the coroner.

Just at that time, the body sat up. He opened his eyes and said, "Where the hell am I? I just about passed out from fear. I left the room so quick I caught up with the ambulance drivers even before they got to their office to get the tea. I was shouting, "He's alive, he's alive. Come back quick. Bring some blankets." We all ran back into the morgue. The poor old guy was shivering like hell and in shock. We wrapped him up in the blankets, gave him hot tea and rubbed him down to warm him up. Of course one of us called the doctor. We moved him into the offices where it was warmer."

"The doctor that arrived on the scene was the same doctor who had pronounced him dead. He couldn't believe it when he arrived. In all of his practice, he had never seen the like of this before. He concluded the shock of being placed on the frigid slab had started the fellow's heart into pumping again and this had caused him to revive. After checking him out thoroughly, the ambulance drivers took him to the hospital and took me home. What a night! I couldn't sleep at all that night. And every other body after that unnerved me. I eventually gave up the job. It just wasn't worth it. As a matter of fact I did have a nervous breakdown which prevented me from working for about six months."

There was silence in the room for a few seconds as everyone digested what Jack had just said. Grandma was the first one to recover, "That would have prevented me from working for bloody ever, Jack. What a tale!" Rosa commented she had heard of these things happening before as she worked in the medical department for the veteran affairs as a stenographer.

To continue the conversation, Jack asked Grandma, "What made you decide to come to Canada and make such a big change?"

Grandma replied, "I decided to immigrate in 1947 after our house had been bombed during the War. I was proud of my house and had worked hard to maintain it before and during the War but things got worse after the War instead of better. It was virtually impossible for me to get back what I had lost let alone make life better. Frank, my husband worked for the Birmingham City Bus Corporation as a mechanic. He was extremely clever and he applied for a job in Detroit, USA. His application was accepted. So we all decided we were going to leave England. But at the last moment, Frank got cold feet. He enjoyed his time in England as he liked his job at the bus company and he was also a very talented piano player and singer. He used to tour all of the bars and get his drinks paid for. He just said, "Why would anyone want to leave England. I have everything I need here."

"He might have had it good, but we, as a family, didn't. Now I'm talking about Veron, Rosa and Paul. You see by that time, Peter, my second son, was working for an insurance company up in the midlands and Frank my oldest boy, who was trained as a draughtsman just like Gilley here, had joined the Navy as a third engineer to help the War Effort. After the War, he was allowed to go back to being a civilian. He also fancied Canada so we all decided to immigrate because my sister Rita lived in Winnipeg. She told us it was a great place to be."

"As you know Jack, things were not that good in England after the War. Prospects in Canada looked far more beneficial, especially for my kids. I decided we would come to Canada instead. It was much easier to come here than to go to the States as Canada was still part of the Commonwealth. I decided to leave bloody Frank Sr. in England to pursue his dreams. I always hoped one day he might follow. I had already sold everything in order to start our new life in Canada so proceeded with the plan minus Frank. I had heard about British Columbia and in particular, Victoria and how much like England it was. I decided then and there Victoria would be our destination.

We traveled by ship to New York and then by train came to Toronto where Frank Jr. decided to settle as he had been offered a job with Imperial Oil. If, for some reason, it didn't work out, he would join us out west. From there we went to Winnipeg and met up with Rita and after several days I realized Victoria was really where I wanted to be. Winter was approaching and I don't like snow. We boarded the train and continued west.

Once we arrived in Victoria, I put Veron and Rosa to work immediately at the Empress Hotel. Paul, who was still eleven, and couldn't work, went off to school. I decided to get my own business, a second hand store. I had always wanted to do this and Victoria was prime territory for such a business. I rented a building with a store front and a residence above. This way I could attend to Paul and to my business and there was no time wasted traveling in between. It was also a place for the girls to stay till they got established. I used my last savings to acquire stock. Eventually, Rita moved out here and went into competition with me. In fact, she only thought she was my competitor but never really came into the picture. She's retired now like I am."

Gilley was intrigued by this information. He sat listening attentively and as Grandma finished up her story, his gaze fell on Rosa who kept butting into the conversation yet adding no real information. As a matter of fact, she was getting quite into her cups. She began complaining about how hard her mother had made her and Veron work when they got here. "We worked all the time and had to turn our wages over to Grandma" grumbled Rosa. "If either Veron or I brought a friend home for dinner, Grandma would make us pay for the friend's dinner. If a man friend came over, not only did we have to pay for his dinner, but we had to put up with her flirting with him at the same time."

Grandma was beginning to get a little annoyed with Rosa's complaints. "It's time you went home, Rosa. I've heard all I want to hear from you tonight."

Gilley decided to offer to drive her home. (There was no way she could walk by now). Rosa responded, "There's no way I need a bloody man to take me home. I can walk,".

Knowing Rosa's stubbornness, Joy offered to walk her home instead and since Joy was a bit of a favourite of hers, Rosa accepted this offer.

Joy, gave Gilley a look that said, "You'd better come with us too, but walk behind."

As Rosa was leaving, she said, "Why the hell you brought us to this bloody place I don't know. We should have stayed in bloody England with Brother Peter. He's doing very well for himself and we would be too. Joy, you make sure that you go back to England. You'll do much better there."

At this stage, Joy agreed just to save the peace. "It was Gilley that made the decision to come here."

Gilley jumped in here at this point, "It wasn't my decision. It was your parents' decision we should come back here for two years to taste the life here and see if we liked it. And up till now, I think it was a good decision of theirs."

"Ah, bullshit," slurred Rosa. "Let's get out of here. I've had enough of this conversation tonight." At that point, she staggered to the door, threw it open and stumbled down the stairs. Joy ran after her and Gilley followed up the rear to make sure the women were safe.

Arriving back at Grandma's after seeing Rosa home, they discovered everyone had gone to bed. "It's time for us to relax and have a beer by ourselves and watch a bit of TV," Joy said. Gilley agreed with that. Eventually, they made their way to their sleeping quarters. It was a makeshift corner of the living room with very little privacy.

"What a shame," thought Gilley.

The following morning started bright and happy with Grandma preparing breakfast. Nellie and Jack soon arose. The clinking of teacups woke Gilley up. "Come on, you two, you can't stay stinking in bed all day. Time to get up," Grandma yelled.

Gilley did as he was told and stepped into his pants. He made his way to the shower looking for that magical rejuvenation. It was a little disappointing as this shower was not as strong as the one at home. It did the trick somewhat however and got rid of those cobwebs. Joy, being stubborn, was not going to move.

After breakfast, Grandma ordered everyone to come with her for a walk along Dallas Road and through Beacon Hill Park, saying to Nellie, "This is what you're used to doing in the morning, isn't it? We'll leave Joy to fend for herself. She's not the best in the mornings and I should know. After all, I brought that girl up and that's another story."

Grandma grabbed her shopping bag and it seemed to be full of something that was bulky and of course she set the pace and the direction. It was a warm summer morning with blue skies and white puffy clouds and very few people around at that time of day. As they came to the first garbage can along the road, Grandma immediately pulled out a brown paper bag from her shopping bag. This looked suspiciously like a bottle. She looked around a bit to see who was watching and quickly dropped it into the can. "Well, that's one down, two to go." Nellie, Jack and Gilley looked at each other questioningly. Surely she had a garbage can at home?

Jack decided to brave the question, "How come you don't dump your bottles in your can at home?"

Grandma responded, "Garbage men are nosy buggers and are gossipers. I don't want them to know about my drinking and spread it all over the neighborhood. In any case, when you have a few people over and the bottles build up so every morning I like to take a walk and get rid of the evidence. You never know, if someone thought you were drinking a lot, especially an old woman like myself, living alone, they might try to take the advantage of you. If anyone is going to take advantage of me, I want to be the one to choose him."

As they walked along the beach road, she rambled along telling many little stories. They reached Beacon Hill Park and stopped for another drop-off. She stopped and recalled, "I once saw a chap in a black raincoat standing behind that tree. I had a feeling he thought he'd give this old lady a thrill. Sure enough, he threw his raincoat open. There he was standing so proud. I was afraid of what might happen, but I looked into his eyes and said, "I wouldn't be so proud, young man, I've seen bigger and a lot better than that." With that he closed his coat and ran off in the opposite direction. I showed him that it's not wise to mess with Grandma."

Arriving back at the house, Joy was up and ready for the next stage of the trip—Butchart Gardens. She had already cleaned up the dishes and made the beds. Everything was back to normal. Grandma said, "Didn't I tell you I raised her right?" After many "Thanks" and "Goodbyes", Grandma looked a little sad. It was obvious Joy was her favourite granddaughter as she had been her first grandchild and she would have enjoyed spending more time with her.

The foursome loaded into the car and began the hour-long trip to the much-anticipated Butchart Gardens. After everyone settled into their seats, Jack and Nelly asked more about Belle (Isabella) which was what Grandma preferred to be called. They asked Joy more about her upbringing in Victoria and some of her experiences as a young girl. Joy was pleased to be able to tell her story to people who seemed genuinely interested in her.

Joy told them how she lived in Victoria until she was eleven years old. Jim and Veron moved to New Westminster as Jim had gotten a new job as superintendent of the buildings and grounds for the New Westminster School Board. The territory he would oversee comprised of seven elementary schools and two high schools (Vincent Massey and George Pearson—these eventually amalgamated into one huge school called New Westminster Secondary School)

Before moving to New Westminster, most of her young childhood had been spent with Grandma in her secondhand store, which had competed with her sister, Rita. Joy also had the privilege of going to the auctions with Grandma, Veron and Jim. She remembered how often Jim's car would be loaded up with goods and she had fun being stuffed in amongst the prized purchases as they headed home celebrating their victories over the other auction attendees.

Things seemed picture perfect to Joy. She was the center of attention of the adults in her life. The only thing which was a little confusing was that Mom and Dad would move into a house, work like hell to fix it up to their satisfaction and by the time the house had reached that level, they would decide to sell it for a profit. Then the cycle would start all over again—buy, fix, sell. In total they lived in four houses she could remember—the first house being on Admiral's Road; the second house which was called Tattersall, had a large swimming pool which filled naturally from a spring and had a large back yard (Joy's favourite house of them all); the third was on Vancouver Street and the fourth was on Rockland Avenue.

In the midst of these years of buying, fixing and selling, Sally was born when Joy was about four years old and Anne came along a year and a bit. This accounted for the reason why Joy spent so much time with her Grandmother until she got older and could look after her two sisters. Grandma would often ask if Joy was available to help her around the store. This would provide a reprieve from her babysitting duties. It was exciting as Grandma often asked her to be the detective in the store, watching for customers shoplifting.

The move to New Westminster was at once sad and exciting for this young girl of eleven. In her own words, here was another house that needed to be fixed and that meant Mom and Dad would be very busy and she would have to baby-sit. On the other hand, this would mean a new job for Dad, which he was very excited about and it also meant a new adventure for them all. Much to Joy's surprise, her family stayed in this house. All through her high school years, she kept expecting to be told the family would be moving again. Dad did the usual fix-up and made the house look great, but there was no mention of a move.

This presented Joy with an entirely different experience. Instead of having to move from school to school, she could stay in one place—something she had always wanted. Well, she found staying was much harder than she thought. Going to Vincent Massey High School presented the greatest challenge of her experience. She found most of the kids she wanted to befriend already belonged to groups and clubs. These kids were not open to newcomers, as they had gone all through elementary school with each other.

Eventually, she became friends with Linda, Liz, and Lorraine and a few others. She was also eventually invited to join one of the prestigious sweater clubs. (These sweater clubs only invited in a rare few at a time.) It was considered a mark of honor to be invited even though the initiation rites were often embarrassing and difficult.

By this point in Joy's story, they arrived at the Gardens and the topic changed immediately. Finding a parking spot was the typical challenge they had encountered in Victoria. Getting out of the car after being successful in the endeavor, Joy said to Gilley, "Don't forget your camera. I really do want pictures of this part of our trip."

Butchart Gardens had been an old quarry pit from which limestone had been extracted to make Portland cement. This enterprise was owned and run by Robert Butchart. As the quarrying took place, stripping the land of its natural beauty, Jennie Butchart requisitioned tons of topsoil from surrounding farmlands and built these spectacular gardens. These gardens included a Japanese garden, an Italian Garden and a Sunken garden. Mr. Butchart was so impressed by his wife's endeavor he added his own touches. His hobby had been to collect exotic birds and birdhouses. He had these strategically placed throughout the Gardens.

This all began in 1908 and by the 1920's more than 50,000 people had been to visit her creation. It has become one of the most visited attractions in Canada. The only surviving portion of Mr. Butchart's Tod Inlet cement factory is the tall chimney of a long vanished kiln. The chimney can be seen from The Sunken Garden Lookout. The plant stopped manufacturing cement in 1916, but continued to make tiles and flower pots as late as 1950. The single chimney now overlooks the quarry Mrs. Butchart so miraculously reclaimed.

Jack and Nelly wondered the grounds like children in fantasyland. They had never seen such beauty and such originality. The floral arrangements were beyond description. Fortunately for Gilley, the camera seemed to be working properly and he took the shots Joy directed. Three hours later and after a spot of tea and lunch, the group, leaving the miraculous gardens, traveled north over the Malahat Highway toward Nanaimo. It was another hot day. As a matter of fact it was the hottest day of their trip so far however this portion of the drive showed another spectacular part of British Columbia.

Arriving in Nanaimo, they discovered they had just missed the ferry back to the mainland and they had a two-hour wait until the next ferry boarded. It was 104 degrees Fahrenheit, the hottest day in Nanaimo's history to date. This just about killed Jack and Nelly and Gilley and Joy weren't too far behind. There was no shelter in which to get out of the oppressive heat let alone no pub to pop into for a quick one. The one saving grace was there was a little café serving beverages and snacks. A cup of tea was always Nelly's idea for quenching one's thirst. This time they all took the plunge and found out she was right.

Eventually, the ferry arrived (none too soon for the foursome). It was a refreshing journey as the wind on the waters blew away the heat accumulated on the tarmac. Arriving at Horseshoe Bay, they looked north to snow capped mountains. They could see another part of BC that would have to wait for another visit. Gilley explained to his parents this was the Squamish Highway leading to Whistler Mountain and to his first experience in a logging camp and a meeting with a real Native Indian.

Driving off of the ferry, Gilley decided it wouldn't hurt to take Mom and Dad on a final tour of West Vancouver before they headed home to New Westminster. This little side trip took them up to the

British Properties. This area held some of the wealthiest homes in British Columbia. Gilley spotted a lookout and stopped the car.

From this point they could over look English Bay and the Lion's Gate Bridge. The view was another spectacular display of ocean, islands and coast land. One could see all the freighters and tankers waiting to dock in Vancouver as well as the private sail boats which dotted the blue waters. Gilley explained the Lion's Gate Bridge was built by the Guinness family (one of the original founding families in the area) in order for them to have easy access to their properties which eventually became the British Properties. This family had owned this land before it had been developed and were instrumental in the establishing of this exclusive neighborhood as well as opening the corridor to Whistler. Gilley also explained the sales manager for Swann's, Dennis Shears, lived in the Properties and he had been promised a visit soon.

Back into the car and continuing on, the tour wound down the mountain and went across the Second Narrows Bridge. Joy exclaimed, "Gilley, you should be familiar with this part of the highway as this is the route you took when we were coming from Linda and Howie's." She then explained to Nelly and Jack that Linda and Howie live in Millardville, which was on the other side of New Westminster and that somehow, Gilley had ended up driving over here looking for home, which had been about a mile away from their point of origin. He also ended up going across the Lion's Gate Bridge. It had been a miracle he had found his way back to New Westminster and that there had been enough gas in the car to take them on this escapade.

Gilley's remark was, "But I was going in the other direction when I made that trip. How am I supposed to recognize the area especially since it was night time?"

Jack said, "You sure have done enough driving over here even since we've been here and you've done a good job."

Nelly, jumped in, "Yeah, Gilley and at least we didn't get stopped by another police man."

"Mom, you mean the RCMP", retorted Gilley. "Mind you there are many different police forces. In Vancouver, New Westminster, and Port Moody, they have their own force. The RCMP are Canadian forces and are only in places not patrolled by local forces."

Arriving back at the apartment, it was time for dinner and cold beers (and tea of course). It was Sunday and tomorrow was another workday. It was also coming to the end of Jack and Nelly's trip. Five more days and they would be heading home. In two more days, though, more visitors from England would be arriving at Jim and Veron's. This would be Jim's sister Eunice and her husband Edmond.

CHAPTER 13

EDMOND AND EUNICE COME TO CANADA

NELLIE AND JACK HAD never met Edmond and Eunice and everyone was expecting that things should be quite a lot of fun. Edmond was Polish but he had gained his British Citizenship by marrying Eunice, but was still a socialist at heart. Now along with Jack being a socialist, this could conjure up a few good discussions as both Jim and Veron were not of this belief. Gilley and Joy could see fireworks in the making.

Monday morning was back to Vancouver in the Duster. Business was not moving along as Swann's had anticipated. The goal was to acquire the wire rope building and solve the overcrowding problem which was due to abundance of contracts. The contracted timelines were becoming more and more delayed due to the delay in the availability of new facilities. In order to help out, the owners of the two companies had compromised and some shop floor space for the winch program was allocated ahead of time.

Now this program came about due to the North Sea Oil and Gas becoming a major development in Europe. The greatest need for this project to succeed was to have supply vessels. These ships not only supplied the necessary apparatus and other commodities to the oil rigs, but they were essential for moving and positioning the huge platforms.

Most of Europe had taken on the task of building the oil rigs thus overtaxing the industry and leaving a gap in the area of supply vessels. This created the opportunity for other countries such as Canada, to participate in this great endeavor. The Canadian Government, seeing the potential, promoted Canadian shipyards. They did so by providing subsidies to those companies who could qualify in building the necessary vessels and to those who could support this building program by providing the necessary equipment. Vancouver was already knowledgeable in the manufacturing of similar types of vessels and had the necessary naval architects experienced in building coastal and deep sea tug boats. With this knowledge and experience, it wasn't a long reach for these companies to design and build the needed ships. Swann's had the ability to support these shipyards with the large winches and deck equipment needed.

Allied Shipbuilding was the major contender for building these vessels and was bidding on five ship sets for IOS (International Offshore Supply) out of Britain. Allied had specified all of the deck equipment would be manufactured by Swann Winches. The other shipyard was Bellaire and it was bidding on three ship sets for another offshore supply company and they also wanted Swann's to supply the deck equipment. With all of these orders Swann's had to increase their engineering staff. The offices were becoming rather crowded during the hot summer weather and this necessitated the move to the wire rope building. The agreement between the two companies was a welcome relief.

The local watering hole, The Waldorf, with its air-conditioning, became the most favoured place to be during lunch and after work by both management and employees alike. As the Longshoremen's Union Hall was in between Swann's and the Waldorf there was often competition for who got there first. The laws in Canada insisted there be no standing in any beer parlour so seats became a premium. The other strange rule in Canada was that your beer had to be served by a waiter. Gilley got a bit of a giggle here as it reminded him of the bus conductors in England with their change bags at their waist.

This Monday back at work was an exceptionally hot day and the lure of the Waldorf hung in everyone's mind all afternoon. Gilley had to fight off the temptation to drop in for just a quick cool one, as he knew family obligations awaited him back at the apartment. Nellie and Jack still had things to do and places to go before their return to England. This Monday night was a trip to Queen Elizabeth's Park and the famous Bloedel Floral Conservatory. These attractions were located together in the southwest part of Vancouver. The park was a delight to see with its sunken gardens and fabulous flowers. It was smaller than the Butchart Gardens by far, but the two of them had something in common—they both started out as a quarry and were turned into a thing of beauty.

The thing that set this Park above others was the panoramic view of the North Shore Mountains and Vancouver. That night the foursome saw a spectacular view as the sun, setting in the west, sent streams of light on to the local coastal mountains turning them a variety of colours.

The Conservatory boasted of tropical plants, flowers and birds. It was set up on the high knoll of Queen Elizabeth's Park and served as the crown for this venture. By the time everyone headed home, Nellie said, "That was spectacular. What a beautiful city. Thank you for taking us to all of these places. However, Jack and I would like to spend our last few days with the two of you at the apartment, visiting and resting up for our return trip. We need the time to pack all of the things we've acquired during our stay as well. That is going to be quite the feat.

Joy answered, "I understand, Nellie. Besides the reasons you've said, Eunice and Edmond are coming two days before and you'll have a good time getting to know them. We have many plans in the works for you both. For example, I have a dinner planned for Tuesday night to give the four of us an opportunity to be alone and chat as well as for you to be able to do your laundry before you return. Then, on Wednesday night, Veron has organized a welcome to Canada and going away from Canada dinner for all as Eunice and Edmond are arriving Wednesday morning. So your request fits right in with our plans."

Tuesday night came along and it was not as hot and clammy as it had been previously. Joy opened the patio doors and the back door and to everyone's relief a nice breeze came through the apartment. After dinner everyone settled down with their favourite beverage (tea and beers). It was time to recap the trip and catch up on things that had gone by the side.

Jack began, "Have you made any good friends here yet Gilley?"

"Not really", said Gilley, "I haven't had the time to get to know any one the same as I did back home. The pace here is different and I have been busy getting used to the Canadian way of life and getting myself established in my career. I have met some very nice people and I golf every Saturday with Jim, Eric and Brian.

"Unfortunately Brian will be leaving for New Zealand this fall with his wife Marva, so my working buddy, Dave Mosley, whom I have gotten to know fairly well also, will be joining our foursome. He was the one who sold me this very good camera for $20.00. Even though it's not as good as Jim's it still takes great shots as you have seen. He's got a great sense of humour. By the way, he's from England."

"Oh really, what part of England", said Jack?

Joy jumped in, "He's from Windsor, one of my favourite places."

Nelly, not to be left out, said, "You'll never have friends equal to the ones you have in England because you grew up with them. These friends are part of your history."

On this point Gilley had to agree. "Bill Wakefield, one of my pals from childhood and one of my drinking buddies, has announced he will be getting married next year. Joy and I plan to come over for his wedding. He has asked me to reciprocate and be his best man. It would be an honour. Joy however, is not pleased with this marriage as she always thought he should marry Liz, her best friend as well as her drinking and traveling buddy in England."

"We saw Liz not too long ago. She is still living with Aunt Phyll and teaching computer classes in Newcastle. I was talking to her and she plans to come back to Canada one day soon. She really enjoys England, but there are some things she is homesick for," replied Nellie.

"I really thought Liz and Bill would hit it off. It would have been fun to have Gilley's best friend and my best friend get married and move to Canada. My dad said that Bill would have no problem getting a job here in B.C. with his qualifications in horticulture. As a matter of fact Dad would give him a job with the School Board. They are always looking for qualified landscapers."

Jack jumped in, "He's a fool not to take this chance. From what I've seen of Canada, this would be a great place to start a life and raise a family. But love is blind. With him marrying Christine, I doubt he will move over here now. She is very committed to her family in England."

"Of course," added Gilley, "Bill has a large family too and he might find it hard to leave them behind as he is the eldest and feels responsible for his mom and dad. I know Neil is back there with you two and if anything happened he would be there to see things are done immediately, but of course I would come home as soon as I could to help out.

"Now, my other friends Ray and Margaret thought about coming over here too. It's a different story for them. What with him being a printer, jobs are very difficult to get as the Union here makes it hard for people from overseas to gain a membership and one has to be a member in order to get work in British Columbia. Ray would have come over here and take some other type of work until he could get in. Also, it is not easy for anyone to immigrate to Canada who doesn't have a guaranteed job or a family member to sponsor him.

"Dave Wright, who is a teacher, has sent many applications over here and not one has been accepted. He hasn't even gotten an encouraging response even though Jim has put him in touch with right people. It seems that it's again a very protective Union situation. Dave has also applied to Germany to teach the children of the British Troops who are stationed there. He's getting married this fall and is eager to get something going other than teaching in England."

Nellie surmised, "Well, Gilley, it looks as if there are very few who can join you here in your new life. Have you heard from John and Val Palmer lately? What are the prospects of them coming over here?"

"No chance. Val is pregnant and she is the only child. With John being the only child in his family too, they are bound to stay in England or close at hand in Europe. I also know that John has had an offer from Stanley Miller to move to Saudi Arabia to be the head Quantity Surveyor for their Saudi operation. This would mean a very good salary and they would be closer to their families. This company gives leaves of absence to their employees and families so they can return to their native land for long periods of time in order to reconnect. I don't think John and Val are going to move there until late 1972 or early 1973."

"Well, you were best man for John Palmer first, then Ray Cowie, and now you're going to be best man for Bill. Dave will be a bit upset you're not going to be his best man."

"There's nothing you can do about that is there? He did ask me, but he also knows I'm fully committed here until next year. I did promise to come back to England after two years and we are planning to do so. We can't return any earlier than that."

Joy jumped in here, "You know, I never really wanted to come back to Canada in the first place. I would have preferred to have stayed in England and made our life there. But to be fair to Gilley, I said we would give it two years here and if he likes it after two years, we will stay here. Or he will stay alone, depending on circumstances."

At that moment a knock came at the door. It was Jim and Veron and Tinker. They were out for an evening stroll and thought they would come in and have a drink.

Jim said to Jack, "Well, what do you think of Canada?"

"Everything is so big here. What really impressed me was the size of the lorries or trucks as you call them here in Canada on the ferry. How the hell they get onto that boat and it doesn't sink, I'll never know. But I know my son in-law, Bill Bates, Iris's husband, would be thrilled to drive these lorries over here. After Iris's death he remarried to a lovely girl called Dot. She looked after our granddaughter, Valerie, as if she was her own. Then they had two of their own children, Robert and Carol. Lovely kids. We still see them frequently and they are looking forward to hearing about our trip. That's why I wanted Gilley to take a photograph of one of those big trucks. Bill won't believe it if I just tell him about them."

"What happened to Iris? How did she die? Do you mind me asking?" queried Veron.

"She died when she was thirty-four." said Nellie. "That was in 1963. She caught Rheumatic Fever during the War from the air raid shelters we had to stay in. They were often very damp and this created a heart condition for her. She had to be very careful. Just after Valerie was born, it became worse. She was one of three at that time to do a valve bypass in her heart. It was very experimental, but she was the last of the three and was doing very, very well until she caught a bad flu."

Gilley joined into the conversation at this point. "I remember the last time I saw Iris. She was at home and I had popped down to see how she was doing. Bill was away on a long distance drive for the company he worked for and Iris had been feeling poorly with this flu. I put on a nice fire for her and made a cup of tea. I told the lady next-door Iris was not well and I would be taking Valerie up to my mother's for the day. This neighbor often looked in on her. Iris asked if Mother could come down to see her as soon as she was free. However, before Mother could get there, she passed away."

Jim, wanting to change the subject, said," What would Neil think of Canada, Jack? Would he like to move out here do you think?"

Jack, grateful for the distraction, said, "Well, Jim, Neil was in the Merchant Navy and traveled to many places during that time. He visited Canada, but that was on the East coast. He has very fond memories of that time. He has a good job, he plays golf every week and has a young family, Brenda and Christine.

Course, Joan, his wife, is an only child. Her mother is Bella, whose husband died when Joan was very young. She visits every weekend and she is a real character. She looks after the kids for them. Neil is envious of Gilley because Gilley has left him with all of the family problems. Yet, they don't think he will be here forever. They full expect Gilley to return home one day."

Veron couldn't let this go by, "What's wrong with Canada? There are plenty of good opportunities here and very many more than in England for a young man to make good of himself."

Jim agreed, "When I came to Canada right after the war, this was the land of opportunity. One could do whatever one set his mind to and it would succeed. It's a hard land as it doesn't have many of the refinements you would find in Europe, yet it has its own raw beauty and unexplored potential. It has the need for the pioneer spirit."

Jack agreed with Jim and Veron, "If I were younger, I would immigrate here. Everything is so big and full of promise."

Nellie, on the other hand, felt that one should live where one felt comfortable and for her that meant England. She liked what Canada had to offer but as she put it, "It's a nice place to visit. Some of the things I would love to have in England are these electrical gadgets you have here. For example a built in washing machine with an automatic dryer, plus that dishwashing machine you have is a great time saver and I would dearly love to have one of those little toaster ovens. One would not have to heat the entire kitchen just to cook something small."

Jim joined in, "Unfortunately, Nellie, all of our appliances run on 110 volts rather than the 240 you have in England. And most of these electrical gadgets couldn't be used in Europe. There are adaptors available, but these are generally for short-term use only. Hair dryers and shavers for example are things one would use only on vacation and not on an ongoing basis. I'm sure one day these appliances will be available in England. Having said this, many of the houses in England were built before electrical power was available to them. It's difficult to adapt them for these luxuries but I'm sure the newer, more modern homes come wired with electrical power."

"One thing I would like to have in England," Jack said, "Is more television stations like you have here in Canada. I'm not much for the adverts, but there is a greater variety of things to watch here. There are many stations that seem to operate for twenty four hours which is very handy for people who work shifts or for those who cannot sleep at night."

Jack continued, "I have enjoyed the various news broadcasts which are also available. One can receive the Canadian and the American perspective as well. That would have been handy in the War. Mind you, I've noticed that they don't give much coverage of world issues. It seems to be more national news that is available."

"You mentioned the War, Jack," said Veron. "Did you serve in the First and Second Wars, Jack?"

"Only the first War and that was enough and I cheated to get into that one. One had to be eighteen to enlist and I was born in 1900. I changed my birth certificate to 1899 but I only saw 6 months of active duty in France, in the trenches of course. They were wet and miserable places, they were. The stench was horrible and the gun fighting was enough to frighten the hell out of the devil so I was relieved when the war was over and I could return home. I had thought there was glory in fighting, but I learned my lesson. I did all that for the uniform, as one did look smart in it."

"The ironical thing is how lies catch you up. To my surprise, when I was sixty-four, the Newburn Council, whom I worked for, received my retirement papers from the government instructing them to retire me. They were surprised as well, as they hadn't expected these for another year. Along with this fact, my superannuation pension wouldn't mature for another year. This set the cat among the pigeons. It took me nearly three months to convince the government it was my doing which got me into the Army in the first place, by changing my year of birth on my certificate. They needed my disclosure so they wouldn't be held at responsible for allowing an under aged man into the war.

"So Jim, what did you do during the War?"

"I was in the Fleet Air Arm. I was a lieutenant in navigation, which took me into many parts of the world. I spent a great deal of time on loan to the American Navy. Along with Eric Godden, I was stationed out of Hawaii. But the time I was stationed out of Ceylon was very different. We did have fun, but we also were involved in daily combat and flew alongside many that never returned. I was in reconnaissance aircraft, shooting photographs of the aftermath of the bombing. This was done to see what damage had been inflicted and how successful the air raid had been. These photos were also to determine whether or not another air raid was warranted.

"Once I returned to base, I was responsible to develop the negatives and to turn them over to higher powers. This one time when we were successful, Eric, (Ann's husband and Gilley's now golf partner) and I escaped with the squadron's rations of booze. We went into the local town and rented a hotel room. Once the word was out, everyone joined in the fun. We ended up throwing the furniture out of the window in order to make room for everyone. There was one room that had a huge fan to keep it cool. This fan became the focus of our fun that night. As we drank away the booze, it became a game to see who could throw chicken bones into the blades of the fan and have the fan throw them out of the window. The person who got a bone out, got an extra drink.

The following morning, the hotelier was quite upset. He was waiting for us in the lobby. He demanded we compensate him for the damage we had done. My friends buggered off leaving me to deal with this gentleman. As I had spent all of my money, the only thing I could do was to write him a cheque. The only paper that was strong enough for this was the toilet paper, that wax-type, Jack.

At first, he wouldn't accept it, but when I told him to go to his local bank and deposit it as it was legal tender he insisted I go with him. Sure enough, he was cashed out. It wasn't until I returned to England and the bank manager motioned me aside that I realized this hadn't been such a good idea. The bank manager took it as a slur against the bank, what with it being toilet paper and all. He would not tolerate this in the future. It's strange how we only remember the good things of the War, eh Jack."

Veron jumped in, not to be outdone, "Well, I worked during the War. I did my part for the country too. I worked for the arms factory and I was an overhead crane operator. This crane was capable of lifting 50 tons and it was my responsibility to make sure the slinging was to my satisfaction before I lifted the load. It was a great job as I was my own boss and many times I was stationed between the two ends of the factory waiting for my next lift or my next break."

"The only embarrassing time was when I had to go to the toilet. I had to move the entire cab to one end or the other in order to climb down the ladder. Of course everyone knew where I was going. I often got many cheers descending the ladder, as many times, just as I was about to disembark, they would call for a lift."

Nellie said, "That's the other thing I can't get used over here. They call toilets washrooms."

"I remember one time during the War, Neil, Gilley's brother would have been about thirteen. He was very attached to his bed. This was so much so that even during the air raids when the sirens went off, he would not leave it. He would say if the Germans were going to get him they would get him in his nice warm bed.

Well, one night, just after dusk, we heard a loud growling sound in the sky. No sirens had gone off, so Jack and I went to the front door to see what was happening. Just as we opened the door there was this great big explosion which blew open the windows, blew the cat right to the top of the stairs and blew Neil right out of his nice warm bed. He came running down stairs, shivering. He stood near the fire shaking and said, "I'm not scared, Dad. Really, I'm not scared, I'm just cold."

To find out what had happened, Jack went off to investigate. It turned out a stray German bomber had dropped a bomb in the dean. Fortunately for everyone, the trees in it and the soft earth absorbed most of the shock. The most damage done was windows blown out of many of the houses. Luckily, no one was really hurt apart from minor cuts and bruises and, like Neil a bit of a fright."

Joy jumped in here, "What's a dean?"

Gilley had been anticipating this question from her. "The dean is a deep ravine filled with trees and shrubs with a small stream running through it which we call a burn. It is thought that when the Romans were building Hadrian's Wall some of the stones were excavated from this area, creating the dean."

Joy said, "I didn't realize it had such significance in building the Roman wall. I remember the ravine now and I remember the Wall, walking from Walbottle to Throckley. Isn't part of the Wall on the premises of a farmhouse close to the dean? Just in behind that farm, was the Secondary Modern School Gilley went to? I miss being close to all of that history. Here in Canada, we don't have anything that is as old or as interesting as what is in England. And so close and intermingled with everyday life."

"It has been quite a lot of fun reminiscing about old times," said Veron, "but we must get going home now. Eunice and Edmond are coming tomorrow and I have to organize a little party."

"Just a moment," said Jim, "I have a little gift for you, Jack. You remember that cowboy hat you had admired? Well, I found another one today along with a western tie. I thought you might want to wear them to the party tomorrow night." With that he gave over the best gift Jack had received.

"My friends in England will really have something to talk about now." Nellie chuckled in the background.

Jack spent some time admiring the hat and trying it on to everyone's delight. "It fits well," he exclaimed. "Now for the tie! That's better. I look like a real cowboy now. My friends in England will have something new to talk about when I appear at the club with these on."

Nellie said, "If you go out dressed like that, don't expect me to come along. Do you think I want the whole town talking about my husband the cowboy?"

Jim asked, "Jack, one question I've wanted to ask you—Gilley told us so many stories about his magpie, Pete. Is it true that Gilley's magpie traveled with you on the bus to work?"

"I don't know what Gilley has told you about Pete, but its true he used to travel with me to work and then be waiting for me at the bus stop when I came home. You see, I used to work a split shift. More often than not, he would accompany me to work, fly back home and then accompany Gilley to school. He was quite the character. Everybody in the village knew him. They would tell us weekly stories about his ventures. It was a sad day when we realized he wasn't coming home again. However, years later it's believed Ralph Hunter, one of our neighbours, saw Pete at a Newcastle match. He knew it was Pete as his left claw was damaged in his early days when the shed door closed on him. He could only land on his right claw, then bring his left down for balance. His other distinguishing feature was he could only hop.

Ralph was at the match that day. Pete was being a real pain. He was flying low around the pitch disturbing the play and annoying the players. So the story goes, the officials trapped him using a large net. They locked him in a small room intending to let him go after the match was over. However, the Magpies won that day against the odds. The players attributed their win to this magpie who had been caught, so they decided to keep him as their mascot. Whether this is true or not, I don't know, but it wouldn't be unlike Pete to do something like that. Even though it was far from home, he may have followed Gilley on several occasions when he went to the matches so he knew the way."

This was not the answer Jim had been expecting and he said, "Jack, you tell an even more amazing story than your son. I now know where he gets it from."

Grinning, Jack said, "I can tell you many more tales about our Pete . . ."

Nellie chimed in, "I can tell you stories too. Our Pete was part of the village for years. Even now people occasionally talk about him and his antics. It's generally thought the magpie's life span is anywhere between four and six years, but it has been known for one to live up to sixteen years."

Just then, Veron jumped in, "Jim, it's time to go home. We've heard all these stories before and I have a party to plan. Let's go."

The following day was full of busy for everyone, including Joy as she had to make her famous potato salad as well as working the entire day at the bank. Fortunately for her, she could come home at lunch and get things organized and started enough to just finish up when she got off work. Jack and Nellie were busy packing, as they had to leave the following day. Since they were going back with more luggage than what they came with, they were struggling on where to put everything and how to organize the lot.

The time for the party came very quickly. As normal, Gilley came home late. He had wanted to work some overtime since he was taking part of the next day off in order to take his mom and dad to the airport. With all of the food and drink to carry and the lateness of the hour, Gilley decided that they would drive over to Veron and Jim's instead of walking. They didn't want to be late after all.

Eunice and Edmond had arrived earlier in the day and were down in the bar waiting for the guests to arrive. Gilley introduced his parents to them as he had met them in England before. Drinks all around and then the fun began. Anne and Sally were not to be left out of anything. They were downstairs with the crowd and immediately engaged Gilley in a game of pool. Everyone else got involved in taking on the winner. This was the first time Nellie had ever held a cue in her life and proved to have some potential once she had the rules sorted out and knew which ball to hit.

Jack and Edmond discussed the English politics of the day, as they were both Socialists and very interested in the working conditions of the laborer. Eunice did not share Edmond's beliefs as enthusiastically and this had caused many problems with her side of the family. None the less, Edmond hung onto his beliefs. As the conversation heated up between the men, the others found playing pool much more enjoyable. As the volume and intensity of the discussion increased, Jim, being the good host, broke up the conversation by challenging them to a game of darts.

By the second round of drinks, Veron announced dinner was ready. She informed them it was smorgasbord style and everyone should just help themselves. This was another novelty for the English visitors. Smorgasbord was not a common word in England and it wasn't until they saw the way the food was laid out, they understood what was expected.

Of course, Veron out did herself again. She had done an enormous salmon as she knew Jack, Nellie, Eunice and Edmond would really enjoy this treat. She had barbequed the salmon and served it with a green salad along with cold cuts and fresh buns. Joy's potato salad was superb as usual and complemented the banquet magnificently. For dessert Veron served fresh strawberries and cream over a freshly made vanilla cake.

The end of the night came too quickly. Jack and Nellie, along with Joy and Gilley had to retire early as the latter two had to work in the morning. This suited Eunice and Edmond as they felt jet lagged. It was a good thing Gilley had to bring the car, as they left with more food than they could have carried. Veron always made more than enough.

Thursday morning, Gilley left for work early so he could take the afternoon off to take his parents to the airport. By 1:00 PM the three of them were on the road. Unfortunately, Joy could not take the time from work, yet she still was able to have lunch with them and say her goodbyes. The trip to the airport was a quiet one. Everyone was lost in thought and subdued. It seemed no one wanted to say goodbye.

At the airport, it was sheer comedy. Nellie had her TV tables and their hand luggage intending them as carryon luggage. Their suitcases were bulging with souvenirs and presents and were over the weight limit. That didn't matter. They willingly paid the extra charge. Jack had his cowboy hat on and Gilley was hard pressed to keep a straight face as he said his goodbyes. He had never seen this side of his parents before. He was able to laugh out loud finally as he watched them struggle down the walkway towards the waiting area for the overseas flights. It would only be another year before he would see them again.

Driving back to work, Gilley's mind was with his Mom & Dad and their return to England. He knew his mother and father would be full of their experiences bursting to tell their friends in the village all about the trip. He could imagine his brother, Neil, picking them up in Prestwick Airport in Scotland, how he would react seeing them disembarking with all their goodies, especially the TV tables. They would flood him with tales of their trip and all of their adventures. This made Gilley glow with pleasure. He would finally have something over on his big brother.

All too soon, Gilley arrived back at work and entered into the hot and dusty offices. It didn't take any more than two seconds for him to wish their new extension would be finished quicker than promised. They were told later that afternoon however, it was actually going to take longer. It wouldn't be until the fall that they could move the offices next door. This was because of the building codes and safety requirements regarding the sprinklers. These had to be added throughout the building, especially in the engineering office, as it was upstairs above the main machine shop. Everyone groaned inward as this news was shared.

What would this mean for the next few months? Things were already very chaotic as the manufacturing of the winches had already moved to the new building and the engineering offices were spread in two different places. Purchasing, accounting, estimating, sales, etc were everywhere but close at hand. This stalled the opportunity to promote the company to its best potential and created a lot of frustration for most of the employees and a financial burden on the company, as their goals could not be met as promised.

Yet the company and the employees persevered as the sales manager, Denis Shears was selling winches all over the world and the orders were pouring in faster than anyone anticipated which created other organizational problems. Gilley was having to work harder than ever and often didn't get home until quite late. This benefited Joy and Gilley in that the overtime was an extra bonus to their savings for England.

On top of all this work, Gilley and Joy were babysitting Anne and Sally, (not that they really needed babysitting, just overseeing as they were teenagers) and were staying at Jim and Veron's. This was because Edmond, Eunice, Jim and Veron were on a road trip around British Columbia just like the one Gilley had taken his parents on. The girls and their friends were well behaved for the most part. All except Sally's boyfriend Al, that is. He would pester her day and night, even to the point of throwing rocks at her window at 3:00 AM especially after he'd had a few to drink. This was one problem Joy insisted Gilley deal with.

Gilley decided the best way to handle this was to confront Al when he was annoying Sally, so he waited in the back garden for Al to show up. Sure enough he was on time. He was about to propel a small rock at Sally's window when Gilley said, "This is going to be the last rock you ever throw, My Lad." With that, he approached Al aggressively. This shocked Al as Gilley had always been friendly with him. He stood there with an open mouth waiting to see what would come next.

"This is not the right way to improve your relationship with any of the elders in this house. I've had to stay up almost every bloody night what with all of your foolishness. If you continue this juvenile behaviour, I will have to take more drastic steps to stop you so I can get a good night's sleep." Gilley was quite emphatic by this point. Al dropped the rock and turned tail and ran. Gilley found out later, through Sally, Al had really tied one on that night and had thought Gilley was a bear or something at first. Somehow, this experience stayed with Al and he never returned for his nightly escapades at Sally's window.

When everyone returned, Eunice and Edmond had been so grateful for the trip and for all the sights they saw, that she and Edmond wanted to take the whole group out to a special celebration. Jim suggested the Medieval Inn in Gastown in Vancouver. The Medieval Inn specialized in creating a dinner which represented that period in time. Patrons would reserve a table, not knowing where they would be sitting when they arrived. The fun of the adventure was that certain patrons would be selected to be seated at the head table acting as the Lords and Ladies and guests of that period. The rest of the patrons would be the general guests, but be of less stature and further down the table.

"This is very similar to a place in England called Seton Deleval Hall in Northumberland." Gilley explained. "Joy and I wanted to go to this place when we were in England, but it was too bloody expensive over there. Here, it is quite affordable even if it is not as authentic."

"The Medieval Inn it is then," declared Veron, "Would you call and make the reservations for the six of us, Joy? Choose a night that is most convenient for the two of you as we four are available anytime. Gilley, you can drive."

The only day reservations were available was the following Thursday night. Off they all went, Gilley driving of course, but in Jim's blue Ford Torino. The ladies were dressed in their good dresses, but Jim and Gilley sported their new polyester Leisure suits, complete with open necked flowered shirts. Edmond felt al little underdressed in his casual slacks and shirt.

Upon arriving at the Inn, they were shown to a nice table. To Eunice's dismay, no one in their party was picked for the head table. What this meant was they had to perform in order to be allowed to go to the washroom. Of course, it was impolite and embarrassing to publicly declare that one had to use the washroom, so if one needed to go, then one would have to ask if he or she could partake of the salt. The phrase to be used was, "My Lord, could I please partake of the salt?"

It was then up to the Lord's discretion what he would require the person to do. He could ask for a song, some poetry to be recited or a joke told—even a funny story to be told. If one did not oblige, then he had to take the long route to the washroom. This meant he or she had to walk to the head of the table and kneel before the Lord and ask humbly for the salt. The person would have to take the salt, apply it to his meal, and then return it to the head table. If the person was fortunate, the Lord would then grant the request for the washroom. If not, the process began again.

Many people would try to sneak out of the room and avoid this whole affair. However, the "wenches" (waitresses) were prepared for this and would yell at the offender. The "punishment "would then be even more hilarious especially for the spectators. Even if one successfully escaped and got to the washroom, he or she would be caught coming back.

Another feature of the restaurant was that everyone had to eat his or her food from wooden boards and were only given a knife with which to eat. There were three selections, chicken, ribs and steak. Each selection came with potatoes and vegetables and a loaf of bread. The beverages were wine and beer, which flowed non-stop during the feast.

No sooner had everyone settled down with their choice of entrée, than Veron had to ask for the salt. She was not up to saying anything, so Eunice volunteered to do the entertaining for her. Without batting an eye, she reeled off a funny story from the English stage, just as though she was a performer. The crowd loved it and applauded. This warmed her up, so as soon as Veron came back, she asked for the salt. This time, she was asked for a joke. Now Eunice had a talent for telling the dirtiest jokes in the most lady-like fashion. She would begin nicely with the topic and slam the audience at the end. Well, this brought down the house.

Soon after that, it was Jim who found it necessary to vacate himself from the room. He asked for the salt and was in turn asked what entertainment he could provide for this prized possession. Jim was a very proud man and would never ever go to the head table and ask for the salt. His upbringing was quite upper class in England. So he decided to tell the story of Archibald Arsenbroke. Now this was a tongue twister that required great talent and a good speaker to pull it off. By the time Jim was done, the audience was in stitches and the Lord of the Manor even allowed Edmond to escape to the bathroom.

About 20 minutes passed and Gilley realized he was not going to make it through the evening without having to ask for the salt. He decided to sing the Geordie National Anthem, that being "The Blaydon Races." Once he started the first stanza, much to his surprise about 10-15 people stood up and sang along with him. These people were obviously from his neck of the woods and knew their stuff. The Lord of the Manor was somewhat taken aback. He thought this was so novel he allowed the whole group to go to the washroom. Gilley was thanked prolifically for saving so many from having to stand up and entertain the crowd, especially Joy as she was dreading to have to ask for the salt.

After awhile, a slight problem began to occur. Joy was the only person at the table who had not yet asked for the salt. She was extremely shy and had decided by hook or by crook she would attempt sneaking to the bathroom at the most opportune time. Well, much to her embarrassment, she was caught right away. And the Lord commanded her, "Come here young lady, and beg for the salt."

She stood there wishing a hole would open up and swallow her. To her surprise, Eunice came to her aid. She stood up and asked the Lord permission to speak for her. Because Eunice had already entertained the group twice, the Lord granted this request and most of the crowd was in complete agreement yelling, "Tell us more! Tell us more!!!" Joy escaped, gratefully to the washroom not even hearing the joke which earned her, her reprieve.

As the night went on, the salt was requested less and less. The reason for this was people just left for the washroom and, as the novelty had worn off, the Lord and guests didn't care anymore. Everyone was having too good a time with other things to worry about being entertained in this manner.

At the end of the night, everyone piled back into Jim's car and Gilley, the designated driver (who really should not have driven that night) took the wheel and headed for home. Jim's only concern was they reach New Westminster without incident. The New Westminster Police Force quite understood about people attempting to make their way home after a good time. Often, they would just have the party pull over, park the car and then would drive the offenders home themselves. The main reason for this was public transportation in New Westminster was non-existent by that time of night. The trip fortunately was uneventful and all made it to Jim and Veron's safely.

After arriving back at Jim and Veron's a few more drinks and a recap of the evening ended the wonderful experience. Gilley and Joy left for home as the remainder went off to bed. Gilley and Joy drove their own car the few blocks home, tumbled into bed and woke to face the next day of work. The magical shower was great, but didn't quite fix everything up for poor old Gilley. Joy almost called in sick, but could not because if her mother found out she called in sick due to a hangover, there would be hell to pay. (Veron's daily walk took her past the bank and as sure as God made little green apples, she would drop in to visit the day Joy wasn't there.)

Fortunately for Joy, that turned out to be the day Veron brought Eunice and Edmond in to cash traveler's cheques. Veron introduced Eunice and Edmond to the bank manager as Joy's aunt and uncle. After polite conversation, the manager said, "Well, your daughter can look after you. She is a very competent employee." Joy sighed a relief she'd chosen to come in after all.

The next day being Saturday, was golf day as usual for Jim and Gilley. Of course they always played at Newlands, weather permitting, and this day dawned very fine. Since Edmond didn't play golf (and the foursome was full anyway) the plan was that Eunice, Edmond, Veron and Joy would join the golfers after the game at Anne and Eric's for a drink allowing the boys to get washed and changed. Since Anne and Eric were from England as well, Eunice and Edmond enjoyed swapping stories of their home-towns.

After a very nice visit with Anne and Eric, the eight departed for a new adventure. Eric had planned a surprise dinner at a secret restaurant. It turned out to be dinner at a German schnitzel house called *The Black Forest*. Knowing that Jim was not a fan of Germans (neither were Germans of him,) Eric had intentionally set him up for a laugh. One story that had always illustrated the relationship between Jim and Germans was even German Sheppard dogs growled and barked and chased him even when they seemed to like everyone else.

At the golf course, for instance, there was a German Sheppard dog. Jim was so apprehensive about this dog he would always make sure someone was between him and the dog. This was after a peculiar incident in which the dog ran out of the bushes next to the number ten hole. He stood on the tee box area and waited for the foursome to come up to it. Everyone else shot and then it was Jim's turn, he placed his ball on the tee and began addressing the ball. The dog made its move. Jim stepped back thinking the dog was going to attack him. Instead, the dog walked over to the ball and peed on it after which he walked off proud of his accomplishment. While everyone was in stitches over the dog's action, Jim remarked, "Thank God he didn't bite me. As a matter of fact, this might bring me luck. I'm going to play this ball." Much to everyone's amazement and a shower of mist as Jim hit the ball, it landed right on the green and Jim put it for a birdie.

Everyone pulled up to the restaurant in their respective cars and got out. Jim, realizing the destination was a German restaurant, said to Eric, "You bugger! You know there will be trouble tonight especially if there is a dog around." With that, Eric smirked and slapped Jim on the back.

Gilley had never experienced German food before and when they were seated, he wasn't too sure what to order. The house specialty was veal schnitzel and Veron, looking after the well-being of her son-in-law suggested that he order that for his first experience. She ordered that as well. Eventually, everyone else decided on the same thing, as this seemed a safe bet. The beer came first and of course it was German beer. It was very good. With the food, came the wine—German wine which flowed steadily. Everyone enjoyed their meal tremendously. (No one more than Gilley, who helped Joy, finish hers off). To top things off, there was Black Forest cake for dessert.

It became obvious it was time to go home as they were the last ones in the place. Saying good night and getting back into their respective cars, everyone headed for home. Gilley was driving their car of course and no sooner had they gone a mile down the road, he discovered he had to pull over to the side of the road. He couldn't believe it. He was sick to his stomach. This brought back memories of his exploits with Brian and the greasy pork chop at the logging camp. Of course, Jim and Veron had been following behind Gilley and Joy and pulled off alongside to see what the matter was. Poor Gilley, he couldn't get away with anything. Joy was so mad as she was embarrassed her parents and their relatives saw what was happening. Veron however came to Gilley's rescue. "Don't worry, lad, it must have been all that rich food. Your English stomach just isn't used to it yet."

Jim said, "Those bloody Germans will get you every chance they can."

Edmond screamed, "Everyone out of the cars. I remember when I got sick on a German apple. The next thing I knew a bomb was going off."

Gilley managed to drive the rest of the way home. This time the magic shower had to happen before he went to bed. He thought as he toweled off, "Thank goodness tomorrow is Sunday and I don't have to go to work."

The next morning, Joy rudely awakened him. This was not her usual style. What was going on? "Come on Gilley, up you get. Remember Eunice and Edmond are coming over for dinner to our place. Mom and Dad are busy tonight with a school function. We have to clean house and I have to prepare dinner. You will also have to make a trip to our bootlegger as we are almost out of beer."

Groaning, Gilley complied. He jumped into the shower. This time it truly worked and saved him from the suffering he had envisioned. He followed Joy's directions to the letter during the day and all was ready when Edmond, Eunice, Jim and Veron arrived at about 3:00 PM. (Jim and Veron came up for a drink before they left for their function.) Of course the topic of conversation was Gilley's night-before. They had to admit that they were surprised at the good shape Gilley was in. They had expected him to be more than a little yellow around the gills. Gilley solemnly vowed he would never ever eat another schnitzel again. But he would eat Black Forest cake.

Joy had prepared lasagna for dinner with loads of salads as the day was still hot and muggy. Edmond was enthralled with Joy's array of budgerigars. She had a grand total of six now and they were of various colours and hues. He asked how it was that she had so many and what did she do with them.

Joy explained the original idea was just to have two so they had something living to add warmth and atmosphere in the apartment. The next time she was in the store to get food, she had spotted this poor little albino budgie with a cleft foot. Of course she couldn't leave this one behind. With this addition, the standard birdcage was too small. Gilley and Joy decided to buy a large white pagoda style cage for their new companions. As Gilley helped install the birds into their new cage, the albino with the cleft foot reminded him of his magpie Pete. He was struck with a pang of nostalgia.

Once Jim and Veron saw the beautiful white cage, they decided three birds looked a little lost in this big cage. Two more would be ideal. Then that brought the total to five. One day Jim had gone out to the back deck for his morning tea. What did he spot lying on the deck, but an unconscious little budgerigar? Of course he had the perfect home for this lost soul. That is how there came to be six.

It was Gilley's habit and the birds' routine to let them have a bit of freedom in the house once everyone arrived home from work. He would open the cage door and one by one they would climb out, have a bit of a fly around the room then would perch in various areas around the living room.

By the time Eunice and Edmond arrived for dinner that Sunday afternoon, the budgerigars had not yet had their little fly about and were squawking and making one hell of a racket. Gilley realized in the rush of getting ready for their guests, the birds' routine had been neglected. After getting drinks and settling his guests, he said, "You two don't mind if I let the birds have their regular fly about, do you? It's their custom in the afternoon." Before anyone could reply, he opened the door and the birds flew out.

"This'll keep the buggers quiet until after we finish dinner."

"As long as they don't fly over and drop something in our drinks or food," replied Edmond.

This did not sit well with Eunice though. Unknown to Gilley, she had a phobia about birds flying into her hair. She voiced this loudly to her host and hostess.

"Don't worry," Joy replied, still not understanding the gravity of the situation, "They never fly into anyone's hair. They just fly around the room for a bit and then settle down in certain favourite areas. Eventually, they wander all by themselves back into their cage."

Eunice was not at all sure of this, but wanting to be polite, in spite of her fears agreed. Dinner was a success and the birds did as Joy predicted and went back into their cages, without depositing any gifts onto the diners.

As the evening passed, the foursome got talking about music. It turned out this was Joy's other passion. As they were discussing different melodies, Eunice noticed this big old piano in the hallway. "Joy, do you play? Could you play us a little tune?" Joy evaded this question, kicking Gilley under the table, wanting him to change the topic.

He decided to change the topic by saying, "I'll tell you that piano has caused so many problems just getting it into this apartment. 1) it wouldn't fit in the elevator, so we had to turn it on its side to get it in. 2) It wouldn't go through the front door of the apartment, so we had to remove the doors and 3) while that was being done, the pressure from the castors broke through the plywood floor in the entranceway to the apartment. With all of the humping and pumping, what with getting it out of its original place in a basement suite, it is well out of tune. We haven't had a chance to have it tuned since we moved in."

Eunice said, in her characteristic bravado, "Well, come on Joy, we'll play a duet. It doesn't matter if it's not in tune. I can sing in tune or out of tune if you want. We can play just for fun and for our men." With that she got up and raised the keyboard cover and noticed how they were exquisitely made. After admiring them, she brought Joy over. As they sat together on the piano bench she began with a lavish string of chords. The piano was so out of tune and she played so loudly that she frightened the birds. They flew madly out of the cage and tore around the room.

Well, this was too much for Eunice. She had held her composure during dinner, but with this sudden surprise, it broke completely. She screamed, covered her head and dashed into the bathroom, slamming the door shut. It was quite some time before the three of them were able to stop laughing enough to catch the birds and return them to their cage so that Eunice could come back to her piano playing, this time with the door of the cage firmly locked.

In spite of the unexpected entertainment, the evening ended nicely at about 8:00 PM. Gilley and Joy walked Eunice and Edmond back to Jim and Veron's for a night cap where Eunice took to the stage again (before anyone else could) and explained her ordeal with the budgerigars. She forever referred to this adventure as "Six and Twenty Budgerigars Baked in a Pie".

At 9:00 PM precisely, Jim got up from his chair and headed up the stairs. "Well, Everybody, I'm glad you had a good time at Joy and Gilley's. I must say good night now as it is time for my nightly bath. It's an early start tomorrow morning. Have a nice walk home, Gilley and Joy." It was his unswerving habit to have a bath at this time every night, regardless of what else was happening (unless a party was in full swing.) This was the cue for Joy and Gilley to return to their apartment. It was just as well, as they had to work Monday morning and the other four were to get up early to take the ferry over to Vancouver Island to meet Grandma and the Victoria group.

As Jim and Veron were going to be away for the week, it had been arranged for Gilley and Joy to oversee Anne and Sally while they were away. The girls were in their teens and certainly did not need babysitting in the true sense of the word, however, they still were not of the age where their parents felt comfortable leaving them totally to their own devices. Thus came the arrangement for Gilley and Joy to oversee them. In addition to this, Jim and Veron had a new renter, Lila. They felt it was important she have access to assistance should she need it.

Now as it turned out, Lila was not shy of introducing herself to Gilley. For example, one evening early on, as Gilley was cutting the grass and Joy was grocery shopping, she asked him to come into the suite to take a look at the dryer. She claimed it wasn't working. Being the gentleman he was, Gilley gamely went and checked out her problem. He discovered the fuse had been blown and remedied the situation immediately. Well, Lila, being very grateful, invited Gilley for a cool glass of beer.

Gilley could hear Anne and Sally giggling outside as they watched through the window so he suggested they enjoy their drink in the bar instead of at her dining room table. You see, Lila had a reputation of inviting many men friends over to visit her and this just seemed too good to be true for the two girls.

No sooner had Gilley finished his first beer than he heard Joy pull up in Veron's car. Then he heard Anne and Sally say, "Gilley's downstairs with Lila. She asked him to fix the dryer and now they're having a beer." Joy thundered down the stairs to make sure things were on the up and up. Hearing her coming, Gilley asked as soon as she appeared at the foot of the stairs, "Joy, have you met Lila? She's the lady your parents have rented our suite to. Would you like a beer?" He stooped into the fridge to get one out for her, getting rid of the eye-to-eye contact.

As he poured her beer, he explained to Joy about Lila's dilemma with the dryer and how he was able to fix it since it had been an ongoing problem from when they lived in the suite. Lila, being a very astute, decided to admire the bar and she thanked Joy for having such a generous husband. He was one who would quit cutting the grass just to come and solve her problem.

At this point, Anne and Sally, giggling like the schoolgirls they were, came downstairs asking when dinner would be served. Gilley, in turn, offered them pop from the fridge and introduced Lila to the girls. Giggling even more, the two said they had met Lila on several occasions already since she lived in their house. To save Gilley some embarrassment, Lila declared that, yes, she and the girls and met before, but this was the first time she had had the opportunity to visit the bar. Joy said, "Dinner will be ready when Gilley is finished cutting the grass." Since he was also getting hungry and this gave him an out, he went back to his chore leaving Joy and Lila together.

Once he had finished the grass and tidied up the lawn, he went back through the basement to get another beer before going on upstairs. To his amazement, Joy and Lila were still there. They seemed to have struck up a great conversation while he had been away. In addition to this, Joy had invited Lila to have dinner with them. They were having lasagna Veron had left in the freezer for them. All Joy had to do was to add a salad and some garlic bread.

Sitting down to supper, the two girls had a look of disappointment on their faces. They had been certain Gilley would be in deep trouble for having been alone with Lila and that fireworks would fly. They had never anticipated Joy and Lila would get on together. For her contribution, Lila had brought a bottle of wine for the adults. Dinner turned out to be a very civil affair. Soon after dinner, Lila declared that she had to retire to her suite as she had an early morning the next day.

As soon as she was out of earshot, Joy turned to Gilley and sarcastically whispered, "You haven't heard the end of this yet."

The week went on in an uneventful manner apart from a letter which came from England. It announced that Bill Wakefield was getting married in October 1972 and that he would very much appreciate it if Gilley could be his best man at the ceremony. Well, this clinched it, England was calling. Joy was so excited she would have an opportunity to return to England (perhaps for good). "Gilley, accept the invitation right away. I'll make the travel plans and begin saving for our trip. We have just over a year to save up. Looks like you will have to work a bit of overtime in order to make sure we can pay cash for everything. We certainly do not want to borrow any money for this trip."

When Jim and Veron and Eunice and Edmond returned on the following Sunday from Victoria, Joy told them the news about Bill Wakefield right away. This was good news because Eunice and Edmond said; "You can come and stay with us for a few days when you come over. We'd be delighted to see you back again at Tatra. We'll have a few pints at the Red Lion."

Veron replied, "Did anything else happen while we were away? How were the girls? No more problems with drunken boyfriends I hope."

Right away, Anne and Sally vied for the floor, "Mom," they shouted in unison, "Gilley was in Lila's apartment downstairs and he had a beer with her."

Joy came to Gilley's defense, "No, you're wrong; he was in the bar with her having a beer after he fixed the dryer for her."

"He fixed the dryer for her alright, "Sally said, "but that was after he had been drinking with her in her suite."

The entire place just went quiet as they all turned and stared at Gilley for an explanation. "The girls are right. I did have a beer that she had given me outside as I was cutting the grass. It was very hot that day and she came out with this beer as a refreshment for me. Then she wanted me to see how she had decorated the suite since Joy and I had left it."

"Yeah right," declared Jim, "You bugger, you probably had stripped to the waist and were showing off your muscles."

"Yeah, that's right, "Anne and Sally confirmed. "He was stripped to the waist cutting the grass."

"There's nothing unusual about me cutting the grass without my top on. It was very hot and besides, Jim often does it too."

Not to be left out, Veron jumped in, "She's a hussy, alright. She'll have any man, but not my son-in-law. Jim, get rid of her. We don't want any temptations in our home."

"Now, now," Gilley said, "There's no need to go that far. Nothing happened between her and I. It's the girls just wanting to have a bit of fun, you know. She invited me in because she wanted help with the dryer. Jim, you really should get that fixed permanently, as it could become a real fire hazard. You do remember when Joy and I were living here, I had to fix it almost every time Joy did the laundry."

Joy jumped into Gilley's defense. "I had a few drinks with Lila myself in the bar that night. She seems like a very nice lady and she ended up having dinner with us. I didn't see any attraction from either side."

Gilley, wanting to propel the conversation in this direction said, "That lasagna was great Veron. The best ever tasted."

With all of this excitement going on, Eunice and Edmond had been left out of things for a bit. Eunice, not to be left behind, said, "A little flirtation doesn't hurt anyone. One should never, ever lose the fire."

By this time, the fun had gone out of this conversation and things turned towards how the trip to Victoria went with Grandma and the Group. As usual, Grandma and Rosa drank their concoction of brandy and wine and the conversation had deteriorated accordingly. Grandma had then taken Eunice and Edmond for the walk in the Beacon Hill Park for the usual drop off of bottles. This had caused some entertainment for Eunice and Edmond.

And Grandma had told them about the story of the time when Veron, Rosa and herself were having a few drinks in her house and the phone rang. Grandma was the one who answered. It was an obscene call. This man on the other end of the line was breathing heavily. So, as the story goes, Grandma immediately said to the man, "Hold on Pet, this call is not for me." She then gave the phone to Veron, "Here you go Luv, this is for you."

Veron listened for a few seconds, and then said, "Mom, this call is for Rosa. You are always getting us mixed up."

Rosa got on the phone and listened for a second. "You dirty old bugger," she said and then handed the phone back to Grandma.

Grandma said to the man, "Well, Pet, I hope you've had your jollies tonight. We have and you have given us a good laugh." At that she hung up the phone.

After the laughter died down, Veron reminded everyone there was a going away party for Eunice and Edmond on Monday night. Edmond said, "Could you invite Lila? I'd really like to meet this young damsel."

"I'll see what we can do for you Edmond," Jim jested. Turning to Gilley, "Did you get her phone number lad?"

"Cheeky bugger" said Gilley. "You should have her number yourself as you have known her longer than I have."

On that note, Joy and Gilley left for their abode and a good night's sleep as they suspected that tomorrow would be a long, long day and sure enough their suspicions were confirmed.

By the time they got through work and a very hot draining day, that magical shower was a must for Gilley. This gave Joy enough time to finish off her specialty—potato salad. First to the liquor store as its traditional in Canada to bring alcohol to a party one is attending and then onto the party. When they arrived, there was no parking available anywhere. "Who the hell did Jim invite anyway," thought Gilley? There's always parking around here."

"Gilley, just drop me off at the door and go find a spot. I'll take the salad in and help Mom out," said Joy. That was fine with Gilley as he felt he didn't need any further "help" finding a parking spot. After some touring around, Gilley finally found somewhere to park.

As he entered the house caring two cases of beer, the answer to Gilley's parking question became clear. Jim had invited a large number of associates from the School Board as well as the usual family and friends. As Gilley descended the stairs into the bar Jim shouted, "Where the hell have you been Gilley? Get over here and help me behind the bar. For those of you who haven't met my son-in-law, he'll introduce himself as the night goes on." With this he left the serving position and joined his guests, leaving Gilley to manage the bar. Joy was whisked upstairs by Veron to help put the finishing touches on the banquet.

Eunice, in one corner, was in her best form this evening, telling all sorts of naughty jokes and stories to entertain the crowd. Edmond, in the opposite corner, equaled her in volume regaling everyone with his politics and war stories. This, along with the record crowd made for a very noisy environment. Then Harry and Gwen appeared. As soon as Harry had his first drink in hand, he was after the women and young ladies, doing his best to tease them and make them giggle.

After making his initial rounds with the women, he spotted Eunice. Right away he discovered that he wasn't the only party maker in the crowd. He finally had run into some stiff competition. He immediately made his way over to where she was holding center stage and embraced her. "You must Eunice, Jim's sister. I'm Harry and I've heard so much about you. As soon as I saw you I knew we'd have a great time together."

Jim, over the din, shouted out, "Now, now Harry, you watch yourself that's my sister. She'll talk circles around you if you give her a chance."

Gilley was doing his best to keep up with the orders and he became increasingly concerned as the booze was going down quickly, but it was the beer which was in an emergency state already. After informing Jim of the situation, Jim said, "Oh, our favourite friend isn't here yet, I'll give him a call."

After making the call, he returned with the good news. "The situation is under control. The solution will be here in ten minutes. For the usual reason, he will be leaving it at the back door before they come in the front. Serve the hard booze and delay the beer drinkers."

Upon overhearing part of the conversation, one of the school trustees called The Colonel, leaned over to Jim and Gilley, "If you are in need for more beverages, I have a case of my homemade wine in the trunk of my car just for emergencies such as this, Jim.

Jim responded back, "It's not the El Crappa Special is it?"

"Of course it is Jim, I keep the best of it at home," returned Colonel Bill.

"By the way, Colonel, this is my son-in-law Gilley and this is his wife and my daughter, Joy. Gilley, Colonel Bill is one of the best School Board Trustees. He knows a good idea when he sees one. He often supports my proposals and makes sure that the others understand where I'm coming from and why I do what I do."

"You know, we military men, even if we served in different countries, have to stick together," The Colonel replied to the compliment. He turned to Gilley, "How did you serve your country, Gilley?"

Gilley immediately shot back, "I served my time."

This took The Colonel aback somewhat, "What prison was that?"

Everyone around the bar stood back in silence. Jim came to Gilley's rescue, "Gilley didn't mean he served jail time. In England, when one gets bonded as an apprentice it is like being in the military as one is committed for five years. This is called serving your time. Do you think I would have an unsavory character behind my bar serving my guests their drinks. Come on Colonel, I thought you knew me better than that."

Gilley replied, "I couldn't have explained it better, Jim."

At this point Veron shouted down to the guests, "The Smorgasbord is ready. Come and get it." With the guests' attention drawn away from the bar, this gave Gilley enough time to sneak out to the back door and bring in the new supply of beer. It would be nicely chilled by the time dinner was over.

The dinner was usual banquet with ham, chicken, roast beef and salmon. In addition to these basics, there were curried prawns, curried eggs, and curried rice. There were so many different types of salads that Gilley could not identify them all—except Joy's wonderful potato salad, his favourite. Then along the side the dessert table groaned with cakes, bars and other delightful sweets.

Gilley watched as people lined up, took their plates and cutlery and made their way around the table, taking what they chose. This was interesting as no one had given any instructions as to how to proceed. It seemed everyone but he knew what to do. Little did he know Eunice and Edmond, being the guests of honour, had been instructed earlier by Veron about how to tackle a smorgasbord. After all, they were the guests of honour and were to go first. The line up moved quickly and people stood against the wall, sat where ever they could and ate the huge pile of food they had heaped on their plates. It was amazing to Gilley what people could eat and he made sure that even though he was last in line, he wouldn't be outdone. One other amazing thing occurred—no one spoke for about 15 minutes. The din which had filled the bar downstairs had disappeared as everyone focused on their dinner. All one could hear was the clink of cutlery against the china plates.

After dinner was over, each person carried his or her plate into the kitchen to help with the clean up and then returned to the bar for more drinks and fun. Unfortunately, it was a Monday night, so many people ended up leaving early as they worked the next day. However, there were the usual diehards that partied on. Edmond had been teasing Jim about Lila not being at the party. Jim finally gave in and knocked on Lila's door, inviting her to join them.

Lila accepted the invitation but asked if it would be alright for her to bring her friend Suzie. This really got the party going as Lila's friend was every bit as attractive as she was. They headed straight for the bar to get drinks and to chat with Gilley, smiling at everyone as they went. The Colonel took Jim aside, "You increasingly surprise me, Jimmy. Let me go and get my wine from my car. I do believe I have one or two of the better bottles stowed there as well."

As the Colonel arrived back at the bar, so did all the ladies who were cleaning up in the kitchen. They were surprised to see the two women sitting at the bar chatting to Gilley. Gilley was very thankful he was behind the bar as one could cut the tension with a knife. These two ladies had stolen the attention not only from the other guests, but from Eunice and Edmond as well. Edmond took the credit for the commotion being caused and said," I asked Jim to introduce his tenants to us all. Everyone, meet Lila and Suzie. I certainly wouldn't mind having them as my tenants, Jim. Perhaps you girls would consider moving over to England."

Now it was Eunice's turn to be noticed again. "Are you two ladies hairdressers, by chance? If you are, you could come to England and do hairdressing for me in my salon. I am always looking for talented young women."

"Who's got the wine glasses?" shouted the Colonel, now bent on serving up his best El Crappa for everyone especially the ladies.

This eased the tension somewhat and Veron and Joy went upstairs to fetch the requested glasses. Gilley moaned to himself as he cleared the bar to make room for the wine tasting, "This is going to be a night to remember or better yet to forget. We're in for it now."

A number of the guests excused themselves from the wine tasting, knowing what was to come. There was the core group left-The Colonel and his wife, Emma, Mickey and Elaine, Harry and Gwen, Eunice and Edmond, Brian and Marva, the two girls, Lila and Susie and of course Gilley and Joy as well as the hosts, Jim and Veron.

By this time it was about 10:00 PM and no one was feeling any pain. Edmond was flirting with the new guests, along with Harry of course and Eunice was still trying to hold her own with the remainder of the crowd. All of a sudden the doorbell rang. "Who can that be at this time of the night," Veron announced. Joy ran up the stairs to see who it was. Much to everyone's surprise and pleasure, it was Mike Cassick. Unknown to Veron, Jim had invited him along and since he had an earlier engagement that evening, he could only pop in just now. He really wanted to see Eunice and Edmond and Jim had promised Mike he would be a celebrity if he showed up as the couple from England had never seen anyone so huge.

Sure enough, he was a hit. Of course as soon as he saw Lila and Suzie, he immediately began to chat them up, too. (This being after he had gotten his drink of course). Gilley immediately gave him two beers, as he knew what Mike's drinking habits were. There was the time he had arrived at a party and declared he was very thirsty. He had picked up a full twenty-six once bottle of Rye and had downed it as if it were water. Everyone at the time watched carefully for him to show signs of drunkenness, but it never came.

Eunice had a very strange reaction for one her age. As soon as she laid eyes on Mike, (she was to later confess to her friends back in England) she fell immediately in love with him. Her reaction was so strong, she was very tempted to change the departure date by more than a week or two from its original time. However, common sense prevailed and she ended up just flirting with him for the remainder of the night.

Mike didn't stay long as he lived far away and he had an early day in the morning working for Jim. He was quite aware he was at his boss's house and didn't want to make a fool of himself. He thought he would leave before things got out of hand.

Mickey and Elaine were next to leave, then the Colonel and his wife. Brian and Marva also said their goodbyes. Things were clearly winding down so Lila and Suzie bid farewell as well. This left the eight diehards to discuss the success of the party and to have a few more drinks.

Joy and Gilley eventually made their farewells, too and left the party. They went to their normal parking spot and discovered the car wasn't there. At first, Gilley thought someone had stolen the car. Then he remembered there hadn't been any parking close to the house and he had to park elsewhere, but the question now was where. He walked up and down the street and couldn't see it anywhere. At this stage, Harry came out to get some fresh air.

"Hey, Old Boy, What are you doing still here? I thought you had left ages ago."

Gilley had to confess, "I can't find the bloody car and Joy is so upset she has started walking home. I can't for the life of me figure out where I put the damn thing."

"Let me help you out, Buddy. I'll get my car and we can drive around and look for it. That's much better than walking in circles trying to find it," declared Harry.

This was an experience in and of itself. "Driving with Harry—oh my goodness," Gilley thought, "Will I live to see tomorrow?" Harry was driving all over the road and up on the curb and over the boulevards. He did this for about fifteen minutes and much to Gilley's relief he spotted the Duster. "There it is," he shouted. "Pull over here. Harry, my boy, maybe I should take you home. I don't think you know where you are by now."

Harry belligerently said, "I know exactly where I'm going. I'm going back to Jim and Veron's for another drink."

Gilley thought, "I should follow him just in case he really gets lost." He proceeded to do just that minus the swerves and bumps which continued to occur as Harry made his way back. At last they were back at Jim and Veron's. Everyone was out on the front lawn. Gwen had gone looking for Harry and had become quite alarmed when she discovered the car was missing.

"Where is that bugger now? He had better not have gone home without me again." She fumed.

Gilley had to take the fall. He explained how Harry had driven him around to find his lost car and that indeed they had found it as was evidenced by the presence of the Duster.

Of course, Veron, being the good mother, asked after her daughter, "Where's Joy in all of this confusion?"

"Well," said Gilley, "she got mad and decided to walk home. I was going to follow and pick her up, but Harry seemed to be so lost after he helped me find my car, I couldn't let him out of my sight. I had to make sure he made it back here at least."

"Are you telling me Harry is more important than your wife and my daughter? You had better hope she made it home safely. You just wait here while I phone the apartment to see if she's there."

Jim chuckled, "You're in it now, Lad. There's nothing worse than an angry mother-in-law."

Harry and Gwen decided to go. In spite of Gwen's pleas to drive, Harry got behind the wheel and then did seem to navigate better than he did when looking for the Duster. Gilley commented to Jim regarding this fact.

"You wouldn't believe what Harry has found the morning after a party in his car," said Jim. "He has discovered pieces of trellis, fence pickets, clotheslines and clothes. He is a bit of a wild one and everyone knows it. Thankfully he hasn't hurt anyone or himself when he's driven home in that condition."

By this time Veron's anxiety was at a peak. "You had better get on your way home, NOW! I've called Joy and she'd not answering the phone. You'd better make sure she's arrived home in one piece. Call me when you find her so I can sleep tonight and remember, we will see you at the airport tomorrow afternoon to see Eunice and Edmond off. That is if you don't lose your car between now and then again."

Back at the apartment after Gilley arrived, Joy was not at all impressed he had embarrassed her in front of her family and friends by getting so drunk he'd lost the car. She was especially angry that Veron had phoned to see if she'd arrived home safely. "I knew it was Mom calling," she yelled at him, "But I was in the bathroom and couldn't answer. You had better call her back and let her know things are fine. If you don't you'll never hear the end of it and I won't either."

"Do you want a beer," responded Gilley? He had to think fast as he knew he was in big trouble. "I will phone Veron right now and let her know things are fine."

"What did she say," asked Joy?

"Your dad answered and told him everything is fine. You made it home safely and so did I. Please tell Veron."

"It's nearly 1:00 AM, Gilley. We have to go to work tomorrow. Have you not had enough to drink tonight?"

"I need another drink after driving around with Harry and following him. You wouldn't believe how he swerves and dodges all over the road when he's had a few too many. Even after we found the Duster and I followed him back to your mom and dad's he continued to jump the curbs a few times and even drove over that boulevard in front of your parent's. I've never been in a car or followed a car when someone has driven like that," explained Gilley, cracking two beers"

"I had to make sure he found his way back to your mom and dad's. I'm convinced he didn't know where he was. When I arrived back there, everyone was out on the lawn looking up and down the street for him. Gwen thought he had buggered off home and forgotten her. Then when your Mom saw me and that's when all bloody hell broke loose. She stomped into the house and called you and then ordered me home. I came home straight away to make sure you'd arrived home safely."

Joy, still trying to show she was annoyed and yet that she sort of understood Gilley's predicament, decided to let it go for the time being. She joined Gilley in a beer and couple more cigarettes. Finally, they went off to bed.

The next morning, that shower had to work extra hard to produce its magical effect for Gilley. Work also seemed a little bit of a drag as the night before was taking its toll. Leaving work early in order to see Eunice and Edmond off at the airport, he drove to pick Joy up. On the way, he began to recognize a pattern developing-always picking people up or seeing them off. It never seemed to be their turn to fly out and return. Joy commented on the very same thing as they were driving home.

"I just love flying," she sighed. "I also love it when the plane takes off and you feel that exhilaration of going somewhere. Our turn is coming next year when we go back to England for Bill's wedding. I can hardly wait. Who knows, maybe we'll stay there. By that time you will have given Canada the two years you wanted to."

"We'll see what happens," said Gilley. "You never know what tomorrow brings. It will sure be nice to get back into a routine now that all the visiting is over with."

Chapter 14

Partying Has Finally Come to An End?

WELL, "TOMORROW" CAME AND along with it came the Swann Floor Hockey Team and an invitation from Allan Pickering, the organizer. Gilley was quite excited about joining the team. This was because he felt the need for physical activity especially participating in a team sport. He was also feeling out of shape (after all, his father had commented on his gaining weight). A night out with the boys was good for Gilley especially after all the partying that had gone on since his arrival in Canada.

Floor Hockey was an entirely new game for Gilley. It was played with sticks and a ring and the object of the game was to get the ring into the net. The sticks were like a broom shanks. It cost two dollars a night each to rent the gym and the normal game time was Wednesday nights from 7:00 PM - 8:30 PM. Fortunately, this location was east of Swann's at Willington and Hastings. Unfortunately the closest watering hole was the Waldorf which was back toward Swann's and inconvenient for most of the players. A few cases of beer brought in someone's trunk stood solved the problem. It was only 20 cents a bottle same as it would cost for a glass at the Waldorf. This was considered a bargain as the bottles were a bit bigger than the glasses.

After the first game, Gilley got home round about 10:00 PM. He had taken a few hits from the boys and given his fair share back. He was feeling pretty good about his performance. Not knowing the game and the rules, he decided to impart his new knowledge to Joy. After he had gone into a long explanation of the rules, the techniques etc, Joy turned to him and said, "That's a woman's game, you know. It's called Ringette and I used to play it back in high school."

Now Gilley was in for a bit a ribbing as Joy told Jim and Veron on the weekend about Gilley's new activity. Gilley was to find out that Sally and Anne also played the game and Sally was considered quite good in the league. Jim decided to come to Gilley's rescue, "I thought Soccer was your game Gilley? As a matter of fact I mentioned to Jim Arthur, one of our school trustees, that you were quite good at the game back in England. His son in law, Kirby used to play for the Canadian National Soccer Team. He also played for the New Westminster Royals. He had to quit soccer due to a leg injury. He may be able to give you some contacts for playing soccer. It turns out on Sunday we have been invited to Jim Arthur's place for cocktails and he has extended the invitation to you and Joy. Joy, you will want to come, as I'm sure you'll want to see their home in Victory Heights. Gilley, you don't know this, but Victory Heights is a very upscale part of New Westminster."

Veron, not to be out done, mentioned that Audrey Arthur was a member of the same elite women's health spa as she was. Veron was very proud of her fitness as she used to go frequently. Of course, she knew most of the members.

Gilley was intrigued about this offer more for the opportunity to play soccer again than anything else. He really was not interested in the politics which might come with the game. What he really wanted to do was to kick that ball again and feel the rush of scoring a goal.

Sally did not want to be left out of this because she felt she had some investment in the conversation being one of the star Ringette players, "Gilley, you realize, don't you, that real men play ice hockey or lacrosse. They would not want to play with rings and sticks."

With that comment, everyone had a giggle. Joy replied, "Ice hockey time is very expensive and so is the equipment that one needs in order to play the game. We just can't afford Gilley's playing hockey at this time as we are saving to fly to England next year. On top of that, he doesn't even know how to ice skate. That would be a sight worth seeing, wouldn't it?" With that remark, the laughter increased.

Gilley had to do something to salvage his bruised ego. He decided to change the subject. "What is Lacrosse? I've played basketball, rugby, tennis, golf, badminton, cricket, soccer, squash, snooker, darts, lawn bowling, Coyts, table tennis and rounders in England, but I've never heard of lacrosse. Here I thought I was a fully rounded sportsman. Since coming to Canada, I have played golf and found out there are more sports like American and Canadian football (which are a form of deviant rugby), baseball (which is like rounders) and ice hockey of course. But I have never heard of lacrosse."

"Never seen lacrosse," exclaimed Veron? "That's Canada's National sport and you have never seen a lacrosse game? How long have you been here? Jim, what have you been showing this lad that he's never seen a Salmon Bellies game? We had better rectify this as soon as possible."

Jim jumped in, "Now that you people have had your say I want to ask what is Coyts, Gilley?"

Gilley explained, "Coyts is a game where you have two iron rods in the ground about 22 feet apart. You have a round ring approximately six inches in diameter. The object is to get the ring over the iron rod."

Jim sniggered, "That sounds like our game of Horse shoes."

Gilley retorted, "Yeah, if we couldn't find rings, we used horse shoes too. It looks like we have another game in common and I'm going to play soccer which is actually, in England and Europe, called football as its play with your feet. American football has a ball that is shaped like a rugby ball and the only time your feet touch it is when it's kicked off and kicked through the goal posts. Otherwise, you play with your hands. So why isn't it called hand ball?"

Everyone had a good laugh at that because there was no logical answer. Jim jumped in, "I used to play cricket in Victoria's Beacon Hill Park when I first came to Canada. I was working as a surveyor for the BC government. There are more cricket clubs in BC than what one would think. Quite a good club now is the one at Stanley Park in Vancouver. It's called the Brockton Point Cricket Club."

Gilley was quite intrigued with this new bit of information about his father-in-law and immediately asked, "What bat were you?"

Jim responded, "Number three and my field position was in the slips."

Gilley was even more impressed now, "I think the best batter for me was number six and I played many field positions. My worst experience was playing silly-mid-on."

Of course the Canadians were lost with these terms, "Are you two speaking a foreign language? Don't you know that's rude?"

"Only the Queen's language of course," responded Jim. "Terminology is one of the most important things in all sports because if you don't know the terms, you can't play."

"It's typical of the bloody English to have their own bloody rules, isn't it," Veron joined into the conversation.

"Howzthat, Jim," Gilley shouted over the noise?

"I'm not out, we've only started playing," Jim laughed, carrying on the sport's language. This annoyed Veron to no end, but she held her tongue as she didn't think it would make a difference to the boys.

The evening carried on and as Gilley and Joy were leaving for home, Jim slapped Gilley on the back, "Golf tomorrow. I'll cook breakfast, if you meet me here. Howzthat"?

"You have a deal Jim. I'm the designated driver tomorrow as Joy and Veron are going to get their hair done together for the big event at the Arthurs' on Sunday."

On the way home, Joy asked Gilley, "What was that term you said to my dad as we were leaving? It sounded like 'How's that'?"

"Oh, 'Howzthat'. It's a term we use in cricket when the bowler beats the batsman and knocks the bails off the wickets."

"What's a wicket and what's a bail?'

A wicket is three stumps in the ground with two bails or bits of wood loosely balanced in the top of the wickets. If the bails fall off the stumps, the batsman is out. And when the bowler generally hits the wickets the bails go flying along with the stumps."

"It's all too technical for me," said Joy, "You and dad can commiserate about cricket to yourselves."

Sunday, three o'clock arrived. Jim, Veron, Joy and Gilley as the designated driver, arrived at Jim Arthur's in Jim's blue Torino. In spite of the fact they were right on time so was everyone else it seemed. As a result, parking was at a premium, even in Victory Heights. This surprised Gilley, as there seemed to be lots of room in this affluent neighbourhood. He dropped his passengers off at the door and wondered where to park. Once more, after driving around and around, Gilley found himself parking several blocks away from the party.

He arrived well after Jim, Veron and Joy and felt a little uneasy as he knew no one and could not see his group. At that stage, a dark, good-looking guy came up to him out of the crowd. "So, you're the soccer star Jim has been telling us about, eh?" At that stage, Gilley didn't know which Jim had said what, so, feeling somewhat more awkward than before, replied, "You can't believe all Jim tells you."

Then, the dark haired man introduced himself with a laugh, "I'm Kirby Carter and this is my wife Susan. Welcome to our party. Let me get you a drink and I'll introduce you to everyone. The rest of your party is on the patio. It's been a great September this year. We were hoping today would be sunny as we could make use of the patio and yard one more time this year."

At the bar, Gilley ordered a beer, which was poured into a chilled beer glass for him by a man dressed in a black and white outfit. Kirby took Gilley to where Joy was standing and said, "I'll talk to you later about the soccer, how's that?" and off he went to greet more guests.

"This is a bloody posh place, man," Gilley expressed as soon as Kirby was out of earshot. "They've even got a man serving beer in a tuxedo type suit. You wouldn't catch me serving drinks dressed like that behind your bar, Jim. I don't care how much you'd offer to pay me. This place makes me feel quite nervous. I've never been in such an expensive home. Man, everywhere you look, money drips from the walls. And here I thought your home was elegant. What does one have to do in order to live up here in this Victory Heights?"

Jim began, "Here in Canada, Gilley, a garbage man could live beside a doctor if he could buy the house. It's not like in England where there are districts reserved for certain classes. Here anyone with enough money can live wherever they want."

This got Gilley thinking, "Really! Well now!!!." The possibilities here in Canada were endless. All he had to do was save enough money and a place like this could be his. For a while he just stood there looking around and taking it all in, imagining the possibilities.

As this was very unusual behaviour for Gilley, his ever-vigilant mother-in-law soon noticed it. Veron gave him a sharp nudge in the ribs, "What's wrong with you, Gilley? Looks like you have diamonds in your eyes or something. We're fresh out of drinks. Go and get us a refill would you? That would be two martinis shaken, not stirred with a green olive. Joy, what are you having? The same? Gilley, make that three martinis and get that silly look off your face."

Joy expressed her amazement at how many people, along with their parents, she knew from high school. She was quite relieved she was appropriately dressed for this occasion. When Veron had suggested this outfit, Joy had argued it was much too formal. She was now grateful her mother had pressed her into wearing it. She grabbed Gilley's arm and offered to help bring the drinks back to their party. "It's Ok, Joy, you just stay here and I'll get them. If I have any difficulty, I'll get that guy in the monkey suit to help me out."

As Gilley made his way to the bar, he came across a lady dressed in a similar uniform to the man behind the bar. She was carrying a huge tray of cold shrimp and a dipping sauce. She offered the tray to Gilley along with a nice smile and a napkin. Not knowing what to do, Gilley passed on the invitation. This was something he'd never run into before. He stood there for a moment and watched the woman as she made her way around the room. He saw all of the guests were helping themselves to the tidbits on the tray. He also noticed there were about five other men and women doing the same thing and on each tray there was something different. He also noticed there were ladies who were serving drinks too.

Gilley arrived at the bar and placed his order. The response he got was not what he expected. The man behind the bar asked, "Sir, is there something wrong with the service out there that you had to come and get your own drinks?" Gilley, embarrassed and not too sure what to say blurted out, "Well, no, I just didn't know the rules. You mean I could just ask one of the waitresses to bring me a drink and they would?"

"Or you could ask me and I will have them sent to you, sir. What is your order?"

"Three James Bond drinks and a beer for me. We are standing on the patio over there."

The waiter arrived back at the patio, just as Gilley did. (He had followed a few of the waitresses and sampled the appetizers on the way back). The waiter stated, "Where is Mr. 007?"

Jim looked at the waiter, "James Bond? Is that who you're looking for?" The waiter, Gilley and everyone started to laugh, but only Gilley knew the real reason why this was such a joke.

Eventually, Kirby and Susan joined their group. As introductions had already been made, the men launched into talk about sports and in particular, soccer. Kirby said, "I apologize, Gilley, I know you call the game football in England. But here in Canada we have to distinguish this game from the other so we call it soccer."

Kirby and Gilley had a great time discussing soccer and the various players. Just before the end of the evening, Kirby and Susan invited Gilley and Joy to supper next Saturday at their apartment. Kirby had wanted to continue this discussion, "And by that time, Gilley, I will have arranged a trial game for you. It will probably be with the Westminster Royals in Queen's Park."

Time to leave and time for Gilley to find the car he thought he had parked miles away. He had no idea where he'd left Jim's Torino, especially after a few drinks. He set out in the best direction he could remember and to his surprise, he came across the Torino in short order. "How did that happen," he wondered? "Maybe I'm getting used to this Canadian way of living and having to park miles away from the party." He collected his passengers and driving home, Veron said, "Gilley, I saw the way you were looking at that house and the things in it. Don't you forget that not all that glitters is gold. Many of these people are in deep debt and only live to keep up with the Jones."

"Don't worry, Veron, I'm not like my magpie who only goes for the glitter. I can differentiate between the gold and the glitter."

The week passed according to routine and Saturday came in short order. Before Saturday, Gilley had at least one more game of floor hockey to get into shape and he also did a bit of jogging to increase his fitness. He soon realized just how out of shape he really was. "How could that happen so quickly," he puzzled? "Maybe it's all the cigarettes, the drinking and the fabulous foods I've constantly been eating."

Dinnertime at the Carters was set to be at 7:00 PM. Gilley and Joy showed up promptly on time with the customary case of Labatt's Blue and a bottle of Blue Nun white wine. Joy was quite impressed at the apartment. It was a brand new building with all of the modern conveniences. She went into the kitchen with Susan to drop off their contributions and Susan invited Joy to tour the apartment, much to Joy's delight.

While the women were doing this, Kirby and Gilley got down to the real business—talking about soccer. This word soccer was still difficult for Gilley to apprehend, as he always had related this game to the title of football. Kirby understood this and did his best to help Gilley through the transition. As they talked, they shared their past soccer histories.

Kirby told Gilley about his playing with Canada's National team and the thrill of this. He also shared that while he was on the national team, he sustained fairly serious hamstring injury. "I got one of those injuries which cut my career short. If I didn't take care of it properly, it would reoccur more and more frequently and get to the point I may have a permanent disability in my leg. Too bad. I had hoped for a longer career playing my favourite game. Tell me about your soccer days, Gilley. What experience did you have?"

Gilley said, "I know how you feel, Kirby. Let me tell you about the time when I was nineteen, playing for a local amateur team called Newburn AFC. I also had sustained an injury which cut my soccer career short. This happened when I was heading a ball and suddenly I saw double vision. Eventually, it was diagnosed as a detached retina and the only cure was an operation. Even with the operation, I was also told that I should never play soccer again as this could result in permanent blindness in my eye."

"There was a very long recover rate for this type of injury (five months) and during this time I gained 70 pounds and lost much of my fitness. I was bound and determined not to stop playing soccer though. When I was able, I began retraining and was able to gain back much of the level I had previously. However, due to the eye injury and the fear of re-injuring my eye, I had decided that I would not head a ball again. This limited me to the teams I could play for. Ah, eventually, I captained my factory team and played the position of center forward."

Kirby interjected, "Strikers over here. Were you always a striker?"

"No, the position I played was called center half, which I think they call a center back over here."

"You're correct, Gilley." Kirby responded.

Just then the ladies came in and Susan announced dinner was being served. Kirby asked what Joy and Gilley wanted to drink with their dinner. Joy went for the wine and of course, Gilley went for another beer.

The first course was a delicious looking salad with green onions, chopped hard-boiled egg, celery and croutons. Topping the salad were lots of bright red cherry tomatoes. Gilley knew these were explosive little buggers and one should be careful when eating them. He was dutifully eating the salad and just as dutifully attempting to pay attention to Kirby and the dinner conversation.

Gilley asked Kirby what he did for a living. Susan replied, laughing, "You will never believe what my husband does for a living. He sells "LEGGS" panty hose. Most people can't believe it. Here he was a national soccer player, very good looking and in good shape, and he is able to have a job where he's encouraged to flirt with all the women in order to sell his product."

"What a dream job for any man," replied Gilley.

"It's not as good as it sounds. I do have to sell my product on commission, you know," said Kirby.

Joy sided with Kirby, "I can see how difficult this might be for you and how you could get yourself into trouble if you weren't careful. Why, someone might think your salesmanship was a come-on and take you seriously. It could get quite complicated." Looking at Susan, she continued, "Because women can be very foxy and cunning when it comes to a good looking man."

Susan said in reply, "You are quite right there, Joy. I work for BC Tel on the switchboard and I hear lots of gossip and with Kirby's position, I've learned to just take it with a grain of salt. Most of the gossip spreading women in my department idolize Kirby and are always kidding me about bringing Kirby around to give them a demonstration of how well he sells "LEGGS".

At this point, the inevitable happened. No matter how careful he had been with those little buggers, a cherry tomato exploded his mouth shot a stream of seeds and juice across the table and onto the window. To Gilley's amazement, no one noticed. This led him to think of the time, in England, he had attempted to scoop some hard ice cream out of a dish and the little ball shot out of the bowl, bounced on his forehead and dropped back down. He had quickly wiped his brow and no one saw that accident either.

This time, though, he was almost caught. The combination of the current event and the remembered one caused him to begin laughing out loud. He couldn't help himself. The giggles overtook him. Susan, Kirby and of course Joy looked at him then wondering what the hell was going on with him. Now he knew he was in trouble. Thinking fast on his feet, he began his explanation (once he could get control of himself again of course).

"I was just thinking of the expression on my mates' faces when I tell about your job. They won't believe me. Who wouldn't want a plumb job like that? Being with women, getting to flirt with them to sell your product and getting away with this while being married."

Joy started to laugh too, "He's right. Knowing John, Dave, Ray and the lot, they wouldn't believe him. He's already written them about some fantastic things that go on over here, but this one will stretch them to no end." Gilley said a very heartfelt thanks to Joy in his mind. He'd gotten out of that one.

Much to Joy and Gilley's delight, the next course was lasagna. Gilley had really developed a liking for this Italian dish and he tucked in without another word. Just as he thought things would be winding up, Susan announced, "Now for Kirby's specialty. He loves to make this dish almost as much as he loves to eat it."

With that she brought out elegant bowls filled with hard ice cream, a bowl of cherries in a sauce and a bottle of brandy. Kirby proceeded to scoop the cherries onto the ice cream and then he poured generous amounts of brandy over the top. With a flourish, he then lit a match and touched it to the top of each dish. These burst into flame. What a sight! Four bowls of flaming cherries jubilee, tumbling over the edge. "That should get rid of the hard ice cream at least," thought Gilley as he watched the tomato juice and seeds slowly sliding down the window.

Fortunately, Gilley was able to maneuver his way through dessert uneventfully. After dinner, everyone retired to the living room for a liqueur and hopefully more soccer conversation. As the talk did turn in that direction Joy asked Susan if she could help with the washing up in the kitchen. Having had enough soccer conversation around dinner, Susan readily agreed.

Kirby then asked Gilley, "What team do you support?"

"Newcastle United," Gilley quickly replied. "They are nick named the Magpies."

"Why's that," asked Kirby?

"Well, the Newcastle strip is black and white and in that part of England, there is an abundance of magpies. As you know, these birds are also black and white and since they frequented the stadium in the old days they were thought to bring good luck. I had a magpie when I was young that my father and I raised from a fledgling. Apparently it frequented the stadium as well. Interesting birds, magpies are. Do you have a favourite English soccer team, Kirby?"

"Yes, I tend to follow Chelsea. What do you mean by interesting? I don't think I've ever heard of a magpie."

"I'll tell you about that later on. You do realize that Chelsea is a southern team and that Newcastle is an extreme northern team. This makes them archrivals as in England, the north and the south have competed for years whether it be soccer or any other sport. There is even an animosity between the people."

"It's the same here in Canada. The east and west are always competing for things, but I'm sure this won't affect our friendship," Kirby finished up laughing.

With that, it was time to leave. Joy invited Kirby and Susan for dinner at their apartment in two weeks time. Kirby said, "That's good timing because by then I will have spoken to the coach and given him some of the background on your soccer career."

On the way back home, Joy expressed how lavish their apartment was and that it would be a bit embarrassing for her with their simple furnishings. "Well, I'm sure they will understand. We've just come to Canada and one has to start somewhere, right? Besides, they don't have a piano and five budgerigars."

"Well, how are you going to out-do that flaming cherries jubilee?"

"Don't worry, I'll find something better than that. I'll ask around and someone will tell me what to do."

That week brought another surprise. Dennis Shears, who was the sales manager of Swann's invited Joy and Gilley to a party at his house for the coming Saturday night. He lived in West Vancouver in the British Properties. This was where the very wealthy lived-the "old money" as one might say. When Joy announced the invitation to her mother, Veron grumbled, "You guys are really trying to out-do me now, aren't you?"

Gilley explained there could be a possibility for him to be offered a job in Singapore running Swann's operation over there. This was presently being run by Don Howath who was a legend in himself as he was one of Swann's leading designers of winches and had done a tremendous job in the East as Swann's representative. His contract was almost up and he was looking forward to returning to Canada. This left his position open for the next up and coming designer.

Joy was thrilled with this idea where as Gilley had a few reservations. He was still trying to become accustomed to the Canadian way of life and he wasn't sure he wanted to take on a new culture just yet. But again, one could not pass up an opportunity of a lifetime like this. It was Dennis Shears who was promoting Gilley for this position even though he had only been with the company for less than a year. Jim, who was usually very reserved in his opinions, thought it was a tremendous opportunity for Gilley and Joy. His nephew Jeremy Barr was residing in Hong Kong which isn't too far from Singapore. Jim was sure he would love the fact his cousin would be close by.

Jeremy, who had lived in England at the time of Gilley and Joy's marriage, had struck Gilley as a bit of a snob and he had decided he didn't like him. Joy on the other hand, loved Jeremy as he was the one who had taken care of her when she first arrived in England. He took her under his wing and showed her the London lifestyle and as well as the local pubs. Veron on the other hand, agreed with Gilley (for once) and also thought Jeremy was a pompous ass.

Joy was feeling more than a bit nervous about attending a party in this setting. Since they had just received the invitation that Tuesday, and she was working all week, there would be no time to go shopping for a new dress to wear. Jim, attempting to reassure her said, "Remember when we went to the Arthurs' two weeks ago? The place where you will be going will be similar to their house but probably on a much larger scale."

Veron also reassured her, "What you wore to that party was fine. You will be having your hair done as usual, Saturday morning. Just add a bit of jewelry, such as your pearl necklace and you'll fit right in. Under dressing is much more elegant than overdressing."

Saturday arrived and Gilley went golfing as usual, but this time Dave Mosley would be joining the foursome. This was becoming more and more regular as Brian and his wife Marva were getting ready to immigrate to New Zealand in the next few weeks. With Dave being Gilley's colleague and Dave not knowing about the invitation to Dennis's place or the Singapore opportunity, his playing golf at this time presented a bit of a dilemma for Gilley. Gilley felt uncomfortable as Dave had been with Swann's much longer.

It was the usual rush to get to the golf course and Gilley had not thought to prep Jim about this situation. Of course, by the time he had thought of warning him, it was too late as the game had begun. Hoping, hope against hope, Jim would not say anything, Gilley just played the game. He thought he had escaped this pending uncomfortable situation and began to relax. Everyone went into the clubhouse afterwards for the usual beverages. The conversation went around as usual until Jim announced to Eric, "See my son-in-law? He's going to a posh party in the British Properties tonight. He might be going to Singapore for his company and him being with this company for under a year. Quite the accomplishment, eh?"

Eric sarcastically retorted, "Well, he must be brown nosing someone to get that one! What do you think, Dave?"

Dave, in his English, southern accent leaned back in his chair, "Well, I feel a bit sorry for the lad. I was stationed in Hong Kong during my stint with the RAF and I would not want to go back to that part of the world to live.

I had heard a rumor at work that Don Howath was coming back and they were looking for a replacement. It doesn't surprise me they would consider Gilley for a post like that. But Gilley, whose party are you going to tonight?"

Gilley, under the strain of it all, blurted out, "Shears house."

"Oh, you mean the mansion on the hill? But you guys do know Dennis Shears' home town is not far from Gilley's and those Northern people do stick together."

Eric piped up, "Especially those Geordies. I should know because I married one. Do you notice that when you come over for breakfast who gets the special attention?" With that everyone laughed and Gilley breathed a deep sigh of relief even though he was in the company of three Southerners.

On the way back to New Westminster, Jim began laughing, "You should have seen your face when I mentioned the party and the Singapore job. I am sorry for putting you in that spot. I didn't think when I mentioned it, but now it's out in the open and you don't have anything to fear. Besides, it was worth it to see you squirm like that."

"Thanks a lot, Jim. You don't know Dave. By Monday coffee, the entire crew will have my bags packed and be seeing me off, even though there hasn't been a decision made from the top."

Arriving at Dennis's house, parking was a problem as usual. Gilley dropped Joy off at the house and spend a great deal of time looking for a place to put his car (as usual, the spot he was able to find was a few blocks away.) He took special care to remember where he had parked it as he did not want the embarrassment of losing the car tonight. Joy, in her high heeled shoes, waited at the top of the driveway for Gilley's assistance down the steep incline.

The house, a Tudor design, looked as if it were three houses in one and to Gilley looked like a small apartment block. However, upon entering through the large double oak doors it was obviously one huge, magnificent place. Irene, Dennis's wife, greeted them at the door as if they were old friends. She took Joy's coat and directed them towards the party room.

The party room was situated above the double garage and designed like an English pub. It had all the features of a pub back in England including all the artifacts found in a typical country pub as well as a nice long bar. The illusion was perpetuated by all the different English accents Gilley could hear-Cockney, Yorkshire, Lancaster, Scottish, and also Geordie (along with many others that had mellowed with being away from Britain for many years).

To make Joy feel more comfortable, Irene took Joy on a tour of the house. The stunning feature Joy reported back to Gilley was the magnificent view. She said all the windows at the back of the house were really large and gave way to this panoramic view of Stanley Park and the University of BC as well as the endowment lands. It was breathtaking. One could also see all of the ships at anchor waiting to go under the Lions Gate Bridge to birth in one of the docks on Burrard Inlet.

Returning to the main party, Irene then introduced Joy to the guests. (Gilley had introduced himself, while the women were touring the house.) As the women joined him, it was immediately apparent to Gilley Irene was also from the northeast. "Irene, thanks for taking Joy around your home. It's very impressive."

With that, Irene said, "My pleasure. Please feel comfortable to mingle and enjoy yourselves. I have a few things to attend to." With that, she disappeared into the crowd. "Come and meet Les Coward. He's from the northeast too."

Les was one of the principles of Allied Shipbuilders. He had worked in many parts of the world but had never lost his Geordie accent even though he was from Middlesborough. He had taken a shine to Gilley as they had sung *The Blaydon Races* while Joy was on tour of the house. This song was historically the national anthem of the northeast and of the Magpies, the Newcastle United soccer team. As the night progressed, the noise became just like that of a typical English pub as everyone enjoyed the banter and the sing-alongs. Hearing this made Joy and Gilley feel quite nostalgic.

Dennis, in his usual fashion was being a very good host. He was talking and cavorting with all of his visitors, making sure everyone was taken care of and they didn't lack a thing. Irene was the perfect match for Dennis. She made sure there was no lack of food and the bar was always fully stocked with anything anyone could request. Gilley and Joy were watching this fascinating couple and were beginning to see themselves in this role.

At one point Dennis and Les were chatting it up with Gilley when Dennis said, "Les, I think it's time to introduce Gilley to the idea of going over to Singapore. What do you think?"

Les immediately took the cue, "What a great idea, Dennis, you already have that office over there and Don Howath is due to return soon, I presume. Gilley, you would make a great representative for Swann's over there. Opportunities like this come up from time to time for a young man like you in Canada, but seldom would one see this happen in England." Joy could hardly believe her ears. Les continued, "By the look on your wife's face, it looks like she wouldn't mind going there either, would you Joy?"

Joy said, "I love to travel. I went over to Europe with the intention of traveling around there for a time, but I met Gilley during my first few weeks in England and that was that. Now I'm back in Canada and I would just love to go to somewhere like Singapore."

"I also know Swann's has an associate company in Australia. That could possibly be the next step for you if you like traveling. You can never tell," said Les, "but if you are both willing to travel, that opens opportunities all over the world. It makes it so much easier when both parties like to go places and don't mind being transferred around. Its possibly one of the best ways of climbing the corporate ladder and the financial benefits are great. In addition, you have the opportunity to visit the surrounding countries. That would go a long way to satisfying that bug you talked about, don't you think, Joy?"

"When can we go," she responded?

Dennis was quite pleased. Not everyone in the company was as competent as Gilley and also had a wife who was willing to travel. "We think it could be within the next nine months. Not sooner than six though as there are things to be worked out. We would give you sufficient time to make all of the necessary arrangements for an extended stay."

Gilley, feeling a bit overwhelmed and not wanting to show it said, "Thank you very much for considering me for this post. I won't let you down if you decide to send me."

By this time, the party was starting to wind down and Gilley and Joy took their leave as they did not want to overstay their welcome. Gilley was also aware he'd had enough to drink and he still had to find that car (again).

As they left the house, Joy had to lean heavily on Gilley's arm as the driveway was very steep going up. "I wouldn't want to have a car up here in the winter," Gilley remarked. "It would be hard enough getting up the hill but you could have a good time coming down. Mind you, the front door might need replacing from time to time in that case."

Once up on the main road, Gilley thought, "Now where did I leave the bloody car? Was it to the right or to the left?" Unfortunately, the cars he had used as landmarks had already left. There he was again, standing there with a very unhappy wife.

"You've forgotten where you parked the car again, haven't you," Joy chided?

"I don't think so, but it looks like it was further away than I had thought as I was anxious to get to the party."

As they wondered up the road smoking their cigarettes, apprehension was increasingly having its affect on Gilley. By now he was quite unsure of where the car was and the more he thought about it, the more unsure he became. Joy stopped and said, "How far away from the house were you when you parked the car?"

"A long way, but I remember parking on a corner."

"Hopefully, it wasn't illegally parked as the people up here wouldn't stand for that. They'd call and get you towed away right away."

As they turned this little corner in the road, there stood the Duster. What a relief! And no ticket was attached to the windshield. Double relief for Gilley as he knew he'd never live it down if that had happened. Joy observed, "You are a lucky so and so. You are almost too close to the corner and could have been towed."

On the way back to New Westminster, coming down Taylor Way Joy dozed off and Gilley had his chance to dream. "That could be my house in the near future if I play my cards right. I'll go to Singapore and to Australia or where ever I have to go if I could have a house like that." He continued to drive along and to daydream. Suddenly he came to a light and back to reality. He was once again in Stanley Park having taken yet another wrong turn. Even though it was late at night he recognized the area from the time he had driven Veron's car all over the Vancouver area in an attempt to get home.

"Not this time," He vowed, "I know where I am and how to get home." Well, famous last words. Gilley took the turn that led him across the Burrard Street Bridge and down into Richmond. By this time, Gilley was totally lost and didn't know where he was. He had a very hard time telling east and west from north and south at night time. During the day the mountains gave him the clue he needed. He was just about to wake Joy up when he recognized he was at Marine Drive. "That'll get me home." He knew this was the way he'd traveled many times to the airport and back. He finally knew where he was! He confidently turned east and headed in that direction and for home.

At this stage, Joy woke up, "Where the hell are we?"

Gilley replies, "Marine Drive—on our way home."

"This seems to be the long way around. Did you get lost again? What time is it? It's past 1:00 AM. We left the party at 12:00 AM. We should be home by now as it's only a 45 minute drive. You did get lost again."

"Well, I wouldn't call it lost," said Gilley, "I just took the wrong turn and I managed to navigate my way through Stanley Park and Vancouver again. Then I ended up on this Marine Drive and I knew this took us to New Westminster."

"Could you hurry up home? I've got to go pee."

Just then, Joy spotted the White Spot. "Gilley, stop there! It's open. I'll go pee there. Pull into the drive in and order a White Spot Triple O burger and fries. I'm starving."

Gilley did what he was told and ordered two of each. Unfortunately for Joy, she took too long and the order came quite quickly. By the time she returned to the car the food was there and the long serving tray was across the seat hooked on both windows. This, once again, taxed Gilley's ability to balance things. In order for Joy to get into the car, he had to lift the tray from his side of the car and leaver it without spilling anything until she could wedge her way into her seat.

"Why did you order the tray? We could have gotten this to go and eaten it on our way home," Joy grumbled.

"I didn't fancy driving and eating at the same time. These White Spot burgers are very sloppy."

"You've got a good point there," she conceded. "But I didn't think you would be hungry too after all of the food I saw you eat at Dennis's."

"All of this bloody driving makes one hungry, you know. Besides, I can't turn down a Triple O and fries. These White Spot fries are as good as any I got in England."

The following day was a typical Sunday. It was down to Jim and Veron's for the traditional roast beef and Yorkshire puddings. Gilley was getting used to having his beef done to between medium and medium well. In his household, any color was not natural in beef. Veron still would give him the outside portions of the roast, hoping one day that he would make the full transition to have his meat quite bloody.

Of course, before dinner, it was down to Jim's bar for drinks and a game of pool. This Sunday, both Jim and Veron were full of questions as to what had occurred at the party the night before. Joy was very eager to share her experience. "Mom, Dad, you should have seen the view from this house. It was absolutely spectacular. It overlooked English Bay and Stanley Park. One could see as far as the UBC endowment lands, even though it was quite dark.

The house itself was the largest house I've ever been in. It was huge. There were more rooms than I could count and all of the rooms that faced south seemed to give one a different perspective of Vancouver. There was every modern convenience you could imagine. Their party room was probably one and a half times the size of what you have here.

It was done up as an English style pub, yet somehow, it didn't have the character or warmth your bar down here has."

Veron jumped in, "Well, have you invited them back to your place for dinner?"

"Not yet, we haven't. But we are likely to do so fairly soon as it looks like the job in Singapore is probably going to happen and if so, it'll be within the next six months. It seems as if Gilley is the prime candidate for it." Joy replied, eying her mother a bit warily.

Jim came next, "Well, it'll be a bloody shame if I lost my golfing buddy and be back to the only male in the family. You do know Tinker is an 'It', so he's no support for the male gender in this family."

Veron turned abruptly to Jim, "All you can think of is golf at a time like this. He should take this chance. Who knows what it will lead him to? If you don't go you don't get." This remark created a little bit of tension in the room.

Gilley suddenly became aware that this remark might have been prompted by a bit of envy on Veron's part. He thought she may not like to see her daughter in a position where she was out of her element socially and where she, as her mother, would not be there to assist if need be. At the same time, he wondered if Veron might also be pleased with her daughter and son-in-law's success but, couldn't bring herself to openly celebrate for them as this would mean a loss for her. She was becoming more and more attached to them as a married couple and had looked forward to the influence she'd be in their lives.

In an attempt to ease this tension and include her in the process, Gilley said, "You know this is a great opportunity for the entire family. It will be great for you and Jim to come out on holiday to see us. And if you hadn't made it possible for me to come here by buying us the one way tickets this opportunity would not have come my way. So, it's thanks to you two we have been presented with this. Let's all have a drink to celebrate."

Jim said, "Did you bring any beer?"

"Well, no," said Gilley. "We came over as soon as we could to tell you the good news. Tell you what, Jim, you supply the beer this time and I'll make it up to you. After all," Gilley bantered, "It's your bloody fault I'm here, so it would be nice if the house bought the rounds."

At this point, Anne and Sally barged down the stairs for a game of pool with Gilley before dinner. Veron told them about Gilley's news and his possible promotion to Singapore. They both looked at each other and Anne said, "Does this mean we get to go and visit Gilley and Joy when they get there? After all, we weren't allowed to go to their wedding."

Sally, tagging along enthusiastically agreed with Anne, "Yeah that would be cool. I wonder what the boys are like over there."

The oven bell signaled the roast was done. As Joy and Veron went upstairs to serve dinner Veron said, "It's going to be a few minutes until dinner is served. So play your game but make sure it's a quick one. No dilly dallying on the way." As usual, the dinner was a classic.

Arriving back at their apartment, the telephone was ringing. It was Kirby Carter. "Well, Gilley, you have a chance to try out for the Westminster Blues. Come Wednesday night to the field opposite the Columbian Hospital. Ask for Don Wilson and mention my name. He doesn't promise you a full game, but he will let you play a bit as it's a practice match among themselves. Unfortunately, I won't be there that night, but you should be there by 6:45. Give me a call afterwards and let me know how it went."

Gilley felt a little bit nervous about this upcoming try out. He really didn't know any one and he wasn't very sure what level they played at and what they expected of him. Joy sensed Gilley's change of mood and asked, "Who was that on the phone?"

"Kirby. I've got a game Wednesday night."

"You should be really thrilled, right? This is what you've been waiting for."

"Well, yes, right. This is what I've hoped for. But, I'm not match fit, so for the next two nights, I won't be having any beer and I'm going to go jogging after work. I've got to get somewhat prepared. I thought I would be invited to a few training sessions first so I could get a feel for the standard of play they have. Plus the fact I haven't kicked the soccer ball for some time. I don't even own a soccer ball. At least I've got my soccer boots and kit from England."

"You've got nothing to lose. And if you didn't go, you'd be wondering for the rest of your life. Knowing that, we should have an early night tonight, unless you want to have a quick jog around the block right now."

"That's a good idea, but not on such a full stomach. I think bed is a better idea right now."

The next morning at work, Gilley had a new experience—personally meeting a sales representative. In England, the engineering and drawing offices never were exposed to outside salesmen selling mechanical applications and goods. These people were always seen by the head engineer or the head buyers. However, in Canada, things were more relaxed and any of the draughtsmen could ask for a sales representative of a company to come and explain his products. Often enough, they would just drop in as a courtesy call because many of them traveled province-wide never knowing exactly when they could be there.

Gilley was sitting at his drawing board when suddenly he heard this loud voice coming into the room wishing everybody good morning. It had a broad Yorkshire accent and was greeted fondly by everyone. Upon turning around to see this person Gilley was met by the sight of a short, stocky, well dressed man. He was about forty years old and was dressed in a typical English tweed jacket and matching tweed hat. He sported a thin moustache reminding Gilley of a British spiff (gangster) even though this was typical dress for manufacturer's representatives.

He introduced himself as George A-Minns and his broad Yorkshire accent brought fond memories back to Gilley. He decided to talk to George about the type of clutch application he had in mind for a new winch design. In doing so, Gilley recognized this man was not only very knowledgeable about the products he sold, but he had some kind of engineering background. Meeting this company rep was the new experience for Gilley. He was able to get the information he needed and more, directly from the horse's mouth, so to speak. This was important as George walked his way through the catalogue highlighting all of the areas Gilley needed to know about to complete the design.

Once business was out of the road, the socializing and joking began and George had the latest and greatest jokes to tell. After he left, Gilley stood there amazed at the professional, yet friendly and knowledgeable manner in which George presented his products and interacted with all of the office staff. Gilley thought, "Wow, that's the way to sell products and you can have a good time doing it. I think I'd really like to try my hand at that type of career in a few years time after I return from Singapore. The next time George comes in I'm going to ask him how he got into the business."

Anxious to get home so he could begin his training, short as it may be. His plan was to jog before dinner, not smoke or drink and go to bed early. The jogging, planned for an hour, ended in twenty minutes as he could no longer breathe. He could not believe how out of shape he'd become in such a short amount of time. Getting back to the apartment, Joy was surprised he got back so early. "I thought you'd be gone for an hour?"

"Yes, I thought so too, but then I thought it would be better to do some stretches and leg exercises before supper, then do something else later. Vary it up you know."

"Hrumpf, sure Gilley. Just don't forget to shower before you sit down for dinner. I don't want to smell you while I eat. You are absolutely saturated right now. Do you really think you'll be ready for Wednesday night?"

"Sure I will, I'll have a jog before my morning shower. Then I'll work out again when I get home. That way I'll make the best of my time."

"Right" was Joy's last comment on the subject.

The next morning, Gilley could hardly move. "I have to do at least ten minutes running to get rid of this stiffness. It's all coming back to me now." And off he went running down the street. He was back in ten minutes, sweating like hell and huffing and puffing. He entered the shower he thought, "I do have to stop smoking if I really want to play soccer." After his magical shower, he felt invigorated again and set off for work. He was able to resist smoking until his first coffee at work. "Well, I'll just have one instead of two." He surprised himself by cutting his smoking in half by the end of the day. And he was able to jog for forty minutes before he thought he'd pass out this time. "Great, things are improving," he told himself. "I may be able to pull this off after all."

Wednesday came and Gilley didn't want to be late for his soccer trial. First he had something light to eat, relaxed on the chesterfield (no beer), didn't smoke that full afternoon, and then stretched and went for a little jog around the block to loosen up. Off he went to the soccer field as directed. He didn't want t be too late or too soon. He waited patiently in the car until he saw what he considered half the team had shown up.

Sitting in the car might have been a mistake. He had a chance to think. Am I too old? Did I do the right thing? Do I still have what it takes to play on a team such as this? Why did I decide to try out? How good are these players anyhow? Perhaps I should have come to a game or two before I came for a trail. Then, in typical Gilley fashion, he decided "What the hell, it's now or never."

Strolling onto the field with his kit bag, he looked for Don Wilson. What he looked like or who he was, Gilley didn't know. Kirby had given a vague description, but it could have matched half of the players on the field. He decided to ask this little guy who was putting his boots on, "Could you tell me where I can find Don Wilson?"

In a Scottish accent the guy replied, "He's not here yet. Have you come for a trial cuz your face doesn't look familiar."

"Yeah, I came out for a bit of a run around and see if I can fit into a team here in Canada. How long have you been here in Canada," asked Gilley?

"I came over two years ago and I've been trying to get a full time position with this club for the past six months. I live just around the corner which is real handy. I haven't had much success yet other than playing in practice matches like this one today. They have a fairly good standard of soccer here but it takes a long time to get recognized, unless you are really exceptional," he replied. "When was the last time you played?

"About a year and a bit, I'd say," replied Gilley. "The last ball I kicked was for my local team back in Newcastle."

"That wouldn't be for Newcastle United would it?"

"No, I never attained that level of play. Of course, I would have loved to." said Gilley.

"Well, best thing is to tell them that you tried out for Newcastle United. A bit of bull shit goes down good in Canada," he replied with a chuckle.

"I seem to be finding that out in many areas. But unfortunately, a friend of Don Wilson's, Kirby Carter, knows the full truth."

Just at that time, Don come by. "You must be Gilley. Kirby Carter told me you'd be here tonight. You probably need to warm up. It will be later in the first half that I'll bring you on as a second striker. Just warm up with Scotty here. He knows his way around."

At this point, Don carried onto the rest of the team and began organizing the game. This entailed splitting the team of twenty two players with his best defense facing his best forward line. This gave them a chance to really show what they were made of against a better team in the league.

Scotty and Gilley were the only two that didn't have a position. Gilley asked Scotty if they could go over to the side and practice with the ball. He confessed to Scotty that he had not really had a ball in his hands for over a year and needed to get the feel back again—fast. Scotty thought this was a great idea, so they began to warm up and practice, passing the ball back and forth and doing a bit of juggling. The feel didn't take long to come back. Gilley asked Scotty, "What position do you play?"

"Outside right, on the wing," Scotty replied.

"Well, we might get to play together tonight," Gilley said.

"I don't think so as he will probably put you into the second string of forwards as he knows my ability already and I will probably go into the first string."

About thirty-five minutes into the game, Scotty got called into his normal wing position on the first string. Five minutes later, Don called Gilley up and put him into the second string forward. Immediately, the ball came to him. A voice shouted "Put me through."

Gilley heard the command but his opponent was holding him tight, knowing it would be difficult for Gilley to execute the play. He moved in to intercept the ball before Gilley could pass it to the player calling for it. This created an opening and Gilley took advantage of it. He moved to the right and pushed the ball forward around the defense men and into that open space. He saw the opportunity to score and hammered the ball with his right foot. It went right across the goal mouth and it went out of play.

No sooner did that happen, then Don came over to Gilley asking him why didn't he put the ball through when he'd been asked for it?

Gilley replied, "I wasn't able to because, by you shouting, my marker moved forward for the interception and opened up the position for me to move to his right. This gave me the opportunity to pass the ball across the goal mouth. Just no one was there to intercept."

"Next time I call, please execute," stated Don and with that he marched away!

Gilley shrugged his shoulders and wondered, "Could I have made that pass? Have my reflexes slowed down that much in a year? At twenty-six, it shouldn't have done." The game continued until then the whistle blew for half time.

At stage, Gilley thought Don would come over and talk with him some more and explain what he expected of him in the game. Little Scotty came over instead and said, "Nice move. You have to be careful, he is the coach and it has to be done his way until he understands your ability. It'll be the same teams for the second half. You'll probably get another 10 minutes."

The whistle blew and the game began. Gilley remained on. Not much action for him during the first 10 minutes this time as most of the attacking was being done by the first string. Gilley, getting a bit bored, went digging for the ball and fortunately, it came to him. Moving ahead, Gilley saw his counterpart, Don and realized he was in a good position. Gilley pushed the ball through to Don very fast. Gilley then moved into the open space and shouted, "Don, put me through!!" By this time, though, Gilley was offside. After a few more minutes of play, Don substituted Gilley.

About five minutes before the end of the game, Don recalled Gilley. He had just gotten into position when a great opportunity came to his right foot. Not thinking, but acting on instinct he hammered the ball towards goal. To his surprise, he saw the net bulge and was ecstatic. No one else was. He didn't know he was not supposed to score a goal on his first night out with this team. At full time, everyone headed towards the changing rooms and Scotty came up to Gilley, "Nice goal. I think you may have made no friends tonight. You show good ability. With a little bit more training and match practice, they wouldn't be able to refuse you, but you would be replacing someone's friend. I don't go into the changing rooms, because I just live close by and work evenings. Hope to see you next week."

Entering the changing rooms, Gilley felt a definite chill. No one spoke to him or even acknowledged that he was there. He decided to just change his shoes and go home. This was not the place for him tonight nor would he be joining the team even if they asked him to. It just wasn't comfortable.

Back home, Joy wondered how things went. Totally out of context, she noticed he had not yet showered. This made her a bit wary. He was also quite quiet, which was unusual for him. He excused himself while he went for a shower. After he came out, he grabbed a beer and a smoke and said to Joy, "I think it's probably time for me to hang my boots up. Not that I don't have the ability. I scored a goal tonight. No one congratulated me. Canadians play a very different game and don't have the comradeship they do in England. If a total stranger had come for a trial at a practice, our team back home would have welcomed him with open arms and made him feel part of the team. We would have made sure he came with us for a beer afterwards. I walked back into the changing rooms and no one spoke to me. As a matter of fact, they all ignored me. No one cheered when I scored, even. What would anybody think? Do you think I should go back for a second attempt?"

Joy said, "You are not going to find the same friendliness over here in many areas. It can be very cliquey here. As a matter of fact, when I went to school at New Westminster High, there were so many clubs and organizations and if you were not in the right ones, you were out totally. It's too bad you had to find out this way. The game you love so much is out of bounds for you in New Westminster. You could play if you decided to try out for another team in another city. However, you may find the same problem. It's up to you and how determined you are to play soccer."

"Well, it was always my ambition to play professional soccer. When I had my eye surgery it became clear this profession was out of reach for me. Now I realize I've reached my peak at twenty-six. I should be at my best. I know if I trained, I could make the team, but would I ever be accepted?"

"Probably after a few years of sitting on the sidelines. Is that what you want," replied Joy?

"Yeah, I should have realized what was going on after talking to Scotty. He's been coming out to practice for a long time and has yet to play a full game, but he is now one of their reserves. He's a pretty good soccer player. I don't think I could do that. It's just not me to not play the game I love."

The following week, Gilley did go back for Kirby's sake. He watched the game for fifteen minutes and then said good-bye to Scotty. He knew he had made the right decision for himself as playing soccer not playing politics was what he wanted. Time would tell if he wanted it bad enough. There were lots of teams around, but thinking to himself, "Most of the games would be played on Sunday and Saturday is golf day. I don't think Joy would allow both things to happen. Besides, she enjoys watching golf (especially Jack Nicholas) and there is a good possibility she might take up the sport one day, whereas she definitely would not take up soccer. So maybe it's just as well to let it go."

Gilley didn't have much time to belabor this decision as things at Swann's were heating up quickly. To Gilley's surprise when he arrived at work Thursday morning, the office was abuzz with the news that Swann's would be taken over by ABC Packers. It was to be a clean take-over and was to help Swann's to further their interests in Nova Scotia, Singapore and Australia.

This sounded like good news at first. As the day went on, though, bad news began to trickle through the grapevine. First of all, in the late morning, Barry Freeke advised the engineering office he had decided to resign Swann's along with Art Burgess. Apparently, Swann's acquisition by ABC Packers wasn't as clean as was first thought. That afternoon everyone was in turmoil. What was going to happen? Who is going to be the next president? Who is going to be the next chief engineer? Are any of us going to have a job tomorrow? Late that afternoon, Bill Robbins, the general manager, made the official announcement to everyone that Art Burgess and Barry Freeke had resigned from the company. There would be no other resignations nor would anyone else be laid off. "We will have a new president as of next week. His name is John Cleaves. He comes to us with great credentials. He was responsible in making Quadra Steel the company it is today. Everyone can leave tonight with ease, knowing you have a job tomorrow. We are considering some others for the chief engineer's position and will announce it as soon as possible."

That night Gilley arrived home wanting to tell Joy the news, but thought it would be better to wait another day or two until things had really settled down.

The following morning, Bill Robbins approached Gilley and asked him if he would consider the position of chief engineer. Now this put Gilley in a bit of a quandary. Here he had been offered to go to Singapore, now he was offered this position. At twenty six years of age, he never expected to be offered any of these positions as in England, typically one would have to be in their forties to even be considered. It was at this age a man was considered to be mature and worth of respect.

However, Barry Freeke had explained to Gilley earlier in the year many companies in Canada offered positions such as this one to someone who had the right qualifications. These qualifications were taken from the Professional Engineer's Association of that particular province. Barry had come from Ontario but couldn't operate in BC until he had been accepted by the Professional Engineer's board of examiners in British Columbia. Barry was only two years older than Gilley, but due to the fact that Barry had a Bachelor of Science in mechanical engineering from Leed's University in England made it easier for him to pass the board exams.

This offer presented Gilley with a big decision. He went for a walk down to the docks to clear his head. He thought to himself, "Right now I'm earning $700.00 a month. They'll probably give me another $200.00 a month to do this job. If I don't succeed, it'll be at least three months—that's $600.00 in me pocket. I really don't think the transfer to Singapore is going to happen now, with all of this going on. I think I'll take this job. Better is a bird in the hand than two in the bush" With that, he immediately went back to Bill Robbins and said, "One question, how much does the job pay?"

Bill said, "Nine fifty to start."

"Thanks for this opportunity. I'll take the job on two conditions; I have to be the one to tell the other draftsmen and engineers I will be taking this position before it's to be announced. And I, instead of calling the position Chief Engineer, I would like it titled Engineering Manager. We have professional engineers on board and I don't want to ruffle their feathers. Secondly, I have arranged to take a trip to England for a good friend's wedding. I'm to be his best man. The trip is planned for October next year. I would want to still be able to follow through with this trip."

"Well," he said, "Congratulations on your speedy decision. And of course, there won't be a problem for you to go back to England and I like how you think. You're taking the welfare of the company and its employees into consideration."

"Another question-why did you pick me? I'm the last one hired here".

Bill's reply was straight to the point, "It was Barry Freeke who recommended you for the job as you have been better trained and have a better academic background than the others. You have already shown your organizational skills."

"That's very flattering, thank you. When would you like me to start," beamed Gilley?

"I'll have your business cards printed right away so you can announce it tomorrow. Then I will formally hand out a letter of notice regarding this decision."

At that point Bill invited Gilley to join him in a drink at the famous watering hole, the Waldorf Hotel, but instead of the beer parlour, it was to be in the cocktail bar where Jim and Gilley had eaten lunch previously. As Bill sat down, he was automatically given his favourite drink by the waiter who knew him—a Manhattan. The waiter then asked Gilley "What would the young man like"?

"A Labatt's Blue please," replied Gilley.

Then the waiter turned to Bill and asked, "Mr. Bill, would you like anything to eat?"

"Let's see, I think we'll have some of those deep fried shrimp to share for now, thank you."

Gilley always thought Bill was easy to talk to and felt at ease with him. He knew he could talk to him about most things whether personal or work related. However, today Bill was determined not to talk about work. He wanted to get to know Gilley better. He wanted to know about Gilley's experiences in England and how he was enjoying his new life in Canada as well as to get to know Joy better. Too soon it was time to return to work. Bill impressed Gilley by telling the waiter to put everything on the company tab. Bill explained to Gilley this was one of the perks of the job. Once a month, the company would reimburse the Waldorf. This made it very convenient when one had to take customers out for lunch. It insured one would never be caught in an embarrassing situation.

Gilley thought to himself, "Maybe one day I will be able to run a tab too. That would be a step up the ladder. I can just imagine taking Joy down here and saying, 'Put it on me tab.' On the way back to the shop, Bill suggested it would be good, since tomorrow was Friday, to begin moving into the new offices right way and this would take the focus off of all of the changes which were occurring in the upper management. It would be a progressive move as all of the technical people would be in one location. The staff had been waiting for a long time for this move to occur.

"I know I can leave this move in your hands, Gilley. If you need any help, just ask." With that statement, Bill left Gilley to return to his duties. Gilley, as he was walking back to the office, had the feeling the management was behind him one hundred percent.

Upon returning to the office, everyone was wondering where Gilley had been. Upon brief reflection, Gilley decided that now was the time to break the news of his being made the Engineering Manager. He did this with little fanfare. Most of the staff congratulated him on this promotion, but one did not—John Pendry, the present Chief Draughtsman. He felt somewhat slighted and that he really deserved this position. He didn't hold anything back. Since it was the end of the day and everyone was leaving, he took this opportunity to express his thoughts loud and clear. "Gilley I clearly don't understand why management would have picked you for this job over me. I've been here for over three years and worked myself up to this position. Here you come along and you haven't been here yet a year. I don't understand their thinking and don't think it's right."

Gilley understood how John felt. He said, "I understand how you feel, John and it puzzles me a bit too. However, it will be made official tomorrow morning. You can assist me or you can fight me. But tomorrow, we are all moving to the new offices. So any work you have planned for the boys will have to be put on hold until next week. If we all pitch in and do our best, I think we can be moved and settled by tomorrow night. We can start fresh Monday morning on our projects. I will need your assistance to organize this move along with the work we presently have on hand."

Gilley then did something that was not characteristic of him, but he felt it had to be done, "If you don't like what's happened, John, think about it tonight and we'll talk tomorrow. Perhaps we will have to get upper management involved." With that statement, John turned on his heel and left the office in a huff.

On the way home, Gilley was lost in thought. He needed to have some time to think about all that had happened during the day in order to get his mind cleared enough to deal with tomorrow. He felt as if he didn't need to have any more input from anyone. With this realization, he decided not to tell Joy about what had happened as this would just promote a celebration with the in-laws and not give him any time to readjust to the new position. He decided to phone Joy and tell her he had to work overtime that night. He would be home about nine o'clock. With that he stopped in New Westminster at the King

Edward beer parlour. With book in hand, and a couple of beers, he started to write down his plan.

Gilley took into account that the company was now short two draughtsmen, himself and Allen Pickering as Allen was now going to work with George Strut, in the mixer division of Swann's. (These mixers were used in the mining industry and this industry was booming.) Don Howath would be back from Singapore next week ready for work. He was originally the Chief Draughtsman. Hugh Christy, who was a professional engineer, responsible for the diesel powered winches. Pat Sullivan was a US draft dodger. He was a very capable engineer. He was responsible for the Gantry Crane division. Hartwig Diener, a German draughtsman. David Mosley, Gilley golfing buddy and another draughtsman. Danny Ellis was a general technical illustrator and also used in draughting. Rudy Maros—he had been hired by Dennis Shears and was until now an unknown quality, but apparently a good engineer from Czechoslovakia. Of course, an immediate problem was John Pendry.

"What the hell have I let myself in for? Maybe I should just stay here and get drunk. Well, I'll feel awful tomorrow morning and I don't think the magical shower would do much to help out and I need a clear head to deal with everything. I knew it wouldn't be easy when I said 'Yes'. I guess I didn't factor John's strong response into things. I think I'll tell Joy tomorrow night at Shakey's Pizza Parlor. Everyone meets there Friday nights. That'll give us the weekend to celebrate and to settle into this new venture. It's time to go home, have a bite to eat and go to bed. Tomorrow will be a bit of a day. I'll need to get in early—before everyone else—to get set up."

That night was not easy. Gilley was constantly thinking about all of the things he had to do tomorrow. Joy noticed his restlessness and inquired about it a few times. He decided to stick with his initial decision and not tell her until the weekend. This made matters worse in that Gilley now understood a wife can always tell when something is on her husband's mind. Joy was no exception and, being Joy, did not give up easily.

Eventually, Gilley came up with the excuse that it was a big day tomorrow due to the fact they were moving the office and the work load everyone was under was extreme. Hopefully, once they got themselves settled in their allotted positions with all of the engineering being in one location, the pressure would ease off considerably. The other problem which had presented itself was the shortage of skilled draughtsmen. This was also putting pressure on the engineering department as they were constantly working extra hours every day. The orders kept coming in as the company was expanding its product line and it was also becoming recognized as a leader in winch design for the off shore supply vessels. Since each winch was a custom design as many of the supply vessel companies had their own ideas for their specific operations, there was no standardization.

Gilley was normally a very laid back person and these types of things did not bother him as a rule. Joy, not having ever seen this side of him, accepted these explanations reluctantly and gave up her probing (much to Gilley's relief). She thought there was more to things than he was letting on, but decided to let it go. She would find out eventually.

That night he tossed and turned as his mind went over all of the things he anticipated to occur the next day. The fact of this new responsibility brought into question whether or not he would find any more opposition within the company once everyone knew of his promotion. He wasn't used to having someone such as John Pendry so hostile towards him and this was a source of concern for him.

He rose earlier than normal, showered, breakfasted and was just about to leave an hour earlier than normal. As he kissed Joy good-bye, she said, "I hope your day is a good day and maybe tonight you can tell me what is really going on and what is bothering you."

Driving to work, Gilley felt a little guilty that he hadn't explained the entire story to Joy. He was basically an honest person, but until now he really didn't realize how powerful a wife's intuition could be. "What a surprise she'll have tonight," he thought.

Arriving at work, Gilley was the second one in. The other was Bill Robbins. Gilley confided in him that he had told the engineering personnel they would be moving into their new offices today. He explained he had reasoned this would be a new start for the staff in many ways and it would also be a bit of a distraction for them. Plus the fact Monday would be the start to a new week and a new outlook. People would have had the weekend to get used to all of the changes and would, more than likely, come to work in a more positive mood. (Generally, Mondays were always blue days)

Gilley also explained he was already having some problems with John Pendry. John had reacted in quite a hostile manner yesterday.

Maybe today, he would have changed his tune. Bill said, "Some people take it harder than others and with you being the younger member with the least time on the job here, I'm not surprised someone reacted that way. There may be others who are not as vocal about their unhappiness. Don't worry about it too much, you have our backing and things will work out. We will go along with any decision you make. This is your department now."

"I think it was a hell of a good idea to get things moving today. I knew I had chosen the right man for the job. You think well on your feet, Gilley. The other departments will offer as much help as they can with your move. To start with, we can take all of the drawing boards over on the forklift for you. They are quite heavy and that will save time as well as energy. I'm afraid you fellows are on your own to get them upstairs. Perhaps we can pull some manpower from the shop floor."

"Thanks so much," replied Gilley. "I was a bit nervous about this day as there is a lot riding on it and there is a lot to do."

Things went very well that day. By mid-day, all of the office furniture was in place. The engineering staff had a great time arranging their new home. It went so well, there was time for people to organize their work for the following week. By 4:30, Gilley invited everyone over to the Waldorf for a few beers on him. Even John Pendry came over. He sat at the far table from Gilley, but he had participated in the day's activities without any further confrontation. Perhaps things would work out after all was said and done.

Driving home, Gilley had a feeling of relief and of a job well done. There had been no further tensions among anyone. Even the rest of the staff and the shop floor had congratulated him on his promotion. Bill Robbins had come through with his business cards. These said, "Engineering Manager".

He was running a bit late and knew Joy worked until 6:00 PM on Friday nights. Generally the bank staff would meet at Shakey's Pizza Parlour for a beer and pizza. Knowing this, he drove straight to the pizza parlour. Upon his arrival, Joy looked sternly up from her beer. It was approaching 6:45 PM. He was more than a bit late and had not phoned her to let her know. He held his hand up as if to stop her from speaking, and said to her, "I have some news that will explain it all."

"I knew you were holding out on me. It had better be good news."

Gilley handed her his new business card, "I just received these today."

Right away, Joy responded, "How long have you known this? How long have you been holding out on me? I knew something was up. Come on, out with the entire story."

All the bank staff paused at her statement. They knew something was coming and didn't want to miss a thing. Gilley never failed to provide entertainment and something to talk about.

"Well, I only found out yesterday morning from Bill Robbins. I told you Barry Freeke and Art Burgess had left. Barry had recommended me for the job. It does pay another $300.00 a month." Gilley offered in his defense.

"Don't just stand there. Get a glass and pour yourself a beer from this pitcher. Did you hear, everyone, Gilley got himself a promotion. Maybe you should order another pitcher in celebration. We'll have our pizza and then we have to get over to Mom and Dad's to tell them the good news."

Generally, Friday night was a quiet night at the Wilson's. Jim would come home, put his feet up and unwind. Tonight would be different. After stopping at the liquor store on the way there, Gilley and Joy arrived unannounced. This was quite unusual and of course was a signal to Veron. Immediately upon their entry, Veron exclaimed, "What's wrong? What happened now?"

Joy replied right away, "We have some good news. Let's go down to bar and have a beer."

"You're pregnant, aren't you," Veron guessed?

Gilley retorted, "That's not good news, Jim. That's a prison sentence."

"True," replied Jim under his breath.

After everyone was settled with their beers, Veron with her gin and tonic, they said in harmony, "Alright, out with it. You can't keep us waiting forever."

"Give them a business card, Gilley," Joy instructed.

He did. Well, the celebration started. Everyone wanted to know all of the details and Veron's first response was, "How much more does it pay?"

"$300.00 a month more", replied Joy.

Veron turned to Jim and said, "Well, at this rate, he's going to surpass you, Jim. He's been here just over a year and he's almost doubled his salary with the opportunity of going to Singapore. They must be willing to pay him more for that."

Jim, in his laid back manner, said, "I hope he ends up making twice as much as me. Then he can take care of us all. I've always wanted a son-in-law who could take care of us when we get old."

"Oh, Jim, I didn't mean it like that." But underneath Veron's exterior, he knew she didn't like the fact that her daughter would end up surpassing her in her social standings. In spite of this undertone, it was a fun night. As the night grew on, Jim reminded Gilley golf was tomorrow and they would have to on the road by 6:30. "Chop, chop, time to be off as my bed is calling and tomorrow comes early."

As usual, everyone met at Eric's. This time Dave Mosley joined the group as Brian was getting prepared to go to New Zealand. (Jim and Veron were holding a surprise party for Brian and Marva that night.) Jim immediately informed everyone of Gilley's promotion before Dave arrived. Eric's typical response was, "It must be paying more money, so the beers are on you after the game."

Anne, who was very compassionate, said, "That's great news, Gilley. Congratulations. I'm going to make you an extra fried egg sandwich for that. Is your friend Dave coming today?"

"He will meet us at the Pro shop as it's a bit early for him and it's a long way for him to drive from Richmond."

"Oh well, I'll make a fried egg sandwich for him too. You don't mind taking it along, do you? How's that"?

Jim said, "Don't give it to Gilley, he'll eat it. I've never seen someone eat so much."

At the Pro shop, Dave appreciated the egg sandwich. Eric, who was one to stir things up a bit, said to Dave, "Well, do you like your new boss, Dave? Do you want to play with him or against him? It doesn't matter what you choose, you'll not win."

"Oh, nice" said Dave in his southern English accent, "Nice."

He decided to play with Gilley. In this golf game, it was quite vicious due to two factors. Not only did one play in pairs, but the other object of the game was purely money. It was a nickel for whoever got onto the green first, a nickel for who was closest to the pin, a nickel for first down, and a nickel for the lowest score. At the end of the game the person with the lowest score won $.50 extra from the others and the pair with the lowest score won $1.00 from the other team.

If one didn't have a good day, he stood the chance of being out up to \$10.00, not to mention taking the ribbing from the other three. Generally, one would lose two to three dollars and the winner would be generally Eric or Jim. Gilley and Dave, being much younger focused on having a good game and a low score. Jim and Eric focused on winning the money. They had figured out how to win at this game, especially since they had come up with it. But that day was different. Gilley and Dave took the prize money. How had they accomplished this? It was never to be known. Eric would never have thrown the game. Was it just good luck or had the youngsters begun to figure out the system?

Once in the club house, known as the 19th Hole, Eric was in a bit of a mood. He was not used to being outdone. He challenged Dave and Gilley to a game of shuffleboard. This was sort of a mini board game of curling. Again, a similar game in England would be called Shove Half Penny. Obviously Eric and Jim thought this would be an easy task to regain some of their losses. To their surprise, the youngsters whipped them at this game too. Next—cribbage. Dave wasn't very knowledgeable about the game, but luck prevailed and the youngsters matched their other wins.

By this time, Eric was really sarcastic and to some degree blamed Jim for their losses. He was a man that was not used to losing, especially so many games in a row. He was getting desperate. He challenged the group to a Snooker game. Unknown to the younger men, Eric was a champion Snooker and Billiard player plus the fact that no one knew there was full size table at the back of the club house. By this time, Dave and Gilley were feeling quite fortunate that luck was on their side today. They heartily agreed to the game.

In the back room, the lights above the table were operated by a coin box system. This was very typical in most billiard halls as well as the ones in England. Now, Eric expressed to Jim, "Now Jim, you are going to get the opportunity to play on a man-sized table not that midget thing you have in your basement bar."

Now Dave or Jim didn't profess to be great snooker players, but Gilley fancied he could hold his own when it came down to it as he had played many games in his youth. He had not played on a full sized table since he'd left England. The game proceeded with Jim and Eric on one team and Dave and Gilley on the other. Eric broke the reds and positioned the white ball back in behind the green.

It didn't take Gilley more than a second to realize this guy was no amateur, unless this was just a lucky break. Something told him this was not so. Gilley then took his shot taking the white off the back, up the side and touching the red. Eric's immediate response was, "So you think you are pretty good at this game, eh? Holding back on me eh, Jim, not telling me your son-in-law knows a bit about this game." As the game proceeded, it quickly became obvious the game was really between Eric and Gilley.

After the table opened up, and it was Eric's turn, he showed his prowess in the game as he sank red, colour, red, colour one after the other, getting a break of 46. The most frustrating thing of the game for Eric was he followed Dave and Dave took a defensive play. Eric was determined he would not leave a break for Gilley. The best Gilley could do was three reds and three blacks which totaled 24. Obviously, Jim and Eric were back on their winning streak.

Now, not to be outdone, Gilley challenged Eric to a game of billiards. That was his next mistake. What he should have done was congratulated Eric, bought him a beer and left well enough alone. Billiards is a highly skilful game, not that Gilley didn't have the skill, but Eric, again was a master. Gilley should have known. The game ended up with 101 to Eric and forty to Gilley. After the game, Eric then invited Gilley to come to the legion some day and familiarize himself with the large tables. He graciously indicated, "You do have potential Gilley, but you obviously lack time on the table. Where did you learn to play?"

"In a little village called Walbottle. They had a two table institute where the old men taught us how us how to play in our early teens. This lasted until we got to eighteen, the legal age in England for drinking and drinking became more fun."

Time was creeping on. It was about 3:30 PM in the afternoon and the going away party for Brian and Marva was that night. Since everyone was expected to be there, they all felt they needed to get home before they got into trouble from their wives. Jim and Gilley left and stopped at the liquor store in New Westminster and stocked up with beer and booze and wine. Once back at Jim's the ladies were waiting for them. "Jim", Veron said, "You were supposed to be picking my mother and Rosa up at the bus depot. Where have you guys been? They took the 2:00 PM ferry and were to arrive at the depot at about 4:15 PM. It's now gone 4:30 PM."

Jim replied defensively, "We stopped and picked up all of the booze for the night and I thought you had decided you were picking them up."

"You knew we wouldn't be picking them up as Joy and I were at the hairdressers today and we were organizing the spread."

Jim then turned to Gilley, both of them feeling no pain, "Why didn't you remind me, Gilley?

Gilley, quick on his feet responded, "I thought the bus didn't arrive until 5:15 and that we had lots of time to pick up the booze and fill up the bar."

"Gilley, you take your car and go and get the two of them. I'll unload the booze and get the bar stocked. By the time you get back here, things should be in order."

As Gilley drove away in his Duster, he was pretty sure he knew where the bus depot was. It was next to the Royal Towers, was it not? He got to the Towers in quick enough time but he could not find anywhere to park (so what was new, he'd been here before). He didn't think to look for the customer pick up and it was not well signed. After finding a spot, of course, miles away, he made his way to the terminal and attempted to locate his in-laws. They were not to be found. He phoned Veron. "They are not here. I'm sure I'm in the right place. There are Greyhound buses everywhere."

Veron suggested, "Try the Cloud Nine Cocktail Lounge. It's at the top of the Towers. They probably got tired waiting for you and decided to go for a drink."

"Great idea," Gilley headed into the lobby of the hotel and took the elevator up to the Cloud Nine. No Grandma or Aunt Rosa.

"Maybe they went into the beer parlour," he thought and then proceeded down the elevator making his way into the beer parlour. Now this location was much harder to search as it was full of men, smoke and no women could be found. Now he was getting a bit upset. "Maybe they are in the restaurant. I'm sure they could get a good pot of tea or maybe a drink."

No Grandma or Rosa was to be found in that place either. In frustration, Gilley asked the desk clerk if there were any other places that two women could go to wait for their ride. "Try the lounge off the side of the building here. It's actually a bit hidden and hard to see. Look for the carved wooden doors which are just around the corner to your right."

As Gilley opened the two wooded doors, he could hear laughter and Grandma's was the most distinctive. Sure enough Rosa and Grandma were in men's company. Gilley didn't know what to do. Here he was ready to whisk them away to the party and they looked like they were having a party to themselves. Gilley's dilemma was he didn't know if these men had come over with the two women in order to attend the party or if the women had just picked them up for a bit of entertainment while they waited for their lift.

Cautiously approaching, Gilley made his presence known. Rosa saw him first and immediately responded, "Come join us for a drink. We are having far too much fun to leave here now."

Grandma yelled for the waiter, "Bring a round of drinks here and a beer for the new one."

"Oh boy, now what do I do," thought Gilley? He decided to say, "Well thank you Grandma, I'm sorry I'm late. I've been running around the hotel looking for you in every possible spot but this one. Veron is waiting for us."

Rosa quipped, "I'm not sorry at all. That bossy sister of mine can wait. Sit down and make yourself at home." She then proceeded to introduce Gilley to the two men. Sure enough, she and Grandma had picked them up after they had entered the bar to wait for their ride. They were flirting shamelessly, like young girls. The two men were obviously not comfortable with the situation, and once they finished their drink, excused themselves from the table graciously picking the tab up and wished Gilley the best of luck.

Grandma said, "Go and get the car while we go to the ladies room. Pick us up at the front door." Having gotten the car he waited at the front door as instructed. As time passed and the ladies didn't appear, Gilley wondered if he should call Veron to let her know what was happening. Just as he was about to get out of the car, he heard Grandma's laughter coming from the same bar.

He got out and went into the bar. Here they were sitting down again with a couple of different men. Luckily, they hadn't been able to order yet. Thinking fast on his feet again Gilley shouted, "Grandma, your ride is here. Come on let's go. They are all waiting for us."

Rosa answered, "One more for the road!"

"We can't. I'm parked illegally and the car is running."

"Well, I hope you can catch it in time. Then park it legally so you can come and have a beer with us."

The time was passing on, Gilley was well aware of this and of his responsibility to get Veron's sister and mother to the house before the other guests arrived. He also had to go home, shower and change as he was still in his golf gear. Now he was getting nervous. He realized Rosa could get quite belligerent very quickly and her voice could get very loud. Any more drinks and things would just get worse. Grandma, to Gilley's relief, decided it was time to go and told Rosa to come along. Thank God!

Reluctantly, Rosa said her goodbyes and got into the car. By the time Gilley pulled up in front of Jim and Veron's it was gone 6:30 PM. Entering the house everyone was frantic, especially Veron as she knew her Mother and sister too well. Instead of getting a tongue lashing for delivering them late, Gilley received a small smile of relief from her. She quietly said to Gilley, "I do know what they're like when they get into a bar. That's why it's always imperative to be early to pick them up instead of being late. Go home and get yourself changed and get back here no later than 7:00 PM to look after the bar for us."

"Right on, Veron" said a much relieved Gilley. "I'll be back. Does Joy need anything from our house?"

"She's already there waiting for you." replied Jim.

Back home, things were not as pleasant. Joy was somewhat upset it had taken Gilley so long to run this simple errand. He went into the whole explanation of the situation. This had some effect on her before he went into the shower and by the time he had emerged, shaved and changed, she had come around, realizing again what her relatives could be like, thank goodness.

As the night went on, it was obvious the party was a great success. Brian had been sent off royally and given a very unique parting gift—a custom made golf club. This was to help him as he had great difficulty avoiding water when he played golf. It seemed as if his balls were magnetically drawn to any type of water. Jim and Gilley had designed a golf club with the center cut out so that the club could just glide through any water hazard. They had fashioned a net made of stainless steel wire inside this hole and this would allow the ball to be carried from the hazard.

Of course, unknown to most of the guests, Rosa flirted shamelessly with Eric and caused a bit a disturbance with Eric's wife, Anne. Jim diplomatically saved the night. Grandma behaved herself, by and large, but detested Eric because she thought he was an arrogant English Southerner. It was well known the North and South of England very seldom agreed. Of course she had to let her feelings be known. Thank God for Veron, stepping in as the referee.

During the night as Rosa was sitting at the bar, the wig she was wearing became more and more twisted. She actually became quite funny what with her remarks and this sliding hairpiece.

Of course Aunt Rosa was not the only one who was entertaining the guests. Harry was in his glory. He chatted up all the women as his wife Gwen smiled pleasantly and made small talk with the other wives. She knew he was harmless. All told, there were about 24 guests, 75 percent of them smoked and the room was filled with a blue cloud. The bar took on the look of an old English pub with the talking and laughing between parties and the jokes being shouted across the room.

While doing the barman's job, Gilley had the opportunity of stepping back to observe what was happening. This took him back to the days when he ran the bar at the Bay Horse in Cramlington, operated by his friends Stan and Wynn Crone. Many good parties were held there and of course the best one of them being the wedding reception for Gilley and Joy. Just at that time, some music came on. It was one of the songs which were played often during those days in Cramlington. As it came on, Gilley asked Joy, "What does this remind you of?"

Joy said, "Of course, the music and the atmosphere tonight remind me of England, but it's not the same as being there. It makes me feel as if we should never have left."

"Well you wouldn't have a party like this in a house in England."

She turned around and said, "The parties at John and Val Palmer's were pretty good, but they didn't have a bar. But I sure miss all of your friends and the fun we had. All we seem to do here is work and party with my parents and their friends."

"One day, if we're here long enough I will build a bar that has the English pub character and one day we may have all of our friends there from England," replied Gilley

Rosa had wondered over to the bar at this time and had overheard a part of the conversation, "What's these two love birds doing talking and looking at each other as if it was the first day they had ever met?"

Grandma immediately jumped in, "Leave those two alone, Rosa. You've made enough of a scene tonight. Maybe it's time for you to go to bed?"

"I would go to bed of I had man like Gilley." Turning to Joy, she said, "You'd better watch yourself with him. If I have my way, I'd be off with him." While she said this she snuggled up to Gilley, pushing Joy to the side. This totally embarrassed Gilley. Fortunately, people began screaming for drinks and he was able to make a hasty exit from that scene.

Rosa turned to Joy and said, "See, he's a popular man and everyone wants his attention. You'd better keep his attention on you."

Joy shrugged her shoulders, did an eye roll and said, "He's just not that type of person. He is a flirt, but I know at the end of the night we go home together and I don't mind doing a bit of flirting either. I think it's good for one another as long as you know how far to go."

As the party began to wind down, Rosa and Grandma were getting into their typical squabble (something that happened every time they had been drinking). It was quite embarrassing for Veron. Jim tried to hustle everybody out before things got too bad. Getting rid of Harry was a bit of a problem as he was still flirting with anyone who was still there. Eventually everyone left and Gilley and Joy cleaned up the bar. Veron looked after her mom and Rosa. Jim appeared at the bar totally bedraggled. "Gilley, one for the road, man? That was quite some party."

Gilley replied, "Yes it was. Brian and Marva were sent off like royalty. So Grandma and Rosa have gone to bed? Is this a regular occurrence, then?"

"Oh yes. Every time they get drinking, but at least they will sleep it off and be OK by tomorrow. This sort of thing is inherent in the family". Turning to Joy, "I hope you don't have the same problems with your mother, Joy. She can be just as bad as the other two together."

Joy replied, "I've seen my mom in action. It's not a pretty sight. I don't think Gilley has yet. So watch out, you have something to look forward to one day."

Sunday was typical and uneventful as everyone was recovering from the party and the previous week. Monday came before Gilley knew it and he was back to work for the second week in his new position. Arriving early as normal, Gilley made the coffee and then sat in the empty engineering room and thought about his new situation. How had this happened to him so quickly? Canada was indeed a land of opportunity. It offered so much more than England. The excitement, the customs, the money—he could not believe his good fortune. He knew Joy wanted to go back to England and stay there. He also knew he didn't. How was he going to solve this problem? Somehow, the situation with John Pendry paled in comparison to this one with Joy.

The staff arrived, had their coffee and chatted about all the changes that were taking place. Gilley had been right. They had used the weekend to get used to the management changes and had come to the conclusion on their own, that Gilley was the man for the job. He didn't need to convince them any further. He just had to maintain their confidence in him by making good decisions.

As fall arrived and the typical wet west coast BC weather began, chess took over the normal outings on coffee and lunch breaks. The men in the drawing office had begun to play during their breaks and the new offices were perfect for several games of chess to be happening at one time.

Business was good and morale was very good. The staff at Swann's had their routine and in spite of all of the changes, things were running smoothly. The new president, John Cleaves was due to begin during this week and all the staff were waiting for the official announcement. However, instead of following the standard protocol, he took it upon himself to just wander through the company and informally introduce himself to all to the employees on an individual basis. Due to the new location of the engineering office, word had not yet reached them that this was happening. That day several chess games were in full swing, (it was lunch time) and lo and behold, Mr. Cleaves popped in. Not knowing who this stranger was, Gilley walked up to him and said, "Hello, can I be of any assistance to you. We don't get many visitors up here as some people don't even know we exist. Are you lost?"

To everyone's dismay, especially Gilley's the neatly dressed man said in his very English accent, "I don't want to disturb you on your lunch break. I just wanted to take this opportunity to introduce myself. I am John Cleaves, the new president of the company and I was wondering where this famous engineering office was." Looking around the office, he said next, "Ah, chess players, are we? Who is the current champion?"

Everyone turned at one time and looked to one man, Pat Sullivan. Pat was a draft dodger from America, but one hell of an engineer. John walked across the office to his chess board and asked Pat's partner if he could make the next move for him.

John Pendry jumped out of his seat. "No problem, sir. Be my guest."

John looked at the board for a few seconds made a move and Pat just looked at him as said, "Holy mackerel. You've played this game before."

"Well, just to be fair to you all and not to brag, I'm a Grand Master."

Everyone was taken aback by that. Some were elated and some were embarrassed. John continued around the room and introduced himself to everybody. By the time lunch was over, most of the men were feeling a bit more comfortable with him around as he had a friendly, approachable way about him.

As he was leaving, he made the office an offer, "I'll come back next week some time during lunch and I'm prepared to play six games." Turning to Gilley he said, "You just let me know when they're ready. By the way, we have a manager's meeting at 3:00 PM today and I would like you to attend." His departing words were, "Sorry for interrupting your lunch break. Do finish your sandwiches before you begin working again. Is that OK with you, Gilley?"

"Of course. Thank you for stopping by. We'll look forward to seeing you next week for that match up," replied Gilley, "And of course I'll see you at 3:00 PM."

During the entire time John Cleaves had been in the office, Gilley was aware of the undercurrent emanating from John Pendry. He returned to his office pondering what to do with John. He had a feeling things were not going to go well, despite the outward calm. Just at that time, another stranger walked in and headed straight for Gilley's office—a second stranger in less than an hour. Even though his reputation had preceded him, no one knew what he looked like.

"Hello. Gilley I presume? Don Howath here. When do you want me to start? I just arrived back from Singapore yesterday."

"Nice to meet you, Don," said Gilley, relieved it wasn't another executive, "I knew you'd be coming this week, but wasn't quite sure what day. I've heard quite a bit about you and am pleased you'll be working in this department. We have a lot of new winches to design. When would you like to start?"

"Today, if it's OK with you."

"Sure it is. I'll just introduce you to everybody. I have an office at the corner which can be yours. I know you know a lot of people on the shop floor. Since its gone 1:00 PM, just visit for the day and get yourself reacquainted with everyone. I have a manager's meeting at 3:00 PM, but if you're around after that, I'd like to take you for a beer at the Waldorf."

"That would be great. It'll give us a chance to get to know each other," said Don.

"Well," said Gilley, "I do need help and your expertise will be greatly valued. My job is to make sure we can design the equipment in an orderly fashion so we can meet the tight deadlines we have. We have lots of new contracts and thus new winches to design and the men here are working as hard as they can. Your experience will assist us all greatly."

After introducing Don to the men in the engineering office, Gilley and Don went down to the shop floor. Gilley had to check out a few things with the foreman before going to the manager's meeting and Don wanted to see his friends. On the way down, Don mentioned he had felt there was a bit of tension between John Pendry and Gilley during his introduction.

"You are a very observant man, Don," said Gilley. "Now is not the time to discuss it. That's part of what I'd like to talk with you about over that beer tonight."

"That sounds like a good idea. I've run into this type of thing before. Let's meet in the Hawaiian Room at the Waldorf at 5:00 PM." With that, Gilley left for the manager's meeting.

This was Gilley's first manager's meeting. What could he expect? With having no experience and not having time to ask anyone, he thought this is when his Father-in-law, Jim would have been rather helpful. Jim was used to being at meetings due to his position at the school board. He wondered what he should bring? Well, he knew from past experience that taking a pen and a note pad couldn't hurt.

The meeting was held in a large room reserved for the president's purposes. It was fairly formal in décor with a board room type table and leather chairs. Instead of sitting at the head of the table, John Cleaves sat in the middle of it. This was, he said, in order to relate better to all of the participants.

At the meeting were all the important people such as Dennis Shears-the Sales Manager; Bill Robins-General Manager; Mel Newth - Controller; George Strut - Director of the Mixer Division; Lorne Hughes - Shop Foreman; Mac Harrison - Hydraulics and Installation Forman; John Clarke - Head Estimator; and Jim Hunter - Purchasing Agent.

The meeting started with John Cleaves welcoming all in attendance and stating what a privilege it was for him to be named president of such an up and coming company. He also said he was impressed already by the quality of work and workmanship he had observed as he had toured the plant. He commended everyone on what a good job they had done in continuing to keep things going through out this transition period.

Stating his faith in the future of Swann's, he declared that the company had a full order book and the amount of future billings and sales looked very bright. Along with the fact there was an operation in Halifax, and an office in Singapore, they were also looking at purchasing a company in Australia. The need to be international was the future, especially with the exploration of oil in the various seas around the world, in particular the North Sea. He announced Swann's was in the design stage of building five deck systems for Allied Shipbuilding, who in turn was building the offshore supply vessels for I.O.S. This was along with two other winch and gantry systems for Bell-Aire Ship Yard. In addition to these orders were various towing winches for John Manly Ship Yards. There was the potential to be awarded a full deck system for an ice breaker for the US Coast Guard which was being built in Lockheed Ship Yard in Seattle. This would be a joint venture with a well known hydraulic company called Rucker Controls out of Oakland, California.

"So, our books are full and according to Dennis Shears, more opportunities are available. It's nice to have all of this work, but are we profitable? That is the bottom line for the owners." At this, he turned to Mel Newth for his input.

Mel was an Australian with a very definite accent and was responsible to the directors of ABC Packers who were the sole owners of Swann's.

Now ABC Packers had their own large fleet of fishing vessels to supply their canneries. It was the intention of ABC to become more diversified. Mel was an up and comer and had been associated with them for some time. His background was in accounting and since computers were starting to become very significant in this field, he was in the forefront of this trend. John Cleaves was, of course also very much in favour of the new age of computers and accounting. He had just left the steel distribution company, Quadra Steel which had made a big impact on the local market with the aid computers.

Mel began, "I know you fellows have heard of the benefits of computers from me before this meeting. You have also no doubt heard about some of the down sides. With the research and the advances coming fast in this area, the downsides are dwindling and we believe this is the way of the future. Of course, you'd be familiar with computers in the field of accounting. But in addition to this, we have used computers to do research out at UBC through Norm Johnson on simplifying the design of the gear drives of the winches into a standard format. This would give us the benefit of economizing the design by utilizing past products and thereby increasing profits."

"Today, as you know, we build each winch as a custom product. To enable us to enter the International field, we have to streamline our products and methods. I want you to know this will not deter us from building custom winches, but what it will do, is let us produce standardized products such as gear drives, hydraulic systems, spooling drives, brake systems and so on, thereby saving us engineering time and streamlining the production. I know Dennis Shears would agree as he is the one who has to sell the products. He believes having standardization will make his job easier and provide the customer with a product he can more readily afford and we will have the satisfaction of having the delivery on time. This also gives us the advantage of having spare parts in stock readily available for replacement when the need arises. As you all know, spare parts can be the bread and butter of a company. It is important to know what spare parts can be stocked economically and provided to the customer in record time."

"By introducing the computer into our company, the computer will be able to log man hours to specific segments of each job with more accuracy. It will also record material usage and purchased items—basically everything that goes into building a winch. You may be wondering why we don't just stick with the system we already have. It has worked fine up till now. There is nothing wrong with it except it is slower and the history of each produced item can get lost after the paper work is finished and approved by the departments. Also, with the old system, if we want to recover information in order to build another similar product, it would take an enormous amount of time to find the files."

"With the computer, this information is stored and catalogued for future use with a minimum amount of work by the office staff. The nice thing is when we take on major projects, the breakdown of the labour, materials and outsourcing will be readily available. In financing any of these winches, we can more effectively estimate very quickly where the money has to go. John, I give the floor back to you."

John Cleaves got up to bring the meeting to an end. He asked of anyone had any questions before they left. "Please know that if you cannot think of anything today, the door is always open to come in and ask whatever you like. If I'm not here, I know Bill Robbins is of the same mind as me and he will be available. One last note, we are starting a new adventure with George Strutt of Industrial Mixers. These mixers will be predominantly used in the mining industry. According to the market research, this should prove to be a good extension for the company. There will be no further staff changes in any departments. If we are all finished, I would like Bill, Gilley, Dennis and Mel to stay behind. Thank you for your time."

After everyone had left, Mel took the chair. "The reason why we are here and why we asked you all to stay behind is to adopt a new control system which will enable us to coordinate pricing and the cost of our products along with promoting a better production system. This will alleviate some of the pressures put on estimating, shop flow, and purchasing. If we can develop a system that can be tracked from the drawing number, which in turn could be a part number, we feel this will be a good starting point. We need to do this in order to keep up with the future and our new computer system which is coming on line soon. This will enable the company to move into the future and have a competitive edge.

The system which seems to be the most flexible is the three-three-three digit system. I have a great deal of experience and success with this previously. With John Cleaves coming from the steel distribution industry, he knows how important it is for us to move with the times. Already the steel industry is moving toward total computerization. I have discussed this with Dennis and John and we know that you, Gilley, have had exposure to a similar type of system in England. It would help us if you could put some of your time in the next few weeks towards developing a method that would work in the drawing office and that will be compatible with this digital system."

Gilley had caught this new vision as Mel spoke and was already visualizing how this next step could be utilized in his department. In his exuberance, Gilley said, "No problem. I have already been thinking about a system and I will go through this idea with you Mel, possibly some time tomorrow. Do you have a time when we can get together?"

"That's very interesting, Gilley." said John. "Mel, can you make some time in your schedule for this tomorrow? Thank you for your enthusiasm."

Mel replied, a little surprised at the suddenness of this turn of events, "I have time from 11:00 AM to 12:00 PM. Does this suite you, Gilley?"

"I'll make it work."

John, closing the meeting said, "It's time to call it a day, gentlemen. Thank you for your time on such short notice. Have a good evening."

Pulling Gilley to one side, John said, "Just before you leave, Gilley, you know you are going to have to put your house in order. I can feel the tension in your department. And I know its early days for you, but a kind word to you is this, 'Get rid of the disease before the disease gets you.' I know it's not going to be easy, but it's the best for everyone in the end."

"I agree, and I will need some time in order to do it properly so as to not affect the ongoing work in the department. The person in question has a very important project on the go at this time. I will give him a deadline to meet so things don't drag on." Gilley left the room experiencing for the first time what management was really like. He was looking forward to that beer with Don.

At the Waldorf, Don had a beer waiting for him. "How did your first meeting go? My guess is you're very thirsty."

"That's quite true, not that I talked very much. Cheers, Don, here's to the first of many, I hope."

Don, straight to the point, said "I do not want your job for love nor money. I will be more than pleased to help you in whatever way I can. But I do like to design and be my own man. I'm used to that after being in Singapore for so long. I do know you have to get rid of John Pendry as soon as you can. The both of you are on a collision course. I can feel the tension when you're together. When either of you are not there, there's no tension. It will eventually effect the department."

"I know what you mean, Don. Let me bring you up to speed on what has happened so you have some background. You must understand I was put into this position by others. John Pendry took offense as he thought he would be the next in line. He's having a problem with this turn of events. He was used to acting as the assistant to Barry Freeke. When Barry was not around, he would check on everyone's projects and also be responsible for his own work. Since I've been put in charge, I've decided each man is to be responsible for his own projects only and is to report to me directly. I'm a firm believer of a team approach. We all have gifts and talents to contribute and need to be acknowledged for that. The company also benefits from utilizing the strengths everyone brings to the table.

That's not to say we cannot help each other in time of need or benefit from one another's expertise, but I believe more work will get done using this new approach. I explained this to John Pendry and he disagrees even after I explained to him, that he is like the others in that he is responsible for his own projects. He is not the second in command as he was under the other system. He still retains his current salary but without that added responsibility.

My new function is to act as the liaison between the various departments. This is to get the work to the floor in a timely manner and to give the particular work to the best person for that project. I'm trying to create a method whereby the designs get to the shop floor in such a manner as to utilize the man power to the most effective means. Since we have so many different projects and time restraints, it has to now be controlled by one person acting as liaison between the various departments."

Don nodded his head, "I now understand what's gone on and why the tension is there. I know what you're getting at and I agree with these changes. That's why I don't want the responsibility you have. I've done it and I don't like it. I just want to be left in my corner to do whatever designs you want me to do. I wish you all the best, though. You are in the middle between the staff and the upper management. It's hard to keep everybody happy. You're welcome to those politics. Keep me from them, please, and I will support you in every other aspect of the job. Now, it's time for another beer and time to talk about other things." With that he raised his hand and ordered another round.

The next few days were very chaotic what with the new systems being implemented and the meetings that had to be attended. On top of it all, the day arrived when John Cleaves wanted to have that game of chess with everyone. Six boards were set up. The players were Pat Sullivan, John Pendry, Dave Mosley, Don Howath, Garry Dean and Hardwig Diener. All of the players except, Pat, were novices to the game and over several weeks of playing had become quite good. Pat had been in several championship matches over his lifetime. He was the department champion. No one had beaten him yet.

On the agreed upon day, John Cleaves arrived. At the first table, he picked white and made his first move. At the second table, he was black and made his move. He went around to all the boards in a like manner. They were well into the lunch break before the losses started to accumulate. One by one, the challengers gave way. Only Pat Sullivan remained in the game. It took ten more minutes before he too fell to the master chess player.

No one had ever seen such skill demonstrated. John could keep all six games in his head and remember what moves to make in order to win. He did this without any errors on his part too. When it was all over, he thanked everyone, especially Pat and said to Pat. "I was lucky with that last move, you could have given me a hard game, but in the game of chess, one always has to be two to three steps ahead of his opponent. Gentlemen, keep practicing and remember some of the moves you made today and do as much reading as you can if you want to improve."

During the next few weeks everyone was intent on these chess games at lunch, practicing what had been recommended. Coffee breaks even started getting out of hand. Things between Gilley and John Pendry were also deteriorating. John's productivity had dropped by at least 50%. Gilley knew he had to do something but was not sure just how to go about it as he had never fired anyone before.

One day, Gilley caught John staring into his drawer. He noticed John was oblivious to everything else around him. As he watched, he decided to time John. He found this went on for a good half hour. He realized this was not the first time he had noticed John staring into his drawer. It was the first time he noted how long the incident took. Gilley also realized John was staring into this drawer for a reason-he was deciding upon his next chess move. Usually, John realized what he was doing and closed his drawer to avert suspicion if anyone approached him. This day, he was so engrossed in the game, he was oblivious to his surroundings.

In all fairness to him, Gilley had called him aside previously and had discussed the drop in production and the lack of enthusiasm towards his work. This day, Gilley purposely walked up to the desk and made a point of indicating he knew what was going on. John looked up at Gilley and in his amazement, went to close the drawer. Gilley said, "That's your last move, John. I will go down to Harry Tressel, the bookkeeper, and have your severance and holiday pay arranged while you pack up your things. I'd like you off the premises by 4:00 PM today."

John couldn't believe his ears. He let loose a barrage of words that would make the sailors on the dock blush. He did what he was told, though. After Gilley returned from Harry's office, the whole engineering department was in disarray as John banged and thumped his way around the place. He glared at Gilley and proposed that he and Gilley should sort this out in the car park after work tonight. "If it would make you feel any better, John, I don't mind seeing you in the car park. This was not an easy decision for me and I thank you for the opportunity you gave me. But I would prefer you go home, think about this whole incident and call me tomorrow. If you still feel any injustice due to my action today, I'm prepared to sit down and talk it over with you."

John sneered, "You Northerner, you just can't get on with the Southerners and I suppose what is true in England is true in Canada."

"I hold all Englishmen with the same respect as I do with my birthplace. Here we are in a strange land which is seven times the size of Britain with about 10% of the population. Wouldn't you think we could get on as our basic lifestyles are the same? But you were prepared to buck the position I was given. Now I have to put the company first and that's the end of the story. You were not doing your job and it was affecting the rest of the office and I was becoming the laughing stock. Maybe you are right; I don't like to be made a fool of. Your behaviour has even drawn the attention of John Cleaves. It was that out of hand."

"Well, I would like to go and have a talk with John Cleaves," retorted John.

"Be my guest, I will set the appointment up right now."

Gilley followed through with his promise and off John went to see John Cleaves. When he returned, he was somewhat subdued. Things had obviously not gone the way he thought they would. He left the premises in a hurry, pointing at Gilley, "I'll get you for this."

Once this was all over a sigh of relief could be felt throughout the office and things settled down. Soon, the office personnel congealed and the work started to gain momentum. Dennis Shears kept bringing the orders in. They were coming in so fast Gilley had to hire a couple more draughtsmen. They were not too easy to find. He decided to hire one more young man who was from BCIT, the technical institute in the lower mainland. This person was Ken Boyle, a friend and colleague of Garry Dean, one of the chess players. Gary had been working on a temporary basis for Swann's in the hydraulic end of things and was very capable. He had impressed Gilley. When he recommended Ken, Gilley decided he could give this young man a chance.

In addition, Gilley worked closely with Mel Newth to develop a computer system called the three-x-three digit system. This system would start in the drawing office, as most things did and would automatically be registered by all other departments, giving Mel the end result he needed-cost analysis on every item Swann's produced. Gilley was so involved in his work that fall passed quickly and the Christmas season was on him before he knew it.

CHAPTER 15

CHRISTMAS 1971— A CANADIAN CHRISTMAS

HALLOWEEN WAS OVER AND the Christmas decorations in the stores were up. Gilley couldn't believe it. He hadn't had the Carter's over for the promised dinner nor had he followed through on his promise to Dennis and Irene Shears. "Well, this will not do," he thought as he wound his way through the traffic on his way home. "Tonight Joy and I will have to make definite plans to rectify this oversight."

Arriving home, Gilley was expecting to have the promised Chinese stir fry. Joy was a good cook and Gilley didn't have trouble wondering if he would like the dinner, he just had the occasional problem identifying some of the ingredients as Joy loved to take him around the world on his stomach. As he entered his apartment he heard familiar voices. "Hmmm, there's always a surprise when I come home," he thought. Jim and Veron were seated comfortably on his couch, drinks in hand.

"Gilley, what took you so long," asked Jim? "We've been waiting for you to get home so we could try Joy's new experiment. She's been watching that TV show, 'Cooking with Won' and she went and bought his cook book. She has this wonderful Chinese meal planned but she can't start cooking until we're all here. Come, grab a beer so she can get started. We're starving."

"Oh . . . . Well . . . Traffic was bad tonight," stuttered Gilley.

"What night isn't it bad," Joy declared. "I don't think he's ever been home at the time he promises. He's always late and always has an excuse. The traffic one is pretty common. Lucky for him, Chinese dinner doesn't take long to cook."

Getting his own beer, Gilley thought, "Now how am I going to play this one? I have to make the plans with the Carters and the Shears now or it'll never get done?"

Before he knew it, dinner was ready and they were all seated eating this marvelous culinary experience Joy had created from her new cook book. Truly, he had never had Chinese food so delicious. His in-laws were equally taken by their daughter's talents. He decided this was the right time to introduce the topic. "Joy, I just realized we have to have Kirby and Sue Carter over for dinner soon. It was August we were at their place and I really think we need to have them here for dinner before Christmas."

"You're a little late there, Gilley. I have the menu all planned and have invited them over for this Saturday night. I was wondering when you would clue into having them over. We're going to have baked salmon and wild rice. By the way, don't you be late from golf on Saturday."

With that Veron said, "It's about time you two got into the social scene. Joy, I've always told you that you won't get ahead in this world just waiting for your man to lead the way. We women have to take the initiative and do the planning for them. Now, are you going to cook this wonderful meal for them or are you going to go with something more Canadian?"

"Never mind what she's cooking for the entrée, I have to outdo Kirby's flaming Cherries Jubilee. How are we going to do that?"

At this, Veron got very excited, "I have just the answer. You raved about my trifle. How about if I serve the version of it that got Jim his job on the school board? I had the School Board Trustees over for dinner and served this version. It was after that they appointed him to Superintendent of Grounds."

Gilley looked over at Jim for confirmation. Jim just smiled. "OK, Veron, you're on. I have every confidence in Joy's menu plans and like mother like daughter, I'm sure your dessert will be the winning touch. Now, what do you two have planned for Dennis and Irene Shears?"

"I thought you'd never ask," said Joy. They're coming over on the third Saturday night of November. That would be November 20th. Since the Shears don't know the Carters, I plan on having the same menu. Mom, would you also make the same dessert? After all, Dennis Shears has more influence over Gilley's career than Kirby Carter does.

"I will make my lime version of this dessert for Dennis and Irene. The vodka in this one is what really makes it a hit."

"Well," thought Gilley, "What was I worried about? Now that the women have everything under control, what better can a man ask for? Well, how about another beer?"

Saturday came quickly enough and believe it or not, Gilley wasn't late. Joy was quite relieved as she had given him a list of things for him to do on his way home. The first thing was for him to stock up the beer and liquor supplies and secondly, stop at Jim and Veron's for the trifle. She and Veron had planned on an almost fool-proof way of packing it so it would arrive at the apartment in the same condition it left the house in. They all knew what condition the banana splits from the Dairy Queen arrived home in. The plan worked and to Joy's relief everything else went as planned. Her baked salmon and wild rice was a hit. Sue duly impressed, "Joy, I've never been brave enough to serve salmon to company. This was delicious. I also can't get over your budgies. You have five of them. Most people I know who have birds only have two at the most. How did you come to have five?"

Joy said, "That's an interesting story, Sue. How about if I tell you the story during dessert? Gilley, it's your turn. Bring on the dessert." With that cue, Gilley went into the kitchen and returned with a tray of four large parfait dishes filled with multicoloured layers of delight. There was custard, cake, fruit, whipped cream and of course sherry. Veron had outdone herself as there was a huge mountain of whipped cream topping it all off with a maraschino cherry on top. Gilley gracefully placed a serving before each person as if he had done this for years.

Once everyone began to eat, the aroma of the expensive sherry wafted through the room. No one spoke until the bottoms of the dishes were reached. Once that was accomplished, Kirby and Sue tripped over each other with compliments. They had never had a dessert like this.

"Would everyone like a coffee and a liqueur? We have Grand Marnier and Kailua," asked Joy. "Gilley, you pour the liqueurs and I'll get the coffees. Let's all relax in the living room." With that everyone did as suggested. The conversation turned to soccer for the men and budgies for the women.

Kirby wanted to know how things had gone for Gilley at his soccer trials. "Well, Kirby," said Gilley, "It's a fairly high standard you guys play here in Canada and I've been out of it for about a year now. It seems it would take quite some time for me to become fit enough to participate and, you must realize these players, having played together for quite some time, have their own way of interacting with each other. I felt a bit like an interloper. Understandably for them a stranger in their midst might not be welcome."

"My job has changed quite a bit since you and I originally talked and I need to focus my energies at Swann's right now as things are exploding on that front. I've been made Manager of Engineering and this is demanding all of my time right now. Soccer has to come second place at this time in my life. In the future, recreational soccer would be fine.'

Kirby said, "Hmmm, I agree with you. It will be hard to break into the network of players as they all know each other. I did have chat with Don who said you were a very capable player but would take a while to adapt to Canadian style. He can't understand why you haven't come back."

"Well, to be very truthful, I wasn't given any inspiration to return. No one communicated with me. I was left on the outside, like Scotty, who is a very capable player. He, after one year, still turns up, session after session, hoping one day there will be a place for him. I don't want to spend that time waiting. I either play or I don't play."

"I'm glad to hear you being so candid, Gilley. I wish more people would be like you. I wish I was still playing. I would have made sure, to the best of my ability that you were made to feel welcome. I didn't realize so much of a clique had formed. I would not have sent you there if I had known. I apologize."

"Oh it's not for you to apologize. I appreciate what you did and I also have learned what the game is in Canada. There are so many teams comprised of other nationalities in the mix, I can see why many teams keep to themselves. The only way you could get into a team here is if you were a well known superstar. I think the future in recreational soccer is to have multiple substitutions. That would enable everyone to have at least one run out."

"Thanks, Gilley. I do appreciate you saying that, and I agree with you about the subs. I foresee a day when that happens because a lot of players will still want to play when they're over thirty. I can see the day when there will be an over thirty league."

"Interesting opinion you have there, Kirby. I never thought about players over thirty years old playing. Perhaps there will even be an over forty league which would encourage older players to come back into the game and have fun. Knowing myself, I would rather play soccer than go jogging to keep fit. It looks like it's time for another drink." And sure enough, just at that juncture, Joy came over to see if she could refresh their drinks.

"That would be very nice, Joy. One more and we'll have to be on our way. It's been a delightful evening," replied Kirby.

The next social engagement was slated for the following Saturday, November 20th. This time, Joy's cooking, even though she planned the same menu, was even better. Gilley thought, "Practice makes perfect." The conversation was lively amongst the four of them and an added attraction was the invitation to walk down to Jim and Veron's. Gilley was eager to show Dennis Jim's English style bar. He had bragged that Jim had pool table and dart board as well.

Arriving at 1806, Jim and Veron were also entertaining a couple of guests and they fully expected Joy and friends to join in. It was quite interesting as these friends, Joan and Bill Cummings, were visiting from Galliano Island. (Galliano Island is one of the Gulf Islands between Vancouver Island and the Mainland). Joan was from Kent in England and Bill hailed from Canada, but had spent many years in the Canadian Air Force stationed outside of London. This was where they met and married and afterwards decided to settle in British Columbia after the War. Jim had met Bill through the School Board—at a conference to be specific as Bill was a supplier for grounds equipment. The two had gotten on well and eventually a friendship had developed between the two families.

Joan was a music teacher and since she had met Gilley at the wedding reception was fascinated with his voice. Even at the party, she declared she could make him a great tenor if he would submit to her teachings.

The new arrivals were greeted with enthusiasm and drinks all around were handed out along with introductions. Dennis was duly impressed with Jim's bar. He particularly liked some of the memorabilia Jim had brought over from his visits to England. He especially liked how Jim had incorporated the pool table into the English style. He stated it was done so skillfully, one would have assumed pool tables were a common thing in English pubs. Jim smugly declared it wasn't easy to mix such different cultures as the American and the English and make it look like they belonged together especially here in Canada. "After all, the original size of such a table was eight foot by four foot. This one is three by six. It's small enough to fit in this room and large enough to have a good game."

After everyone had a good time playing games and visiting, Joan piped up loudly, "Gilley, its time you showed us what you can do with that wonderful voice of yours. I insist you sing us a song. What do you know?"

Irene and Dennis were enthusiastic about this suggestion and called for "The Blaydon Races" a traditional Geordie song that inspired Newcastle United (the Magpies) to many a victory. With all of the encouragement and the beer Gilley felt he had no choice but to oblige his audience and launched into the requested song. After he was done a hush fell over the crowd. Joan broke the silence finally, "Gilley I knew you had potential, but you need a lot of work. You and I don't live close enough to accomplish that. But if you're really interested in developing your talent, you and Joy are welcome to come to Galliano Island." The party ended shortly after that and the foursome walked back to Gilley and Joy's, all having had a wonderful time. Gilley felt quite relieved that all of his obligations were now fulfilled thanks to Joy.

It wasn't too long before the hustle bustle of the Holiday Season was in the air. It was amazing to Gilley how early the Christmas decorations appeared in the stores. People started to decorate their houses and some even their yards. With all of the new responsibilities, including a course on hydraulics Gilley had taken on at the British Columbia Institute of Technology (or BCIT), he couldn't believe Christmas arrived so quickly. He began to wonder, "Was this Christmas going to be as big a celebration as last year or was last year put on just for my sake?".

This year was different, but not in the way that he thought. It became very cold. Joy and Veron especially were commenting on how unusually cold it was. They were even talking about a 'White Christmas'. This was something very rare, Gilley learned, in the moderate climate of the lower mainland. "In actual fact," he thought, "one did not have to go very far to experience a Christmas with snow." As he observed all of the mountains surrounding Vancouver were always covered in a thick blanket of snow from November to March.

It was a skier's paradise. There was Grouse Mountain, Cypress Bowl, and Seymour Mountain. These were within an hours' drive of the Vancouver area. The new addition, Whistler Mountain which was between an hour and a half to two hours' drive depending on the weather conditions and of course Mount Baker, even though in the United States, was a popular ski destination. Gilley was fascinated by the name Whistler Mountain and so asked Jim one evening over a rare quiet beer.

Jim replied, "Did you know Whistler Mountain used to be called London Mountain because of all the fog and rain it received? Then back in the 1960's, the developers decided this was not good for tourism and changed the name to Whistler Mountain. This was after the whistling calls of the marmots which are prolific in the area. They want it to become an international ski resort such as Switzerland with chalets and the sort. I can't see that happening because of the population and the location is not yet well known. Who would rather come to Whistler Mountain instead of the Swiss Alps? This will take a lot of promotion on the part of the developers."

"Would you think it would be a good idea to invest in property in that area, Jim? After all, stranger things have happened and Vancouver is getting a good name throughout the world."

"Oh, no, I don't think so. It's a photographer's paradise I suppose if one wants to drive that far. However, I think you can get beautiful pictures just here with our local mountains. I'm sure you've noticed how beautiful sunrises are here when the mountains change from blue to red to orange."

"Oh yes. You don't have to tell me about the sunrises. Early morning is one of my favourite times of the day. As I take my magical shower, I look out my window and watch the mountains change colour as the sun rises. It's particularly beautiful during the winter with the snow reflecting the sun. And then there's Mount Baker to the south. Now that is a sight to behold. It didn't matter what time of year it is, there is always snow on its majestic peak and it's always changing depending on the time of day and the season of the year. It's hard to believe it is over a hundred miles away as the crow flies as there are days it seemed as if one could just reach out and touch it-a trick of the atmosphere, I suppose."

"Now you're talking. Baker's a ski resort with potential and the Americans know how to sell a potential. That's the place I would invest my money in if I had enough.

By the way, I think we may have a white Christmas this year. You know what that means? It's going to spoil our golf game. Remember last year? We played right through the winter even though we had to change courses due to the snow in Langley."

"Maybe you should teach me how to ski. Then we could get away for the morning anyway."

"I don't know how to bloody well ski, man. If you want to ski, you have to ask Sally or Anne." Just then Joy and Veron appeared.

"What do you mean ski, Gilley," Joy stated. "There's no time for that. We have lots to do this year to get ready for Christmas since we have our own place this year. There are a number of traditional festivities here in Canada we need to invite our friends to. Anyhow, you don't even know how to ice skate. Why would you want to go skiing?"

Gilley replied quickly, "Well, I do know how to roller skate and was good at it. Ice skating shouldn't be a problem. It's only a matter of balance. I think the thrill of coming down the mountain, plowing through the snow would be worth the trip. I never thought I'd get to do something like this. Back home only the rich can afford to participate in this sport as they go to the Alps. The mountains are right here in our back yard. Why shouldn't we take advantage of it? It would be a shame to say you've never done it."

Veron chimed in, "I suppose you're going to say you want to go hunting too. You have to choose what you focus your energies on here in Canada. There is so much to do here and you still have to maintain your family obligations and responsibilities. Gone are the days you could bugger off as you please."

Joy jumped in, "You could just be like your brother Neil. He likes fishing and often takes off just to satisfy his needs. That won't happen here."

Jim came to Gilley's rescue, "The way he plays golf—he already incorporates the fishing and the hunting as he's often fishing his ball out of the water hazards or hunting for his ball in the rough."

It was now almost two weeks before Christmas and the calendar was chalk full of parties. There was hardly an evening free to do the shopping. Jim and Veron were especially busy as Jim's job required them to attend many social functions. A sure sign Christmas was coming, besides the decorations, was Jim's bar. It was filling up with all of the presents his associates and suppliers were giving to him. Gilley thought it took on the look of the liquor store downtown. That was a bit of alright with him, as he knew he wasn't going to be asked to do as many booze runs as normal. If only Jim's customers would also give cases of beer as gifts, things would be perfect.

Getting the tree was Jim's Christmas duty—one in which he took great pride. No one could tell what surprise he had in store for the latest tree. Would it be a tall bushy one or a "Charley Brown Tree?" Decorating the tree was left to the girls, except for the lights and of course the tinsel. No one could put tinsel on like he could. He made sure it was put on strand by strand and heaven help the person who put on a clump, in the name of saving time.

Gilley soon found the answer to his question. Christmas in Canada, in British Columbia was a huge celebration no matter what. It was much bigger and more done up than in North East England. Last year was typical of how British Columbia celebrated this season. And what a celebration it was. It turned out to be very snowy and that made driving home after all of the partying an adventure in and of itself. The gifts were extravagant and wrapped in the brightest paper with bows and ribbons. It was a tradition that the stockings which were hanging over the fireplace could be opened anytime Christmas morning (and everyone had one, including the adults), but everyone had to be present for what was known as the 'Gift Opening'. This could only happen after a huge breakfast had been cooked by Jim and fully consumed by everyone else. Jim's theory was with all of the drinking and snacking that would go on during the day, it was important to start the day with a full stomach.

Not to be outdone, Joy had decorated the apartment with a live tree in a stand of water to keep it fresh. Gilley had to follow in Jim's footsteps and help select it. He was to learn this year that this selection was a tradition in and of itself and was a very important one. The successful selection of the tree forecast the success of the rest of the holidays for the man of the house. It came as a great relief to Gilley that in his house though, this important selection had to be OK'd by Joy as she didn't often agree with her father's choice of tree. He also could see himself putting on the lights every year, as Jim had as long as they were chosen by Joy as well. It seemed as if this was the contribution to the Christmas preparations the man of the house made. Gilley was happy with this as living in the apartment required a minimum of work for him as compared to what was expected of Jim and some of his friends.

Christmas rolled into the New Year with the partying never ending it seemed. The culmination was New Year's Eve. Now in England, First Footing was the tradition. This was where a tall dark stranger would knock on one's door and present the owner of the house with a piece of coal. This would ensure this house would have heat for the rest of the year. In return for this gift, the home owners would give the stranger a drink and a bowl of soup. Of course, Gilley and his friends loved to play the strangers and would go from home to home with coal for their friends, having drinks and eats, often not returning home until daybreak.

Jim and Veron, being from England, decided they would surprise their friends with their own version of First Footing. Gilley was to leave the party at about five minutes to twelve o'clock and knock on the door with his gift of coal. Veron had somehow managed to find some coal somewhere. Most people had abandoned using coal to heat their homes and used gas furnaces and if they had the fireplace on, they used wood as it was in abundance in British Columbia.

Gilley was all for this idea as it was right up his ally. At five minutes to twelve, he left by the back door and went around the house to the front door. He waited until precisely twelve o'clock and began knocking on the door. Well, everyone inside was whooping and hollering and banging pots together and making a great noise. The rest of the neighbourhood was doing the same thing. Poor Gilley, no matter how hard he knocked, he could not be heard over the hoopla. He stood out on the front porch in the snowy, cold weather for at least 10 minutes. Eventually, Joy realized her husband was missing and remembered the new plan. She flung open the front door, laughing, "We all forgot about you in the excitement. Come on in and get warmed up."

"It's a drink I need and I'll begin to thaw out. I don't think First Footing is a good idea here in Canada as no one can hear the knock." He joined the party downstairs and had to explain to all of the guests why he was carrying that piece of coal. "It's for good luck, if I can find a fire to put it on." No fire was to be had.

Jim came to the rescue. "The fire upstairs is ready to light. Let's go upstairs and light it up and put the coal on. That way we have luck for the rest of the year as Gilley has promised." Everyone thought this was a wonderful idea so the entire crowd tromped upstairs following Gilley and Jim. Jim got the fire lit with much encouragement of the spectators. Of course, drinks all around had to be refreshed. By the time this occurred the fire was ready for the coal. Gilley, having a bit of the theatrical in him, with much pomp and circumstance as he could muster placed the coal into the fire. Applause erupted and shouted "Speech! Speech!" everyone shouted.

Gilley turned to the group and responded, "This piece of coal which we see burning away in the fireplace, will ensure you will have heat and good fortune in the coming year. Here's to 1972!" Raising his glass, he toasted to the New Year. Everyone cheered and raised their glasses too. Next they all raced back to the bar for refills.

The following morning Gilley had invited Jim and Veron for New Year's breakfast. He insisted it was right to start the New Year off right with his family's traditional breakfast. Since he had taken part in the Canadian celebrations he stated it was only right he share some of his English traditions with his family now that he had his own household. He would cook breakfast and it would be the famous bacon deluxe buttie with lots of coffee and tea. Of course there would be a wee drammie included.

Nine o'clock came with loud rapping at the door. Gilley was showered and ready for the response, but Joy growled underneath the covers, "It's your fault they're here. You invited them. I don't want a bacon buttie," she complained. "You entertain them."

That was fine with Gilley. He offered his in-laws coffee with the drammie, which they readily accepted and he proceeded to build his famous bacon deluxe butties. These consisted of fried crispy bacon, fried tomatoes and a fried egg with a slightly soft center. All of this was served on thickly sliced and toasted white bread spread generously with butter. Once it was all put together, each side of the sandwich was spread generously with butter again and warmed by frying again. Since Gilley had had so much practice in England, it wasn't long before he set his favourite breakfast proudly before his in-laws.

Jim responded first, "Gilley my boy, this is fabulous. I didn't know you had it in you."

Veron said, "This is a heart attack on a plate. But it sure looks and smells good."

With that, they all tucked into breakfast. The aroma and the laughter finally got Joy out of bed and she demanded one for herself. Gilley, chuckling, was all too happy to make this for his wife. As he was doing so, Jim asked for another, along with another of Gilley's special coffees. "You sure can, Jim. How about you, Veron?"

"No, no, Gilley. This is enough for me. I'll have to work out at the spa an extra day as it is. I will have another of your special coffees though."

"Well, Jim, I don't want you to eat alone. I'll make myself another one too. Joy, how are you doing with yours?"

"I'm fine, Thanks. One is enough for me. Could you please make me a nice cup of tea, this time with no additives?"

"The pot is already on, Sweetheart."

The morning went off as well as Gilley had hoped. The foursome sat around drinking their coffees and teas and reminiscing about the night before. Just before they were about to leave, Veron reminded them they were expected to come for dinner. Ham was on the menu, along with scalloped potatoes, especially for Gilley. "Come over early. We'll have some games in the bar with the two girls."

All too soon the holidays were over and it was back to work. Gilley had been off work since December 24, a Friday. This year Christmas and New Years had fallen on a Saturday. Swann's had closed at noon on the twenty-fourth and were scheduled to open again on Monday the third. The company had decided to give the employees the two extra days off as they had worked so hard making the move to the new facilities. They had known full well not much would be done during those two days in any case. The men were able to enjoy their families during that week.

Monday morning, as Gilley was getting ready for work, Joy said, "Gilley do you realize that its only eight months before we go back to England for Bill Wakefield's wedding. We are going to have to get our plans and money together. We need to pay for the airline tickets I booked through Sears. I can hardly wait until I see English soil again. You can imagine how much of a good time I had in England and I wish we could go back forever."

Gilley was taken off guard. Eight months would fly by in no time. He responded, "This really is the land of opportunity, Joy. Just remember what my father said, 'If he was twenty years younger and had known this paradise existed, he would have immigrated here in a flash.' I would never be earning the money in England I am here in Canada plus I would never have been given the position I have today. The system would never have allowed it. Canada is for the young and ambitious."

Joy just looked at Gilley. She had realized quite awhile ago she would have to do some significant convincing in order to get him to move back to England. She knew he was correct regarding his job, but she believed once he had been reunited with his friends and family and had seen his soccer team play again, he would change his mind. He would see things were better in England overall. He would realize how much he missed the English beer and his fish and chips. Those things did not compare here. "Well, I'm not going to worry about it now. I'll bide my time and when it's right, I know I can convince him that returning to England for good is the best thing for us."

CHAPTER 16

THE UNEXPECTED

LATE SATURDAY AFTERNOON, AS usual, Joy and Gilley were sitting in the bar with Jim and Veron having a beer. Sally entered the room looking quite troubled. "I need to talk to you Mom." She was obviously trying to keep herself under control. Veron immediately pardoned herself and took her upstairs. When Veron came down, she too looked very upset.

Jim said, "Well, what was that all about?"

"Sally's pregnant," she blurted out! "She wants to get married to Doug this summer. They've already discussed it apparently and they have their minds set." Everyone sat stunned for a few moments. No one had expected this news. Turning to Joy, she said, "Joy, would you talk with her about this. She's so young and having a baby at this early stage in life could ruin her future. Try to talk her into having an abortion. It would be in her best interest. And no one tell Anne about this yet. When she finds out it should be from Sally herself."

Suddenly Gilley piped up, "Well, you know you can't trust these skinny guys who can eat a twenty ounce steak like Doug can. Now we know where he's putting all that energy." This comment broke the silence. Everyone nodded in agreement and smiled.

Jim concluded, "Let's have one more drink and be off to our beds and see what tomorrow has to bring."

Veron was very disturbed and she could talk about nothing else. She talked about the fact that this would bring a great embarrassment to the family and hardship to Sally. She pleaded with Joy as a big sister, to try to talk some sense into Sally. "You know, Joy, an abortion is the best way to deal with this kind of situation. That way, everyone can start all over again and no one will know anything about what has happened."

She added, "Sally is only eighteen and has just started working as a girl Friday. She has some potential to move up in her new company. This will start her off on the wrong foot, not only financially, but in every other aspect of her life as well. It's very hard for mothers with small children to keep a good job these days. And as far as Doug goes, well, at least he works for Avco Financing and has a bright future. I am led to believe this job requires him to be transferred to different branches in the province in order for him to advance. What kind of life would that be for any child—moving all the time?"

"Well," Jim interjected, "Today is a far more liberal day than when we were brought up and if this is what she wants to do then we need to give her all our support. I agree this isn't the best start for a young couple, but it's hardly new. And Joy as her eldest sister may be able to persuade her of the alternative. But you know Sally, she is stubborn and I think she will do it her way. I do believe we should just all sleep on it and revisit this tomorrow. It will also give Sally a little time to compose herself. I think she was really brave to have come forward so early. How long has she been pregnant?"

"Approximately two months," said Veron.

"So if we have a wedding it will have to be before the end June so she is not showing too much girth," decided Jim. "The quicker the decision, the quicker we can begin the arrangements as this summer we have the school board conference in July and we are very involved with organizing that. I wonder if Doug has told his parents. Let's call it a night, eh?"

In the next couple of days, Joy talked to Sally extensively, but Sally was undeterred. She had made up her mind that she and Doug would get married and they would have this baby. She realized this particular order of events came with some embarrassment, and wanted to keep this from Anne as long as possible as Anne was one to announce things to the world. Veron quickly became reconciled with Sally's decision and stepped into the role of mother of the bride to be quite naturally. She came to look forward to her first grandchild in spite of all of her initial protestations.

Gilley found it hard to believe, but life just became even more complicated. In spite of his earlier misgivings, he found he became fond of Doug. One of the things they discovered they had in common was cars. As it turned out, Doug had a Triumph TR-6 and on several occasions allowed Gilley to drive it. Doug seemed to be fairly well heeled. The other thing he had in common with the family was he enjoyed a few beers. Interestingly enough, with announcement of the coming birth, Sally and Doug were inadvertently elevated to adult status. This gave all a chance to share these commonalities.

Gilley stressed to Doug that he, Gilley, was Number One son-in-law and he also let the whole family know this fact. This started a bit of a competition. So at any opportunity, Gilley set it up so he and Doug would have challenges that needed winning. It could be pool, darts, and cribbage-any basic game. The family relished in these little battles and even began to keep a bit of a running score (especially Jim, who would instigate the matters even further by creating a hierarchy, with himself being the elder, he was automatically the top dog).

Veron, not to be outdone created her own hierarchy by working on Joy. She inferred it will be nice to become a grandmother at such an early age and she had hoped it was Joy who would have given her the first grandchild. Especially since Joy was the first born and the first to be married and married for well over a year by now. "What is wrong," Veron lamented? "When are you and Gilley going to make me a grandmother? It seems as if Gilley is doing quite well. Perhaps the problem is both of you working? Too much work and not enough fun?"

Joy came back to her mother, "Mom, we're not sure about our stability right now. Gilley may be going to Singapore to work and we are going back to England this year. We wouldn't to bring a child into that uncertainty, now would we?

It suddenly seemed it didn't matter to Veron what plans Gilley and Joy had, such as possibly going to Singapore and traveling to England this year, plus getting their home set up properly, buying a car etc. What became important was having a baby and nothing could outdo that.

During this period of time, Veron especially vied to be in control of every situation and if she perceived her control was threatened, she would do whatever it took to regain that control. Joy found herself being the brunt of her mother's embarrassment over Sally's predicament. In spite of the fact Veron needed Joy's help in the wedding arrangements she would continually badger Joy into doing things for her no matter how willing Joy was to participate. She would never give Joy's ideas the credit they deserved and would turn them out as if they were her own. It was a very difficult time for Joy and Gilley as often Gilley had to take the brunt of Joy's frustrations.

The wedding was planned for June. It was decided that since there wasn't much time to arrange a hall, it would be held in the back yard. All the necessary arrangements were put in order by Veron. Jim had his orders to redecorate the house and put the garden in order. One big project to be done was the large patio deck. Jim had the idea to make concrete squares of different colors. These squares would be approximately three by three feet square along with a sliding patio door from the dining room. Of course, Jim, being the builder he was had everything designed and drawn out. The first thing to be done was to knock out the window and the wall and install the sliding patio doors. This was a great experience for Gilley and a great laugh. One incidence Jim was never to live down came after Veron had stressed some stickers needed to be put onto the sliding door part as many people couldn't tell whether it was closed or open. He kept putting her off.

Well, one afternoon, after a few beers, he was adjusting the balance of the door he had just finished installing and stood back to look at his masterpiece. In celebration of the event, he lit a cigarette and decided another beer was in order. He also knew Gilley wouldn't say no to a beer. He decided to go to the bar through the new opening he'd just finished. It just happened Veron, Joy, Anne, Sally, and Gilley were inside admiring the accomplishment. "Time for a beer," Jim announced and walked straight into the door, smashing his cigarette all over his face and the new pane of glass in the door.

Totally embarrassed, Jim said to Veron, "Now you don't have to get those stickers as I've already marked door with my cigarette butt. And if I'd been walking any faster, it would have blood as well." Then he turned to Gilley, who was in total fits of laughter, "No smart remarks out of you, Gilley. Next week you're pouring concrete instead of playing golf. Golf is on hold until we get this done."

"The nights are getting longer, Jim. Maybe we could do one square a night and then we could still make those tee times." Gilley responded.

"Well," remarked Veron, "If you miss just one weekend of golf, this whole deck could be finished in a couple of weeks."

"What a good idea, Gilley," said Jim, ignoring Veron's comment. "If we pour three squares on Monday night, we have to let them cure for at least forty-eight hours. That means we can only pour the next three squares on Wednesday, let them cure and pour again on Friday. We then have to miss Saturday and pour on Sunday when we can pour six, filling the voids we had created during the week. We have approximately thirty-eight squares to do and, given this schedule, we can get them all done in time for the wedding and not miss any golf. Sunday is the best day to pour concrete anyway as we can get more done that day. We can't pour on Saturdays as all the squares have to cure properly. Otherwise, they'll crack. Now we don't want that."

"I already have the sand and the cement being delivered here tomorrow. The school board has a mixer I can borrow and I can have it dropped off after work by one of the boys. This way we can get going right away. Now, Gilley, what you and I have to do is to lay out the partitions tonight so we know where to start pouring tomorrow. I think we can get Veron to cook enough supper for you and Joy on those nights."

"What have I got to do with this? I hope you don't expect me to help with pouring the concrete." Joy objected.

"Joy, we have lots to do," said Veron. "We have the menu to plan, food to make, dresses to pick out, the invitations to address, flowers to make etc. I'll keep you busy enough so you don't get roped into the manual side of the business. On top of that, the boys will need refreshments. Gilley will especially need sustenance as his job will be to carry the buckets of cement from the ground up to the deck where Jim will do the finishing work."

At hearing this was to be his job," Gilley chimed in, "Where is number two to be son in law. I think he could be here to help."

Sally answered that quickly enough, "Doug is going to be away until almost the wedding day. He's to be at a training course for Avco Finance which will better his chances at becoming a branch manager."

"Thank God, because you will need it with a baby on board. I hope it pays good money." Veron said.

"Mom, that's why he's taking it," Sally said, coming to Doug's defense.

At that point, the conversation turned to the wedding plans. "Sally, have you decided who will be your Maid of Honour," asked Veron?

Anne jumped in and said, "I don't want to do it. I don't know what to do and besides, it sounds like too much work."

Joy volunteered, "I'll do it."

Sally said, "Great, there's that one solved. I didn't know who to choose."

"Doug's family, who is quite religious, have a relative in Calgary who has offered to perform the marriage ceremony. He's a pastor in a large church there. Next Saturday, Doug's parents, Peggy and Robert Woodward are coming over here for supper in order to meet us all. Bruce, Doug's brother is away in Europe somewhere right now. I guess we'll have to wait until the wedding to meet him," Sally informed them.

Anne was dating a guy called Art who was a bit older than her and came from a large family. The family lived in Millardville, which was predominately a French speaking community a few miles from New Westminster. His mother was a seamstress and had agreed to make the wedding dresses for Sally, Anne and Joy. This took a great pressure off Veron.

Art was on the short side and had a very entertaining personality. He loved old cars and motorcycles. He would often arrive in his old vintage Ford from the thirties. This was his baby. He kept it in immaculate shape and had invested quite a bit of money into restoring it to its original state. As a matter of fact, Anne was the only one who was allowed to be a passenger. This excluded any possibility of using the car as part of the wedding.

The patio project was coming along as planned (and the golfing was able to continue uninterrupted). Yet Veron tried to speed the process up as she wanted to impress the Woodward's family who were coming over for dinner that weekend. She dearly wanted to have them see the project at its finished state. Jim tried to explain to her that the total deck would take over one ton of concrete and Gilley would have to mix and carry the buckets up to the deck. Each bucket weighted approximately forty pounds. "Even though Gilley is a young, strong lad, it doesn't matter, it is my time that needs to be paced as I have to trowel and level every section. On top of that we have to allow curing time for the cement. If there is insufficient time allowed for the curing process, the concrete will crack and crumble in no time at all, making this a wasted effort."

As much as she would have loved to, Veron could not argue with this reasoning. After all, building was Jim's forte and time after time, he had proved to be right. She would just have to have her dinner party with a partially finished deck. Jim reassured her that what was finished would look very good, especially with the sliding door with the cigarette butt sticking to the glass (which still hadn't been removed—waiting for Veron to get the stickers. It did serve its purpose, both to warn people and to remind Jim of his clumsiness.)

At Gilley's work, Dennis Shears had outdone himself in selling winches to most of the local shipyards and had also obtained an offer for tender for the icebreaker being built for the US Coast Guard in Washington State. The hydraulic and deck equipment had been awarded to Rucker Controls out of Oakland, California. He had been able to obtain this tender partially due to his good relationship with Rucker and the Canadian Consulate.

Rucker had no experience in deck equipment, but their hydraulic system and controls were preferred by the US Coast Guard and they desperately needed a winch manufacturing company of Swann's capabilities. Another bonus was that the Canadian government was very prominent in obtaining work from the USA as a trading partner. They would assist in the technical aspects and with some financial guidance.

This guidance would involve the input of the Canadian Department of Supply and Services (CDSS). The specialty of this department was to interpret the Coast Guard specifications to Swann's engineers in terms they could understand as the Coast Guard, like most government bodies, had a lot of red tape. These specifications needed to be interpreted by people who understood government language.

As the Engineering Manager, Gilley had to spend quite a bit of time with CDSS, especially with Harry Blackwell who had emigrated from England in 1948 (much like Jim had). Harry had worked for the Canadian Navy and then had moved onto this government branch as many others had done. The other person assigned to this task was Al Austin. He was from eastern Canada and headed up the BC Branch of the Department of Supply and Services. His main interest was building his retirement home on one of the Gulf Islands. Both men proved to be invaluable assets to this project for Gilley yet the final purchase order for the project would not be placed till the fall after all of the "eyes" were dotted and the "tee's" were crossed in accordance with the US Coast Guard rules and regulations.

This was along side of all of the other responsibilities of running the engineering office. All of the members of the engineering staff were very understanding of the amount of work they had on their collective plate and proved themselves over and over again to also be invaluable to the company. This allowed Gilley to have the extra time to give to these time consuming projects of which many, besides the Coast Guard, had to be taken home to be done.

British Columbia had started to boom. The north was opening up with timber and gas as well as hydro electricity. New dams were being built. In addition to this mining was taking off with overseas markets wanting what BC could offer—that being coal, copper, molybdenum with gold and silver being smaller yet just as valuable. The gold and silver often paid for the operation of the mine where other ores were being sought after. In the lumber industry, besides exporting timber, pulp and paper mills were expanding to meet world demands. This was having a wonderful effect on the economy of BC. Jobs were plentiful and paid well.

The down side was skilled labour was scarce. People with technical skills were also in short supply. As Swann's was desperate for more technical assistance, they tried every avenue to woo the needed staff. But there was no one to be had for the needs of this company even at above average wages. Gilley often wondered if letting John Pendry go was the right thing as it meant more work for everyone. Of course, on further thought he realized this decision was important for the morale of the office.

Work was starting to get busier as more and more winches were being ordered. Shipbuilding was at an all time high. The lack of skilled men made the situation worse. Subcontracting to other companies just put more and more pressure on the personnel. Everyone wanted the Coast Guard job as it would be a big feather in the cap of the company.

Gilley was at the helm and even though he felt very competent to fulfill the contract with the assistance of the Canadian Department of Supply and Services, the pressure was on as other contracts vied for his attention.

A visit from the Rucker Controls chief buyer, Jim Grady, was imminent. The only reason for this visit was to bring the contract for the sale and have it sighed by Swann's and the Canadian Department of Supply and Services. To prepare for him, Gilley, along with the Department of Supply and Services, had found out everything there was to know and felt very comfortable with the presentation they were to make. The staff, in spite of the additional pressure had come through again. It seemed it was no time at all and everything was ready for the meeting.

Dennis Shears picked Jim Grady up at the airport as he was Rucker's purchasing agent and liaison. It was decided Dennis would also be the one to present the contract for signing. After Jim's arrival at Swann's and a brief tour, he was escorted into the main board room for the presentation. Along with Dennis was John Cleaves, Bill Robbins, Harry Clarke, and of course Gilley.

One of the main topics of importance for Jim was knowing the procedures of welding the steel for sub zero temperatures. This vessel would be operating in these extreme temperatures for long periods of time and of course, how the welds stood up to this punishment was of great importance. Normal welds wouldn't withstand these temperatures. Luckily for Gilley, the Department of Supply and Services had brought this need to his attention earlier and Gilley had been prepared to answer this query.

Once Grady was happy with the explanation, he insisted that two test pieces one inch thick by six inches wide by six inches long be welded together following the procedures that Gilley had laid out and tested in the laboratories in Oakland, California. Jim had been very impressed with the way Gilley had been able to answer the question so thoroughly. Another stipulation to this request was that Gilley present these to the lab in California and he wait for the results. During his waiting time, Gilley would go over the basic engineering design with their engineering department.

The signature to the purchase order would finally be applied when this test was completed successfully. In typical American fashion, he stated, as he left the office, "The quicker the better, Gentlemen." He turned to Dennis and added, "I would appreciate it if you would drop me off at the hotel where you have me booked. It's been a long day."

Dennis replied, "Jim, if you are not too tired, we had planned to have Gilley and his wife Joy, join you for dinner tonight at the hotel. They have a wonderful restaurant on the top floor called the Three Green Horns. Would that be alright with you? Unfortunately, I am flying out of town to Singapore and cannot make it. As you have seen, Gilley will be more than capable of looking after you tonight and he will make sure you get to the airport tomorrow."

When Gilley had proposed this to Joy, she was thrilled to get the opportunity to participate in supper on the company's behalf and of course, get a wonderful meal on the company's expense account. Upon meeting him, Jim Grady was not what Joy expected. He was short and rotund and had the typical American style crew cut hair. In addition to this he had heavy rimmed glasses even though he well dressed, he did not come off as the executive type.

When they arrived at the restaurant for dinner, Jim's first request to the waiter was "Beefeater on the rocks!" This was not a common drink in Gilley and Joy's experience. He explained this is the only drink he wasn't allergic to and it was a good gin after all. The restaurant lived up to its reputation and the food was out of this world. And Jim expressed that for such a small town in comparison to San Francisco, he liked what he saw in Vancouver and could tell it was an up and coming place and a place where anyone who invested money would be sure to make good.

The dinner went on for a lengthy time with Jim asking many questions about Gilley and Joy and Vancouver in general. He came to the conclusion it was a marvelous place for young people to start their lives as there were untold possibilities in the upcoming expansion of the city and the province. Gilley could tell Jim was well read and had done his homework by the types of questions he was asking. He was obviously of the same opinion as Gilley that British Columbia had a tremendous future with its resources and natural harbours along with a fairly diversified workforce. This was one of the reasons that brought Rucker Controls to Swann Winches.

After dinner was over, Gilley offered his services to run Jim to the airport in the morning. This was accepted graciously, "Taxis can be hard to come by. I hope you don't mind that my flight leaves at 7:00 AM? I travel light, so as long as we're there by 6:30 AM we should be OK."

By the time they got home, it was gone 1:00 AM and Joy was quite perturbed because Gilley would have to be at the hotel by 5:30 AM which meant he would be leaving New Westminster no later than 5:00 AM. This gave him less than 3 and a half hours sleep. Gilley would then drive directly to work and put in a full day there. Who knew when he would be home and the condition he would arrive in what with all of the changes going on at this time in Swann's history? Gilley had no such concerns. He had every confidence in the magical shower. It hadn't failed him yet and he would make it successfully through the day no matter what came his way.

After picking Jim up at the hotel, dinner's conversation continued with Jim stressing the importance of having the welding samples known as 'coupons' ready by the following week and having them in California within the stipulated time. This was due to the US Coast Guard and the regulations they had imposed upon Rucker Controls.

Gilley had realized he would arrive quite early at work and had planned to start on the welding specifications. After his conversation with Jim and the importance he'd placed on having these done on time, Gilley made it a priority to begin this project. Thank God Harry Blackwell was coming in today as he knew the proper procedures Government bodies, especially the US Coast Guard, would require.

CHAPTER 17

THE SAN FRANCISCO TRIP

WHAT WITH THE WEDDING and their vacation back to England coming up, plus the extensive work load, time was just flying by. Before Gilley knew it he was on his way to a country he'd never been before—the United States of America. (Well, he had been there when landing in Seattle and driving to Blaine and coming across the border into Canada. But that didn't really count as he was in the back seat of his father-in-law's limousine surrounded by his new in-laws.)

Gilley was to fly to San Francisco and hand-deliver the two welded samples to Rucker Controls for testing and analysis. This was a prerequisite laid down by the US Coast Guard, the end user. All deck equipment which was to be fabricated for their ice breaking ships had to withstand subzero temperature testing. The welding procedures used and set out by Gilley himself would be under total scrutiny and testing by an independent group. For Swann Winches it was very important that the results were in their favour as this would lead to a huge contract and a large feather in their cap.

Gilley arrived at the Vancouver International Airport with these two large coupons as per the agreement between Swann Winches and

Rucker Controls. He was Swann's representative and would hand deliver these coupons directly to Rucker's. Rucker's would then deliver these to the independent lab with Gilley being the witness. Now, each of these plates weighed 26 pounds and Gilley had rigged up a sling type method for carrying them, one in each hand. In addition to these, he had a brief case and small suit case with him.

The agent at the ticket counter had said Gilley's carry-on luggage, including the coupons, was OK. It was a different story when he got to the security gate. These plates caused all sorts problems. Surrounded by security people, Gilley had to explain what it was he was carrying. He had had these plates well wrapped and it wasn't obvious for the casual onlooker to know what they were. (And Gilley really did not want to unwrap them as they had been so hard to wrap in the first place.) Trying to explain to the uninformed security force it was imperative these plates travel with him *on* the plane rather than in the luggage compartment was a challenge. He explained they were worth a lot of money, not just in and of themselves, but for the future orders of his company. Also, Rucker Controls had insisted he keep them within his possession as part of the business contract.

Gilley began to fear he might miss his plane as the questioning and haggling went on for so long. After they had torn part of the wrapping away in order to determine that what Gilley was carrying was not bullion, they finally all came to an agreement. The security forces insisted Gilley relinquish the coupons. However, the coupons would be put into a security locker in the cargo, with an identity number which only Gilley would have access to. He would then personally to pick them up at the security counter at the San Francisco airport. This made everyone happy and Gilley was able to catch his flight.

As Gilley boarded the plane, he realized there was a lot more to flying than just buying a ticket. He sat down in his seat and began to reflect on his ordeal with security. They were there for a good reason and not just to cause inconvenience. He could have been smuggling bullion or something more dangerous and it was their job to make sure the plane was safe. He also knew the security people understood this was his first flight to America and he did not know what the rules were. They had actually been quite helpful in the end, after they realized he was not trying to smuggle contraband across international borders, but was just an ordinary business man attempting to do his job. He started to chuckle realizing the security had thought he might be carrying gold bullion. The coupons would have been at least three times the weight of what they were if that were the case.

As the flight took off, and the non-smoking sign was taken down, he lit his cigarette and relaxed back into his seat. This was a trip full of promise. Who knew what opportunities would come out of this venture? After savoring his cup of coffee, the gentleman next to him decided to open a conversation by saying, "Well, you're a happy guy. Did you get lucky in the airport?" This man was curious as to the reason for the continuing smile on Gilley's face.

Gilley replied, "Yes, actually, I was lucky I got through security." Gilley proceeded to tell him the story. The biggest laugh was they thought these plates could have been gold. If that had been the case then Gilley would have been carrying over $125,000.00 as carry-on luggage. The guy was astounded Gilley had figured out the price of the plates as if they were gold.

"Well, my friend, you amaze me. You figured out the price so quickly. Do you deal in gold?"

"No, as a matter of fact I don't. My Father-in-law has just bought some ounces of gold and I am aware of their price just now. I think it's $62.00 an ounce, is it not?"

"It is actually $59.00 an ounce according to the stock market today." Just at that time, the stewardess interrupted them for breakfast. This was another surprise for Gilley. He was given scrambled eggs and sausage. This breakfast was consumed at a record rate and the two men returned to their conversation.

By this time, they had decided to introduce themselves properly. As they did this, they did the normal thing of exchanging business cards. Gilley's was self explanatory, but Wayne Fraser's was not. This led to another round of discussion. As it turned out, he was a precious metal dealer, but the card said, "Exclusive Investments". Questioning further, Gilley discovered he was now in for another level of education-the world of precious stones and metals. The remainder of the flight passed quickly as both men got on well and Gilley was particularly fascinated by Wayne's occupation and he absorbed all of the knowledge he could glean from him. This was a world that had always fascinated Gilley, but one that had never presented itself as of yet. What a great opportunity!

At the conclusion of the flight, Wayne instructed Gilley to buy as much gold as he could possibly afford. He could see within the next ten years or less, gold would hit a high of around seven to eight hundred dollars per ounce.

On Gilley's way to pick up his "bouillon", Gilley had another chuckle at the thought that if this was gold, and the prices did go up as Wayne predicted, then he would be carrying over a million dollars in his hands in the helicopter to Oakland. Ironically as Gilley handed the coupons to the pilot, the pilot commented, "These are so well wrapped and so heavy, you might think they were gold." This just added to Gilley's amusement and he thought, "What fun it might be if they really were." As he contemplated this, his magpie spirit awoke and thoughts of glittering gold and gems entered his mind and his imagination took off. He had to get his hands on some of that glitter. Here he was just about two years out of England on his second air flight and going on a helicopter for the first time. His thoughts drifted to Pete, going in search of all that glittered. Was he, Gilley, looking at the glitter of the magpie or was he being responsible? Was the Magpie spirit prompting him to take a gamble? Would this gold investment be what would make his family comfortable? Was this prediction Wayne had told him following the Magpie? Was he being irresponsible in wanting to follow the gold and glitter that Wayne had talked about?

Upon their take off, the helicopter was quite noisy and shook like hell. Not wanting to show his fear, Gilley just looked down into San Francisco Bay. He had read a lot about the famous Golden Gate Bridge and Alcatraz, the notorious prison. Being, the only person on the flight with Gilley, the pilot pointed out these wonders and Gilley was quite pleased that his research had paid off. The flight only took about half an hour. It seemed they had just gotten up in the air, when they began to land at their destination, the airport at Oakland California. As he stepped off the helicopter, he quickly remembered he had to keep his head down. The pilot unloaded his luggage and handed the coupons to him. He could see all of these items were a bit much for one person to handle, so he offered some assistance as they walked crouched and headed to the terminal.

There, at the terminal, were the two Rucker personnel, Len Murphy and Harry Jacobs who were from the engineering department. They were pleased to see Gilley and welcomed him warmly. As each one took a coupon, they exclaimed how heavy they were, not having realized the weight for one person to carry them as well as all the luggage required for the trip. A new respect for this Canadian/Englishman was beginning to develop already. Gilley, smiling to himself, said, "It's a good thing they're not gold bullion. Then we would all be in trouble." Everyone agreed, laughing and commenting they were so securely wrapped, they could have been.

First order of business was to get the testing of the coupons underway immediately as it was imperative to keep the timeframes. After a quick inspection of the facilities and an explanation by the technician of the testing required, one could see why two plates were necessary. They were told it would take between eight and fifteen hours to complete the testing. Then Harry said. "The quicker the better as we have to get this young man back to Canada in three days. We are on a tight delivery schedule."

Just as they were leaving the lab, Len said, "It's lunch time already, Harry. Let's grab some lunch. We'll take Gilley here to our local haunt." Turning to Gilley, "I wonder if you have ever had meat loaf sandwiches and if you have, you have never had one like the one they serve at this place. It's a small café with home cooked food and today the special is meatloaf sandwiches on sourdough bread." Gilley's first reaction to this menu suggestion, never having had meatloaf and really not knowing what it was, was disgust, but he smiled and said that even though he had never had meatloaf sandwiches, he would be delighted to give it a try.

"I've never had sourdough bread before, but I understand San Francisco is known for this specialty," replied Gilley.

The café was a quaint, homey little place. Gilley thought at one time it must have really been a home, just by the design. An enterprising person must have turned it into this café. The place was packed, but a special table had been reserved for Len and Harry. As they sat down, the waiter automatically brought over two glasses of Budweiser beer and asked Gilley what he could bring him. "I'll just have the same, thanks."

When he brought Gilley's beer, he asked, "Would you like something off the menu this time, or are you going to go with the usual, the special of the day. You must know today its meatloaf sandwiches on sourdough bread." This he said more for Gilley's benefit, as the other two were regulars and could recite the menu by heart.

"The Special of the Day would be great for all three of us," said Len as he took a good long drink of his beer. The other two nodded in agreement. Both Gilley and Harry were thirsty too and in no time, they were all ordering a second round.

This is when Gilley stated, "I was told the best beer in California is Coors."

"That's right," said Harry, "tonight you are staying at the Holiday Inn and in their lounge they serve Coors on tap. That's what you want to try. It's really good and you'll like the atmosphere."

Len piped up, "You sure won't find any of your English Ale down here. If you do, they serve it cold. I don't understand how you Englishmen can drink warm beer. It must be an acquired taste."

Gilley replied, "Well, gentlemen, if you've never had it any other way, what would you have to compare it with? It's true that warm beer tastes different, but it's a good difference. You can taste the flavours of the various ales when they are served at room temperature. In Canada, it's difficult to differentiate the tastes of the beer when they are cold. I suppose it's the same here in the States."

"We'll give you some good samples tonight," responded Len and Harry together.

When the sandwiches were delivered, Gilley could not believe his eyes. He thought Veron made a huge sandwich but this was beyond imagining. If only he had brought his camera. One could have fed all three of them with leftovers for supper. Instead, they each had one of these of monstrosities. Len and Harry expertly picked up one half and tucked in. Not wanting to look out of place, Gilley followed suit. It was out of this world. The onions, the spices in the meatloaf, the mayonnaise and of course, the famous sourdough bread combined to make this lunch one he would remember for the rest of his life. The beer was perfect and washed everything down.

The waiter didn't waste any more time and dropped three more glasses of beer and the bill. He knew his clientele. It was obvious these men didn't waste much time either. Gilley was already beginning to realize the pace was much faster in San Francisco than in Vancouver. After the bill was paid and everyone got into the car, Gilley kept talking about this fabulous sandwich. "I can't believe I ate the whole thing. It was a good job I was hungry. I've never seen the size of anything like that. If only my friends in England could see me now. I'm famous for putting anything between two slices of bread. This would be the ultimate for them."

Len replied, "On busy days like this, we have very little breakfast and we have a late supper. We have to fuel up to keep going for the afternoon." Back at the office, they got right down to the other reason why Gilley had come. Len then explained Rucker's was only interested in the hydraulic package of this contract yet the Coast Guard insisted the hydraulic package include the deck equipment. This consisted of Anchor Windlasses, Capstans, and the Towing Winch. This came about from the Canadian Government, the Department of Supply and Services to be exact, who were promoting Canadian businesses and were prepared to assist small manufacturing companies with financial and technical aide. The government had a list of qualified hydraulic equipment suppliers throughout Canada along with a contact name for each company.

Dennis Shears was representing Swann's who were deck equipment specialists. They manufactured hydraulic driven equipment using Sunstrand Hydraulic products. As Rucker's were the applications engineering group for Sunstrand Hydraulics this would be a good marriage. Along with all of that, the Canadian and U.S. governments had an understanding they would work together to promote specialized companies as well as ensuring these companies would be able to complete the contracts on time and to the specifications required.

Gilley had known that the Canadian Government was behind this contract, but he was surprised at the intricate connections Rucker's had made. He realized these Americans did their homework and they wanted to work with the best companies available. This realization also explained why he'd been treated so royally. The office they gave him to work out of was a dream come true. It was nicer than John Cleeve's office back at Swann's and had air conditioning of all things. The windows were huge and allowed in all the light needed to view these plans. Gilley was glad this office was air conditioned, as he was beginning to feel drowsy, what with the huge lunch and the beer, not to mention the early morning to the airport and the flight down.

He did his best to assess the plans given to him, smoking one cigarette after the other to keep himself awake. Just as he was about to lose the battle, in came Jim Grady. "Well Gilley, you made it at last. Welcome aboard. I see it hasn't taken long for the boys to get you working. You know you are booked into the Holiday Inn for the next two days on our tab. We normally finish here around about 6:00 PM, but I'll come back about 5:00 PM to take you to your room. That will give you time to freshen up and be ready for dinner. Len and Harry are going meet you in the bar of the hotel and take you down to Fisherman's Wharf. I would love to join you, but something unavoidable has come up. I hope to do so tomorrow night. By the way, you must try this new beer called Coors. I hear that it's quite good and I know you Englishmen like your beer."

Five o'clock could not come too soon. Relief had actually come in the form of coffee about 3:00 PM, but that still was not enough. Perseverance saw the job about fifty percent completed by the time Jim poked his head back into the office. "How's it going? You look about done in. I think it's been a long day. Let's go."

"I think I have enough done for the meeting in the morning. Can I just leave my brief case here or should I take it with me?"

"You aren't going to do much work tonight. It should be fine here. Do you have the rest of your luggage nearby?"

"Just around the corner in that little space," replied Gilley.

Jim returned with the luggage and they headed towards the elevator and the car. Fortunately the hotel was only a few minutes' drive from the office and as Jim dropped Gilley off, he said, "Now don't go walking around here at night time. It's OK during the daytime, but night can be dangerous. Remember I'll meet you here at 7:00 AM for breakfast in the dining room. Len and Harry should be here about 7:30 PM tonight to take you for dinner. Try that Coors beer if you have a mind to. Don't keep Len out too late as both of you have that important meeting with the Coast Guard at 9:30 AM. See you tomorrow. We can go over the plans for the meeting when we arrive at the office." And he was off.

Gilley trudged to the elevator with his bag, looking forward to some shut eye. He reasoned he could take an hour's kip and be ready on time for the boys. As he entered the room, he was impressed all over again. The Americans really knew how to do things up. The room was quiet and well furnished, but more importantly, at this moment, it had a large queen size bed just like his one at home. He immediately took off his shirt and shoes and lay down. Suddenly he woke up. It was darker and he scrambled for the clock. Six thirty! Whew! He had not overslept.

Looking around the room as if for the first time, Gilley took a moment to appreciate his first stay in a hotel. This was much different than the motels he had stayed in with his parents on their trip around British Columbia. The room was nicely appointed with a large queen size bed and matching drapes that reminded Gilley of a James Bond movie. It had an easy chair and a desk with a telephone. All of this was impressive, but the large TV was what really caught Gilley's attention. This was the biggest TV he had ever seen. Sure enough it worked and, taking a moment, Gilley flashed through the many stations they had in the states. Promising himself to explore this modern convenience more, Gilley moved into the bathroom.

Now this room was more than sumptuous. There were two sinks and a long vanity but it was the shower Gilley focused on. He needed one of those magical showers tonight as jet lag was beginning to catch up with him. He had to be alert for his next meeting. Looking into the stall, he saw he had nothing to worry about. There was a large circular head and plenty of fluffy towels. He had enough time for a shower and shave. Well, this shower was nothing like he had ever had before. Gilley discovered this shower head could deliver various pressures of water. There was a slow gentle setting, a normal setting and best of all a pulsating setting that did the trick superbly. Refreshed and ready to go, Gilley dressed and left his room for more of the American adventure.

He went down to the bar and looked for his hosts, but since it was not quite 7:30, they were not to be found. Gilley found a seat where he could see the entrance and where Len could find him easily. He decided to take Jim Grady's advice and order that new beer. As he looked around and got his bearing, he immediately noticed the waitresses were dressed in short skirts and low cut tops. Wow, what a place! Gorgeous women! It only took a second when he noticed one of these gorgeous women walking towards him. "Hello, Sir, can I get you a drink from the bar?"

In his strong English accent, Gilley said, "Aw, yes, I would like a beer called Coors, please." The waitress cocked her head and said, "I'm sorry, sir, but I can't understand what you are asking for. It sounds like you want "a Bayer called Coarse". We don't carry anything like that." She seemed embarrassed that she couldn't understand what Gilley wanted. She asked another waitress to come over to help. "What accent is that and where are you from?"

"The accent is English and I'm from Canada." Immediately upon hearing this she waived the others over to her. "Come and listen to this guy's accent. It's so cute. I can't make out what he's saying, but I could listen to him all night. It sounds like he wants a "bayer called course", but what do you think that means," she giggled?

The three waitresses were standing around Gilley, giggling and trying to figure out his request, teasing him and asking him to speak some more in his delightful accent. At the same time, Gilley was getting rather frustrated and embarrassed. He was trying to modify his speech the best he could when Len walked in. "Well, you certainly didn't waste any time making out with the waitresses did you?"

"All I'm trying to do, Len, is to get a beer that Jim recommended. Coors, I believe he said."

"OK, girls, two glasses of Coors draft, please. The gentleman has been asking for beer all along."

"Sir, could you let him ask us, now that we know what he wants? It sounds so cool the way he says it in his English accent." Gilley complied and with that, the beers arrived and the girls departed, much to Gilley's relief.

Len commented, "By the way, Harry sends his regrets. Something came up at the last minute and he can't make it. Also, I'm not surprised that your accent is a hit with the girls. The American girls think anything that comes from England is cool especially since the Beatles made such an impact over here. I think they actually did figure it out, but wanted to string you along a bit just to hear you talk. On top of that, you're not such a bad looking guy either what with your athletic build and being over six feet tall. You would be quite the catch for most of these girls and you could have a lot of fun on this trip if you are inclined that way."

Hearing this, Gilley didn't know what to say. His face turned a deeper shade of red. This was his first time on his own in North America and away from Joy. He had never even entertained the idea Len was suggesting. This was a business trip after all. Of course he had heard the guys bragging over coffee, but had always thought they were exaggerating. Well, maybe this was more than male bravado.

"Well, Len to tell you the truth, I'm happily married and I have enough problems with this one without complicating things by bringing more into my life," Gilley was finally able to reply.

Len agreed. "I'm happily married too and wouldn't cheat on my wife, but there is so much promiscuity these days, it's hard to know where people stand these days. Did you see that film, Bob and Carol, Ted and Alice?"

"No, what was that about?" asked Gilley.

"It was a story about neighbours' wife swapping. They ended up in bed with one another. It caused quite the controversy in our circle of friends. Maybe it hasn't made its way up to Canada yet. I don't know about you, but I'm hungry. Finish up your beer and I'll take you down to Fisherman's Wharf for a great seafood dinner. You must know San Francisco is famous for this wharf among other things."

"Oh yes, the city's reputation had reached all the way to England and to the small part where I grew up. I've been really looking forward to this trip and to seeing the sights. I used to watch 'Have Gun Will Travel' with Richard Boone who played Paladin. It was one of my favourite shows. I believe it was set in San Francisco's Hotel Carlton were he awaited responses to his business card: over the picture of a chess knight "Have Gun, Will Travel . . . Wire Paladin, San Francisco."

"I remember that show. It was one of my favorites too. Let me drive you past the Hotel Carlton. It's still standing on Sutter Street and is a bit of a tourist stop because of that show."

On the way to the Wharf, Len drove Gilley passed the various tourist sites, pointing out things like Knob Hill, the Golden Gate Bridge, and the infamous Alcatraz Island as well as the Hotel Carlton. There were many others as well, but hunger and fatigue were beginning to distract Gilley's attention. Finally, Len pulled into a parkade (as it was called in California). They wandered down the Wharf, taking in the sites and all of the various venders and restaurants along the Wharf. It seemed like this place never slept. They finally wound up at their destination, The Crab's Nest.

"This is the best place in the entire city to get specialty fish such as Abalone, freshly caught tuna and shark as well as their famous crab done in almost any way imaginable including steamed with garlic butter and lemon juice."

Len had reserved a table by the window, overlooking the harbour. The view was spectacular. The Pacific Ocean was right at their doorstep and the sun was setting on the horizon. The waitress brought menus and the wine list over along with steaming sour dough bread; fresh butter and two bottles of ice cold Coors. Between the fragrance of the bread, the sunset and the overwhelming menu choices, Gilley realized that he was in another world.

Never ever having known about most of the items offered he had no idea what to order. Of course, in England, cod, halibut and haddock were common menu offerings. Here, the exotic names left him breathless. Of course he had had crab and lobster since coming to Canada, but names such as Abalone and shark were a bit intimidating. Not wanting to appear too ignorant, Gilley started the conversation, "Well, Len, this seems to be your place. It appears to me you come here often. What would you recommend for someone who is a novice at eating the variety of seafood offered here tonight?"

"Believe it or not, Gilley, the specialty here tonight is English fish and chips. And it is very good. You could try it and compare it to the real thing in England."

"Now, that sounds like the very thing. I've never had a good fish and chip dinner since I left England. What are you going to have, Len?

"I'm going to have the Abalone," he said. "What sort of wine would you like with your dinner, Gilley?"

"I'm quite happy with beer. It goes best with fish and chips in my estimation, but what wine would you recommend?"

Len replied, a bit relieved, "You know, I'm happy with beer too. Abalone can be quite salty and beer has a way of washing it down really well, especially Coors. Did you know it's called the 'wine of beers'?"

When dinner came, Gilley could not believe his eyes. The size of the battered fish was unbelievable. He didn't know if he was given cod or halibut. However, upon his first mouthful, he knew instantly this was the best cod he had ever eaten. The chips were freshly cut large slices of potatoes, deep fried to the ultimate golden brown crispness. Just like his mother had made them. Len's meal looked like a work of art. The different vegetables and the rice were sculptured around his plate with the abalone as the center feature. Just looking at Len's dish made Gilley almost wish he had ordered the same thing. However, no piece of art could replace this wonderful trip back to his homeland.

Much to Gilley's pleasure, he found Len to be a kindred spirit. The sumptuous dinner, the jokes traded back and forth and the stories told made the evening pass quite quickly and before Gilley knew it he was back at the hotel having had a great time. Len said as he dropped Gilley off, "I really enjoyed this evening, Gilley. I'm going to just drop you off here as we have an early start tomorrow. A bit of a warning though-don't walk around this area at night. It's quite unsafe, especially for strangers to town." Waving Len off and going into the hotel, Gilley decided he would have a bit of a nightcap. He wanted to know if he could pronounce "Coors" any better after having been with Len all night. It was about ten fifteen, enough time for him to have a couple of beers and then phone Joy at 11:00 PM as he had promised.

It turned out things did not happen the way he thought they would. No sooner had he entered the bar and found himself a table, than the waitress he had encountered earlier came over with a Coors on her tray, "Sir, I will give you this Coors if you will ask me for it in your neat English accent."

With that Gilley, in his strongest English accent, replied, "No problem, sweetheart, could you give me what you have on your tray, please?" With that she laughed so hard Gilley thought he might end up wearing it instead of drinking it.

When she finally recovered herself she said, "The next one is on me, sir. You just have to let me ask you some questions about England since it's a bit quiet right now." Gilley agreed to that. After all, it meant a free beer. What he was not prepared for was the line of questioning she took. She asked if he knew the Beatles, or had seen them in person. Did he grow up near them at all; after all, England was such a small country? Then she asked about the Animals and the Rolling Stones etc.

It turned out Gilley could not be of much help to her and he felt he had let her down somewhat. Other than the fact the Animals were from Newcastle and his friend Ray Cowie had worked with Eric Burdon before he had become famous, Gilley didn't think he was much help. He said, "Well, Ray and I often had a beer together with Eric in a pub called the Printer's Pie. But no one knew then what Eric would become."

"Oh my goodness, you drank beers with Eric Burdon of the Animals! I can't believe it. What was he like back then?" Gilley didn't know how to answer, but he was saved as the bar suddenly became busy because the late shift of patrons came in. Since it was going on 11:00 PM and time to call Joy anyway, Gilley quickly finished his beer and, saying goodnight to his new found friend, he made his escape to his room and made his call. Tomorrow would be another interesting day, he was sure of that.

The following morning after experiencing the pulsating shower again, breakfast with Jim Grady was yet another adventure. Gilley thought the breakfasts in Canada were huge compared to England, so he was not prepared for what was placed in front of him that morning. He followed Jim's lead and ordered the All American Breakfast; the house special. It consisted of two eggs, easy over, three links of sausage, three strips of bacon, hash browns, fruit, and two four inch pancakes and all the toast he could eat. Orange juice and endless coffee were also included.

Nothing much was said during this spread. Jim tucked into his plate as if he had not eaten for a few days, but Gilley didn't know where to begin. How in the world was he going to be able to eat all of this? He had been taught it was bad manners to leave anything on one's plate especially when one is a visitor. The pancakes were the challenge for Gilley. He had never seen them served with a full breakfast like this before. He waited for Jim's lead and sure enough, Jim spread them with butter and then smothered them with syrup as if they were the only thing in front of him.

Gilley was suffering by now. He had always been accused of having a big appetite, but Jim had him beat. Those back home would never believe he decided to leave the pancakes in spite of the risk of having "bad manners". Making the best excuse he could think of, Gilley said, "I'm sorry Jim, I never have liked pancakes. Would it be acceptable to leave them?"

"Of course, Sonny. Pass them over here. There's no point in wasting good food. This might be my last meal until supper time, if I get home in time and besides, when you get to my age, you don't care much anymore about your waist line. As you can see, it's been "wasted" a while ago." With that declaration, he reached over and forked Gilley's pancakes onto his plate repeating the same ritual with the butter and syrup.

By the time it was time to leave the restaurant and get to the office, Gilley wasn't sure if he would be able to walk to the car. Trundling to the car, he thought to himself, one would have to be really careful about one's weight here in The United States of America.

Back at the office, the Coast Guard officials were waiting patiently for everybody to arrive. Gilley and Jim were the last to arrive. Len said, "Jim, did you introduce him to the Breakfast?"

"I did and he did well. He may not want lunch this afternoon though."

Gilley replied feeling a bit intimidated by the surrounding brass, rose to the occasion, "One has to rise early to do justice to the size of breakfast which was served this morning. However if I get an opportunity to have those meatloaf sandwiches again, I will definitely be able to make room for them. I will have to get back to Canada, though, before I explode, what with all of the good food and large portions that are served here in the United States." This got quite a chuckle from Len and the boys. With that, everyone was invited to sit around the large board room table and the meeting got underway.

It wasn't long before the Coast Guard was demanding the finalized physical sizes of the deck equipment from Rucker. Gilley, knowing full well most of the final design had not been completed, decided to present the footprints of the equipment needed for the Naval architect to finish the structural design of the deck. Even though he felt defensive about answering this question, he decided the best tactic was to take the offensive. "Gentlemen, you realize many of the test requirements set out by the Coast Guard are number one priority and that's why I am here today. The final weight of the equipment and the physical size are not due until next week. This is according to the agreement set three months ago."

The Coast Guard representative responded, "We would like to bring everything forward from that agreement. How could you provide us with a shorter delivery schedule of the equipment? It has become imperative this be done much sooner than we predicted. We have a smaller window to do the testing than predicted."

Gilley responded, "The equipment schedule is six months after acceptance of the deck foundations. We have finalized all the designs and we are waiting now for the test certificates from the coupons I brought here yesterday. This is for the subzero Charpy tests and x-rays of the welds. These things cannot be hurried if you want us to follow the specific detailed procedures you have laid out in the original order. What I can do when I get back to the office is to see if we can improve the six month turn around. The alternative is to give us a timeline for each piece of equipment so we know what you want first. I can tell you this would not necessarily speed up the final delivery of the last piece of equipment, but it could possibly improve the shipyard's delivery of a finished vessel as the builders would not be waiting until all of the equipment was finished before completing any vessel.

And this solution could possibly give Rucker's the opportunity to hook up the hydraulics as each piece of equipment becomes ready. I cannot speak for Rucker's, but I know we have done this in the past with other shipyards and it seems to speed up the finished product."

After a bit more discussion, the Coast Guard decided this was the answer. They decided to return to the shipyard along with Rucker's and obtain an orderly sequence of the equipment as it would be needed. Now it was lunch time. The Coast Guard representatives excused themselves explaining they needed to get back to headquarters. Gilley was still feeling quite full and did not expect lunch, especially after the remarks Jim had made at breakfast about working all day without a break.

Jim thanked Gilley for his input and solution, but said he would have to excuse himself from lunch as he had to follow up on Rucker's side of this possible new delivery arrangement. "Can you get back to me next week, Gilley? I need to know the schedule your company can arrange so we can be ahead of the Coast Guard. It'll take a week for them to finalize the decision anyhow.

You see, Gilley, it's a good job you booked out of your hotel this morning. I believe there is a 7:00 PM flight back to Vancouver tonight. Since you have an open ticket, you could go on standby. The test results will be ready by 3:00 PM and if all is well, we can proceed with production."

Just then, Jim was interrupted by a page over the intercom. "Excuse me, Gentlemen I will be back right after I take care of this." After about three quarters of an hour had passed, he returned with a smile on his face. "You passed all of the tests. You can take your samples and parts back with you if you like."

"You are welcome to the samples, Jim. After all I went through with security and all getting them here, I don't care what happens to them. All I need is the test results and I'm happy."

"The tests are ready for you to pick up anytime. Len will drive you to the airport and I will take my leave of you now. Before I go though, Gilley I would like to have a quick word with you before we say goodbye." With that, he pulled Gilley to one side.

"You did very well today and if you ever think of moving to the States and working for Rucker's I know Len and I could make things happen to ensure you would get a working permit which could lead to a green card if you ever wanted to live in the States. Now remember, when you get back home, you are the project leader for this contract and I will be writing a letter to Swann's to indicate this is our wish and part of the agreement," Jim said emphatically. "Len will take you back to Oakland where the helicopter will take you back to the airport. By the way, how did you enjoy the helicopter ride? Many people find it a frightening experience. It's the noise that gets them."

"Thank you for the job offer, Jim. I think we have to get this job finished first as it's our priority. Then we can talk. About the helicopter, it's sure a good way of seeing the harbour," Gilley replied. "The flight path is closer to the ground and I was able to get a good look at the layout of the city as we made our way from the airport to the landing pad. It was great seeing Alcatraz too. Thanks for this opportunity. My wife has never been on a helicopter before so that's one up for me."

Jim replied, "It'll take more than that to keep ahead of her. She is one smart lady."

Arriving back at the main airport after another good helicopter ride, Gilley stood in standby for the Champagne Flight. The holding area for standby was right next to the bar and of course, Gilley thought it was a good idea to have a couple of those Coors again as he didn't know when he might be in the U.S. As he was drinking his first Coors, he noticed someone familiar walking into the bar. It was Wayne Fraser, the precious metal broker from his flight down. He waved Wayne over, "What a coincidence we should meet in the airport," exclaimed Gilley. "I am assuming you are on your way home as well. Would you like a beer?"

"There's nothing wrong with a beer at this time of day. I think we might even have time for two or three as out flight isn't due until 7:00 PM. That's if we get on it. I take it you are flying standby as well," replied Wayne.

"That's right. My business was finished earlier than I thought and I decided it would be a good idea to come here and attempt to get onto the first flight home."

With that, the waitress came over to get Wayne's order. He ordered a Coors, too and Gilley ordered a second one to keep up. They commenced updating each other on what had brought them respectively down to San Francisco. Both had been successful in their business dealings and were feeling the flush of triumph. The talk eventually turned to gold. This was in Wayne's area of expertise and Gilley had definitely tried to steer the conversation in this direction. He had not forgotten Wayne's advice of, 'Buy gold, as much as you can' as they had departed a few days earlier.

"Have you bought any gold yet, Gilley?" asked Wayne.

"Not yet. I haven't had time to think about gold the last two days. I've had the Coast Guard and my company on my mind, but will definitely look into it when I get home."

Wayne came back with, "It's just not gold that will pay off shortly, it's silver as well. It would be worth your while to buy as much as you can while the prices are at this level. When you buy it, make sure you get the actual gold or silver in hand. Many people will offer to buy it for you and then keep it having given you a certificate of ownership."

He continued, "I'm not suggesting there would be any underhanded dealings, but I personally would prefer to have it in my own hand. Remember people are in the business to make money and they could sell it prematurely or could encourage you to sell it prematurely. If you have it in your possession, in a safety deposit box, it's often more work to get it out and you will think twice before you go down there, take it out and sell it. It's kind of a psychological thing, but it works for me and my friends. I believe gold will hit six hundred dollars U.S. per ounce. It will drop here and there, but will never go down to where it is currently again. Believe me. I've worked in this industry for years and can read the signs. As a matter of fact, I just purchased thirty-two ounces of gold and one hundred ounces of silver today. You don't need a big safety deposit to hold a small fortune."

Just at that time, Gilley heard both of their names called over the PA system. He could not believe how fast the time had gone. The two men boarded with their carryon luggage and much to their surprise, they had seats beside one another at the rear of the plane. As a matter of fact, they surmised these were the stewardess's seats as they were small and uncomfortable. The announcement came over the PA, "Good evening, this is the Captain speaking. We would like to welcome you aboard our flight today. As you can see, we have a full flight today, Ladies and Gentlemen. Unfortunately, there will be a slight delay of about an hour as we have missed our take-off spot due to a boarding procedure lasting longer than normal. We should make some time up as we can catch a tail wind on our way to Vancouver. Arrival time in Vancouver should be approximately 10:30 PM. Ladies and Gentlemen, enjoy our champagne flight."

It didn't seem to take an hour for the plane to take off as Gilley and Wayne were engrossed in their conversation about precious metals and gems. Before long, the stewardess interrupted them with the offer of champagne. That was just the first glass and it kept coming. It seemed to Gilley his glass was never empty. About half way through the flight, the stewardess approached Wayne and Gilley, "Gentlemen, are you enjoying your flight?"

"Very much so," they replied in harmony.

"That's good. However, we have a bit of a problem. There are so many extra people on board tonight that we are running out of dinner for each passenger. It seems everyone wants to eat tonight and I was wondering if you two are hungry or if we could just give you a snack and send you home with a magnum of champagne each instead. The snack would be a bag of chips and some peanuts."

Gilley remembered he had split a meatloaf sandwich with Len on the way to the airport. Len did not want to let Gilley go without having him taste another one of these American delights and had taken a detour just for this purpose. Therefore he was more than willing to give up his dinner in exchange for the champagne. Wayne also agreed. Both men however, asked if they could have more than one bag of chips and peanuts. The stewardess, smiled and said, "I will take care of my two very special passengers. Don't you worry!" And they didn't.

Before long they were touching down in Vancouver. They ended up with one magnum each in hand and at least that in their stomachs. The stewardess had shown them how to stash it so that they could pass customs. Both were successful at customs and Wayne's wife was there to take him home. Gilley, however, had left his car in the parking lot underground and had to drive home. The two men exchanged farewells and Wayne told Gilley to give him a call next week as tomorrow he would have to leave for Toronto and then London, England.

As Gilley approached his car, he was very relieved he remembered where it was parked as the morning before he had left it in a rush. Getting into the car, he thought, "Why isn't Joy with me now. I usually loose the car and leave her standing on the curb waiting for me. Here, I find it right away and she's not here to appreciate it." With that he started the engine and turned the wheel. Looking out of his rear window to make sure he cleared the cars beside him and there is no one coming up behind him, he cranked the wheel to get out of the spot. He moved back slowly to exit and was very surprised when he heard a loud metal crunching sound and felt a distinct vibration. Turning towards the sound, he realized there had been a huge concrete pillar right by his front driver's fender and he had turned so sharply he had crushed the fender just over the wheel against the concrete pillar.

Groaning inwardly, Gilley got out and inspected the damage. He was surprised at how much metal had been dished in. He was also mad at himself by this time. He had never had an accident all the time he'd been driving. The only mark on the car was over the rear wheel well and Joy had done that when she had had trouble parking at Woodward's. This was more than five times more visible than that incident.

Gilley, to his surprise, managed to get home without the usual 'detours' around the city and without further incident. It was approaching midnight when he pulled into the assigned parking place at the apartment. This spot had a light that shone fully upon the car especially on the driver's side. Gilley decided to back into the spot this time. This was so that when Joy looked over the balcony she could not see the damage on the car. Gilley didn't have a hope in hell of coming up with an explanation for the damage or any way of softening the news if she did. His only hope in doing this was to postpone the inevitable until he felt more able to deal with it. However, immediately upon entering the apartment, Gilley knew he was in trouble—more trouble than he had been in a long time. Instead of asking how he was doing or how did the trip go, Joy sarcastically said, "Why did you back the car in? Are you hiding something?"

Trying to buy some time, Gilley slurred, "Look what I got for you off the airplane today-a magnum of good champagne."

"I don't care much for champagne. You know that. What are you trying to hide?"

"Nothing, I just have to get going early tomorrow and I thought it would be easier to drive straight out in the morning. I thought you liked champagne, especially when it's free."

"Gilley, you never back the car in. I think you've done something to the car. I can see you've had a bit to drink. Did you stop somewhere?" Joy was straining to see out the window by this time.

"Nope, I came straight home."

"Were you drinking on the plane? Where did you get the champagne?"

"I got it on the plane. The stewardess gave it to me."

"Why would the stewardess give you a magnum of champagne?"

"Well, she didn't have enough food for us, so she gave us peanuts, chips and this champagne."

By now Joy was really upset. Gilley was hardly making sense and she just knew something was wrong with the car. She shot back, "Gilley, stewardesses do not just give out magnums of champagne to everyone. Why you? What did you do on the plane?"

"Nothing," said Gilley holding his hands up as if under arrest. "I met this man, Wayne, whom I met on the way down. He told me I should buy gold and silver. She gave us both a magnum because they ran out of food."

"So what's that got to do with the car?"

"Nothing. The car is fine. We had a few beers at the bar waiting for the plane. Then they ran out of food and all we got was chips and peanuts along with our champagne. I have to buy gold."

"What do you mean you have to buy gold? Tell me about the car. You never back in."

"Well, gold is $62.00 an ounce today and it's going to go up to $600.00 an ounce in the next few years. I have to buy gold tomorrow."

"Now I know you're drunk. We don't have enough money to buy half an ounce right now. All our money is set aside for going back to England. You never acted like this in England."

"Joy, we have to buy gold. Do you have something to eat? I'm famished. I got this champagne instead of dinner. Let's have a beer."

By this time Joy realized she could get more flies with sugar, so she bargained, "I'll make you a sandwich and have a beer with you if you tell me about the car."

"Jim Grady says 'Hi' to you by the way. He thinks you're smart. He told me this today."

"I'll go make your sandwich. Here, have a beer."

With that Joy went to the kitchen and began the sandwich. She decided to make his favourite night time snack—a fried egg sandwich. While Joy was busy, Gilley realized he was not going to win this battle. Jim was right, she was one smart lady. He would have to tell her about the car when she finished making his meal.

"OK Joy, I confess. While I was backing out of the car park at the airport, I hit a pillar. I was in such a hurry to get home to see you, I wasn't paying close attention. The guy who parked next to me didn't leave me any room to maneuver. Besides, I hardly touched it, but when you see the damage, you'd think I'd been hit by a truck. I can fix it."

"I knew something had happened," growled Joy. "Do I have to go out and have a look at it?"

"No! No! No! I can fix it. These cars are made of thin metal and it takes nothing to smash them in. Don't worry about it. It'll be fine."

"You were on that champagne flight and that's probably why you bashed up the car."

"No, I didn't drink that much on the flight. Why don't you just sit down and listen to all I have to tell you. I mean it when I say we have to buy gold. I learned some great information today that could put us ahead for the rest of our lives. Let's have another beer and a smoke."

"This had better be good, Gilley. You'll have to make up for the bashed fender."

With that Gilley proceeded to tell Joy about Wayne and the information he disclosed to Gilley about gold and silver and how investing in this would be the best thing they could ever do. Joy's response was, "You talk as though we have a lot of money. We're going back to England this year and we have furniture payments and car payments. And that's not to mention all of our daily expenses along with car repair bills now. What do you think we would use to follow this wild advice you are giving me?"

"We could borrow the money", replied Gilley

"Where from?"

"We could borrow from the bank as this would be considered an asset. Gold is not going to go down, right? The collateral would be for the bank to hold the gold for us. Surely the bank would see this as a solid investment. You work at the bank and with your connections surely we could get a loan for some gold or silver. Remember that Wayne said that it would go up to six hundred dollars an ounce. We could get it for only $59.00 an ounce right now and that would be a profit of over ten times our investment. It's on a bit of a lull right now. But, according to Wayne that's just temporarily. In another month, he predicts it will begin to climb steadily and then will shoot up rapidly. Your dad bought some already, a bit high, but he would be wise to buy some more now anyway. Or we could talk to your father. He's interested in gold and is associated with an investment group that that is focused on commodities. He just bought some for $72.00 an ounce. He will understand the value of this information." Gilley felt he was on a roll.

Joy could see that Gilley was very determined and he would not be put off easily in this mood he was in. She replied, "Tell you what. I will ask at the bank tomorrow and then we can talk with Dad on the weekend. He does belong to that investment group. He will steer us straight." With that, she got up and went into the bedroom. Gilley saw there was no point in discussing this further tonight and he followed her. She did inquire about the trip and its success before they drifted off to sleep.

The following morning, Gilley really needed that magical shower to get him going. The champagne did not react on his system the same way beer did. He was anxious to get to work never the less, in order to report on the success of his trip and the new things he had discovered in the United States of America. He wondered how many of his mates knew about Coors beer for example and meatloaf sandwiches on sour dough bread.

To his amazement, most of the Canadians had had both of these things and meatloaf sandwiches were quite the thing in BC as well. Gilley wondered who started the fad, the Americans or the Canadians. He was discovering the two countries had much in common.

His biggest task after this trip was to coordinate the delivery required by Rucker's for the deck equipment now that they had the green light. Much had to be done. Firstly, patterns for wildcats (the anchor lifting sprocket), capstan heads and gears had to be finalized to enable the foundries to cast within the six week window that had been agreed upon. Secondly, all the specialized steel plates had to be ordered.

Thirdly, it was imperative that the coordination of outside suppliers, such as the foundries and the gear cutting shop be done so the finished product would come together on time.

On top of all of this, the designs for each piece of equipment had to be completed and finalized along with other orders which were pending. This took a lot of extra time and energy on Gilley's part. In spite of all of this, Gilley's mind kept going back to what Wayne had told him and he continued to try to find a way to take advantage of the gold market. On top of that, Gilley also thought about the offer Jim Grady had made him. He didn't know what to think.

That weekend, when Gilley and Joy had time to connect, he discovered Joy really had talked to the bank manager. She reported the manager had said the bank was not in the position of loaning money for investments. Even though they could keep the investment, they were not in the business of storing them. If Gilley could come up with the money from another source, it would be the best way for him to purchase his gold. This left Jim and Veron. Saturday evening came around and both Gilley and Joy brought up the subject. (It seemed as if Joy was actually warming to the subject.)

After much discussion and beer, Jim confessed, "Gilley, I think I know where you are coming from. But right now, I'm getting out of the investment group as its taking too much of my time. I have to pay for this wedding and I don't see gold increasing in price. I think it's peaked out and will go down. My investment group does not agree, but I've been doing my research. I know what your friend from the plane told you, but how do you know if you can trust him? I bought gold at $75.00 and ounce and its now at $69.00 and that was over a year ago. That's why I don't see any future in the precious metal market." With that Jim patted him on the back. Gilley knew he had reached a dead end here too. However, he was not to be deterred.

CHAPTER 18

SALLY'S WEDDING

WEEKS JUST FLEW BY and suddenly, the wedding was upon them. All of the finishing touches to the grounds, the inside decorations, and the food and beverage arrangements had taken up all spare time. As Veron didn't work outside the home she devoted all of her attentions to this gala affair and expected Jim, Gilley and Joy to devote any spare time outside of work to this as well. Gilley found himself stretched to the maximum. No matter how the men looked at it, there wasn't any way to finagle a golf game in. Jim was sure Veron was onto them as any time he came up with was immediately booked with one errand or another.

The gold fever had truly bit Gilley. Even though he didn't have much spare time, he spent whatever time he could on researching gold. He researched the history of mining, smelting, and refining. The ancient past to modern times all interested him. If anyone had a gold story Gilley was there. As his knowledge of gold and the refining process grew, his engineering mind was applied to new ways of getting this precious metal out of the ground. Ideas spun in his head. He would wake up in the middle of the night with a new idea for a machine.

To make matters worse, Jim kept talking about selling his gold investments to pay for some of the wedding expenses. Gilley would choose his times and he kept encouraging Jim to hang on. "The time will come, Jim. Wayne had nothing to gain from telling me about the price of gold. I do believe he's right."

But Jim kept saying, "Listen Gilley, I know what I'm talking about. After all, I've been doing this for years. Gold is going to go down in price. As a matter of fact, it's dropped three dollars today. I don't have a lot invested so it won't matter one way or the other."

"Well, Jim," Gilley replied, "If you want to sell some of your gold, why don't you invest half that money into silver. It's going to naturally follow the price of gold and if you invest in silver, you won't have as much to lose if it doesn't increase. I don't think I'm wrong."

Finally when Jim could handle the pressure no longer he conceded, "I'll tell you what Gilley, I'll sell my gold and I'll invest 30 percent into silver and you'd better be right." Gilley knew this was the end of that discussion with Jim.

Jim's attitude did not deter Gilley. It actually seemed Gilley's determination grew when Jim or Joy voiced their opposition to his dreams of striking it rich. However, time did not permit Gilley to pursue his dreams much farther. Instead, he had to put them on the back burner for another time. He knew he would one day get involved with gold and mining it.

Before everyone knew it, the day was at hand. Of course, it ended up being Gilley's job to go to the liquor store and bring all the alcohol to the wedding bar. This entailed several runs back and forth between the house and the liquor store. He began to wish he had a delivery truck instead of the Duster. Amazingly, by the time the wedding started, which was noon on a very beautiful, sunny Saturday in early May, everything was in place.

Gilley could not believe his eyes as he stood surveying the grounds. He had been so involved in the details he hadn't taken the time to appreciate the whole picture. Veron had insisted upon lots of flowers. Now Gilley understood why. They were all around and transformed the backyard into an outdoor wedding chapel. She had made sure flowers lined the trees which surrounded the back yard. (These trees had been planted to create privacy in the backyard.) She had insisted pots of flowers be planted beside the driveway, along the sidewalks and of course highlighting where the ceremony would take place under the cherry tree. She had hung baskets off the deck and the bouquets the wedding party carried tied in beautifully.

The music started. The ceremony had begun. The night before when they had had the rehearsal, so many things went wrong Gilley was sure everyone would laugh today. However, when he saw the minister, Doug and the two groomsmen standing under the blossoming cherry tree, waiting for the women to arrive, he knew things would go smoothly. Then he realized why Veron had insisted he shake the tree in the morning. She hadn't wanted any cherry blossoms falling on the wedding party. As he surveyed the tree and the men waiting underneath it, he hoped to God that none would fall. If any did, he would be history.

Turning, he saw Anne, who was the Bridesmaid and Joy who was the Maid of Honour, walking out from the basement and towards the large cherry tree. The dresses the girls wore were a wonderful combination of peach, pink, white and a touch of green and matched everything perfectly. They proceeded to the cherry tree with a dignity he didn't know they possessed. Then came the Bride dressed in a simple yet elegant peach coloured dress, carrying a larger bouquet of flowers. She wore peach rose buds in her blonde hair and looked absolutely fabulous. It was definitely her day. Jim, her father, proudly escorted her to the center of the ceremony—the cherry tree. Gilley began to appreciate all the planning Veron had done. He felt as if he was in a movie, it was that nice (especially if one was to compare his wedding with this one.)

The minister, who was Doug's uncle, had traveled from Calgary just to perform the ceremony. He did more than justice to it as he led the nervous party through their vows. All of the women were in tears and all of the men wanted to head for the bar as soon as it was acceptable to do so.

Gilley was mesmerized by the pomp and ceremony accompanying the wedding. He couldn't help but compare the weddings he had been to in England with this affair and concluded that only royalty would go to so much fuss and hassle. After the ceremony and receiving line, the guests were invited into the house where the speeches and luncheon (or what Veron called the Wedding Buffet) occurred. The speeches were held in the living room and it was Gilley's job to make sure everyone had a glass of champagne for the toasts.

Now, Veron had given Gilley strict instructions about the minister. She had told him to make sure the minister was taken care of. If he wasn't, it would be embarrassing for the family. Well, Gilley kept making the rounds with the champagne as the toasts were happening and observed the minister's glass empty on each occasion he happened by. Not wanting to incur Veron's wrath, he would obligingly fill the glass. Well, by the fourth time passed, he realized the minister was starting to relax. That was Gilley's cue to make sure his glass was always full no matter what.

After Gilley's assistance, the minister was all smiles as the meal started. However, Gilley noticed he had a difficult time maneuvering his fork to his mouth. Veron noticed this too and came up to Gilley asking, "How many drinks did you give the minister?"

"Just as you said, Veron, I kept his glass full. Every time I passed him, it was empty so I filled it up. I was taking care of him."

"Well, I didn't want you to get him drunk. I hope he has the good sense to abstain from more drinks. It would be too embarrassing if he were to fall down drunk at this wedding. So don't give him any more, you bugger."

"Well, he didn't have to drink it, did he," Gilley chucked.

The Buffet was outstanding. Absolutely everything was represented on the groaning dining room table. Roast beef, chicken, salmon, salads, potatoes and multitude of other foods delighted the guests. People were asked to take their plates out to the new deck Gilley and Jim had worked so hard to create. After the feast, everyone relaxed and the party moved down to the bar.

Needless to say, Gilley took his usual position behind the bar. However, Jim came up to him and said, "Gilley, why don't you let me do this for awhile. You go and mingle and enjoy yourself. Come back in a bit and give me a break." Gilley was only too happy to comply. He knew Jim took great pleasure in serving his guests their drinks. As the afternoon went on, Jim was getting funnier and funnier. This was typical of him when he'd had a few. Gilley realized Jim had been behind the bar for a few hours so he offered to take over while Jim took a break. "Oh, no thanks, Gilley," replied Jim. "It's very fortunate to have a sink here behind the bar."

"Is that why it's called a 'wet bar' here in Canada, Jim," laughed Gilley?

Soon it was time for Sally to throw her bouquet and Doug to throw the garter and be off on their honeymoon in Doug's TR6 sports coupe. No one knew where they were going and keeping this secret was quite the feat. It was customary for the best man to find out where the happy couple was going so that the wedding party could disrupt the private night as much as possible. But Doug had won this one. The only clue was they were off to Vancouver Island somewhere.

Back in the bar, the party continued. More and more of Doug's friends showed up. At about 7:00 PM Jim said to Gilley, "We're running out of beer, Gilley, what with all Doug's friends showing up. I'll never let it be said this bar ran dry. You'd better go to the liquor store for more."

"I've got four cases stashed in your workshop," replied Gilley.

"Sorry, Gilley, those are long gone. What do you think I've been serving? You'd better get going."

"When does the liquor store close on Saturday?"

"Thank goodness they're open until 10:00 PM. Otherwise, we'd have to impose on Mickey. I don't want to inconvenience him today as he's having so much fun. Here's twenty dollars. Get whatever you can. I think you can get about eight cases anyway for that amount."

"Alright, Jim. I'll be back as soon as I can."

On his way out, Joy waylaid him, "And where do you think you're going?"

"We're running out of beer. I've got to go by the liquor store."

"Well, don't get lost and don't get a ticket for speeding, eh!"

"Right" and off he went.

Getting to the store wasn't a problem. Gilley knew his way and actually found a parking spot close by. He couldn't believe his luck. However, he realized when he entered he may have another problem. Even though he was dressed in his new suit bought especially for the wedding (and their trip to England) he was under the influence. Here in Canada, they were very strict about serving people who were suspect. Now Gilley knew he'd had a few so he would have to do everything without raising suspicion. He obtained a shopping cart because eight cases of beer were not easy to carry to the cash register. He filled up his cart and headed to the lineup.

As he got into line, the young man ahead of him, sporting a cowboy hat, looked back, "We're all dressed up in our finery tonight, aren't we," he said. "Where's the party? Can I come? I'm sure they won't notice one more."

Not wanting to attract attention through an argument, Gilley said, "If you help me load these into the car and you follow me to the party and I'll make sure you get in. However, that cowboy hat will definitely a problem so how about if you remove it when we get there?"

"Deal," said the young man, standing beside Gilley.

The cashier recognized Gilley, "Back again are we? What's going on today? Are we entertaining all of New Westminster? It must be costing a small fortune."

"You can say that again. My sister-in-law got married today and we're running out of beer as all her husband's friends just turned up even though they weren't invited. My father-in-law won't have his bar run dry, so here I am again. I think this is the fifth time today."

"Well, you know, sir, I believe you're under the influence."

Under the influence or not, Gilley was quick on his feet, "Well, I have my friend here who's driving. I'm just here to pay for it."

The clerk eyed the pair suspiciously but rang the purchase through. As they left the store with the cart, his new-found friend said, "That was quick thinking on your part. I hope you know your way back to the party. I think I've earned my way in after all. By the way my name is Larry and I live in New Westminster so I guess that qualifies me for the invite."

Arriving back at 1806, both men unloaded the car. As they made the last trip, Joy said, "Larry, what are you doing here? I haven't seen you for ages. Your sister Linda is here with Howie. How the hell did you get here?"

"It's a long story, Joy. Who is this guy unloading beer? Do you know him?"

"Yes, he's my husband. We just got married nine months ago in England. Let's get you a beer. I have to hear this one. Whatever you tell me won't surprise me after all the things he's done since coming to Canada."

Down at the bar Linda and Howie were surprised to see Larry. They crowded around as he told his story to Joy. They couldn't believe it but Jim said, "I know when I send this guy out on an errand, he comes through."

"By the way, Jim," said Gilley taking him aside, "I've left two cases of beer in the trunk for tomorrow. I think we'll need them after today."

Jim laughed and slapped Gilley on the back, "Good work."

The party was still alive and well at 2:00 AM. People started for home at that time. With farewells finally said, and the last person gone, Veron and Jim were left to tuck Rosa and Grandma into bed in spite of their protests. Joy and Gilley walked home. Gilley thought it was a darn good thing the next day was Sunday. "We can have a long lie in and relax after all the hectic days we've put in."

Much to his annoyance, the phone was ringing at 8:30 AM the next morning. It was Veron. Gilley couldn't believe his ears. Did that woman never stop? "What time are you guys going to come over here to help us clean up? Jim is presently making breakfast."

"Give me time to take my magical shower because its needed today, Veron, and we'll be there as soon as I can get Joy out of bed, You know what a challenge that can be," answered Gilley.

"Don't forget you left your car here. You'll have to walk over."

"I know, Veron. It was a romantic walk home last night after all the hubbub." Snorting, Veron rang off. Right, thought Gilley. "Come on, Joy, your mother wants us to go and help clean up the place. Get up. Your dad's cooking breakfast."

"I'm not getting out of bed. If you want to go over and help, go ahead. I've done enough and I'm staying right here. I don't care what my mother thinks. If she wants to clean so early in the morning, let her. I'll be over later."

Gilley, wanting one of Jim's great breakfasts with sausages, eggs, bacon, hash browns and toast, left Joy where she was and headed over to the in-laws. The place was a mess. He had never seen it looking so bad. However, Veron and Jim were on the patio, enjoying their coffee and the lovely morning with Grandma and Rosa, both looking worse for wear. They too had been dragged out of bed to tackle the job. After the much enjoyed breakfast, Veron was chomping at the bit to get the house back into order. She took charge like a sergeant-major and set everyone to specific tasks. Anne was not to be seen and Gilley wondered what magic she had performed to escape her mother's commands.

By noon the work was done and just in time for lunch, Joy arrived. Veron, not missing the irony of this, put her to making lunch for the crew. Gilley was just on his way to the bottle depot to return the empties when Jim whispered, "It's time we made a trip to the bootlegger. I've just called Mickey and we can stop on our way back.

He's waiting for us. Come on, let's get out of here so we can get back in time for lunch."

"Don't forget, I've still got two cases in the trunk of the car. I saved them just for today," said Gilley.

"No you don't." said Jim. "You don't remember, but I sent Joy out with your keys to get them as we were running out again. Let's go and once we get back, we can relax and enjoy the day."

Sunday passed with the majority of the family relaxing and enjoying the sunshine. However, Veron was still in her clean up mode and struggled with sitting still. Everyone decided to let her go at it as they recognized this was her way of unwinding from the hectic weeks prior.

Chapter 19

Preparing to Return to Merry Old England

AFTER THE WEDDING, THINGS returned to normal, thank goodness. Gilley could now concentrate wholeheartedly on the Coast Guard project and the rest of his work. No matter how much work there was to do, Gilley could not take his mind off the gold and the information Wayne had given him. He kept thinking of how much money he could make if he could convince Joy to invest some money, no matter how small in gold. She had already explored getting a loan from the bank for investment reasons and they were clearly not interested.

"Gilley, remember we already have a loan with Wosk's for the furniture, a loan with the bank for the car and a credit card payment with Eaton's for the clothes we needed for the wedding and for England."

Jim was of no help as he had sold all his interests to pay for the wedding. He decided to approach Dennis Shears. Dennis was an open-minded man with a good knowledge of the markets. He listened intently to Gilley's proposal. "You may be onto something. Let me give it some thought and we'll talk in the next couple of weeks."

Gilley knew he had to carefully pick the people he talked to so, encouraged by Dennis's response, Gilley decided to talk to George Strut as well. George was manager of Swann's mixer division. Mixers were predominantly used in the floatation system for separating various minerals, including gold. George said, "You have to be very careful when investing in precious metals. It can be a volatile market. But you may be onto something. I'll check with my people and get back to you. If they can see what you're telling me, maybe we can work something out."

But before Gilley knew it, Joy was saying, "Gilley, do you realize it's almost time for our trip to England. You've been in such a busy mode I don't think you've noticed time going by and my packing things. We've only got a couple of weeks to finalize things before our September departure. Do you know what you want to take with you, besides what I've packed already?"

"Whatever you've packed will be good. You have good judgment. Besides, if I forget anything, I'll buy it in England."

"No you won't," replied Joy. "Things are too expensive for you to have duplicates."

Realizing Joy was right, Gilley was jolted into the present. He turned his mind to the impending trip. It would be good to see family and friends again. Besides Gilley was looking forward to Bill Wakefield's wedding. He had received some information about what would be expected of him as Bill's Best Man. Bill had already rented the wedding suits for his attendants and had provided an outline of the ceremony. Gilley had been making notes for the speech he was expected to give and being such a long time friend of Bill's, Gilley knew he was able to tell some funny stories about their growing up years too.

Since they were going to be in the United Kingdom for eighteen days, Joy had been talking about seeing her relatives, Peggy in Teddington and Eunice and Edmond in Sussex as well as some sites she hadn't seen when she was there last time. Of course there was Aunt Phyll, whom Joy and her friend Liz had boarded with on her first stay in England. Gilley's brother Neil had also arranged for them to go to Edinburgh for the weekend. And all of this was in addition to the wedding.

One disappointing bit of news Gilley received was one of his good friends, Dave Wright, had taken a position in Germany teaching the children of the Armed Forces at the base. Because of this, he wasn't able to attend the ceremony and would not be available for a visit with Gilley this trip.

Dave had married Brenda while Gilley was in Canada. Now Dave and Brenda had been dating before Gilley and Joy left for Canada. They met at the Waggon Inn as Brenda's sister Linda worked there and Brenda and her friends frequented the Inn along with Gilley, Dave and their crowd. Gilley remembered John Jefferies who was the only Scotsman in his group. John would buy a box of matches and count them. If there were less than the average stated contents of forty-eight, he would return the box. If the count was over, he wouldn't say a thing.

Gilley knew the old crowd would gather at the Waggon Inn to see them, including John and Val Palmer and Ray and Margaret Cowie. It would be good to see all of them again and catch up on what they all had been doing. Gilley also was looking forward to seeing Fred and Muriel again too. They had been instrumental in Gilley and Joy meeting and in keeping the group going.

Now, Gilley and Joy's animal family had grown from five budgerigars to include two gerbils as well. "Joy, you have acquired all these pets," said Gilley, "Now who do you have looking after them? After all, they can't look after themselves while we're gone."

"I'm surprised you even remembered our pets, Gilley. You've been so wrapped in work. I didn't even think you noticed our two new tenants."

"Well, of course I had. They keep me awake from time to time running on their wheel in the middle of the night."

"I'm surprised anything keeps you awake at night, Gilley. You hit that pillow and you're gone till the alarm goes off. Of course I've made arrangements for their care. Who do you think I am? My mother and Anne will make sure they're cared for. What do you want to get Bill and Christine for a wedding gift? I think we should get them something from here. That's always a nice touch. What could we get them that they would not receive in England?"

"Steak knives."

"Steak knives?"

"Yes. Bill likes his meat and they don't have sets in England like they do here. To my knowledge, that is. I think a nice set of steak knives from Canada would be a great gift. They'll transport easily as well."

"Why Gilley, you have a good idea there," said Joy. "I'm surprised. I'll talk to my mom about what kind to get. We have to take a few things for your parents, Aunt Phyll and Neil and Joan and their two kids too. I already have several cans of salmon and some smoked salmon especially for your mom and dad from Woodward's. You know how much your family likes salmon and it's so expensive over there. We can buy duty free cigarettes and whiskey at the airport too. What do you think we should take Christine and Brenda? What do you think about going down to Gas Town and getting some Native jewelry?"

"Good idea. Instead of us going down to Gas Town, maybe Veron could stop there on her weekly trip to the Bay and get something they might like. Sally and Anne are just a bit older so she'd have a good idea of what might appeal to girls that age."

"Gilley, that's the second time in a few minutes you've had a good idea. What's gotten into you? Is it the thought of going back to you homeland?"

"Maybe."

"We have to remember to get Mom and Anne something nice from England as a Thank You gift for taking care of our pets. I also said Anne could stay overnight here if she wanted to. I think she's a bit lonely with Sally gone from home now."

"I wouldn't be a bit surprised if Jim ends up looking after the lot. I can just hear Veron now, 'Jim, on your way to work, would you mind popping into Joy's place and feeding the pets? Can you make sure the cover is off the birds?"

Giggling, Joy said, "Dad might enjoy that. At least he can get away from Mom for a bit. He could sit here and have a smoke in total solitude."

The week prior to their leaving was filled with tying up lots of loose ends. Even though Swann's had known for months Gilley was going away for three weeks, they still all complained he was abandoning them in their time of need. Gilley made sure his work was completed, at least as far as he could see, for up to four weeks ahead and he had left explicit instructions for his competent workers. He wasn't worried about the work getting done without him as all the men were dedicated. He knew they were giving them a hard time. Yet he remembered what Jim had said. "Make sure some things which are not disruptive have some gray areas that will leave them wishing you were here and hoping it can wait until you get back. That way your staff will know they need you and they will look forward to you coming back. If you make it too easy, they'll wonder why you're there in the first place."

Friday arrived faster than they would have liked. Gilley was looking forward to that long flight back to England. At least, Joy couldn't ask him to run to the drug store or to the supermarket to pick up some forgotten item. He may even have time for a nap.

Jim and Veron picked them up at the apartment, drove them to the airport, had a few pints with them in the bar and saw them off. Of course before heading to the boarding area, stopping at the duty was a must. The allowance to take overseas was two bottles of liquor and two hundred cigarettes each. Two bottles of Scotch and twenty packs of Craven A were ordered. The process for this type of purchase was the buyer would pay for the goods up front in the country of origin and the purchases would be delivered to them before disembarking in the destination country.

Before he knew it, they were in the air, on their way back to England. Gilley's thoughts turned towards his favourite sport, football (soccer). "If the gods are with me and the flight is on time, maybe I can make it to St. James Park and catch the second half of the Magpies game with Tottenham Hotspurs."

Joy was beside herself as plane accelerated off the tarmac and climbed into the air. This was her favourite part of the flight. Looking over, Gilley could see the pleasure on her face as the plane started to climb away from the ground. As it leveled off, she exclaimed, "We are finally on our way back to England. I thought this day would never come. Merry old England, here we come. After all, you kept your promise. We would spend two years in Canada and then return to your homeland to see if Canada is all you've cracked it up to be."

"Oh, oh," thought Gilley, "This is it. What do I do now?"

As often in his life, he decided to just let destiny take its course, but Gilley knew one thing, magpies always returned to the nest but they don't always stay.